In the Fullness of Time

Also by Terry Roberts

That Bright Land
The Holy Ghost Speakeasy and Revival
The Sky Club

The Stephen Robbins Chronicles

A Short Time to Stay Here
My Mistress' Eyes Are Raven Black
The Devil Hath a Pleasing Shape

PRAISE FOR

In the Fullness of Time

"In Terry Roberts's excellent new novel, he describes the topography of western North Carolina with the attentiveness of a skilled landscape painter, but Roberts is equally attentive to the terrain of the human heart. His characters are not one-dimensional 'types.' Instead, they embody the complexities and contradictions of fully realized humans, most of all Clinton Salter, a good man torn between loyalty to the law and loyalty to family. *In the Fullness of Time* is yet another reminder of why Terry Roberts is one of our very finest novelists."

—**Ron Rash**, *New York Times* bestselling author of *Serena*, *The Cove*, and *The Caretaker*

"In the beautiful mountains of North Carolina, in the county that has given us the most distinguished fiddlers, Terry Roberts sets a story of murder, graft, political corruption, and families with long memories and secrets. *In the Fullness of Time* is a novel of betrayal, where crime is close to home, but also of courage, integrity, and long-delayed love, in prose from the place where the music was born."

—**Robert Morgan**, author of *Gap Creek* and *Chasing the North Star*

"You are holding a tale of a Southern mountain sheriff. But beware: Roberts could have made this a stereotype fest, but instead tells a story that celebrates truth, steadfastness, and justice. With a dog or two thrown in for local color. This is a book you need during these fraught times."

—**Wayne Caldwell**, author of *Cataloochee* and *The Shadow Family*

"Terry Roberts's Madison County offers a welcome refuge even in the midst of seemingly inescapable violence. As Clinton and Catherine struggle to start anew, they wrestle beneath the weight of family and the legacy of community. A gorgeous journey from start to finish, this heartrending and insightful novel is shot through with veins of light and wisdom."

—**Heather Bell Adams**, author of *Maranatha Road* and *Starring Marilyn Monroe as Herself*

"Terry Roberts's story had me from page one, drawing me into the town of Marshall, NC, and the lives of the characters there. Like his other novels, *In the Fullness of Time* isn't so much a mystery as a series of enigmas about the longstanding insecurities that spark the most inscrutable human behaviors. Deft, engrossing, and compassionate, the story delves deeply into the ways a place can shape complicated motivations. Roberts's mountain community is poised between the past and the future, between old recriminations and the desire for change. It's about the long arc of families and history, a paean to the intricate relationships between people, time, and place. I loved it!"

—**Julia Franks**, author of *Over the Plain Houses* and *The Say So*

"Terry Roberts is one of those authors who, from the opening page, takes you by the hand and pulls you into the story in a most effortless and wonderful way. In his spell-binding new novel, *In the Fullness of Time*, Roberts brings 1960s Madison County, North Carolina, to life with such vivid detail, such a rich, sensory depiction you are there, sitting alongside Sheriff Clinton Salter as, with common sense and notable decency, he seeks to right a slew of wrongs so generationally accepted as to be woven into the very fabric of the community. Through it all is a tender love story of two good people, of family estranged and moving toward wholeness, of a community healed. Terry Roberts is an exceptional writer and, with *In the Fullness of Time*, a master storyteller at the height of his craft."

—**Cathy Rigg**, author of *That Which Binds Us*

"In Terry Roberts' sixth novel, *In the Fullness of Time*, the big picture is about the mysteries of Time—of what was, is, and will be. The core of this tasty apple—the story itself—delivers barn burnings, grave robberies, murder, 'banjos and buttermilk,' Republicans, Democrats, family stain, family love, and romance. And that's just the core. Thundering through the mountains of fabled Madison County, North Carolina, this novel is a train that's destined to be a lasting tribute to a place that demonstrates how people and land are, in so many ways, the same. All aboard!"

—**Clyde Edgerton**, author of *Walking Across Egypt* and *The Bible Salesman*

In the Fullness of Time

a novel

Terry Roberts

KEYLIGHT
BOOKS
AN IMPRINT
OF TURNER
PUBLISHING

Keylight Books
an imprint of Turner Publishing Company
Nashville, Tennessee
www.turnerpublishing.com

In the Fullness of Time

Cover and book design by William Ruoto

Library of Congress Cataloging-in-Publication Data

Names: Roberts, Terry, 1956- author.
Title: In the fullness of time : a novel / by Terry Roberts.
Description: First edition. | Nashville, Tennessee : Keylight Boos, 2025.
Identifiers: LCCN 2024043172 (print) | LCCN 2024043173 (ebook) |
ISBN 9798887980577 (paperback) | ISBN 9798887980584 (hardcover) |
ISBN 9798887980591 (epub)
Subjects: LCSH: North Carolina--Fiction. | LCGFT: Novels.
Classification: LCC PS3618.O3164 I5 2025 (print) | LCC PS3618.O3164
(ebook) | DDC 813/.52--dc23/eng/20240920
LC record available at https://lccn.loc.gov/2024043172
LC ebook record available at https://lccn.loc.gov/2024043173

Printed in the United States of America

In memory of those who were lost on 27 September 2024 when Hurricane Helene devastated much of the territory portrayed in this book.
And for the courageous survivors who have been rebuilding that world, day by day.

WAS

Doe Branch
February 1931

TIME. AN ANCIENT CLOCK TICKING ON THE MANTEL. The boys' father has been sitting by the fire for most of this long winter afternoon, and now dusk is swirling into the room. He is drinking from a mason jar of cheap liquor, which doesn't bode well for man nor beast.

Clint, the older of the two brothers, knows that the best thing would be to get hot food in his father's belly, which might temper the rage boiling inside the man. Plus, hot food might just put him to sleep, snoring before the hearth.

Their mother ran two years before. Clint does not blame her, for by the time she left, she barely had mind or strength left to fight. He would run too, far and away, except for his little brother, who is only twelve. Clint knows that he is responsible for Willie, and, for now at least, his one goal in life is to keep his father from harming the boy. Later on, he thinks—when Willie is a little taller, stronger, faster—then by God, we'll run for it. And the old man can beat *himself* to death.

Hot food. And so, with Willie's help, Clint applies himself to the woodstove in the lean-to kitchen stuck on the back of the house. He's only fifteen, but he's been doing the majority of the cooking since his mother disappeared down the road. This night, he puts a pot of beans on the old, battle-scarred table, along with hot cornbread and a piece of ham meat hacked into three fist-sized pieces so the old man can't take it all.

He has taught Willie what to do at the first sign of trouble. Straight along past the barn and through the pasture to their sister's house, where she lives with her husband a half mile away. Run like a witch is after you, he has hissed to Willie more than once, and don't look back. The boy nods. He knows.

They sit at the table, lit by the flicker from the fireplace and the oily, yellow gleam from the one kerosene lamp. Their father serves the three plates with a ladle of beans and slides one down to each of the boys. Clint is using his own fork to pry a piece of hot cornbread from the skillet for Willie when the storm finally breaks.

"This ain't fit," his father grumbles around a mouthful of beans. "This ain't fit for the dog." Clint and Willie make eye contact but don't speak. "You should have thrown this mess to the pig and put something decent on the table."

"The pig is on the table," Clint says to his father. "You're chewing on it." Then, when Willie looks up from his plate, Clint cuts his eyes toward the back of the house and mouths the single word, "Window." Willie nods.

"What the hell did you say?"

Clint bites back several words that come to mind but he won't say in front of Willie. "Eat your supper, Pop. It'll settle your stomach."

The old man picks up his full plate, turns it upside down, and slams it down on the tabletop. "Slop," he growls. "You give me slop to eat."

It seems to Clint that the whole room darkens, the air suddenly icy. He looks across at his little brother, whom he loves. "Go," he whispers, "now."

PART ONE

IS

Marshall, North Carolina
1964

CHAPTER 1

"I NEVER ASKED FOR THIS," HE SAYS TO HIS DAUGHTER as they walk from the courthouse back down the one block to the jail and the sheriff's office. "Hell, I never even wanted it."

"Sorry," she says and actually takes his arm as they cross the empty street, an open gesture of affection from her. "You've only told me that a hundred times in the past month. Maybe more." And then, "You've got it now, and deep inside, you know you should do this. What's your office look like?"

He shrugs. "Don't know. I've never been in the sheriff's office before."

"I guess that's a good thing." She laughs as she says it, fully aware of the irony on this cloudy day riven with ironies. "I can read the headline in the *Chronicle* now: *Clinton Salter sworn in as Sheriff of Madison County on December 3, 1964, by District Court Judge*—what's his name—*Lacy Buckner.* Give yourself a day or two. Might decide you like it."

"Never should have let Will talk me into it," he grumbles. "Might resign..."

She shakes her head. "You've never resigned from anything in your life. Too stubborn." She pauses before the squat, two-story brick building that houses the jail and the sheriff's office. "I've got to get back to school, Papa. If I leave now, I can make it by third period, keep the principal happy."

He puts his arm around her shoulders and she hugs him briefly, both aware of the loose crowd of people who have trailed them down the street from the swearing-in. "Are you going to stay in town tonight?" Marian asks. "If you do, I'll fix supper."

"I'll take you to supper," he whispers.

CLINTON SALTER IS FORTY-EIGHT YEARS OLD now. Like many of the Salter men in his line, he is of medium height with a strong build, wide shoulders, and thick wrists. A round, Welsh head on Scots-Irish shoulders. Skin that browns to the color of an old penny in the August sun. A body wrought by years of farmwork and the restless habit of walking almost everywhere he goes. Should he turn suddenly to stare at you, you would sense the brawler he was during his army days. There is intent in his eyes. He loves animals and abides machines, mostly because he spent two war years driving a colonel who became a general through France and deep into Germany. He learned to keep the Jeep running, even under fire, and keep the colonel who became a general mostly out of that fire.

If you watch closely enough, as his daughter does, you can see a hundred expressions flit across his face in an afternoon, the most common by far a barely suppressed amusement at the ways of the world. What you won't see or hear is laughter, not since his wife, Gretchen, died six years before. Nor will you hear him say her name, because he cannot bear it in the past tense.

He is many separate things—farmer, mechanic, teacher, reader, watcher of the seasons, and teller of time—though he views all of these not as separate but as one. He has not darkened the church door since his wife's funeral. Nor has he voted, not since Eisenhower. He trusts neither the kingdom of God on earth nor the kingdom of man. He leaves the latter to his brother, Will, who is tireless in that pursuit.

After watching Marian turn the corner, plundering her purse for her car keys, he pulls open the front door of the Madison County jail. The first room he comes to, barely larger than a walk-in closet, is empty except for a few rickety wooden chairs. Down the hall, he follows an arrow painted red on the wall into a second room, where he comes face-to-face with a thin, fiftysomething woman behind a desk. A frown on her face slowly turns into a wide grin.

"Hello, Mrs. Goforth," he says.

Gloria Goforth nods. "Your brother's in there waiting," she says, and then, after a moment, "I didn't think you'd win, Clinton."

He shrugs. "Neither did I," he admits. "Neither did I."

The inner office, the room actually home to the high sheriff of Madison County, is the largest he's seen so far. There's a wide, wooden desk at the end farthest from the door, with a telephone and little else on its surface. Two wooden office chairs, slightly more solid than the ones out front, push up against the wall to the right. On the left, propped somehow against the wall and resting on concrete blocks, is the back seat from some automobile, Ford or Chevy, which apparently is meant for sitting on.

Behind the desk, leaning as far back in a well-padded office chair as gravity allows, is Will Salter—salesman, raconteur, sometimes farmer, and chairman of the Democratic Party in Madison County. He has both feet propped up on the desk, his eyes closed, his hands behind his head, relishing the victory, another election won, another relative shoved, willing or unwilling, into office.

Clinton smells the lingering odor of cigarette smoke and notices for the first time that there are no windows in the room. He clears his throat and his brother's eyes pop open.

"Goddamn!" Will shouts. "We did it!"

"More like you did it. Now get out of my chair."

Will's boots hit the floor, and he jumps up, reminding Clint of some sort of jack-in-the-box. "Brother, we did it. You are hereby and forever the sheriff, and I plan to celebrate tonight just as hard and just as long as we did on the night of the election."

"As *you* did on the night of the election. I had a good, stiff drink on my own up at the farm that night, wondering just how in the hell I let you talk me into this. *How will it all end?* I kept asking myself."

"It ain't ending, brother, it's just beginning. Damn all Republicans, and damn anybody who won't sit up all night damning all Republicans." On his feet, Will has a kind of electric energy about him, as if he can't stop himself from smiling or talking at you. Taller than Clint, with a hard, clean crew cut of black hair and a thin face, he's almost always grinning. Always with a freshly pressed short-sleeved shirt rolled up over his biceps—he's proud of his arms—and creased khaki pants. He affects cowboy boots to give the impression that he's one with you, the common man, the good old boy just come in from the fields, even though his bootheels are mostly worn from asphalt and concrete rather than good, black dirt. "Twenty-four precincts in this county," he says to Clint. "Twenty-four...and I brought in twenty-one of 'em just for you. And the hell with those rednecks up on Laurel anyway."

"Since you bring it up, I wonder what you promised all those men and women in the twenty-one precincts?"

"The world, brother. I promised them the world. And that together, we were going to get more out of the state capitol for little old Madison County than anyone could ever imagine. Schools, roads, and by God, industry. By the way, keep in mind I got myself elected to the school board at the same time. Between us, we're going to have this place locked down tight." Will is on the same side of the desk with Clint now and moving toward him. Clint realizes that his brother is about to grab his hand and start pumping it up and down as if he, Will, is still running for office, and Clint is just some innocent voter. Will has a painful grip, a salesman's grip, and to prevent this, Clint sidesteps his brother and maneuvers himself behind the desk.

What the hell do schools and roads have to do with enforcing the law? he thinks, perhaps even says aloud, but Will is already at the door, yelling at someone in the outer office. And in a moment, he is gone.

Clint tries out the chair behind the desk and discovers that it's almost impossible to sit up straight in. The previous sheriff, who'd managed to die in office, maybe in this very room, and the chief deputy who'd filled in for him, must have both liked to do their sheriff work tilted flat on their backs. While he is fiddling with the chair, trying to adjust it to something near vertical, Gloria Goforth eases in and shuts the outer door firmly behind her.

"Look here, Clinton—I mean, Sheriff Salter—I got a list of things half as long as my arm to tell you before I go to lunch. Quit messing with that thing and look at me."

He gives up what he's doing, circles the desk, and pulls the two wooden chairs away from the wall to face each other. She stops him even before he can sit, however. Tells him there's paper in the desk drawer.

"What?"

"There's a legal pad and some pencils in that desk. You will want to write some of this down, just in case you have to act like the sheriff while I'm gone to lunch."

He gets the pad and, rather than the pencils, which look like they've been chewed by rats, pulls the ink pen from his pocket. "Okay, Mrs. Goforth," he says as he sits down, "fire away." Once upon a time, many years before, she had been his teacher—his history teacher—at the old Marshall High School on the island in the middle of the river, and he automatically does as he is told.

"First of all, you'd better learn to call me Gloria. Most days, you won't have time for four syllables. Second of all, there's a line of folks down the hall, out the door, and standing in the street, all of whom want to talk to you."

"Jesus."

"They're not here to congratulate you either, so don't kid yourself. They're all here because they want something. Want to know what you're going to do about somebody's dog killing their chickens, or a hunter from Tennessee shooting a bear in their yard, or why you haven't found their husband, who ran off four days ago. A good, round half dozen or so will have a script from their doctor saying they've got to have a dose of corn liquor to fight off the awful pain in their knee or elbow or God knows what."

"Wait, why would they bring a prescription to us? We're not the drugstore."

Gloria Goforth laughs. "Oh, but we are. We are when it comes to liquor. In case you haven't noticed, there hasn't been an ABC store in our fair county since the state shut down the Anderson boys in Hot Springs. For people without a car to drive to Buncombe County, the only more-or-less legal means of taking a dose of hundred-proof anything is to bring your script to the sheriff's office and have it filled, so to speak."

"With what? Have we got some of Uncle Joe Freeman's finest on tap in the back? If we do, I'm going to write myself a prescription."

"Not quite on tap. What do you think happens to the hundreds of gallons of pure corn whiskey—some of it quite good, or so I've heard—that gets confiscated when your lazy deputies actually manage to catch somebody making it or hauling it? It gets stored in a locked room right through that door there. We keep it back here so that the deputies can't drink up the evidence or start selling it themselves. So..."

"I'm not filling any of these damn prescriptions, as you call them, until you get back," he mutters. "What else?"

"What else is the half dozen or so folks in line your brother has made some sort of promise to."

"Promise like what? A job?"

Gloria nods. "Or worse. That you'll arrest somebody or cut somebody loose. That sort of thing."

"You're not going to lunch."

"Yes, I am. Oh—and one more thing. Sometime this afternoon, you're going to have to deal with Tom Runnion. Give it some thought."

CHAPTER 2

TWENTY-SEVEN PEOPLE. OLD, YOUNG; WOMEN, men. All of whom had something, needed something, wanted something. Had been promised something if they would only vote the right way.

Some of the things are small, like a pint of medicine from one of the jugs or jars in back. "Come back tomorrow," is his answer, "with a prescription signed by a real doctor, not your wife."

Some of the somethings are bigger, like *you got to arrest that son of a bitch who stole my tractor.* Which son of a bitch? *My son of a bitch brother-in-law who's had it since last October. Where's the damn law in this county when you need it?* "I'll see about it," is his answer, "or one of the deputies will. What's your brother-in-law's name again, besides son of a…?"

Some things are larger yet. A woman who couldn't stop crying long enough to tell him what was wrong. What had happened. The unimaginable, the unforgivable. He gives her his handkerchief and sits her down at Gloria's desk, thinking maybe she can get something coherent out of the poor woman when she returns.

I come for my pay. "What pay?" *Sol Ramsey told me plain as day that your brother told him to tell me that it was worth a crisp five-dollar bill should I cast my vote for you. Well, I cast it, and here you sit. I want my five dollars.* "Talk to my brother," he says. "I didn't promise you a dime."

Two men who look suspiciously alike and who claim distant kinship with him—*my daddy was first cousin to your grandma on your mother's side*, that sort of thing—claim they are there to be sworn in. "As what?" he asks. *Why, deputies, of course. We was told that you'd be needing help, and we are just the men for the job. Besides which*—one leans forward over his desk to whisper—*we are good Democrats, born and raised, if you know what I mean. And Jeter here is a crack shot.* "Come back on Monday," he says, "and you can both fill out an application." *Does that involve writing?* one asks.

Gloria comes back from lunch after almost an hour and hands him a grease-stained paper bag containing a ham biscuit and cold french fries. She also hands him a Coca-Cola in an icy bottle. "How you like the sheriff business so far?" she asks cheerfully.

"I'm liking farming more and more. This isn't a sheriff's office, it's—I don't know what—social services."

She smiles. "Something like that. Listen, Clinton. I'm going to take up with the line and see what I can do. Tom Runnion is sitting on my desk, holding forth, acting like he owns the place. I'm going to send him in. Get it over with..."

"Wait, Gloria." Clint is nodding but not smiling. She senses that his body is relaxed, but his eyes are cold. Reptilian almost. "Two things. Before you bring in Runnion, call over to Lawyer Gudger's office. Tell him it's time."

"Which Gudger, the old one or the young one?"

"The old one. The one that ain't afraid."

She nods, considering. "You said there were two things."

"You come in with Runnion and Gudger. Shut the door behind you. I want witnesses."

"Well then. You mean to do something?"

He gives her a tight-lipped smile. "I wish there was a window in this room," he says.

BY THIS POINT IN HIS LARGELY MISSPENT LIFE, Tom Runnion has grown into himself. He is the epitome of what some mountain mothers want for their sons. Tall, several inches over six feet, and broad, his shoulders, his arms, his belly right down to his low-riding belt buckle. His butt. Thighs that eventually stretch out the fabric of every pair of pants until they hang bagged at the knee. Size fourteen shoes that they order special for him at Penland's Store.

Runnion's head is small for his body, as if certain items got switched at birth. Somewhere, a reasonable-sized man got stuck with a head like a bucket, and Runnion got that man's reasonable-sized head topped off with a tousled shock of red-blond hair.

He is full of genial spirits, flirting with waitresses, helping old ladies across the street whether they want to go or not, that sort of thing. He also likes to quote the Bible, especially the Old Testament, wherein the enemies of God and Runnion end up thrown over the city walls to be consumed by beasts, their eyes pecked out by ravens.

But always, always, he wants to be certain you know that despite his apparent goodwill, he is a dangerous man. A man not to be trifled with. A man who will have to hurt you if you cross him.

He was the chief deputy in the previous sheriff's tenure and acting sheriff after that man died. When it became obvious that Will Salter and the Democratic bigwigs didn't intend to support him for sheriff, he walked into the Board of Elections, switched parties, and declared himself the Republican candidate. He used the resources of the office to campaign for the office right up until the day of the election. He had known he would win. He had prayed fervently about it, and his mother had seen a vision.

When Gloria shows him into the office, she brings Samuel Gudger along as well and rolls her own office chair in so the former judge will have something decent to sit on. Gudger thanks her courteously and pulls the chair over to the side of Clinton's desk as they had discussed in advance. In contrast to the flood of testosterone that comes in the door with Runnion, the seventy-year-old Gudger is small, composed, neat. When he sits, the chair doesn't screech or scream in protest. Gloria hands one of the two wooden chairs left to Runnion, who is wearing his sheriff's uniform, pants tucked into his boots, and his department revolver strapped to his hip.

When Gloria sits down against the outside wall, a few feet behind Runnion, he is the only person in the room left standing. "This little pissant of a chair ain't much for a big man to sit on," Runnion complains mildly.

"Try the car seat if you want," Clinton suggests. "Although what it's doing in here, I'm not so sure."

Runnion twists around to point with his chair. "That there car seat is a trophy. It come out of the back of a '54 Ford that wrecked out on the bridge trying to run a load of liquor right through the middle of town. My brother unbolted it for me and set it up for a couch."

"It is a handsome thing," Clinton says with a straight face, and Judge Gudger looks down at the desk to hide a smile.

"Well, that's right," Runnion offers, as he sits gingerly down, testing the chair before letting his full weight loose upon it. And then, once he is sure he can actually sit without bursting the chair: "That ought to be me sitting behind that desk, you know, and you ought to be out there on Doe Branch, doing what you do best." He offers this with a twisted sort of grin, as if joking about something they agree on.

"What's that?" Clinton asks.

"Huh?" Runnion grunts.

"What's that I do best?"

"Why, minding your own damn business. That way, I could be doing what I do best—keeping the lid screwed down tight on this county—and you could do what you do best. Hiding out up on that farm of yours. You'd be happy, I'd be happy. Everybody would be happy. Right, Judge?"

Gudger looks up and studies Runnion's florid face. "Perhaps not the fifty-two percent of the voters who chose Mr. Salter," the judge says in what sounds like a whisper up against Runnion's gruff.

"Well, hell, people in this county thought they wanted me until his brother come along and started selling them this political garbage. Vote Democratic, put us in line with the state, all that. But don't worry, I have a plan."

"Be interested to hear it," Clinton says. He cocks his head to one side, so he can see past Runnion's bulk, and is reassured to see that, just as he'd asked, Gloria is taking notes. Word for word what everyone says.

"Well, it's a genius plan, if I say so myself. I'll stay on as chief deputy and run operations out of this office. Sheriff Salter here can check in once in a while but still be free to spend most of his days up on Doe Branch making sure his corn rows are straight and his hogs get fat, while I keep an eye on the county for him. That's the way it was the last six months or so before Sheriff Tate died, and it worked out just fine, didn't it? We won't have to change much of anything."

"You mean even the car seat over there can stay?" Clinton suggests.

"Oh, hell yes. Trophy. Continuous...continuity...that's it. *Continuity* is what people like. Hate change. We can give them that good, old continuity. The forty-eight percent who voted for me and the fifty-two percent who voted for you." Runnion grins and leans back, which is almost a disaster as his chair creaks ominously.

Clinton makes eye contact with Judge Gudger. "What do you think?" he asks, knowing full well what Gudger thinks already.

"I think we have elections for a reason," Gudger says evenly. "And sometimes change is coming, whether people are quite ready for it or not."

"I agree," he says. And then to Runnion, "Your genius plan won't work because of me. I'm not Jimmy Tate, and I'm not dying."

"Well, listen here. I—"

"No, you'd better listen. With both ears. This is your last day working for the county. As of tomorrow, you're no longer wanted. If you like, I'll make a few calls and see if they'll take you on in Yancey or Haywood, but you're done here."

"You can't do this," Runnion growls. "You have no authority."

"Of course he can do it," Gudger says. "He's the duly elected sheriff. You serve at his pleasure."

Runnion is incredulous. "Just because I come out as a Republican. That's it, ain't it? Just because of that!"

For the first time, Clinton can feel his blood pressure start to creep up, his neck start to throb. He shakes his head roughly. "Actually, that's the last reason, Tom. I couldn't care less if you're a Republican or a Democrat or a Tory from old England. It's because you're a—"

"Careful," Gudger whispers.

"It's because we're getting ready to make changes. And I figure to need every man with me, not sharpening a knife behind me."

Runnion lurches to his feet. "Well, the hell with you then. You *and* your goddamn brother." He tosses his chair against the wall, where one leg finally snaps. "I know my own way out, just like I'll know my own way back in four years." He starts to turn.

"Leave your weapon," Clinton says.

"What?"

"Toss that Smith and Wesson on the car seat. It belongs to the county."

Runnion's face is so flushed with blood that even his carroty hair and beard look yellow against the bloated red flesh. "Why, you little shit. I don't need this. I got guns aplenty at..." There's a long pause and the air itself is harsh with the smell of Runnion's sweating body. Finally, he nods and very carefully unbuckles his belt, tugs the holstered pistol off, and tosses it onto the car seat. Carefully buckles up again. The whole time, Gloria says a silent prayer to the gods that hold up men's pants not to fail them now.

Then it is over. Runnion slams the office door behind him as he exits, leaving a trail of heat and stink.

The three left in the room all make eye contact. Gloria shakes her head and grins. Gudger nods. "Just so," the old judge finally says and smiles at Gloria. "The first thing any ruler must do is kill all his enemies."

Clinton nods and winks. "You mean there's more of 'em?" he asks of no one in particular.

CHAPTER 3

THE ROCK CAFE. A LITTLE BEFORE FIVE O'CLOCK. He eats with his daughter Marian at a rear table, on the far side of the counter, where he can sit with his back to the wall and they can have some privacy. The café is only one of two places in Marshall where they can eat more than a sandwich or a pack of crackers, and they're both hungry. Plus, they know Pricey Brigman is in the kitchen, cooking up food from the Brigman farm.

Salad and saltines while they wait for their main plates to come out of the kitchen, which is just getting fired up for the evening. She is drinking iced tea and he coffee, hoping to take some of the edge off the tension behind his eyes.

"Are you done being sheriff for the day?" she asks after a few bites of salad.

"Are you done being a teacher for the day?" He is smiling at her, knowing full well that except for a few days at Christmas and the month of July, she is never done being a teacher.

"I will be in a week or so, when school's out for Christmas."

"So you say. Being a sheriff is worse than being a teacher. I'm not sure I get Christmas Day or the Fourth of July." And then, after a moment, "No, I'm not done for the day. After I check in with Mrs. Penland up on the hill, I'm going to stroll back down to the jail and see what goes on there at night."

"Be careful," she says suddenly, even though she's not sure why. Not sure what to be afraid of.

He nods, and before he can reply, Pricey's husband Page brings their two plates, Clinton's with a double helping of roast beef. "You trying to kill me?" he asks.

The old man shakes his head. "Fortify you," he mutters and grins before swaying back around the counter.

They eat, comfortable with each other as they have almost always been. Letting the separate and braided pressures of their days slowly drain away. As the diner begins to fill up, an unusual number of patrons nod or wave or speak the one word—*Sheriff*—as a greeting. And though neither says it out loud, they both realize that this is the new reality. He has a title, and for the vast majority of people, even those they've known for decades, it has taken the place of his name.

"You know you could have stayed at my house when you want to stay in town," she says. "I only invited you a dozen times."

He smiles. "And I thanked you thirteen times. The truth is that wherever I stay in town, I have a feeling I'll be in and out at all hours of the night, at least at the beginning. And that whatever plans you and Luke have for the evening don't fit so well with your father snoring in the guest room."

She almost blushes. "Luke doesn't stay over all that—"

"Often? Well, if he doesn't, he probably should. And having your father sprawled out on the couch, along with a walkie-talkie squawking on the side table, doesn't make for a very romantic setting. For anybody." And then, after a smiling moment: "Tell me about school."

Marian Salter is the eleventh- and twelfth-grade English teacher at Marshall High School, the only high school in the state that sits on an island. Blannahassett Island is in the middle of the French Broad River, a quarter of a mile from where they sit eating their supper. In only a half dozen years, she has become something of a legend because she demands that her students read closely and well, and she demands that they learn how to write. Reading, writing, thinking. Poetry and prose. Not always something taken that seriously in the mountain coves, but taken very seriously within the four walls of her classroom. And slowly, as her reputation has spread, ambitious parents in other parts of the county have begun to request that their children, girls as well as boys, be allowed to transfer in so that they can have two years of Miss Salter's rigorous teaching.

In 1964, most Madison County students who graduate from high school are either done with their education or they matriculate at Mars Hill, the local Baptist college at the southern end of the county. A very few leave to go further, to Warren Wilson, near Asheville, or even Berea in Kentucky—both Presbyterian work schools founded to educate first-generation mountain students. Or to branches of the state university in Cullowhee or Boone. Two years before, one of Marian's students went as far away as Wake Forest University in Winston-Salem and, even more impressively, stayed. Thrived. This past year, three of her students left the mountains for a university education, and one young woman left the state for the University of Virginia. She has opened a doorway, he tells Marian, to a wider world.

Which she has, but which also means that she works constantly, even furiously, to challenge, to inspire, to raise expectations.

"Tell me about school," he asks again, expecting Shakespeare. Instead, she gives him basketball. "I almost forgot to tell you," she says. "The county basketball tournament is the nineteenth and twentieth, in the gym at Mars Hill, and Mrs. Metcalf asked me to remind you about having a deputy there."

"Who's Mrs. Metcalf?"

"The principal, Dad. My boss."

"Have I met her?"

"Yes, last Christmas. And you were very impressed."

"How impressed?"

"Very."

"Because...?" he asks. He remembers Catherine Metcalf well enough, but he loves hearing Marian talk, the one voice in his world that is almost always soothing to him, even as it is now. He loves that Marian, whose mother is only a memory, works for an older woman she respects.

"Because she's the only high school principal in the county who's a woman, and because of that, you said, she has to be better at her job than any of the rest. And I said that she deals with the idiot sixteen-year-old boys and the...loose fifteen-year-old girls, and the parents who excuse their sons on the first day of hunting season and the last two weeks of school. The morons on the school board, and the... Besides, you said she would be pretty if she ever smiled."

"I didn't say that." He remembers this too. "I only thought it."

"Nope. Said it."

"What else? There's something else."

"She's married to..." Marian leans close to whisper the end of the sentence.

He grimaces. "I remember," he says.

ON THE SIDEWALK OUTSIDE THE ROCK, HE ASKS about her brother, his son, perhaps the one topic on earth that is difficult for them. "Have you heard from Matt?" he says. "Is he doing okay?"

She hesitates before she answers, choosing her words. "I talked to him on the phone last week. Asked about Chrissy. Told him we missed him at Thanksgiving."

Matthew Salter is twenty-six, an attorney. A specialist in something important, who works for the Institute of Government at the state university where he went to law school. He is young, intelligent, idealistic, and he has only been home perhaps a half dozen times since his mother died. And those half dozen in the few years just after her death. In many ways, he favors his father's looks when his father was in uniform, fighting the Nazis, except that Matthew's hair is long and wavy, down almost to his shoulders, and he would never dream of wearing a uniform of any kind. He hates the mountains, or so he says, the backwardness, the ignorance, the willing stupidity about anything cultural. *Cornbread and beans,* he says, when anyone in Chapel Hill asks him where he came from, *banjos and buttermilk.*

"Did you ask him about Christmas?"

She nodded. "Of course. Just like I always do. And he said he was too busy. Chrissy wants him to go with her to Atlanta. That her mother won't have it any other way. He even asked me to go with them, and I declined politely."

"Politely?" He smiles.

"Not really. I think I said *hell no.* But I tried. Said they could come through here on the way back from Atlanta."

"What did he say?"

"Said *here* wasn't on the way to anywhere. At least anywhere he wanted to go." She regrets the words almost immediately. Her father doesn't flinch, but she can feel his reaction, nonetheless. "I'm sorry, Dad," she says.

"For what? You tried."

What neither says, what doesn't need saying anymore, is that when his son, her brother, says he hates the mountains, what he really means is that he despises his father.

CHAPTER 4

Mrs. Penland's boarding house sits up on the shoulder of the mountain behind the courthouse. After supper, Clinton leaves his Jeep parked beside the jail and climbs Hill Street on foot. The old lady shows him around the downstairs of the large stone house and then takes him up one flight of stairs to his "room," which is really three rooms at the front of the house, overlooking the town and the river. Gives him two keys—one to the front door and one to his room—and chats for a minute about the weather before leaving him to go on about her business. He is relieved that she, at least, still calls him *Clinton* and *son*, not *Sheriff*.

After he unpacks, he walks.

Marshall is shoehorned roughly in between the steep mountainside and the river. The only reason there is a town here at all, let alone the county seat, is that the railroad follows the river, and for generations, the railroad was the only reliable road at all. Since he was a boy, Clinton has heard Marshall described as a mile long, a block wide, and hell deep, which he recalls with a smile as he ambles in the early winter dark down to one end of Main Street, back down to the other end, and then across the bridge to the island.

He nods to the few people he meets, takes one hand out of a coat pocket to wave at the two trucks and a car that pass. Out on the island, he walks all the way around the high school, glancing up at the second-floor windows, wondering vaguely which ones open to Marian's classroom. Every ten years or so, the island floods, and rats invade the old building; it happened when he was a student. They got a week off from school, and then the principal let him and his friends hunt down the rats with a single-shot .22 rifle. And now his only daughter teaches in a classroom where he himself read poetry.

Why here, he wonders, *why now?*

After Gretchen died of pancreatic cancer, he continued to talk to her often—in his sleep, in his dreams, during his long day's work on the farm. And often enough, she talked back, blaming him for bringing her to this godforsaken place. Blaming him for not letting her go home to her family in Kentucky to live or even to die. Where there were hospitals, doctors, medicine. Where she could be with her own mother.

He pauses on his way back across the bridge. Cars cross here so seldom at night that there is no danger in standing at the railing, staring downstream toward Tennessee. He can hear the wash of the river below, constant, restless, eternal.

When Gretchen was alive, she had not said these things to him; she had not blamed him for anything. Standing beside her hospital bed in Asheville, he had offered to take her home to Kentucky. But it was too late and they both knew it. *Take me when I'm dead,* she'd whispered, *and bury me beside my father. Take me home,* she said again later. The last thing she was able to say, when there was barely any time left in the room.

He had done it. He and Marian had taken her body by train back to Lexington. Matt was studying for the bar exam and came north only long enough for the funeral. One day and a night was all he could give them, now that his mother was gone.

In the twenty-four hours that Matt did spend in Kentucky, he said some things that sank into Clinton's consciousness only to emerge later, when he looked back at those fiercely sad days. Things he overheard Matt telling others. That they should have brought

Gretchen—Matt called her Mother—home to Lexington as soon as she was diagnosed. That she might have had a chance. What was his father thinking? How could he have been so selfish?

Did Matt actually say these things? Clinton wonders now, or is he imagining them out of some sense of his own regret, his own guilt? *Refused to let her go home...* Clinton is sure Matt did say something like that, more than once. And all that time, Clinton believed she was home, in the mountains.

Home?

Was he here now—suspended in space between the schoolhouse and the jailhouse—because this was his home? Marian was his family? Or had he been washed up here by the river, like a rat after the flood?

Even though it is only a little after nine, the front door of the jail is locked, which seems odd to him. Isn't the sheriff's office like the church, always open, always unlocked to the wayward souls who need help? He walks around to the side door that opens directly into Gloria's office, a thick glass door with the old sheriff's name painted on it. Also locked.

Back around to the front, and he pounds on the door with his fist. He realizes as he does so that the ornate badge he'd been given when he was sworn in is still in its leather wallet in his desk drawer and that he has no ID other than his driver's license. No badge and no keys. He's just a lonely man standing on the step, pounding on a locked door. "Open up," he yells experimentally and again, louder.

After a moment, he can see in the window beside the door a shadow blocking the interior light. The shadow materializes into the form of a man coming from the stairwell. "Who the hell is it?" the shadow man yells. And: "Stop that knocking. Wake the damn dead..."

"Sheriff Salter," Clinton says back, just loud enough to be heard within. "Let me in!"

Apparently, the door locks are more complicated than you might expect, for it takes the shadow some cranking and grumbling to finally pull the outer door open. When Clinton steps up into the foyer, he comes face-to-face with someone he's known for years: Lloyd Maney, a veteran of the war like Clinton. Fought in the Pacific and come home hollowed out by the things he'd seen and done.

"What are you doing here, Lloyd?" Clinton asks softly. He can smell cigarette smoke in Lloyd's clothes and something else. Alcohol of some kind.

"I'm the jailer," Lloyd says and then coughs to clear his throat. "The jailer and the night deputy when nobody else is around. Answer the phone and such, should it ring at night."

"Does it ring at night?"

Lloyd finally smiles and nods with a jerk. "Well, you know, it does. Not often, but when it does ring, you know it ain't good."

Clinton nods. "No, I suppose not. You have any guests upstairs?"

Lloyd shakes his head no, but then pauses, and nods, yes. "There's one. Waiting trial for disturbing the peace, shooting a pistol into a house, but you know, he goes home at night."

"What do you mean, he goes home at night? He make bail?"

"No, no. He didn't make no bail, but he's related to Tom Runnion somehow, second cousin or something like that, and Runnion wrote him out a slip so he could go home at night. He's supposed to be back here by eight in the morning, although he's been slipping in later and later since the election."

"Well, hell, Lloyd. He's not going home at all starting tomorrow. He's in or out. Not half-and-half."

Lloyd nods. "I expected you might say something like that once you showed up. You want to see upstairs?"

The stairs are behind a barred door that opens from the end of the main hallway. The treads are rough, splintered wood, once painted white but faded and scuffed now to a dull gray. At the top of the stairs are six barred cells arranged around three of the four outside walls of the second floor. Solid walls separate each cell from the adjoining ones, and a small, barred window is set into the brick wall at the back of each. All the barred doors are standing open, so Clinton walks into the one he judges is just over the top of his office below. To each side is a low, narrow cot, with a couple of army blankets neatly folded, plus a small, stained striped pillow. In the corner sits a five-gallon bucket and a roll of rough toilet paper. In the hallway is a heavy, scarred bench with some handy chains bolted into the wall for securing prisoners when things get crowded.

"All the cells like this?" he asks Lloyd.

"Pretty much. They's what we call the lady's cell behind you at the front. It has its own flush toilet, and my wife hung some curtains at the window. And they's a bathroom with a door on the other side at the front, so if there's only one or two in here and it's a slow day, I let 'em out so that they can use the john without having to mess with the bucket. The buckets can get..."

"Pretty nasty?"

"Yeah. And smelly."

"You spend the night when there's nobody here?"

Lloyd shakes his head. "Used to be, before Sheriff Tate died, there was a regular schedule, and one of the deputies was supposed to man the downstairs eight hours on and off, answer the phone, go out and see about any trouble. Then I slept at home, but since Runnion took over, the schedule kind of..."

"Fell apart?"

Lloyd nods. "Something like that. So, if there's nobody else here, I'll spend the night. Sleep in the cell right by the stairs, where I can hear the phone."

"Your wife ever come up and stay with you? Don't worry, I wouldn't blame you if she did."

"Well, I mean, maybe. Once or twice. She might bring me a bite to eat and sit with me for a while, if there's..."

"Nobody else around?"

Lloyd nods. "She don't favor for me to be lonely. Once, she brought the dog to stay with me."

He laughs. "Well, hell, Lloyd, I don't favor for you to be lonely either. We'll be back on schedule in a few weeks, so you don't have to sleep here if there's nobody locked up. Go on home tonight and see what your wife is up to. She might just be lonely herself."

"But who'll answer the phone?"

"I will," he says.

CHAPTER 5

FRIDAY, DECEMBER 4. DAY TWO.

After one of the deputies finally arrives around seven, Clinton walks back up Hill Street to shower, shave, and gulp down some eggs and coffee at Mrs. Penland's morning table. When she asks where he spent the night, he tells her. "In jail." And then, because she meant the question kindly, he explains.

By the time he gets back to the office, he sees three men standing in the street beside the jail, smoking. Two he vaguely recognizes, dressed as deputy sheriffs, meaning they're wearing khaki shirts with patches sewn on over the pocket. One man he doesn't know—small, weaselly, blowing smoke out of the side of his mouth. The weaselly man turns out to be Ed Banks, disturber of the peace.

Clinton invites Mr. Banks upstairs, slams the cell door on him and—in front of what is now three deputies—locks it. "You don't have to go to all that trouble," Banks says. "I ain't gonna run off. I just go home at—"

"You're not going anywhere before your trial," he says. "This is your home until then."

"But Tom said—"

"It doesn't matter what Cousin Runnion said. He doesn't work here anymore." Then, he reaches through the bars and snatches the packet of Camels out of Banks's shirt pocket. "No smoking in the jail, Banks."

A quick conversation with Gloria. Get all the ashtrays on the first floor out. Get in touch with all eight deputies and line them up one after the other on the hour. He wants to sit down with each behind a closed door, and Gloria can deal with whoever wanders in off the street. Make that seven; Runnion is already gone.

"Are you going to fire them all?" Gloria asks with a grin.

He shakes his head. "Maybe half," he says. "We'll see."

Dwayne Austin, R. B. Bailey, Danny Fender, Bill Hensley, Balis Norton, Sam Ray, Wayland Tipton. In alphabetical order. His notes read like this.

Austin: tall, thin. Quiet and thoughtful, slight slur in his voice. Served under three elected sheriffs. No complaints on file.

Bailey: short and bow-legged. Always grinning or laughing. Came in with Tate. Reputation for fighting when off duty. Known to rough up a prisoner from time to time.

Fender: medium height, hair like Elvis, long sideburns. Country strong. Speaks slowly and carefully, laughs nervously. Excellent mechanic.

Hensley: portly, blinks like an owl when asked a question. Probably the laziest of the bunch, possibly the laziest human in town. Keeps saying he's a good Democrat.

Norton: medium height, medium build. From Shelton Laurel. Sense of humor. Former preacher. Very good with radios and walkie-talkies. Trained in the army.

Ray: balding, scars on his face and hands. Perhaps burns on his face. Boyhood friend of Clinton's. Tough, determined. Navy vet.

Tipton: small man, wiry. Goes by Way. From Hot Springs. Was reading a paperback book while waiting for his interview. Good with people. Smart.

None of them, except for Tipton, with any special training in law enforcement.

At the end of the day, he calls first Bailey and then Hensley back into the office to let them know that their services will no longer be required. He has Gloria sit in both conversations as a way of easing the tension in the room and to take notes on the whys and wherefores. Bailey is angry but, unlike Tom Runnion, only mutters to himself while he hands over his gun and stomps out without making any threats. Hensley cries. Asks what in the world is he supposed to do to feed his family. When he leaves, Clinton looks at Gloria. "Does he even have a family?" he asks her. "Cats," she says.

As the last formal act of this second day, he calls those that are left—Austin, Fender, Norton, Ray, Tipton—back into the office. Asks Gloria once again to take notes, this time on a schedule. "First off, I count six of us who are left, plus Lloyd Maney, the jailer. Gloria is going to call him in a few minutes to let him know he has a guest upstairs, a real guest who's not going home for the night. On Monday, first thing, we'll post a watch list for the week, and I'll start looking for a few new deputies to fill out the roster. Contrary to what you may have heard, I don't care who they voted for or who they're related to, and I sure as hell don't care whether they're registered Democrat or Republican. So, if you know a likely candidate, send him to me."

"Man or woman?" Austin asks.

He pauses. The thought hadn't occurred to him. Then nods. "We arrest women from time to time, don't we? Then maybe we need a female deputy. Now, for the weekend, I'll be here during the day, and Maney'll be here at night. I need somebody here until midnight tonight, somebody to work graveyard 'til eight, and so on. Anybody got any plans for the weekend that don't involve law enforcement?"

Way Tipton clears his throat. "I've got a funeral tomorrow. Brother-in-law."

He nods. "Can you stay now?"

Tipton shrugs and nods.

"Then here's how we'll play it. Way is here until midnight. Dwayne, relieve him at midnight and stay until eight in the morning. Gloria, are you getting this? Danny, come in at eight?"

He continues, all the way through to Monday morning. When he's done, he looks around the room, judging their body language and facial expressions. There's some tension in the room, the smell of something new going on. But nothing that shouldn't be there. Nothing covert, nothing with a knife's edge to it. "Gentlemen," he says finally. "I'll be in and out all weekend. We'll get to know each other." And then, "Way, I'm going to go find us some supper and bring it back here. We need to talk."

As he leaves in search of food, he walks with Gloria down Plemmons Street. "What do you think?" he asks her.

"I think you're cleaning house," she says. And then, just as they reach her car, "You recall the woman who came in yesterday, crying so hard that you couldn't understand a word she said?"

He nods. "I recall. How could I not?"

"She's married to that Ed Banks you've got locked up."

"Does she want him cut loose?"

"Just the opposite. She's praying we'll keep him."

CHAPTER 6

SATURDAY AFTERNOON. DAY THREE. WILLIAM "Will" Salter.

Clinton and Balis Norton are on duty—Balis out at the front desk, he in his office trying to make sense of the budget and the accounts—when he hears Will out in the front, joshing with Norton, telling a joke he, Clinton, has heard a dozen times. Maybe two dozen. Something about a chicken and a duck that is not funny, but he can hear Balis laughing loud and long—just the sort of response Will requires.

Then Will is in the office, shoving the door closed behind him. Drags the one chair that is left up to his desk and makes himself at home. "So, brother," he says. "What I hear is that you got rid of Tom Runnion first thing. Had to do it, had to do it, I understand. Son of a bitch shouldn't have switched his affiliation. But then we got problems. You can't fire little Billy Hensley. I know he's worthless as a deputy, but he's a rock-solid Democrat and he keeps all his family in line in that precinct."

"You mean the cats?"

"What? No, I don't mean the damn cats. I mean the twelve brothers and sisters he's got up and down Grapevine Road. You got to find something else for him to do. Sweep up or something."

"He's too lazy to sweep up. He couldn't find the broom."

"Doesn't matter. Let him sit on his ass in the corner and scratch his balls. Dole out pint jars of liquor for them that come in with scripts. He can do that. And another thing—are you taking note of what I'm saying? We can't afford to screw this up. You can't fire R.B. Bailey. He's..."

The longer Will talks, the more upset he gets. There's sweat beading at the sharp edges of his crew cut, and there's that vein throbbing in his forehead.

"Does it bother you," Clinton asks, "that Bailey is a sadist?"

"A what?"

"You know. Pulls the wings off flies. Ties tin cans to dogs' tails. Beats and kicks a prisoner when he's handcuffed?"

"I heard about that," Will admits and then grins. "It was only that damn Buckner boy from up on Little Pine. Probably deserved it. What you don't grasp is that R.B. is one of ours. Third cousin or something like. And his father has the Eighteenth Precinct tied up like you wouldn't believe." Will pulls a half-full packet of Lucky Strikes out of his shirt pocket. "You got a match?" he asks.

"There's no smoking in here."

"No smoking? It's a damn jail, for Christ's sake."

"Take it outside."

They stare at each other across the desk for a long time, forty-plus years of older brother, younger brother love and strain, care and competition, sizzling the air between them.

"Listen, Clint. You can say what you want about this one or that one, Billy and R.B., but here's the naked truth. I got you elected to this damn job by turning this county Democratic, one vote and one precinct at a time, so you better, by God, do what I tell you if you want to be sitting here in four more years."

Before he replies, Clinton replays in his mind how many times he kept Will away from his father's fists when they were boys. How many times he took those fists instead, fists and bootheels both. He measures his words accordingly, fitting them to who he and Will were then, as well as who they are now. "Go easy," he says, "with your damn *Do what I tell you*. Here's a little truth for you, in return. I didn't especially want this job. I ran as a favor to you. But now that I'm here, I'm going to do what's right as I see it. Bailey and Hensley are gone. Done. And if and when I replace them, it'll be with the best man or woman I can find. Regardless."

Will stands, reaches across the desk, grabs a fistful of Clinton's shirt collar, and twists it painfully. Snarling, he draws back his other hand and makes as if to slap Clinton.

"Let go, Will," he says quietly, "or I'll make you eat those damn Lucky Strikes."

There is a long moment during which Clinton tries to remember his brother as a much younger man, a boy even, as a way of keeping himself calm.

Then the door to the outer office opens, and Balis Norton looks in. "Everything all right in here?" he asks, and Will hurriedly lets go of Clinton's shirt and tries to pat the collar more or less back into place.

"Just straightening out the sheriff's shirt," Will says jovially. "You know, we didn't have no mama, and I'm not sure the man ever did learn to dress himself. What do you think?"

"Looks fine to me," Balis offers.

"Well, now, that's right. That's right. You're a loyal member of the department, ain't you, Norton? And what I have for the sheriff here is a list of likely replacements for those sorry sons-a-bitches left over from the previous administration. Good men and good Democrats who would make excellent deputies." Will reaches into his shirt pocket and pulls out a sheet of lined notebook paper, which he unfolds and tries to hand to Clinton. When Clinton won't take it, he lays it on the desk. "'Cause you know, good deputies are born, not made. And the men on this list were born to serve the cause, just like Norton here. Good men and true."

Clinton stands and Will sets himself in motion toward the door, still talking. When they hear the door to the street slam, Balis Norton looks back at Clinton. "He always carry on like that?"

"He sells fertilizer for a living," Clinton replies. "What the hell do you expect?" Then, while Balis is watching, he wads up the penciled list of names and drops it into the trash can.

"I thought you was a Democrat," Balis says.

"I am, but it's not a prerequisite to breathing."

Balis chuckles, which sounds not unlike a mule coughing. "Well, since you got all that straightened out, there's somebody else out here wants to see you."

When he steps into the outer room, a tall, thin woman stands up from the chair where she's apparently been waiting. She's not dressed like a mountain woman come to town, but as a professional of some sort, in a skirt and blouse, shades of green, the skirt forest green. The coat thrown over her shoulders isn't made to wear to the barn and back, but rather to an office of some kind. Wool, he thinks.

"I'm Catherine Metcalf," she says, "and I believe that was your brother who just went..."

"Stomping?"

She smiles. "Just went stomping out of here."

"I know who you are, Mrs. Metcalf. You're famous in my family. Would you walk down the street with me and have a cup of coffee? Fifteen minutes with my brother, and I need a..."

"A restorative? I believe the word in this case is *restorative*."

CHAPTER 7

THE ROCK CAFE ISN'T OPEN FOR SUPPER YET, BUT there's coffee to be had at the lunch counter inside Robbins Drug Store. They order at the counter and carry their cups and saucers back to one of the two tiny tables shoehorned into a corner. Cream for him, just black for her.

"So, Sheriff," she begins after blowing on her cup to cool the scalding coffee.

He shakes his head, stirring a teaspoon of milk into his own cup.

She tries again. "Mr. Salter..."

"That's worse. I feel like I know you because Marian talks about you all the time. Try Clinton."

She smiles. Rather, her eyes smile; her lips barely curve. "Does anyone ever call you Clint?" she asks, taking a sip from the cup. Her hands, he notices, are like the rest of her: neat with long, thin fingers; the only decoration a narrow, gold wedding band.

"In the war," he says, "everyone called me Clint. When I came home, I didn't see a lot of people for a long time, and somehow Clint got lost. What do people call you?"

"Seems like everyone I see these days is either a teacher or a student. So...Mrs. Metcalf. But I prefer Catherine."

"Not Cat?" He realizes he is trying to make her smile, really smile, with her whole mouth.

Which she does, and before she manages to get the paper

napkin up to her face, he sees the slight gap between her two front teeth.

"My mother called me Cat. My sister called me Catty." She laughs, then gives up the napkin entirely.

"So, Catherine, not Cat, what can I do for you? Is it the holiday basketball tournament? Marian mentioned that to me."

"Well, there's that. We do need somebody there to keep the peace when the local boys get mean."

"Not the girls?"

"Oh, they're worse. But that's mostly my job. That's not why I disturbed your peaceful Saturday afternoon."

He shakes his head ruefully. "My brother already did that. You're the *restorative*."

She smiles. "Good. I'll try to always drop in right after your brother. No, my problem is that someone is vandalizing the school building at night. We had a fight last Wednesday. A McDevitt boy and an Anderson boy. Nothing unusual. Some of my boys like to fight. But then after school, they got into it again, and by the time I got to the parking lot, it had blown up into a real brawl."

"They each had a brother or a cousin?"

She nods. "So, a couple of male teachers and I waded into the mess and pulled them apart. Bloody noses, black eyes. Right then, on the spot, I suspended them all. The first two for a week, the other two for three days. I went back inside, wrote the whole mess up, called the McDevitt boys' father, and wrote a letter to Mr. Anderson. No phone. Went home and had a..."

"Strong drink, I hope."

"Perhaps. Although I don't think I should confess to the sheriff."

He smiles. "I would recommend brandy, for medicinal purposes. So, you think one or the other or both of these characters, McDevitt or Anderson, are vandalizing the school?"

"Or their fathers or their girlfriends. Lord knows. But it started Thursday night, right after I suspended them, and it happened again last night."

"Rocks through the windows? Paint?"

She glances down, reluctant for some reason to continue. "Threw a concrete block through my office window. And spray-painted *BITCH PRINCIPL* beside it on the outside wall. Misspelled *principal*."

"*p-l-e*?"

"Nope. Left the *A* out entirely. Ran out of room."

He grins and shakes his head, carries both their cups back to the counter for a refill. When he returns with the cups, trying not to slosh the steaming coffee, he asks her how she became principal of a lonely mountain high school on a river island in the middle of Madison County.

She meets his eyes full-on for perhaps the first time. "It's a long story," she says, stirring her coffee to cool it. "You sure you want to hear it?"

Her eyes, he decides right then and there, are a startling, almost unreal, blue. "I'm sure. The way I read it, you're one of the best things that ever happened to Marian. She lost her mother six years ago, and she looks up to you the way...the way I wish my son looked up to me." It's a strange admission to make about Matt, and to this person he barely knows. But even so, it feels good to say it.

"I grew up in Asheville," she says. "But you may have known that. Lee Edwards High School, where I played basketball and read books. Thought about boys, I suppose, but was too shy to do much about them. Went to Chapel Hill and majored in English. Wrote short stories, believe it or not. Had a boyfriend—two, as a matter of fact. Not at the same time; different times. Studied to become a teacher."

"English teacher?"

She nods and smiles. "Math and I are not so well acquainted. Yes, an English teacher. Taught for five years in Chatham County while still living in Chapel Hill. The war years. I felt like I was teaching boys to read when all they wanted to do was escape overseas and..."

"Get killed?"

Again, she meets his eyes. Again, he's struck by the depth of the deep, almost indigo lurking there. "Is that awful? To want the boys and girls you teach to have a life rather than defeat the Nazis and save the world?"

He shakes his head ever so slightly, but he's sure she is watching and sees him signaling no. No, that's not awful. "I have a scar," he tells her, "on my shoulder that is nasty looking, worse than the wound itself, probably. It was as close as I came to shutting it all down. And when I came home after the war, home to the farm, all I wanted to do was sip one glass of hard liquor in the evening and read. After the children came, first Matthew and then Marian, I read to them, leaving off the whiskey till they were asleep."

"That's a wonderful story"—she pauses and then adds his name—"Clint. Not the wound, I mean, not that. But reading."

"Maybe reading is the antidote to shrapnel. And the antidote to concrete blocks flung through window glass. Keep going. What happened next?"

"What happened next, after the war, is that I met this man. An older man who was a divinity student at Duke and worked part-time for the school system. Studying to be a minister, but really didn't want to be a minister, if that makes any sense at all. He was so thoughtful and so idealistic, so sure that he knew answers that the rest of us were too caught up in the world to understand."

"And you married him?"

"I married him. James Metcalf. Not Jim or Jimmy, mind you. James. And his dream was to leave the corrupt, capitalist system behind and return to the earth. Live off the land. He wanted to farm."

Clinton snorts. "Had he ever even been on a farm?"

"Of course not, or he would have known better. But he planned to study seed catalogues, buy a few acres with some sort of house on it, and the two of us—he and I—would return to the simple and innocent ways of our ancestors."

"Why in the world did he pick here? There's not one flat acre in the whole county."

"Oh, because he thought it was the end of Earth. Back of beyond. Didn't someone invent that phrase? He thought this was the least modern place he could find for us. Garden of Eden."

They are both laughing now. She, ruefully, but also glad that he sees the humor in all of this, doesn't seem to resent it.

"And so, you did it. Returned to the Garden?"

"We did it. I kept us alive by teaching school while he tried to farm. Tried to grow everything—corn, apples, beans, cabbages."

"Pot?"

She smiles. "Of course. And he failed at almost everything. Except the cow. He did manage to keep one cow alive for a few years, and he managed to learn to milk her. Kept a few chickens in a lean-to attached to the house."

"So, you had milk and eggs?"

"And what I earned as a teacher."

"Then what?"

"Then one afternoon five years ago, he turned a tractor over on himself while I was at school and"—she tells this part as if it is casual, familiar news, but then sighs before finishing the sentence—"broke his neck and cracked his skull."

There is a pause here, at this delicate point. Both wondering what the other must be thinking.

"But he didn't die," he whispers.

"No, he didn't live, but he didn't die. He never regained anything like consciousness, and he lies there at the Ivy Rehabilitation Center, week after week, month after month, years now in what the doctors call a vegetative state."

"And so you're a widow too. Like me."

"I'm not sure what I am," she says.

CHAPTER 8

"I DIDN'T HAVE A CHILDHOOD," HE ADMITS TO HER when she asks for his story. "At least not after my mother left. Up until then, Will and I had to work, but no more than most boys on a mountain farm. We could still run outside and play when the chores were done and my father wasn't looking." He glances up at her face, which is earnest now, attentive. "Why do you cover your mouth like that?"

She smiles, almost shyly. "It's a habit. Trying to hide this horrible gap in my teeth. But don't try to distract me. Why did she leave? Your mother. And how old were you?"

He exhales slowly. "She ran away because every few weeks, once a month maybe, my father beat her like a drum. And I suppose she just couldn't take it anymore. I don't blame her, you understand. I blamed her then, but truth be told, I don't blame her now. She couldn't stand up to him, and he might have killed her eventually."

"How old...?"

"I was thirteen when she left."

"And you haven't seen her since?" She is incredulous.

He shakes his head ever so slightly. "Oh, I see her all the time, Catherine. In my mind, late at night. Especially when I'm alone on the farm. I see her, even talk to her. But not in the flesh. Before the war, I imagined that she'd come back someday. Just show up again once she heard the old man was dead. But she never did. Never has."

"What happened to your father?"

He looks up from the tabletop to find her studying his face now, perhaps seeing the scars there for the first time, the puckered flesh beside his left eye. "You sure you want to know all this?" he asks her. "Nothing about it is pretty."

She nods. "I do want to know. I told my story. Your turn."

"He died under mysterious circumstances."

"Your father?"

He nods.

She smiles at the serious tone of his voice and then almost immediately regrets it. "Mysterious?" she asks.

Clinton sighs and abruptly stands up. Looks around to see that there's no one else in the drugstore. Even the druggist is in the back room, counting pills. He slowly sits back down and leans forward on the table. "Summer after I graduated from high school," he more or less whispers, "he drowned in a little creek that runs down behind our old house and along the road. He got drunk one late afternoon. I sent Will on off to our aunt's house on some excuse or other. Dad was running from the house toward the road when he slipped and fell into the creek. Struck his head on a rock and lay there face down in the water till he drowned."

"Why in the world was he running?"

He smiles before he looks up to meet her eyes. "He was chasing me with a hammer. And when he fell, I left him there. Walked on down the road, glad to be alive myself."

"Jesus, Clint."

"I asked if you were sure you wanted to hear it."

She nods. "Yes, you did. And then you went off to war?"

"First, I went to Mars Hill. Managed to graduate with a degree in history. Got married to a girl from Kentucky. Built a house, planned a life. And then there was Pearl Harbor. *Then* I went to war."

"Did you want to go?"

He shrugs. "I figured the army needed men like me, Cat. Not accountants and clerks. Fighters. Besides, I got to see the world, or at least a large part of Europe."

"You should call me Cat," she says, smiling with her eyes.

"I just did. Will again."

She pauses before she asks the next question. "What was the war like?"

Now, he stands up for real. Stands up and stretches. When she sees that he doesn't plan to sit back down, she stands as well and takes their cups and saucers to the soda bar. As they work their way toward the door, he notices for the first time that she is only a few inches shorter than he. Willowy, he thinks, is how he would describe her.

As they walk back the one block toward the jail and her parked car, she says, "You're not going to tell me about the war, are you?"

"Not yet," he offers after a few more paces. "Someday. That story requires alcohol."

"For you to tell it or for me to hear it?"

He almost laughs. "Both, I imagine. Telling and hearing."

When they reach her car, a late-model station wagon with wooden side panels, he opens the driver's-side door for her. "Thank you, Clint," she says, bearing down on his name. "I think I'm going to call you Clint when I'm not calling you Sheriff."

"I can stand that," he says. She eases into the driver's seat, taking care that her skirt doesn't slide up. He closes the car door and she rolls down the window.

"One more thing," he says.

She looks up expectantly.

"About the gap in your teeth."

"Oh, God."

"Not horrible."

"It's not?"

He shakes his head. "Not at all. *Endearing* is the word I would use. Your smile is endearing."

She smiles, tight-lipped. And then, realizing what she's doing, manages a full-on grin.

CHAPTER 9

WHAT IN THE WORLD POSSESSED HIM TO TELL her that? About the death of his father, for God's sake. He had never told anyone how the old man ended up in the creek, not even his dead wife.

The good thing about his father is that anyone who knew him knew he drank any sort of raw alcohol he could get his hands on. Until the bottle was empty or it fell out of his insensible hand. And that he was as likely to end up face down in the branch as he was toes-up in the middle of the road or hanging ten feet up in a tree. When it happened, Clinton had only to act shocked and saddened when a neighbor found the body. Had only to tell one lie. *No, he hadn't seen his father all afternoon.* Two lies. *No, I have no idea why there was a hammer in the creek. Maybe he dropped it.*

And now, two cups of coffee with a gap-toothed smile and his secret was out. Well, if not out, shared. His secret was shared. And he'd have to ask her not to share it with anyone else. Even Marian.

FIVE O'CLOCK, AND HE SENDS BALIS NORTON ON home. Around six, Lloyd Maney shows up for the night shift, and Clinton begins to think he might just slip away from the jail, find something to eat, climb the hill to Mrs. Penland's. Or if not Mrs. Penland's, then...

The phone rings and when Lloyd answers, it turns out to be for Clinton.

When he takes the phone from Lloyd and speaks, the voice on the other end is not terrified or enraged or angry, what you would expect when the sheriff's office phone rings at night. Just the opposite. A voice clearly feminine, soft even. "Clint, it's Catherine Metcalf."

"Mrs. Metcalf..."

"Try again."

He motions Lloyd out of his office and nods at him to shut the door as he goes.

"Cat?"

There's a pause before she speaks. "Now that I've got you on the line, I can't quite bring myself to say why I called."

"Are you all right?"

"Oh, I'm fine. I just had a thought, and it was so real that I convinced myself to dial the phone even though it's none of my business." Another pause.

"Go ahead."

"Why don't you go home for the night? There, I said it."

"Why would...?"

"Marian talks about your farm, where she grew up, as if it's the last haven of peace and tranquility on earth. As if you can always retreat there, can always be safe there. Happy even on a winter night. And this afternoon, you seemed so tense, sad even, that I was afraid that you'd left your peace and happiness behind when you left Deer Branch—"

"Doe Branch."

"—Doe Branch behind. And all I did was walk into your office and give you yet one more problem to worry about. I feel guilty for telling you about the concrete block and the principal bitch. That's why I called."

"No reason for guilt. I was actually thinking about going home anyway. Not home to the boarding house, but home. To Doe Branch."

Another pause. As if neither of them can quite think what to say next. He imagines he can hear her breathing, but isn't sure. "Thank you for calling," he says finally. "I might have talked myself out of going otherwise. Maybe I needed permission."

"Well, you have it. From me." He can hear the smile in her voice, and he hopes she's not covering her mouth.

"Can I ask you a favor?" he says after a moment.

"Of course."

"Will you not share what I told you about my father with anyone? You might be the only person I've ever actually..."

"Of course. I know a secret when I hear one. God knows I have my own."

Another pause, this one because neither knows how to end the conversation. More imagined breathing.

"Good night, Cat," he says finally. "I'll see you Monday."

"You will?"

"I'm going to come by the high school to get the addresses of the McDevitt and Anderson boys. Pay them a visit."

Doe Branch. Eight o'clock and midwinter dark.

It's at least a thirty-minute ride in the Jeep from the middle of Marshall down the two-lane road to Walnut and from there down the winding road to the river at Barnard. Across the bridge at Barnard and then to the right up one-lane Big Pine Road, where Salters have farmed for a hundred and fifty years. To the right-hand turn, mostly dirt and some gravel now, a steep climb up to Bear Wallow Gap, and over the gap down into the cove that, for generations, has been known as Doe Branch.

As he drives, Clinton thinks about just how deep and wide is Madison County, especially in the dark, when only the moon and a scattering of stars provide any sort of light. There are few, if any, telephones in most of the isolated coves that make up his territory, and the roads, by just about any measure, are atrocious. It's the twentieth century, he thinks; world wars have been fought, but it still takes two hours to drive from one end of the county to the other. Spring Creek to Mars Hill. Hot Springs to Laurel. Sodom to anywhere. After dark, he imagines that time dissipates, rolls silently backward, and you could easily be traveling the steep back roads in the years following the assassination of Lincoln, rather than the assassination of Kennedy.

Time folds in upon itself in the dark, as do his thoughts. When he eases the Jeep slowly down the curved gravel track from the gap onto his own property, he can sense his father's old house reaching out from the left-hand side of the road through the dark. A light blinks on from the front porch, a bare bulb that throws a filmy luminescence across the yard, casting more shadow than sight. A tenant lives in the house now, half–tenant farmer and half- caretaker who has been with Clinton for ten years, and he's in the habit of turning on his porch light whenever he hears someone in the road along the creek.

Clinton pulls the Jeep to a stop just opposite the house, by the footbridge, and taps the horn. A moment later, the front door creaks open and Randall Shelton eases out onto the porch, his old .410 shotgun held down along his leg. "It's me," Clinton yells to reassure him. Randall waves and slips down the plank steps and along the stepping stones to the bridge. "You done quit your job and come home?" Randall asks when he gets close enough.

"I wish," he replies. "No. I just came home for the night. Check on the dogs. Sleep in my own bed." He points up the cove to his right toward his own house, built just before the war, when the world was poor, but safe.

"The house is likely cold." Randall shifts from one foot to another in the chilled dark. "I keep the furnace stoked up just in case, but the heat is set on fifty or thereabouts."

"That's all right. What I get for sneaking up on you. How would you feel about having a telephone in your house?" He nods at his father's ramshackle place. "I could let you know when I'm headed this way. And if you needed something, you wouldn't have to walk up to the farmhouse to call."

"I don't rightly know how to work a telephone," Randall says.

Clinton laughs. "You can learn. If you can drive a tractor, you can master a damn telephone. You could call that daughter of yours on it too. It'll be a separate line from the one up at the house."

Randall shifts his weight again, considering. "All right," he says after a bit. "How much will it cost me?"

"Nothing," he replies. "I'll pay for it."

YOU CAN'T SEE THE FARMHOUSE FROM THE ROAD because the narrow driveway winds through an ancient stand of rhododendrons—a laurel thicket, mountain people call it—and when he pulls up beside the house and cuts the Jeep's engine, everything is suddenly very quiet. There's no light on in the house, which makes sense, and it's a full minute before his dogs recall their duty and start to bark.

The dogs—a thirty-pound mixed terrier named Jake and a sixty-pound shepherd-husky named Nick—have the run of the valley during the day but are shut up in the house at night to save them chasing a deer or bear into the next county. Nick is smart enough to find his way home across the mountains, but Jake? Jake is a fool—sweet, but simple.

The front door on the wide porch is locked, so he steals around the side of the house and lets himself in through the back door, where he pulls off his boots and turns on a light in the kitchen. The dogs find him there, Jake jumping all over him, while Nick regards him from a few feet away as if to say, "What the hell? Middle of the night?" He turns up the thermostat and lets them outside, knowing Nick won't run if Clinton's there, and he won't let Jake play the fool.

He keeps a case of bourbon at the farm—bought in Asheville where it's legal. He pours himself a tot, adds some ice, and then, glass in hand, walks sock-footed out on the front porch. He can hear the dogs by Nick's occasional bark as they roam up through the orchard, perhaps as far as the cemetery on the flank of the ridge. His father, along with three dozen other Salters and Fortners, Robbinses and Fowlers, are buried up there. Graves that reach back before the Civil War. Hardly anyone now knows that his father's full first name was Lazarus, not Rus, but so far as Clinton can tell, the old man has never risen from the grave. The dogs would tell it if he had. Hell, he himself would feel it where his broken arm healed years before.

Standing, breathing, letting the cold air seep into him, knowing that a hot bath and more whiskey wait inside, he lets his mind wander. A few stray thoughts of Cat Metcalf; he's not sure why, perhaps the husky sound of her voice on the telephone. Thoughts of his daughter: Would she ever marry? Of his son, who is lost. His son, who he could not place, even in his imagination.

Cat again. A woman in full. But then what would he want with a woman? Or she with him, damaged as he is?

CHAPTER 10

Two weeks later. December 19, a Saturday night.

The annual Madison County basketball tournament has just concluded an hour before, and the crowd is mostly gone from the parking lot of the Mars Hill College gym. The championship game was hotly contested, won at the buzzer 62–60 by the team from Mars Hill High over Marshall. A McIntyre boy from Mars Hill scored forty points in the final and had not been shy about letting the Marshall team and even the crowd know just how good he was. There was one loud shouting match in the lobby of the gym between a parent and a ref and two fistfights in the parking lot, but now things have begun to settle.

Clinton has just said good night to Marian and Luke, her longtime boyfriend who teaches at the college. He is leaning against the front bumper of the Jeep, catching his breath. From where he stands, he can see Cat Metcalf's station wagon and imagines that she's still on patrol herself, making sure her own students have all left before she goes home. Maybe they'll spend a few minutes chatting, he imagines, or maybe they'll miss each other in the dark, as they often seem to do.

This night, he keeps his sheriff's badge prominently displayed. He has decided not to wear a uniform in his formal capacity, but at events like this, he turns the leather wallet containing his badge inside out and slips it over his belt so that it's plain to see. In the Jeep, a loaded .45 caliber army surplus pistol is locked in the glove box along with a pair of handcuffs. Behind the seat of the Jeep, a Winchester .30-30 waits unloaded, but with a box of shells in the same glove box. He has already seen enough in two weeks to think that the time may come when he has to arm himself.

He is watching the McIntyre boy and several of his Mars Hill buddies hooting and laughing beside their car, replaying the game and yelling at anybody they know. Suddenly, he hears someone, a familiar voice, scream his name—*Clint!*—and he turns toward the sound. It's Cat, and she's running from the direction of the gym and pointing at a dark figure she is chasing. Again, she screams, and Clinton is sprinting now. He realizes the figure, a man with a stick—no, a rifle—isn't trying to run away, but toward something—someone. Clinton yells at the man to stop, drop the damn rifle. In the splintered moment that follows, the man reaches the McIntyre boy's car just before Clinton and pivots around the back bumper. The boys see what's coming and scatter.

The harsh crack of the rifle.

Clinton is around the front of the car, leaps over the body of one of the boys and slams the man into the car itself. Tears the rifle out of his hands so that it clatters to the ground. The man means to fight, escape, run, and in a rage, Clinton slams his head onto the trunk of the car once, and again, before dragging him to the Jeep and handcuffing him to the steering wheel.

Confusion, shouting. Hoarse voices and shrill screams.

He stuffs the .45, safety on, into the back of his belt and rushes back to the car. It's the McIntyre boy on the pavement, groaning, shot in the chest. Cat is kneeling beside him, people gathering. He falls to his knees beside her, holding his badge high to keep the onlookers back. "Go," he hisses to her. "To the gym. Telephone an ambulance." And she's gone, dashing back the way she came, gasping for breath. "Tell them it's a gunshot," he yells after her.

One of the boys, McIntyre's friend, picks up the rifle and starts toward the Jeep. "Oh, hell no," he says to the boy, immediately shifting toward him. They wrestle briefly, before he pulls the gun out of the kid's hands. "Do something useful," he grunts at the boy. "Take your shirt off and compress the wound."

"Compress the—?"

"Pressure on the wound. Stop the bleeding."

RUSS MCINTYRE SURVIVES THE AMBULANCE ride to St. Joseph's Hospital in Asheville. Survives the emergency surgery to remove the bullet, which, because he dove toward the ground when he saw what was coming, missed his heart and only punctured his lung. Survives ten days at St. Joe's before he is released to his parents. Survives one of the best and worst nights of his life.

The man who shot him is a middle-aged mechanic named Andrew Garland. His nephew played for one of the other high schools in the county, and he was drunk enough to be incensed at the McIntyre boy over the forty points and the defeat. Garland himself spends three nights in the Madison County jail before Clinton convinces a judge to order him moved to Buncombe County for his own protection. Eventually, the same judge relocates the trial to Asheville as well, since there is not an objective juror to be found in Madison County.

CHAPTER 11

CHRISTMAS DAY, 1964.

Dawn breaks cold and bleak, the air frigid enough overnight to start a skim of ice in the eddies along Doe Branch. Clinton is at home on the farm, and when he walks out with the dogs midmorning, he can hear the wind howling like a freight train on the high ridge above the cemetery. "Too damn cold to snow," he tells Nick and Jake when they return breathless from chasing a rabbit through the upper pasture.

Marian and Luke are coming for Christmas dinner in the early afternoon, and he is cooking. Roasting a turkey stuffed with onions and garlic, sliced apples and celery. Baked sweet potatoes and a pot of green beans along with hot cornbread. Marian will bring her famous pumpkin pie. She has hinted that there might be another guest along as well, which puzzles him. He won't let himself even begin to hope for his son, Matt, as that would bring the pain of disappointment. But who, then? Will is taken up with his own wife and children, and they have a new grandchild to play Santa with. Who, then? No doubt a teacher friend or someone from the college. An image of Cat Metcalf flits across his mind, but he won't quite let himself hope for that.

An extra person is fine by him. It's Christmas, after all.

Around noon, he lights the kindling under the fire he's laid in the living room fireplace. Checks on the turkey in the oven. Puts the potatoes in to bake.

Shortly after one, the dogs start to bark, and a few minutes later, Marian's car pulls up in the drive just in front of the porch steps. When he lets Nick and Jake out, they mob Marian first, as she's known them both since they were puppies, then Luke because he's carrying food. And then, finally, they stop long enough to sniff the third person in the car—the mysterious Christmas guest, the unexpected one.

"Dad," Marian calls out to him while petting the dogs. "I made her come, Dad. She was working today, for God's sake. You said there was a turkey, so I told her there'd be plenty of food."

"There is plenty of food," he says to Marian as she and Luke climb the steps and head into the house, the dogs playing around them as if part of the celebration.

He walks down the steps and meets Catherine Metcalf at the bottom. "What the hell, Cat, working on Christmas!"

"I...well, I didn't have anybody really to celebrate it with. I went to see James at the Ivy Rehab yesterday and took him his present. So, I thought it was the perfect day to get a lot done at school." She's serious as she says this, her arms crossed over her stomach, holding her denim jacket together.

He means to be cross with her, stern up against her notion of working on this day, but it's hard for him to keep a straight face. "Christ was born today," he says. He points down to the ground as if to signify that the earth itself knows what day it is. "The donkeys brayed, and the dogs howled, and the cows mooed."

"Sounds like 'Old MacDonald Had a Farm,'" she manages to say with a perfectly straight face. But then, her lips twitch and the corners of her eyes rise into the faintest wrinkles. "And angels were heard to sing on high," she adds.

"They were heard. Why didn't you tell me you didn't have any place to go?" Even as he says it, he realizes just how stupid it sounds. He should have known, or guessed, or asked. He turns and gestures behind him. "This is it," he says. "The last haven of peace on earth. You picked the perfect day to see it."

"Listen, Clint. I'm happy to be here. But I'm not a member of your family. I know that. I don't have presents for anyone, even Marian. I don't have anything to offer for food or warmth or... anything. Wait, I did bring a bottle of wine. I had it in the car and when Marian kidnapped me, I grabbed it." She leans into the back seat of Marian's car to find the bottle.

"For God's sake, come in," he says. "Come and sit by the fire." What he doesn't say is that he dreamed of her several nights before. Forgot the dream when he woke, but is now retrieving it...or rather the dream is recalling itself inside his mind with a strange kind of déjà vu. Of her on the farm, walking, talking, gesturing. He has consciously thought of her in his house, friendly and easy, but then, in a sober moment, wondered just what the hell! What the hell would she do or say to his house? It is beyond rustic, full of books and smelling of woodsmoke. Deer antlers over the fireplace and his grandfather's shotgun hung above the door inside his bedroom. Since Gretchen was gone, the children fled, every inch of this house a man's stronghold protected by his dogs. A retreat. A secret, silent place shut off from the world.

They climb the front steps together. And because the steps are so steep, he reaches out casually to take her arm. At the same moment, she reaches out, their hands meet in midair, surprising them both. Groping and then clasping together.

Since there is no Christmas tree, Marian and Luke place their presents along with his on the ancient chestnut table in the living room. They open Cat's bottle of wine, laughing at her as she explains over and over how cheap it is, that it was intended only for herself, not for...company.

Marian takes great pleasure in showing her around the house, first the living room, dining room, and kitchen. And then, upstairs, where the more secret nooks and crannies are. Catherine is surprised by the number of books scattered throughout the house. History, mostly, but also a few novels—unusual, she thinks, for a man, but then everything about the house suggests that he's an unusual man.

Upstairs, Marian shows off her childhood bedroom and then her brother's—a remarkably sterile place with few personal mementos—and then...her father's room. With the map of western North Carolina and eastern Tennessee, the bookshelf by the bed with yet more books. The windows with curtains tied back, windows that open onto the wide expanse of country behind the house. And yes, the shotgun over the doorway.

This room, Cat decides, smells like him. Not so much a particular odor of cologne or some other bought fragrance, but soap, maybe, and burning candles, the occasional cigar that Marian says he loves. Gun oil and old books, cut by fresh, cold air. Whiskey...maybe. Wool—does wool have a smell? That too. And she asks herself, Does she like the scent? It's a foolish question, really.

She finds that she loves the smell of that room.

Downstairs, the smells are all of food and the fire burning. Marian and her Luke settle into a large, old, very worn sofa in the living room, so she, Cat, wanders into the kitchen and offers to help.

"You can set the table," Clinton says as he takes a steaming hot skillet out of the oven and pours the hot oil into his cornmeal before spooning the mixture back into the skillet to bake. "Four places instead of three."

She looks around.

"Use whatever china you can find in that corner cupboard. It won't all match, I warn you."

"Listen, Sheriff Salter, I didn't mean to interrupt your dinner, I swear."

"You already said that. You're not interrupting. I can tell Marian is thrilled she managed to corral you, and if we have to handcuff you to a table leg to get you to eat, then that's what we'll do. The silver, such as it is, is in that drawer—that one... pull hard."

The terrier, Jake, is on the couch with Marian and Luke, lapping up all the affection he can get. The shepherd-husky, Nick, comes into the kitchen and lies down on a dog bed beside the back door. He doesn't take his dark eyes off her as she works. Nick hasn't made up his mind, she realizes, what he thinks of her.

"Do you know how to carve a turkey?" Clint asks.

She laughs. "Oddly enough, I do. I used to help my father at Thanksgiving. A hundred years ago."

Everything is steaming now, boiling on the stove, and the windows in the kitchen are fogged over against the cold outside. Music comes from the record player in the living room. Nat King Cole maybe...Christmas carols. Does this remind him of his past, she wonders. Music, food, his children. A strange woman?

He opens the pantry, reaches on the back of the door, and hands her an apron. She takes it from him and starts to tie it on, and it is at that moment they both look up. "Shit," she mutters, "it's your wife's, isn't it?"

He shrugs and nods, before smiling. "It is." He glances around the kitchen. "But she won't mind. She's not here."

AFTER THEY EAT, A LOT, MARIAN DECREES THAT she and Luke will clean up the kitchen. And they, Dad and Mrs. Metcalf, Catherine, must sit. "I have a better idea," he says. "We'll take the dogs out. *Mrs. Metcalf, Catherine* can see the farm."

He pulls on his old barn coat—the sleeves and collar torn and raveling—and after a moment spent ruefully regarding the coatrack, hands her a thick jacket with *Madison County Sheriff's Department* emblazoned across the back.

"Seriously?" she says, laughing.

He shrugs. "Consider yourself deputized." He gives her thick wool mittens roughly the size of oven mitts.

The dogs know immediately what this means and have been pawing at the front door, Jake whining, since the coats came off the rack.

AFTER THE HEAT OF THE HOUSE AND THE HEFT of the meal, outside feels like waking up. The air startlingly fresh and cold, the wind above them in the maple tree beside the house, talking more than whispering. From the porch, he points through the laurel stand in front of them. "The house where I grew up is across the creek. There's a tenant lives there now. He went to spend the day with his daughter. I'll take him some of our leftovers for his supper."

He takes her arm again for the steps, protectively.

From any other man, she would have resented it, she decides. But for whatever reason, not him. Protective is just part of his nature.

He leads her around the corner of his house and past the Jeep. They follow a path between stout clumps of winter grass, unshorn since August. He points to the first barn, fifty feet behind the house, and leads her inside. The structure is ancient, at least three stories high, and smells pungently of tobacco, rich and acrid. From the dusty floor, she looks up into row upon row of beams. "I didn't know you grew burley," she says, showing off what little she's learned of farm life over the years.

"Used to," he says, "for cash. One of the few things you can truly turn to cash off the land. What you smell is history. Now, this barn mostly belongs to His Highness." In explanation, he leads her to several stalls that have been closed off at the back of the barn, but when she steps up to the barrier, he pulls her back a step or two. "Not too close. He's a temperamental son of a bitch."

"What in God's name?"

"He's a ram. Daddy Man is his name. We run a flock of about forty sheep and shear for the wool. Sell off the lambs once they begin to look like mutton."

"Do you ever get in there with him?"

"Not sober." He grins for her and steps up to the barrier, with her beside him. Again, protective. "The only creature on the whole place that isn't afraid of him is Nick. And Nick isn't afraid of anything that walks or paws the earth, four legs or two. There's a one-armed sheep shearer that comes in the spring, and it takes both of us plus Randall, the hired man, to shear that bastard. He does his job, though."

"His job is to make lambs?"

He nods. Several things occur to him to say about Daddy Man making lambs, but he doesn't know her well enough just yet to say any of them.

Behind the barn, they open and shut a gate to what he explains is the lower pasture. They follow a rough road through the pasture grass up to the apple orchard.

Where he shows her the several varietals. Early Joe, Grimes Golden, two varietals of Limbertwig, and a half dozen gnarled old trees he calls Pippins. Newtown Pippins. "That stock is from my grandfather's place in Anderson Cove. I've always treasured those trees because they did. My Grandma Robbins in particular."

"When do they come in?" she asks.

"The Pippins? Around Labor Day. They're late, but not as late as the Limbertwigs." They walk on through the orchard. She watches his face as his eyes react every time one of the dogs—Jake—barks. Somehow, he's tracking them as they run.

"What are they telling you?" she asks.

"The dogs?"

She nods. She reaches out to take his arm, but stops herself. *What in the world am I doing?* she asks herself.

He stops and gestures uphill beyond a second barn, a stone barn. He's pointing toward the dogs, she knows. "That's mostly been Jake talking. He loves to chase anything that moves. It's the terrier in him. He'll chase down some small rodent, and Nick will kill it. Swallow it or leave it for Jake. Snakes, Jake is hell on snakes." Now there is a deeper, harsher sound, a barking that means business. "That's Nick," he says. "He's found something bigger. Wrong time of year for a bear. Deer, maybe. Or a bobcat. We've had a bobcat about lately. Killed our barn cats and ate them."

"Isn't that...cannibalism?"

"You'd think, but apparently, old bobcat doesn't recognize the relationship." They are through another gate and close to the stone barn now. "Do you like to ride, Cat?" he asks.

She stops in her tracks. This time, she does reach out and pull on his arm to get him to face her. "I will have you know, Clint Salter, that I showed horses as a girl. And I ride very well. Better than you, I would imagine."

He puts his head back and laughs. "I bet you do. It will please you to know, then, that we have two horses on the place right now. One big gelding that will pull a sledge if you ask him and ride you up the mountain as well. The other a young mare that I took away from a man who was mistreating her."

"Introduce me," she says.

CHAPTER 12

JANUARY 6, 1965. EPIPHANY, WHAT MOUNTAIN people know as Old Christmas.

Clinton takes Way Tipton with him in the Jeep down to Barnard on the river. They stop to talk to the proprietor at Gudger's Store so that Clinton can sort out the various places he's looking for on the far side of the river.

They cross the Barnard Bridge, but instead of turning right up the Big Pine Road toward Doe Branch and home, he cranks the steering wheel around to the left, and they head up Anderson Branch, into Freeman territory along with the Paynes and Caldwells. The pavement runs out when the road veers away from the river, past the Anderson Branch Church and beyond. Clinton points out various landmarks, including Pawpaw Mountain. "We say that so-and-so lives up on Pawpaw." At one point, he stops the Jeep in the middle of the road—or what passes for the road—and points up the ridgeline to the right. "My great-grandfather Ben Freeman is buried up there. Civil War soldier, bootlegger, some say a killer, could write the prettiest hand you ever saw. What's for certain is that he was married to a Payne, Harriet Payne, who is widely believed to have been the meanest woman in Madison County."

Way looks up the ridge and then turns back to Clinton. "That's saying something. I expect there was a lot of competition for that badge back in the day."

"There's a lot of competition for it now, Way. Best not to list names, though."

During the next six hours, they wend their way back through some of the most isolated parts of the county until they eventually come out on upper Little Pine Road. Clinton navigates by dead reckoning and by stopping to talk to most everyone they meet. In this fashion, they find the three farms Clinton is looking for, all of which have one thing in common: Over the past two years, someone burned down the farmer's barn in the middle of the night, sometimes incinerating livestock in the process. The news leaked out of the coves by word of mouth, as barn burning was common enough in previous generations that each incident barely made an inch of typescript in the newspaper, if that.

But there is something different here, or so Clinton thinks, something tying these together. They talk at length with two of the farmers, who were surprised to see the high sheriff himself in their front yard and even more surprised to discover that he cared. They didn't talk to the third farmer or his wife because when they finally located that property, the house was nothing but a scorched foundation over a rain-filled cellar hole. A neighbor, man named Teague, explained that the "matchstick son of a bitch" had come back two weeks after torching his friend's barn and burned the family out of their house. "You best catch him, Sheriff, because if we ever figure out who did it, we'll bury him where you can't find him."

Clinton shakes his head. "Well, if you catch him before I do, I don't want to know where he's buried."

Before they leave, Teague tells them of yet another barn "burnt to hell" off the Little Pine Road, and they stop there on the way out even though it's late afternoon and the winter dusk is looming. Turns out this is a Hagan family, and they speak with Mrs. Hagan as Mister is gone to Marshall. What she tells them would turn your blood cold. Whoever did it deliberately waited until their entire burley crop was hung to dry just last fall. Thousands of dollars of tobacco gone up in flames. Their cash crop for the year. Mister is trying to arrange a loan to get them through the winter, but so far, not much luck. "Send him to me," Clinton tells the woman, "and I'll walk over to the bank with him. Pound on a desk or two. Cosign if I need to."

"You would do that for us?" She is incredulous. "We didn't vote for you."

For the first time since they pulled up in the yard, Clinton smiles. "I don't care about that. If I'm fool enough to run again, vote for me next time."

A mile below the Hagan place, Clinton points out for Way where his brother, Will, lives with his brood.

"Does he farm?" Way asks.

"Pretends to," Clinton replies. "Mostly just talks."

When they pull up to the stop sign on the main highway back to Marshall, Way says, "I guess we can't really call the barn burnings a cold case, can we?"

"Why not?"

"Because they're burnings, get it?"

He regards Way, who keeps a perfectly straight face. "That's pretty damn funny, Way."

"Why you keep me around."

A FEW DAYS LATER, CLINTON ASKS GLORIA Goforth to order the biggest map of Madison County she can find. When it arrives, it takes three of them—Clinton, Gloria, and Way Tipton—to tack it to the wall of his office. When they step back to admire their handiwork, Clinton asks, "Is it just me, or does the whole county look like a clenched fist?"

Way nods.

Gloria says, "I didn't notice till you said it, but now..."

The next time Way is in the office, he sees that there are four red pushpins in the middle of the map: Anderson Branch and Little Pine Road. "You know," Way says to Clinton, "this is how people solved things a hundred years ago. Your neighbor did something you didn't like, you burned his barn. If he's in the way of your boundary line or your pasture fence, hell, you burned his house. It's like the clock is spinning backwards on this."

"What do they have in common, then?" Clinton asks him. "Other than some crazy, old ghost from the past who wanders around at night with a five-gallon can of kerosene and a box of lucifer matches?"

Way considers for a moment. "What they have in common is that somebody is trying to force them out. Cut off their livelihood and these people will have to move."

"If you're right," Clinton offers, "then the next step is to start burning more houses instead of barns."

"That's right."

"Then maybe we best catch them sooner rather than later."

CHAPTER 13

Both Clinton Salter and Catherine Metcalf testify at Andrew Garland's trial in Asheville on a bitter cold day in January. The trial is in Asheville because of the ongoing anger and bitterness from both sides of the case: McIntyre's family screaming for blood, and Garland's family shouting back that the kid started it all by running his damn mouth. Some people need shooting, or so they say. Plus, as it turns out, there was a girl involved. Welcome to Madison County.

The trial only takes two days. On the second day, they drive together in Cat's station wagon since the canvas top on Clint's Jeep is not made for frigid weather. On the afternoon of day two, the prosecution rests, the jury is out for less than two hours, and the whole episode is done, at least as far as the legal system is concerned. Assault with intent to commit murder: guilty. Clinton counts six uniformed Buncombe County deputies in the courtroom and the hallway outside. Enough force to keep the rival factions away from each other.

Standing on the sidewalk outside, Cat with her long, wool coat pulled close around her against the infamous Asheville wind, asks, "Time to start back?"

"I was thinking I might buy you supper in return for driving."

She laughs even as she shivers. "Do you mean a real dinner? Not a meat-and-three from the Rock Cafe?"

"A real dinner. More than one course. Wine, even."

"Lord…I don't know. Let's think about it in the car with the heater running."

In the car, with the windows fogging up, they could be anybody, he thinks, hidden behind the fog. Not necessarily the High Sheriff and the High School Principal. Not two public figures recognizable to half the people in Madison County. Anybody. She's thinking something similar, he decides. That they're far enough away from Marshall to be human. "The Weaverville Milling Company," he says finally. "It's on the way home, more or less. Steaks, pasta. Red wine that could almost have come from Italy."

She smiles at him, at first tight-lipped, but then with her whole mouth.

"It's dark on the inside too, as I recall. Mostly candlelight."

"Oh, Clint. But is it dark enough?"

He shrugs, still staring out through the fogged-up windshield. "What the hell," he says finally. "We'll ask for a table in the corner."

"Or by the fireplace," she says, "if there is one. I'm still freezing."

He directs her along Weaverville Road, past the turnoff to the Marshall Highway. As they drive, it begins to spit snow. He has her turn right onto Reems Creek Road, and a quarter mile later, they pull off beside the creek and into the gravel parking lot. There are perhaps five cars in the lot, a slow night. When she cuts the ignition, she hands him the keys. "I can drink wine," she explains. "In fact, it was the wine from Italy that got me. But Clint, here's the thing. If I drink, you have to drive. I work for the school system."

It is dark inside. And warm. Candlelit. A couple of families and two or three couples scattered into corners of the room. She orders the steak, after asking him if he can afford it. He orders the trout, pecan crusted. Hot bread with rich, salty butter. A bottle of red wine that they agree they will not finish but take with them. Into the cold, into the wild.

"1950," she says at one point after the wine has begun working its way into their bloodstreams. "Fourteen, fifteen years ago. Since..."

"Since?"

"Since I sat in a restaurant at night with a man. Not a drugstore or a diner, but a real, honest-to-God restaurant, where the waiter comes by and pours wine in your glass without you having to whistle to get his attention."

"With your husband?"

"Yes, back before he insisted that I scramble eggs every damn night or get by on peanut butter and white bread. And buttermilk. God, I hate buttermilk."

He shakes his head. "He's a fool, then. To put you through that. Sorry, I shouldn't speak about the man. Not my place."

She grins. "You're sitting here in his place. You can say what you want. How long has it been for you?"

Just as she asks the question, the food arrives, steaming on the plate. Minutes pass, both of them taken in completely by beef and fish, both relishing what it tastes like and what it feels like. Then, between bites, she asks again. "How long has it been for you?"

He considers as he chews. Then swallows. "Since before Gretchen died. Seven or eight years. There was a time a few years ago when Marian kept trying to interest me in women that she picked out, but I couldn't have cared less at that point, and she gave up."

"Is Gretchen your wife's name?"

He nods. "Yes, it is. Or was, rather. It's funny. Is...was? For the longest time after she died, I couldn't say her name. Somehow, I couldn't push the syllables past my lips. I didn't like to hear anyone else pronounce it either."

"You just said it a moment ago, or I wouldn't have asked."

"I know. It slipped out. Well, anyway. She—Gretchen never cared for the mountains, if you want to know the truth. Too cold, too dark, too empty."

Another few bites. "You should have brought her to the Weaverville Milling Company. It's dark, but not cold or empty."

He shakes his head, even butters a roll and bites it before answering. "She would have complained about the food or the waiter or the..." He shrugs. "Something. Maybe that's not really fair? In the beginning, she liked it here, even out on Doe Branch, but after a few winters, she began to miss her home up in Kentucky."

She reaches over and rests her hand, warm now, on his. "We're sort of pathetic, Clint, you and me. Seven years, fifteen years. Do you think we'll ever break out of the slump we're in?"

He nods after a bit. "We're sitting here," he whispers. He pulls up his sleeve and glances at his wristwatch. "At eight thirty-six in the evening on January the nineteenth, 1965." He pauses and points down through the floor to the earth itself, as if the earth signifies time as well as space. "Here, now. And I think we should drink all the wine to celebrate."

"I'll help do that. But drive slow," she says. "That's all I ask."

CHAPTER 14

FEBRUARY, THE COLDEST MONTH OF THE YEAR. The month of icicles along the eaves and the creek frozen over. When Clinton walks out along the railroad tracks to ease the tension in his back and shoulders, he sees that the river is slate gray, as if it were about to freeze into steel before his eyes. And as he watches, he will occasionally see chunks of ice, broken free upstream, crash over the Redmon Dam.

What he discovers during his long hours at the jail is that behind the locked door at the end of the downstairs hallway is a kitchen that runs the entire width of the building. Refrigerator, freezer, an industrial-sized cookstove. A worktable for chopping and blending and mixing. And in the middle of the floor, a stout chestnut table that would easily seat six or eight people. Only two chairs that would hold any weight at all, but he figures chairs can be found.

The evening after he discovers all this, he takes Lloyd Maney back to show him the kitchen. "Did you know all this was here?"

Lloyd nods, which is like watching a puppet's head being jerked by a string. "I did know about it. When I first come to work here ten years ago, there was an old lady who cooked for the deputies and the prisoners. She died."

"I'm sure she did. But why didn't somebody take her place?"

"Well, I guess it was because of Sheriff Tate. He didn't like to eat here, said he preferred his sister's cooking. And he sure as hell didn't like to spend no money. Not to feed all of us. So, over time, the kitchen just sort of rolled over and died."

"I can see that. Let me ask you one more question, and this is the most important one of all. Can Mrs. Maney cook?"

Lloyd commences to nod again, even more violently than before, and his sallow face blushes pink. "That woman is the cook of the world. She can do up fish and game, beef and chicken that would make a grown man cry. Vegetables? Why, that woman never seen a vegetable she couldn't turn into a soup or a stew. And pies. Why, Lord God, Mrs. Maney can make pies that would—"

Lloyd is as skinny as a fence rail, but Clinton doesn't bother to point this out. "All right, slow down. Does she want a job?"

"You mean a cooking job? Here at the jail?"

He nods. "Cook two meals a day. Feed us and the prisoners. I don't think I'm going to hire any more deputies right now, so I've got a little money I could pay her, and we could lay in some supplies from local farmers. Hell, I can grow a lot of what we need."

Lloyd has left off nodding, but is still blinking rapidly. It's such a new idea that it's taking him a minute to digest. "Well," he says finally, "I guess she might like it. Could she bring the dog?"

THE VERY NEXT DAY, MRS. ROSIE MANEY SHOWS up with a basket of cleaning supplies, another of clean rags, and an ancient Plott hound tied with an old belt for a leash. She allows that she goes by Rosie and the hound goes by Brutus. Clinton thinks that Brutus might collapse at any moment.

"You, Sheriff," she says. "I'll commence to get this place clean. And I mean *clean*. You get us some groceries in here and starting tomorrow, you'll have something decent to eat."

"Don't you want to know how much I'm going to pay you?"

She shakes her head. "I reckon you'll pay me what I'm worth. Here's the list for what I need to get started."

He has to get an electrician in the next day to get all the appliances in the new kitchen up and running, but at suppertime, Rosie serves up a giant pot of beef stew, two pones of cornbread, and peach cobbler. There is lemonade to drink and, thank God Almighty, coffee, percolated in a pot on the stovetop. He, plus Gloria and three of his deputies, along with Lloyd and Rosie, eat everything, sopping up the stew with the bread. Brutus eats cornbread soaked in gravy. It is a fine time, with much celebration.

That night, late, a call comes in. Another great barn has gone up in flames.

The next morning, a Sunday, while most of the county is in church, Clint and Way Tipton ride out into the country between Marshall and Mars Hill. Following the directions Lloyd was given over the phone the night before, they turn up Rector Creek and then Rector Branch until they see the smudge of smoke and steam still drifting slowly into the cold sky.

Hollis Rector is a farmer in name only. Rather, he is a banker by trade, one of the men who control how money flows through the county. Not a bad man, but a tight one, with a reputation for turning down the poor and extending the hand of God and mammon to the better off. They walk with Hollis out to what's left of his barn to survey the wreckage. Way asks all the typical questions while he, Clinton, circles the site slowly, looking for any clues as to who'd been there. Sniffing for the leftover stench of kerosene or gasoline.

No, Hollis has no enemies, or so he says. No, he doesn't know who'd want to do such a thing—unless it was one of these goddamned Democrats that have sprung up lately. This last part whispered to Way. No, his neighbors are all fine people. Upright and honest. No, he hasn't lost any livestock; the wife keeps a few chickens these days, that's all. The barn was empty except for an old Ford tractor, which the insurance company will replace.

As they're leaving, Hollis walks with them out to the Jeep. "What are you going to do about this, Sheriff Salter? I doubt that you are aware, given that it happened during the previous administration, but there have been several other such incidents."

Clinton holds up all four fingers and the thumb of his left hand, spread wide. "Five," he replies. "This is number five."

"Well, the good men of this county will expect some prompt action on your part, even though you are new to the office and inexperienced in law enforcement."

Clinton all but laughs out loud. "Well, you tell the good men that I intend to catch whoever's doing this and prosecute him. If some of the less-good men don't catch him first and deal with him on their own."

As they're driving back to town, Way speaks up. "He thinks a Democrat might have done it."

He nods. "I'd say it's at least fifty-fifty he's right. Why don't you find out if the rest of the victims were Republicans? The clerk of court will know."

Way nods. "You find anything?"

"Some very interesting footprints. Our boy got mired up in a mudhole behind the barn. Left his boot prints. Bigger than mine. Size eleven or twelve with a prominent heel."

"Cowboy boots?"

"Square-toe, but yes, cowboy work boots, and the heel on the right boot is worn off on the outside."

THAT AFTERNOON, HE STICKS ANOTHER PIN IN the map. As he's standing and considering, a cup of Rosie's good coffee in hand, his brother puts in an appearance.

Will Salter has been to church apparently, for he is wearing a garish tie around his neck and comes in with his son, Willie, in tow. Willie, aka William Salter Jr., is twenty-four or -five, thickly built and swarthy. He is a student at the Community College in Buncombe County, but Clinton hasn't noticed that he spends much time going to class or studying. Mostly, he does Will's farmwork for him. When the boy was younger, Clinton often wondered if Will was dishing out some of the same treatment to his children that the brothers had received from their own father. He'd seen Will pull out his belt on Main Street in Marshall to whip his son over some minor disobedience and, horrified, Clint had run across the street to restrain Will himself.

Regardless, Willie has grown too big for his father's belt and could fight back. Probably has fought back. He slouches against the wall of Clinton's office now, while his father does the talking.

"Brother," Will greets Clinton, loud enough to be heard in the kitchen. "How you making out with hiring the new deputies?"

"I'm looking around," he replies. "Some of them I want to swear at rather than swear in."

"Well, I didn't come to talk to you about that. Fellow up the road, good man, one of ours, told me you'd been asking around about those barns that got burnt up last summer. Now, you and I haven't talked about it, but I assured our man that you didn't have time for such as that. Hell, people been burning down barns in the mountains for a hundred years. Two hundred."

"True," Clinton admits. "Houses, hotels, churches. Barns just don't seem that important, do they?"

"That's right!" Will exclaims.

"Well, tell your friend that I'm not concerned with the barns. I'm more interested in getting the jailhouse kitchen up and running. First things first."

As soon as Will makes some more noise and then leads Willie back out to their car parked in front of the jail, Clint quietly shuts the door and goes back to regarding the map.

CHAPTER 15

WHAT ARE THE AGREEMENTS, THE UNWRITTEN laws, that hold our fragile human family together? That children are sacred and not to be violated. That elders are to be venerated, listened to, cared for. That a man shall not strike a woman, regardless of the provocation. That a man shall not force carnal relations with a woman. That our kinship to the earth is that of caretaker, not ravager. That life itself is sacred and not to be sacrificed lightly. Yes. To all of these—we say *yes*.

In the final measure, it is Clinton Salter's role, or so he believes, to maintain the unwritten laws first and foremost, so that we might survive. Among these laws...

That the living shall respect the dead and leave them to their rest.

IN JUNE OF THAT YEAR, DURING BROAD DAYLIGHT, someone breaks into the two mausoleums in the Safford family cemetery on a hillside above Hot Springs. They break open the vaults and pull five decayed bodies out onto the ground in order to steal any valuables they can find.

When the call comes in, Clinton is alone at the office except for Gloria. At first, he thinks the call is some sort of prank—grave robbing, for God's sake—but the man on the other end of the line is as serious as he is angry, and Clinton agrees to meet him beside the railroad tracks in Hot Springs.

Thirty minutes later, he drives the Jeep over the French Broad

River bridge and then up and over the railroad tracks. Jimmy Rumbough meets him just on the other side and climbs into the Jeep beside him. They drive together up the long gravel driveway, now mostly overgrown, to the beautiful swale where the Safford family mansion stood until it burned down some years before. There is little left except the ruins of the house in the middle of a wide, sun-drenched meadow. Little left except the family cemetery tucked away in a copse of trees on the edge of a cliff above Spring Creek.

What Rumbough shows him there is horrifying.

Scattered across a clearing in the oaks and poplars are perhaps a dozen graves marked with marble stones. In addition, there are two mausoleums—one built out of rounded river rocks and one more stately edifice built out of marble. A gang of some sort has used heavy tools to tear apart one side as well as the front of the stone crypt. In addition, they have pried open the iron gate on the marble mausoleum and ripped off the marble covers from the front of three vaults.

Once they opened the graves, they dragged the decayed bodies out onto the ground and left them scattered across the leaves and pine needles. Shreds of clothing and shoes still cling to several of the bodies. The three bodies from the marble mausoleum are barely more than mummified skeletons, the bodies from the stone structure nothing but scattered bones, faded to gray and brown. Rumbough points out two skulls among the bones, both with their jaws pried open.

The three bodies in front of the marble vault are the most disturbing of all.

"A woman and two men?" Clinton whispers. He says this based on the scant evidence provided by the decayed clothing.

Rumbough nods. "It's the Safford family. Has to be. Mr. and Mrs. Safford and their son."

"Were you the one found them?"

Rumbough nods. "Out walking with my dog after lunch. I hate to say it, but the dog smelled them first and took off up the hill. Wouldn't come back, and when I chased after him with the leash, he was..."

Clinton nods. "I understand. Have you told anybody else?"

Rumbough shakes his head no. "I figured you'd want to see it...undisturbed-like. Sheriff?"

"Yes?"

"Why do you think they took the other skulls?"

"I don't know, but I'm guessing they wanted the gold in their teeth."

"Bastards."

He, Clinton, nods. "You're right about that. You related to the Saffords?"

"Distantly. Miss Peggy Dotterer is closer. A niece, I think."

"Well, then, let's do this. Let's you and me ride back down the hill and see if we can find Way Tipton."

"Your deputy?"

"Yes. And probably the best one to send after Miss Peggy. We'll use his phone to call back to the sheriff's office so we can round up as many deputies as Gloria can find. Once we take some photographs, we'll...rebury these poor souls however you and Miss Peggy want it done."

"Should we call the newspaper?"

"God no," he replies. "Not until they're back in the ground or back in the vault or whatever. Then we'll let 'em know. They'll want to talk to you and Miss Peggy."

"And you," Rumbough says. "You're the sheriff."

THE NEXT TWO HOURS ARE A CASE OF FAST AND SLOW. Fast: Down the hill to town, where they find Way Tipton reading in his living room while his wife is thinking of supper. Way grasps the weird urgency of the situation almost immediately and takes Rumbough in his car to find Miss Peggy Dotterer, the Saffords' niece. While Way is changing clothes, Clinton calls Gloria at the jail and tells her that, yes, it's true. Grave robbing. To send as many deputies as she can reach in the next hour and have them bring shovels and a camera.

Slow: He drives along back up to the cemetery alone and walks around the whole scene again, slowly, carefully, sketching how everything, including the bodies, is laid out, and taking notes on any and all odd details, strange impressions. As he walks, he steps on something hard buried in the leaves; at first, he draws back, fearing it's a long bone, but instead discovers a rusty crowbar, apparently dropped by the robbers.

First thoughts.

...rain since the bodies were thrown on the ground...water pooled in the metal liners that held two of Safford caskets...three days since the last rain?

...who? Who would be stupid enough...for a half dozen gold teeth and a couple of rings?

...at least one local man...no outsider would know this lost place was even here.

...names, names. The other graves...Rumbough, Henderson, Garner, Izlar, Hill...Is a family member in this? Knowledge of what was buried with the bodies?

...bastards pried open the mouths of the two skulls from the rock tomb...Hell, even a stick left jammed into the mouth of one. Why leave those behind and cut the heads off the Saffords...walk off down the hill with two human skulls in a sack!

...had to be the teeth...unless....

...what looks like the old man's hand, and yes, *the ring finger has been wrenched nearly off...rings and teeth...*

HE IS INTERRUPTED BY THE SOUND OF WAY TIPton's old Chevrolet pulling up beside his Jeep. Way taps the horn twice to get his attention, and Clinton walks back down the hill slowly to meet Way and Jimmy Rumbough leading a well-dressed elderly woman up the faint trace of a road.

As they are introduced, Peggy Dotterer—Miss Peggy—shakes his hand with a warm, dry grip. She is dry-eyed as well, and when he asks her if she is sure she wants to see the open graves and the bodies, she nods. "My husband was buried up here, just last year," she says. "My first horrible thought was that the robbers had done something to him. But as long as he's safe in the ground, then I can stand pretty much anything."

Which turns out to be true. She can stand pretty much anything. She walks into the middle of the site, holding his arm, and although he can see dampness on her cheeks, she doesn't flinch, even at the sight of the half-mummified Safford family.

"What kind of animals would do such a thing?" she whispers, after standing and gazing about for a few minutes.

"*Animals* is right," he agrees. Another piece of time passes. "Would you like us to rebury them?" he asks her.

"Can you get the three back into the mausoleum?" she asks. "And repair the gate?"

He nods. "I've got deputies on the way, and we'll do whatever it takes to make it right."

"Thank you." Again, the naked dampness on her cheeks. "I'm not sure who was in the rock tomb. My Aunt Annie and her son, I think. I should know those bones. Maybe just bury them off to the side?"

"We'll do it just as you say," he offers.

"You know what I'd really like, Sheriff?"

"For me to catch the bastards," he says quietly, so that only she can hear.

She nods. "Yes, please," she whispers. "The penitentiary is too good for them."

CHAPTER 16

LATE THAT AFTERNOON, THREE OF HIS DEPUties—Dwayne Austin, Danny Fender, and Sam Ray—arrive in Fender's Ford Mustang. Gloria Goforth has sent along a fourth man named Pennell or Penland—hard to tell from the way he says it—who works for the funeral home in Marshall. In addition to the tools he asked for, they have also brought gloves for handling the bones.

Clinton sends Way Tipton to take Miss Peggy home and sit with her for a bit if need be. Then he and the deputies, plus Rumbough and Pennell or Penland, set to work. Fender, he knows, is country strong, so he puts him in charge of Ray and Austin and directs them to work out the problem of placing the Safford remains back in the metal coffin liners and sliding the liners back into the mausoleum. Tells them to engineer a way to replace the marble slabs with names and dates chiseled into them. Pennell—for it turns out that's his name—is surprisingly adept at identifying which mummified corpse goes where and behind which slab.

After conferring with Pennell for a few minutes, he decides that they can dig one grave for the bones scattered around the rock tomb. He picks a spot ten feet behind the tomb and to one side, more or less in line with the other family graves, and sets to work with a pick and shovel. It's a relief after the bizarre stress and strain of the day just to let his mind rest in the labor. To let the sweat rise from his skin and run down first his face and then his back and arms.

For most of his forty-eight years, except in the few instances when he was sick or wounded during the war, he has sought solace in work. Hard, physical work. In the war, on the farm. Before and especially after he was married.

This particular work, with long-handled tools in dirt, is where he has always been most at home, in some ways most himself. And the soil under these trees, high on this steep bluff above Spring Creek, is what his Grandma Robbins would call "good, black dirt," meaning that it would grow almost anything. Loam with very little clay. Full of nutrients and strength, he thinks vaguely, recalling her face and her gnarled hands as if she were here now, helping him.

When the hole that he is digging is perhaps four feet square and as many feet deep, he hears Rumbough call out. He pauses and hoists himself out of the hole, his boots, his pants, his shirt grimy with dirt and sweat. He is breathing heavily from the pick and shovel when he walks over to where Rumbough is standing in the trees between the rock tomb and the edge of the steep ravine that falls away to the creek. While scuffling around in the leaves, Rumbough has found two marble plaques with names and dates on them—Anne Dendridge Baker and Bernard Rumbough Baker. He calls Pennell over and together, they decide that the robbers must have wrenched the plaques off the front of the rock tomb to get at the bodies inside.

"You're the expert," he says to Pennell. "What do we do with them?"

"You already spoke to the family?" Pennell asks. "And they don't care?"

He nods to Rumbough. "The niece said to bury the bones and not worry with the tomb. Jimmy here is a distant cousin."

Jimmy Rumbough nods. "So distant that my opinion barely counts, and I don't see how in the world you can tell one set of bones from the other."

Pennell shrugs. "Then I'll tell you what is mostly done in old cemeteries like this. You rebury them, maybe try to put a skull with some ribs, plus some arms and legs, indiscriminate like, if that makes you feel better. And then you place these plaques over them as if they are real markers, just to remind family members who's buried here. Unless you go to a whole lot of trouble and attract a whole lot of attention, that's about the best you can do."

"Then that's what we'll do," Clinton says before going back to take up the shovel. "Let's see if we can't at least get the remains off the ground before dark."

Which they do, barely.

Fender will bring his brother-in-law, who is a mason, back up the hill tomorrow to brick up the gaping openings in the rock tomb and finish cementing in the marble slabs on the three Safford crypts. Fender himself can repair the hinges and the lock on the iron gate that fronts the mausoleum.

There is an odd camaraderie among the men as they walk back down the hill together, as if they've done something hard—physically hard, yes, but more than that. Elemental. Returning the shape of the world to what it is meant to be, the past buried within the past, the present open to the present.

They all pause at the vehicles to sort themselves out. The deputies climb into Fender's Mustang while he fusses about the mud and dirt. Clinton thanks Jimmy Rumbough and offers Pennell a ride back to town. As they begin to disperse, he pulls Way Tipton aside. "What do you think?" he asks Way quietly.

"Somebody here in town knows about it," Way mutters. "Even if they didn't do the dirty work, somebody here saw something or heard something. Hell, probably put them up to it."

He nods. "That's the way I figure it too. Sit tight in the morning. I'll drive up here and we'll ask around."

CLINTON AND PENNELL BARELY SPEAK ON THE thirty-minute drive back to Marshall, both tired and lost in their own thoughts. When he pulls up in front of the funeral home, Pennell reaches over to shake his hand, chuckling as he does so.

"You know, it's sort of funny, really," Pennell says.

"What's funny?"

"It's funny that here we been putting dead people back in the ground all day, and the only way you got to be sheriff was all them dead people that voted for you."

CHAPTER 17

"WHAT IS IT, CLINT? WHAT'S WRONG?"

"Why does something have to be wrong?"

"I can tell by the sound of your voice. You sound bone-tired."

He almost laughs. "*Bone-tired* is the perfect description."

"You need a drink." Cat's tone is decisive.

"I need you," he says and then, when his thoughts catch up to his words: "I'm sorry. I meant to say I need to talk to you."

"Don't be sorry. I can meet you somewhere. You could come up here, but everybody in the county recognizes that Jeep of yours, and my neighbor ladies watch my house like..."

"You can come down here," he says after a moment. "We could sit on the porch at Mrs. Penland's. She won't care if we sit in the dark."

"Clint, are you crying?"

"No." He reaches up to actually touch his cheek. "But if I knew how, I might."

"Oh, Lord. I'll be there in thirty minutes. I have a bottle of good bourbon that I was going to give you for your birthday, and it sounds like tonight is your birthday."

He tries to speak, but the words won't form.

"Isn't Mrs. Penland's that grand house up on the hill behind the courthouse?"

"Thank you," he manages to say.

THEY SIT IN THE DARK. HE HAS BATHED AND changed into the oldest, most comfortable clothes he has in town. She is wearing the same jeans and sweater she had on when her phone rang. There is a light on behind them in Mrs. Penland's kitchen, where he found coffee mugs for them to drink from.

They sip the bourbon straight from the mugs, not bothering with ice or water, sitting in porch rockers, by mutual consent just far enough apart so that they won't accidentally touch each other, but close enough so that only they can hear.

"How was your day?" he whispers when she hands him his mug.

"I'm not worried about my day, Clint. Talk to me."

He does, about the phone call, the cemetery. His voice is hoarse when he speaks. The bones scattered and the mummified bodies. Two missing heads. Digging a mutual grave for the mother and son, ribs splintered and scattered. Forcing the rusty coffin liners like misfit drawers into the mausoleum vaults.

Silence for a bit. One of her gifts is silence, and the moon is rising over the mountain behind them such that the river below glistens silver as it runs north. "What was the worst of it?" she asks.

"I believe in the past," he offers after a long sip of the bourbon. "That the past is real, as real as the present, or even the future."

"Can you see it, the past?"

"I can sense it. All around me—or around us, I should say. As if it is just there." He reaches out toward the town and the river. "Just behind a kind of curtain or a dark, wavering glass. Wavering like water."

"Like the river?"

He nods, which she senses more than sees. "Yes, like a veil made of river water. Constantly flowing, weaving, making."

"I've never heard—"

"The past is all around us."

She thinks of Faulkner—*the past isn't dead*—but doesn't say it. Faulkner isn't here and Clint Salter is.

Instead, she says again, "And the worst part about today...?"

"Was that the sons of bitches who robbed those graves tore a hole in the veil. Ripped it apart. And when they did, the cold air rushed through and what had been living, breathing human beings twenty or thirty or forty years ago fell to dust and bone. Dirt and rotten cloth. The sons of bitches who did that trespassed on sacred ground."

"You mean the past or the cemetery?"

"Both, I guess."

"Maybe," she says. "Maybe the cemetery is a place where the veil is the thinnest, where the glass is almost transparent."

She is with him, he realizes in that moment. Thinking and feeling, sharing the images in his mind even as they flicker to life.

"And you sought to put it back, didn't you? Sew up the rent in the veil where they'd torn it open?"

She can feel him nodding, his rocker beginning to move ever so slightly, flowing, easing him. "Yes," he says. "When we shoveled the earth in over the bones, it was as if we were repairing a torn place in the world."

She pours each of them a bit more bourbon. A healthy dollop for him, only a splash for herself, as she still has to drive. "Will you catch them—the sons of bitches, I mean?" she asks after handing him back his mug.

He sips. "Oh, I'll catch them all right. And when I do, they'll wish *they* were buried under the ground." She is aware of the threat in his voice, the menace that occasionally flashes to the surface of him. And she wonders if she should be afraid of him.

The bourbon is in their blood now and in their thinking. She reaches over finally and takes his near hand, holds it lightly. She can feel the calluses on his palm and fingers, and she massages the back of his hand with her thumb. *Relax*, she thinks, *relax*.

"There's something else," he whispers, squeezes her fingers in return, gratefully but gently, gently.

"Hmm?"

And he tells her about what Pennell, the funeral home man, had said about voting dead people. "Maybe I shouldn't even be sheriff," he offers. "Maybe I should just resign and get it over with."

She stops rocking and leans forward. Turns her head to look at him through the dark, less now as it is leavened by the rising moon. "You are a strange man, Clint Salter, I'll give you that, stepping in and out of the past. But the very fact that you care so much is what makes you a wonderful sheriff."

"But what if my brother stole the names from graves to get me elected?"

"The hell with your brother," she says. "Do you hear me?"

"I hear you." For the first time that night, there is humor in his voice. She imagines his face creased by a grin, and she is glad to be there, to help him.

"Bury him too," she says. "And all the people who would use us and judge us." Her thoughts are addled by the bourbon, and she wonders if she just said too much.

When he walks her to her station wagon thirty minutes later, there is a new presence accompanying them, something looming in the slant moonlight. They are beginning to have a past all their own, the two of them, formed out of moments in the dark.

And as each moment gathers, it deepens.

CHAPTER 18

HE IS OUT EARLY SO HE CAN CATCH HIS BROTHER before he leaves for work. He pulls up into the yard of Will's house in Little Pine and parks beside his company car, an almost new Oldsmobile.

First, he has to make nice with Will's wife and admire pictures of the grandbaby, born to their daughter the year before. Listen to Will brag about being elected chairman of the school board two nights before. And then, after slurping down a cup of lukewarm coffee, he can walk out with Will as he's leaving.

Before he can broach the subject he came to ask about, however, he has to listen as Will talks to his son, Willie, for five more minutes. Standing in the driveway, giving Willie directions for what he wants done around the farm that day. Willie nods without speaking and slouches back in the house, leaving the two of them alone.

"I'm glad you came by," Will says in his salesman's voice, once they're alone in the yard. "We don't see enough of you around here."

"I came by to ask you a question." Clinton keeps his own voice low just in case his sister-in-law is listening at the window.

"What sort of question? You need some wise counsel on how to run the sheriff's office, I'm your man, brother."

He has thought about how he's going to say what comes next. When the words come out of his mouth, they are flat in tone, if anything almost friendly. "I need to know what you did back in the election. Did you stuff the ballot box with people who were still on the rolls, but dead and buried before November?"

Will leans back against the Olds and guffaws long and loud. "You mean to tell me you been in office six months, and you're just now figuring that out? That's rich. Of course we voted dead people. We had to, or you'd still be sittin' up there on the farm wondering what the hell happened. But here's the best part."

Clinton is even more careful now, still keeping a perfectly straight face. "What's that, Will?"

"The best part is that the boys that helped me out—Willie included—we had to find some lost and lonely cemeteries stuck back in two or three of those precincts. They wanted to know why they was working so damn hard and you wasn't helping. But I knew to keep you out of it because of your Boy Scout ways and your high moral character."

"You're right. I would have pulled out."

"See what I mean. Boy Scout!" These last words as full of scorn as it's possible for words to be. "And now you're stuck. The High Sheriff of Madison County. You owe me, brother, whether you want to admit it or not."

Clinton turns and starts back toward his Jeep, but then pauses for a last word. "You may be my little brother, Will, and it may be that I'm in the habit of protecting you from harm. But no more. If you get caught, I'll deny I ever knew about it, and I'll slam the cell door on you myself."

Will laughs. "Bullshit. I made you, brother, and I can unmake you. Just like that!" He snaps his fingers. And then, pleased with himself, he does it again. "Just like that!"

MIDMORNING, HE AND WAY TIPTON BEGIN slowly going house to house in Hot Springs, starting at the end of the village just beside Spring Creek and beneath the Safford cemetery on the bluff above.

They work slowly, talking to people about the weather, about their gardens, their dogs or cats. Slowly working up to the topic of the cemetery, has anyone been talking about it, pointing it out, wondering aloud about what's buried up there. At least half the people they talk with—the younger folks—don't even know it's there. But the older folks, those who remember Mrs. Safford, how kind she was, how awful that her son died so young of typhoid and then her house burned, they know about the cemetery.

And when Clinton or Way finally breaks the news that someone has broken into the mausoleums, turned out the bodies on the ground, they are astonished, angry. One old-timer, working a chaw of tobacco the size of a walnut, asks if they are sure it wasn't bears. Bears might dig up a grave and they are strong as hell. It takes them a moment before they realize he's joking.

Finally, midafternoon, they work their way out of town along the creek, where you can still look up and see the cemetery spot on the ridge above. While Way rests in the Jeep, Clinton walks up to a trailer set back in an immaculate yard. A porch built onto the front of the trailer holds two caned chairs and an aged recliner. When he knocks on the porch door, a woman in her seventies—at least—comes to the door, wiping her hands on a dishcloth. He introduces himself and she comes out on the porch to sit with him. When she does, a large calico cat follows her and begins to rub against his legs.

When they sit, the cat jumps immediately up into his lap.

"That durn animal," the woman says with a grin. "Throw it down if you don't like it. Some people don't care for cats, you know."

"I'm a dog man," he admits. "Always have been, but..." He finds that he is stroking the cat almost without meaning to, and the cat is purring. "I guess all God's creatures need some attention."

"That's right," she laughs. They sit for a bit, relaxing in each other's company while the cat curls in his lap.

"I'll tell you something funny now, Sheriff. That cat is named Bell, and so am I."

"What?"

"My name is Belva, but ever'body calls me Aunt Belle. And when them boys of mine brought me that cat after my husband died, turns out it was named Bell too. Two Bells, if you see what I mean."

"So, if I need to talk to either one of you, just stand in the yard and yell *Bell!*"

"Just so. I'll come running and the cat will ignore you. Cause that's how cats do."

They laugh. The cat purrs as he scratches under its chin. "You know we are related now, don't you?" Belva asks.

"You and the cat?"

"Nope. You and me. Your grandmama was sister to my father up in Anderson Cove. If you trace it back far enough, we're all named Robbins."

"I'm going to call you Aunt Belle then," he says, smiling at her.

They sit on for a bit, again letting the conversation breathe, as mountain people are wont to do.

After a bit, he asks her if she knew Mrs. Safford.

"I did. She and that rich man she married had a beautiful home right up there on the bluff. It was called Loretta, only house I ever knew that had a name attached to it."

"What was she like?"

"Oh, she was a sweet lady. Suffered off and on in life. First husband was a wastrel. Then she married a Mr. Bigelow from New York, but their son, Jack, died young, followed by her husband. Seemed like one hammer blow after another. Even so, she carried on best she could."

"Did you live here then? Meaning the trailer."

"Oh, lord no. I lived way back in Anderson Cove with my husband. But I came into town to teach from time to time. Taught weaving at Dorland Bell. You know, I wove a coverlet for Mrs. Safford once because she admired my work so. I took it to her up at Loretta and she served me tea. She told me she would keep that coverlet in her own room, across the foot of her bed, that's how much she cherished it."

Because Aunt Belle has been so forthcoming and because of the cat, Bell, he tells her straight out about the grave robbers and what they did. When he does, she looks off into the distance for a moment and then says quietly, "That's what I'd call a desecration."

"Yes, ma'am. Can you think of anyone around here who has been taking an interest in the cemetery, maybe the kind of person who is capable of meanness like that?"

When he asks this question, she stares directly into his eyes for a long moment and then glances away. The glance itself is meaningful, he knows, but can't decipher what it means.

"Ma'am?"

She does it again, but this time with a nod, a nod so slight it might be a tremor. Looks into his eyes, the rest of her face still, and then turns to stare at a ramshackle, two-story house across the road from her trailer.

"I understand," he says. "Thank you."

When he stands up, finally, the cat jumps to the floor and then off the porch, out to explore the world. Aunt Belle rises and shakes his hand. "You'll come back and see me, won't you, Sheriff? I'll give you something to eat if you come at lunchtime."

"In that case, you know I will. And by the way, I believe I'll come back tomorrow and visit with your neighbor."

CHAPTER 19

When he drops Way off in front of his house in Hot Springs, he asks him if he's heard the rumors about how Clinton won the election. "You mean your brother resurrecting folks who were already in the ground to vote for you?" Way asks.

He nods. "Yeah, that."

Way shrugs. "Sure, I heard it. Mostly Tom Runnion bitching and complaining about why he lost. But you know what, Sheriff? I don't concern myself with hearsay. And besides, now that we've begun to put things back together the way they should be, I say it's all for the best."

He nods. "I appreciate that. Maybe you're right." And then after a pause, "Why don't you call me Clinton? You being the chief deputy and all."

When he climbs back behind the wheel of the Jeep, Way raps on the hood with his knuckles before he has a chance to crank the engine. "What do you want to do with what Aunt Belle told you? The old Sawyer place she pointed you to?"

"Come back tomorrow, and the two of us will make a show of asking around some more. Then we'll visit with whoever lives there. I don't want it to appear obvious that the last person we talked to before hammering on that door was the old lady and her cat."

"Have you thought about a search warrant—just in case?"

Clinton grins. "I have. I'm going to stop by the magistrate's office in the morning."

His last task of the day? To test his conscience against someone he trusts. Someone who can factor right and wrong.

Gloria Goforth.

She catches the tenor of his voice quickly enough and shuts the door behind her when she comes into his office.

"I've got something I need to confide in you about. Something that you can't talk over around town."

"Does it have anything to do with Catherine Metcalf?" she asks before sitting down.

"No, it doesn't. Wait a minute. How do you know about—?"

She shrugs. "I've heard you talk to her on the phone, seen you walk her to her car. But don't worry, I pay attention when most folks don't."

"That's for another day," he mutters. "This comes first." He tells her about Pennell, the funeral home man. The joke about burying dead people versus voting dead people. "I seem to recall," he says, "that when I was in high school, you straightened me out a time or two."

"More like a half dozen than just one or two." She smiles. "But I always thought the core of you was good. Too good sometimes. You talk to your brother about this voting business?"

He nods. "This morning. He said I was a Boy Scout and likely the last person involved to figure out what was going on."

She shrugs. "He might be right about that. So, what's the question?"

"What the hell should I do?

"What do you mean, What should you do? You didn't know what he was up to at the time."

"No, but maybe I would have lost the election if he hadn't gone creeping through cemeteries, scouting out people who'd died but were still on the rolls. Maybe I'm sheriff under false pretenses. Maybe I should just resign and say the hell with it."

She shakes her head, at first slowly and then almost furiously. "You will recall, Clinton Stuart Salter, that I just got through saying you were often too good for your own sake, even in high school. The first day you ever walked in here, I was afraid you'd fold under the pressure."

"You're not answering the question."

"What should you do? You should be yourself and do the damn job. I have no love lost for that brother of yours; I suspect you know that. But Jesus, Clinton, if he hadn't done what he did, we'd all be stuck with Tom Runnion. I'd have walked away in December and lived off my pension."

"But Gloria, don't you think—"

"I think you need to wise up about this place. This Madison County we all claim to love so much, it's full of simple, kind, even thoughtful people. But the politics are perfectly sordid, and your brother is up to his nicely oiled crew cut in it. The fact that you didn't know what the hell was going on is a compliment to you. You were a history major at Mars Hill, right?"

He nods. "Ancient history, mostly. Through the Middle Ages."

"Did you ever get around to reading Machiavelli? That Italian the judge quoted the day you gave Runnion the boot?"

"*The Prince*."

"Exactly. What's the most famous quote?"

"That the ends sometimes justify the means?"

"Precisely. Well, in this case, the means—which you were too high-minded to even notice—are what got you here. And not only that, the ends are the best thing that could have happened to you, to me, to the county. Hell, as far as that goes, to Mrs. Catherine Metcalf."

"She doesn't have anything to do with it."

"Maybe. Maybe not yet, but she will before it's over, or I'm blind, deaf, and dumb."

"Are you saying I'm in the best interest of the county? The whole damn county?"

"That's exactly what I'm saying. And you need to get over your moral high-mindedness long enough to admit that. So, you slid into the sheriff's office under somewhat suspect circumstances—so what? For your sake and for the sake of all of us, ride with it. You yourself told me you wanted to restore some sort of order to this place that reflects the best instincts of the best people who live here. Your grandparents and mine." She pauses, out of breath.

"Does this fall into the category of you setting me straight?"

"Hell yes. At the very least, reminding you of things you yourself believe."

"You didn't say *hell* when I was in twelfth grade."

"I thought it. Trust me, I thought it."

CHAPTER 20

MIDMORNING. STANDING WITH WAY BESIDE the Jeep after they have visited several houses and a trailer along the Spring Creek Road. There is a search warrant for the residence of Wallace Sawyer in Clinton's pocket.

"How you want to play this?" Way asks.

"I want you to ease through the woods along the creek and up close to the back porch. Where if he runs, you can grab him. Take the rifle from behind the seat. It's not loaded, but it'll suggest we mean business."

"You?"

"I'm going to walk straight up to the front door and knock just like we've been doing. Only I'm going to show him the crowbar we found up by the graves. See how he reacts. I asked around and he's an ornery cuss, not given to disguising his thoughts. If it's his, I suspect he'll show it."

As he speaks, he checks the clip in the army surplus .45 and sets the safety. He lays it on the seat of the Jeep while he slides the holster on his belt and then holsters the pistol.

"You like reliving your army days?" Way asks him with a wink.

"Hell no. But I do like carrying a gun that I'm used to. Let's go visit with Mr. Sawyer, see what he has to say for himself. I'll give you ten or so to work your way around to the back of the house."

AFTER HE CLIMBS THE THREE OR FOUR STEPS TO the porch, he lays the crowbar down on the floor in plain sight, pulls open the screen, and knocks politely. So much paint has peeled off the front of the house that it's mostly gray, mismatched planks nailed up haphazardly. While he waits, he can hear insects buzzing in the hot June sunshine. It's that quiet.

After a bit, he pounds on the door, hard this time, rattling it in the frame.

A hoarse man's voice yells from within. "The hell you want?"

"Open up. Sheriff's department."

He can hear footsteps in the front hall and then the rusty creaking of the dead bolt being pulled. The knob turns and then someone on the other side drags the door free from its frame.

Sawyer is a middle-aged, rough-looking character, pulling his galluses up over a T-shirt that was once white. A strong odor of sweat and stale cigarette smoke hangs in the air, but Clinton's not sure if it's from Sawyer or his house. Maybe both.

"Is Mr. Sawyer at home?"

"He's the only one who's ever at home. Just me."

"I'm Sheriff Salter. I'd like to talk to you about that cemetery up on the hill there behind your house."

"What you bothering me for? I didn't vote for you."

"Doesn't matter. We're talking to everybody up and down the road here, see if they might know something about the Safford cemetery."

"Why? It been broke into or something?"

Your first mistake, he thinks. "Funny you should say that. There was a report of some mischief up there recently." He studies Sawyer's face. Even though he is not a fat man, his face sags from his eyes down into unshaven jowls. Even his lips sag. "By the way, is this your crowbar?" He points down. "I found it lying in the tall grass."

"Looks like mine," Sawyer says. "I been missing it."

"The tall grass up at the cemetery."

"Then I guess it ain't mine, is it?"

"You claimed it."

Sawyer clears his throat, hocks, and spits past him onto the porch. "Screw you, Salter," he says, turns, and runs back through the house, trailing his untied bootlaces behind him.

"Christ," Clinton mutters and starts after him.

Sawyer running shakes the whole house, and since he knows where he's going, he gains a few steps on Clinton before bursting into the kitchen and out the back door.

"Here he comes," Clinton yells. "Grab him!"

Way has apparently been standing close by in the backyard because when Sawyer jumps down the back steps, he's right there, the rifle held loosely across his chest. He manages to yell, "Stop in the name—" before Sawyer runs him over, stomping on him as he goes.

Clinton stops beside Way, unholsters the .45 and holds it over his head. "Stop and drop, Sawyer," he yells while trying not to laugh at Way. Sawyer is neither stopping nor dropping, so he fires off a round into the sky.

The beauty of the .45 is that on a nice, still morning like this, a sweet June morning made for birdsong, the muzzle blast sounds like a bomb going off.

Sawyer looks back over his shoulder, wondering if he's been shot, and runs straight into his own clothesline, strung between two leaning T-posts. The clothesline accomplishes what Way Tipton could not. It drops Sawyer flat on his back and knocks the breath out of him.

Together, Clinton and Way drag Sawyer over to a handy dogwood, lean him against it, pull his arms roughly around behind, and handcuff him to the tree. "Sit your ass there," Clinton says. "This"—he unfolds a paper and holds it in front of Sawyer's face—"is a search warrant. We're going to tear up your house and hope the damn thing doesn't fall down on us while we do it."

"I ain't done nothing," Sawyer manages to catch his breath to say. "It's them boys that work for me what done it."

TOGETHER, CLINTON AND WAY WORK THEIR WAY through the house from front to back, using flashlights from the Jeep because the power has apparently been turned off, and the interior rooms are shadowy dark.

In a paper bag pushed to the back of a kitchen drawer, they find five gold teeth, four rings, and a necklace.

In a cardboard box in the pantry, they find two human skulls, the jaws of which have been smashed.

Way goes outside at one point to throw up in the yard, and as hardened as he is by the war, Clinton feels his own stomach churning as they carry the box and the bag out to the Jeep.

As they are walking Sawyer from the dogwood tree to the Jeep, he again says, "You making a mistake. It won't me. It was them boys who work for me done it." He keeps talking while they cuff him to the stanchion that holds up the back seat of the Jeep. Way starts to slap him out of pure, unadulterated disgust, but Clinton grabs his arm.

"Let him be," he says quietly. "We want him to talk. Take out your pad and start taking notes."

To Sawyer, he says, "Names. Give us the names. Do that and you might not get this whole stinking mess hung around your neck."

CHAPTER 21

THE NAMES ARE AARON GOSNELL AND TROY Rice. Sawyer gives them up later that same day while chained to the bench in the hallway on the second floor of the jail.

It takes them a week to track down Gosnell and Rice, one in Yancey County and one in Buncombe. The two boys—for both are in their early twenties—are at first unsure just what is happening to them, although it's obvious from the beginning that they broke into the Safford family tombs.

Gosnell has a terrible stutter, and when Clinton explains that they're both being charged with trespassing and theft along with "desecrating human remains," he can barely speak at all and begins to cry in fear and frustration.

Rice, on the other hand, only grows more talkative when he grasps that "to willingly and knowingly...open, disturb, destroy, remove, vandalize or desecrate...any human remains" is a felony in the state of North Carolina. Once Gloria Goforth explains to the boy what *desecrate* means, he immediately throws all the blame on Sawyer. When Clinton asks him if he'll make a formal statement to that effect, he responds, "Oh, hell yes."

STATEMENT OF TROY HELTON RICE

MADE THIS DAY, APRIL 19, 1965, BEFORE THE FOLLOWING:

- Clinton Salter, Sheriff, Madison County, North Carolina
- James Ramsey, Chief Magistrate, Madison County, North Carolina
- Way Tipton, Deputy Sheriff, Madison County
- Gloria Goforth, Clerk, Sheriff's Office, Madison County

The following statement was made by Mr. Rice at the Madison County jail, between nine and ten o'clock in the morning on the above date. Mr. Rice declined to have an attorney present.

> Me and Aaron first met up working on the highway road crew up there where the road to Shelton Laurel slid off into the Laurel River. You know where I'm talking about. We worked together for six months or more, right through the winter, when it was so damn cold. When that work run out, somebody told us a man in Hot Springs was looking for a couple of fellows to do odd jobs around his property, so we went up there to talk to him.
>
> Do we stick together, me and Aaron? Yes, we do. You see, once I got to know him, we become friends, and I like to keep him with me if I can because he has a lot of trouble talking, and most people won't hire him by himself because he can't ask no questions nor explain very well.
>
> Well, that man in Hot Springs turned out to be the Wallace Sawyer you want to know about. He had an old barn he wanted us to tear down. He didn't pay us very

much, not nearly what we made working on the road. But he let us stay there at his house when we wanted to, and he'd stand us to a meal at the diner there in Hot Springs from time to time.

So, it all worked out pretty good for a month or so, and when we finished up with the barn, I asked him what next. He allowed as how he didn't have much left until it came on full summer when he'd need some mowing and such. I told him me and Aaron couldn't wait around that long. We'd have to move on to something else.

And that's when he said he had an idea how we could all make some money. He took us back behind his house and pointed across the creek and up to the top of that bluff behind the place and said, did I know what was up there. I said I didn't, and he said it was a cemetery where some rich folks was buried. But it wasn't no common cemetery. It was full of mausoleums and tombs and such as that.

I told him I didn't know what that was, and he said it was where the bodies was buried aboveground and would be easy to get to. I said I didn't know why you'd want to get to a dead body anyway, and that's when he said, for the treasure, you dumbass, for the treasure.

Yes, he called me a dumbass. He talked like that all the time, to me and Aaron both. I didn't like it, but as long as he was paying, I kept my mouth shut.

He claimed there'd be all kinds of gold and jewelry in those graves because of how rich those people were. All of them descended from some Rumbough family that he knew about who used to own the entire town. So, if we was to dig them out of there, we'd find gold and diamond jewelry and gold teeth. Rich people all had gold teeth, or so he claimed.

His plan was for me and Aaron to go up there early in the morning, just after first light, when the town was still asleep, and pull those bodies out of those tombs and bring down all the jewelry and other such, like watches, to his house. He knew where he could sell everything we found, and he would split the money with us.

Well, me and Aaron talked it over. As long as you talk nice and slow with Aaron, he does fine to discuss things. And we agreed it would only take a few days' work, if that, and we could make us hundreds of dollars. At least, that's what Sawyer claimed.

So, one afternoon, along about dusk, he took us up there and pointed out the tombs—there was only two of them above the ground—and the next morning, we went up there and busted those people out of there.

Whose tools? Why, Sawyer's tools of course. That was part of the deal. And he cussed at us for losing his damn crowbar. We brung everything we found back down to his house so that he could sell it for us.

Yes, we brought two of the skulls back down with us in a sack. Two of the ones from that big marble mausoleum. Me and Aaron couldn't figure out how to get those upper teeth out without busting the skulls completely to pieces, and neither one of us would do that. It felt wrong...like that thing you said.

Desecration. Felt like it would be a desecration of those Safford folks. For by then, we'd read their names on the mausoleum, and we felt like we were getting to know them and all.

Did we ever get our treasure money from Sawyer? Hell no. He gave us what he called fair wage. Fifty dollars each. That's all, and when I called foul, he told me to shut up or he'd turn us in to the law.

Gosnell and Rice plead guilty to reduced charges of trespass and theft in exchange for their willingness to testify against Sawyer, the mastermind—if you can call him that—of the whole horrid business.

Of course, only Rice takes the stand during Sawyer's trial in May, but that's enough. That and the two skulls that Clinton brings into the courtroom to submit as evidence. They, the physical remnants of Mr. and Mrs. Safford, stare mutely at the defendant while the judge sentences Wallace Sawyer to fifteen to twenty years for grave robbing.

WAS

Asheville, North Carolina
August 1956

MARSHALL ISN'T LARGE ENOUGH FOR ITS OWN Greyhound bus station, and so the buses stop in front of the Rock Cafe, and they—Clinton, Gretchen, Marian—have made a day out of taking Matthew to meet the bus he will catch east to Chapel Hill, an eight-hour ride.

He is entering the University of North Carolina in a few days, where he plans to study chemistry. His mother, Gretchen, alternates all day between smiling proudly at him and then choking back tears over losing him, her little boy.

They eat breakfast in the café and then, while Marian is in the restroom and Clinton is paying the bill, she has a handful of minutes alone with Matthew. She reaches across the table and takes hold of his arm. "Listen to me," she whispers so the people at the neighboring tables can't hear. "Once you get there, you study. You study like you've never studied before."

"I know, Mama. I plan—"

"Hush. Just listen. Once you get away from here, don't you ever come back."

"Christmas or—"

"That's not what I mean. You can come home for a few days, but you look straight out at the world, and you make your way there. Don't you ever come back to this godforsaken place to live. Do you understand me?"

"I understand, but—"

"You are not limited by this...this..."

"This what?" Marian says as she sits back down at the table.

"Hillbilly backwater," their mother finishes the thought out loud.

"What backwater?" Marian asks.

STANDING ON THE SIDEWALK, IT'S EASY TO SEE why, for the last few years, girls have thrown themselves at Matthew Salter. He's an inch taller than his father, thin and athletic. He struts when he walks and for good reason. He has thick black hair that almost reaches his shoulders and what can only be described as a raffish, lopsided grin. His eyes seem to gleam with cynical humor, even now, as he regards his family.

Clinton and his son share an awkward moment, as fathers and sons so often do—half handshake and half hug. Clinton slips him a crisp new hundred-dollar bill that he's been saving for this moment.

Marian hugs her brother tight and then playfully slaps him. "I'll be on this bus in two years," she says and then, "See you at Thanksgiving."

"Maybe," he replies.

And then it's his mother's turn. As usual, she has claimed the last hug as her right. "Remember what I told you," she says out loud, before briefly pulling him close. "Go," she adds in an urgent whisper, "now."

PART TWO

IS

Madison County
1965

CHAPTER 22

JULY, THE LAST DAY OF THE MONTH, A SATURDAY. Clinton Salter's forty-ninth birthday.

Because Marian is gone to an education conference in Raleigh, the family celebration has been postponed until her return on Sunday afternoon.

Catherine Metcalf does not go to the same conference, although she was registered to attend. She does not go because Clint suggested a week earlier that it might be a good day for them to finally go riding at the farm.

For reasons neither of them will quite admit, they are casually secretive about their plans, almost as if they might accidentally run into each other on Doe Branch on a warm day that just happened to be his birthday. Casual when speaking with each other, neither is calm when alone. He cleans the farmhouse, or at least tries to. She frets about what to wear for walking and riding, and for afterward. Because...

"I'm going to cook supper for you. It's your birthday." This was over the phone on Friday afternoon. It's gotten to where Gloria Goforth automatically shuts his office door when she patches through a call from the high school. And she winks as she does so.

"I thought I might fix some—" he begins to say.

"You cooked last time I was there. Christmas, remember? It's my turn."

"I can go to the store this evening. What?"

"I'll bring what I need. Do you like baked chicken?"

"Lord!"

"Is that a *Good lord, yes* or an *Oh God, no*?"

"Good lord. I'm trying to remember the last time I had it not in some greasy spoon. My mouth is watering just listening to you."

"Then that's what we'll have. You can make cornbread. I can't match your cornbread."

THE GELDING IS NAMED LITTLE JOE BECAUSE HIS sire was Joe before him. The mare is Nell. The dogs range through the upper pasture, while Clint and Cat sort through tack in the stone barn. He only has western saddles, his own and Marian's from years before. It's not what she's used to, having ridden English as a girl, but that life—and that saddle—are long gone, she tells him. And she loves the mare, who is skittish at first, but calms under her hands as she brushes her.

They ride out from the stone barn slowly, letting the mare get used to so many things new—having a rider on her back again, the lay of the land, walking tandem with Little Joe. It's plain from the first moment that Cat was not exaggerating at Christmas when she said she was a fine rider. And yes, more comfortable on horseback than he. Nell is calm beneath her because she is calm. Easy and supple in the saddle.

As they are easy, talking. She asks questions mostly, about how he came into the land? What made him stay here after such a harsh childhood? Did he ever imagine a different life...in a different place? But all of this slowly, as if every few minutes in the saddle invites a new thought.

In addition to what he inherited, he bought land with cash, he says. Acre by acre, as the old folks died and new parcels came available. He stays not just to spite his father, but because his aunts and uncles, his grandmothers and grandfathers are here, here and in Anderson Cove. He points up at the top of the ridgeline in front of them when he mentions Anderson Cove. He was fascinated by Europe, by the ancient cities and springtime landscape, but then it was all blown to pieces when he was there. In many places beautiful, but in many more, a charnel house.

In a slow, roundabout way, he and the horses bring her to the cemetery on the slope of the ridge that folds over the upper pasture. An ethereal blue sky drifts above the deep greens of the woods all around. They dismount. He whistles and calls to the dogs. Jake barks, and in a moment, they are here as well, Nick minding the horses while Jake begs for attention.

He shows her various family graves—not all of the Salters and Robbinses by a long shot, but enough. This includes his father's grave, marked by a bold stone: *Lazarus Salter 1895–1933 May he rest in peace.*

"You paid for that stone, didn't you?" she asks quietly.

He nods. "Later on. After I mostly gave up hating him, started to pity him."

"I can't imagine how you became the man you are if there wasn't some good in him."

He smiles ruefully. "The further away I get from his fists, the easier it is for me to believe that. Who am I to say what pain he felt, what disappointment?" He stares up at the ridgeline above them for a breath. Two breaths. "I hated him at the time for what he did to my mother, and now I don't even know if she's alive. And I still bear him a grudge for what he did to Will."

"You mean what he did to him back then?"

"Oh, he beat us both when he could catch us, but I took the brunt of it. No, what causes me the most pain now is when I think about who Will became." He turns back to her now, staring openly into her eyes. "I've never told anybody this, even Marian, but I think Will was awfully hard on Willie, his son. Struck him with his fist from time to time, maybe, which I hate to even think about."

"Repeated the pattern?"

Clint nods. "I was determined never to lay a hand on either Matt or Marian in anger. Never. I'd cut my own arm off first."

"Clint?"

"Hmm?"

"I should tell you that there were a few times when Willie Salter was in school that I noticed something on his arms."

"What was it?"

"It looked to me like burns."

"Burns from a fire or a stove?"

"No. Oh, Clint, I hate to say it, but they were ugly, small and round like..." She can't finish the sentence.

"Like cigarette burns."

She nods.

"Christ!"

"I wish I'd said something at the time, but somehow I was afraid to."

"I don't doubt you're right. I wish I could argue it was impossible, that Will could never do such a thing. But it's the kind of thing he knew growing up."

"Could it be that you've forgiven"—she glances at the gravestone—"your father and moved on? Laid him to rest in more ways than one? Maybe Will's way of dealing with it all was just to become like him."

"Maybe. Will does take out his anger on the world. Tried to put his hands on me the other day. Always on the outside trying to break in, my brother."

His face at that moment is open, unguarded and sad in a way she hasn't seen before. She wants more than anything in the world to comfort him. She tries a tentative smile. "Is this home, then? Where your ancestors rest?"

"Yes, I suppose it is."

She steps toward him and reaches out to lay her hand against him, aiming for his arm or shoulder, but finding his chest instead. "You have no idea how lucky you are," she murmurs. "No idea."

"Don't you have a home like this?" he asks, realizing even as he says it that it can't possibly be true.

"Of course not. Think about it. That farm that James bought was just about as lonely and barren a place as you can imagine. Nothing like this. You've seen that bungalow where I live now. I only rent it by the year, but that's not—" She stops, for she can feel the tears welling up. Unexpectedly.

"Well," he offers quietly, "you can come up here anytime. You can ride Nell. Explore to your heart's content. If you make friends with Nick after supper tonight, he'll take you anywhere on the mountain you want to go, whether I'm here or not."

She laughs and cries a bit, laughs more than cries. "How much do you own, Clinton Salter? From where we stand?"

He smiles. "You're the first person in years who ever bothered to ask me that. I own to the top of the mountain behind us here, plus the old place across the road. Hundred and twenty acres, more or less."

"My lord, Clint."

"Plus another two hundred acres in Anderson Cove that my grandparents left me. The over-the-mountain place, we used to call it. Not even Marian has ever walked that boundary line." He is suddenly embarrassed, though not quite sure why.

"This is who you are, isn't it? Right here." Her tears have dried up, but the smile remains. She is startled to find that her hand is still resting companionably against his chest, and she removes it to gesture all around them. The fields, the woods, the barns. Sheep in the pasture.

He looks down at the ground, considering, and then up again to meet her blue gaze. "This is who I am," he agrees. "Though until you said it, I'm not sure I had the words."

"That's what English teachers do, Clint. Words."

THEY RIDE FOR MAYBE AN HOUR, ALL TOLD, down the dirt and gravel drive from the cemetery to the road along Doe Branch. He introduces her to Randall from horseback. Randall nods and bows in an obscure, antique way. "Come back to visit," he says to her as they part. "I won't shoot you."

After rubbing down and feeding the horses, they walk slowly back down to the house, stopping along the way to throw some corn to the ram in his stall. There are clouds over the far mountain now, a weight and smell in the air that might mean rain later, but even so, the day feels fresh, open, as if summer might last an eternity...or two.

At the house, she excuses herself to wash up and change in the downstairs bathroom. While she does, he opens all the windows on the first floor that aren't already open, letting the cooler, late afternoon air invade the house. Then he goes upstairs to do the same, propping open the doors to his bedroom and Marian's, so that the breeze can rush through, billowing the curtains. *Wash*, he thinks, she said she was going to *wash up*. So, he goes into his own bathroom to scrub away the afternoon's sweat and change his shirt. *What's she thinking*, he wonders, *about being here?* And then, after a moment, *Hell, what am I thinking? What do I even want from—*

"How old are you?" she yells from the foot of the stairs.

"What?"

"Your birthday! Today! How old are you?"

He's so addled, he has to pause to do the math. "Forty-nine," he yells. And without stopping to consider: "How old are you?"

"Forty-five! Forty-six in September!"

"Why are we yelling at each other?"

"Because you won't come downstairs."

He gives her a brief tour of the kitchen cabinets and drawers, helps her find a pan for the chicken. She then tells him that she has a plan. Which is that he will fix them both a drink—can he make an old fashioned?—and sit at the dining room table while she cooks. That way, they can talk through the open door. He follows these orders and when he hands her the old fashioned, he notices that she's brought an apron of her own from home.

She is marinating the chicken in a bowl when she says, "You're awfully quiet, Clint. What are you thinking?"

"Did you take your ring off?"

"I laid it on the windowsill. Do you mind? It's what I do at home."

He shakes his head. "Of course not. Just don't forget—"

"Some days, it feels like it's cutting my finger off. Why are you shaking your head?"

"I think I'm in shock."

"At me taking my ring off?"

"Of course not. I'm—you're wearing a dress."

"You've seen me in a dress before."

"Not really. Not that dress. You have legs."

She pauses and turns to face him. "Cannot a forty-five-year-old woman have legs?"

He shakes his head. "Not like those. Those legs aren't forty-five. Thirty, maybe."

"Are you paying me a compliment?"

"I'm in shock."

"Well, don't faint. You may hate my cooking."

BUT HE DOESN'T HATE HER COOKING. AS THE late afternoon scrolls into evening, there is red wine—deep and dark—to go with the chicken and the cornbread he makes while they dance around each other in the kitchen, careful not to brush up against each other by stove or sink.

They linger over the meal and as dusk seeps in through the windows, he gets up to light several candles. The candlelight makes her yellow dress gleam. When he sits back down, she asks him about the war.

The sound he makes is more sigh than groan. "Not tonight," he says finally. "I'll tell you sometime, I promise, but tonight feels too much here, too much summer, too much...peace."

Eventually, they carry their dishes to the kitchen. He recreates the drinks they'd sipped earlier while she was cooking, and they carry them into the living room. He brings in the lit candles while she sinks down onto the couch. He sits opposite her in his accustomed chair.

"I'm sorry I didn't get you a present," she says and then takes another sip of whiskey, strong and cold.

"The whole afternoon was a present," he says hoarsely and takes a strong pull just to clear his throat.

"I like being here," she says simply. And then, when he doesn't reply, "But I should probably go in a bit."

Still, he doesn't speak, but grimaces. Then, with some determination, pours the rest of his old fashioned down his throat as though it were cold water. Sets the glass, empty now except for the ice, on the arm of his chair. "No," he whispers.

"What do you mean?"

"No, you shouldn't go. You should do what you want, now and always, but God, how I wish you wouldn't go."

"Just what do you think will happen if I stay, Clint?"

He closes his eyes to consider and discovers himself to be quite dizzy there, the liquor coursing through him. After a moment, he speaks: "The world will probably come to an end if you stay here, Cat. With me. And the world we know will return in the morning. Resurrected as something bright and strange."

She nods, ever so slightly. More to herself, perhaps, than to him. Like him, she swallows down most of the whiskey in her glass. Stands and eases around the low table that separates them. Almost casually, she kicks off her shoes, paying no attention to where they land. When she eases onto him and draws up her legs, the dress pools luxuriously in her lap, and now it's her thighs that gleam in the candlelight.

Her lips are warm and whole. Wet with wonder. For a long while, they simply remember how to kiss, teaching each other as they do. Then she takes his right hand and caresses her thigh with it, until the friction is almost unbearable—for her, for him. Until either, both, are gasping for breath, for more than touch. She isn't wearing much under the thin, yellow dress, so it takes them longer to undress him with their desperate hands.

They find the couch, neither capable of the stairs in this urgent, fleeting moment. They topple there together and lock themselves into place, her arms and legs tight around him. Clinging to each other as if the couch is a small boat swept across the tides. They *groan* into each other and she weeps when they finish.

"What's wrong?" he whispers, breathless.

She shakes her head against his neck to say nothing, *nothing* in the wide and darkening world is wrong. And then, when she can speak, she manages only a single word. "Finally," she murmurs, "finally."

CHAPTER 23

IN *HIS* DREAMS THAT NIGHT, THEY RIDE AGAIN across the nighttime farm. Except now, in the strangely transparent darkness, Little Joe and Nell can fly. Not spinning off the face of the earth into fields of stars, but ten, twenty, thirty feet off the tousled ground, so that together they fly horseback over the fields, the barns, the quiet bleating of sheep, the lowing of a single ox across the branch. The horses gallop through the smooth, velvet air such that they—Clint and Cat—feel the sure exhilaration of flying without ever falling, possessed by this place through all its spinning time. Day into night, dusk and dawn.

In *her* dreams, all within is safety. Within the boundary lines of his acreage, no one can find them, no one can harm them. Within the walls of his house, built with his own hands, they are nestled in quiet. No enemies, no others. When she does wake briefly, she can hear only Nick, his shepherd, stir on the rug that lies on the far side of the bed, and Clint's breathing deep and even. So peaceful that she falls again into some hushed and tranquil place. This place.

HE GETS UP AT ONE POINT DURING THE NIGHT and when he comes back to bed, fits his body to hers under the sheet and thin blanket. She's warm and quiet, barely breathing, or so it seems to him. When he circles her with his arm, he discovers again that she has breasts. Small, warm, the nipples alert to his touch. And he is amazed. That she should be here with him. Peaceful in sleep. Astonished that she should be shaped, made as she is. As if sculpted.

SHE RESTS SO SOUNDLY THAT HE BRINGS HER coffee in bed. He is wearing last night's clothes and his shirt-sleeve is damp with dew. She has no notion of where her own clothes are and doesn't much care. He sits on the edge of bed and tells her that there was a bear in the orchard during the night. Jake sounded the alarm from downstairs where he sleeps and he, Clint, got up to let both dogs out.

"I didn't hear a thing," she says, marveling. And then, "The bear won't hurt them?"

"Not usually, unless it's a sow bear with cubs and even then, they most often head to the nearest big tree, at the edge of the woods. They climb high and safe. The dogs get bored and come home to whine at the kitchen door. Nicky can mostly keep Jake from showing his..."

"His ass?"

"From showing his ass and getting hurt."

"Where are they now?"

"The dogs? Eating their breakfast. I thought I might fix you some as well."

"But it's your birthday."

"Then let's do it together. I brought your clothes up and laid them on the chair."

"I'd rather have your robe," she says. "I have a vague memory of wearing it last night."

THEIR PROBLEM IS WHAT TO DO ABOUT MARIAN. She expects her father to come to her house that evening for a birthday supper with her and Luke. Wine maybe, cake certainly. She's invited Catherine as well, her friend and mentor. Including her as one of the group. But...

"It will show," she says over breakfast.

"What will show?" he asks.

"Oh, please! And you're the sheriff, charged with reading people and solving crimes. *We* will show."

"You mean…?"

"That's exactly what I mean. She'll take one look at you or at me, or even worse, at us, and she'll know that something earth-shattering happened while she was off learning how to teach essay writing."

"Is that a bad thing? That she knows."

"You tell me, Clint. She's your daughter. Most daughters would kill the woman who tried to take their mother's place."

"Are you trying to…" He lets the sentence hang in the air, unfinished.

"No, but something happened. I fully intended to go home last night and sleep in my own cold bed. By myself, thank you very much. And you…got me drunk."

"Care for some whiskey with your eggs?"

She has to laugh at him. "Oh, Clint. What are we going to do? Last night felt like…" She is afraid to say what it felt like and he knows it.

"I'll tell you what it felt like," he says simply. Sitting there, in his shirtsleeves, his hair tousled, two days' growth of beard clouding his cheeks and chin, his eyes gleaming now.

"What?" she says cautiously.

"It felt like the future."

"What do you mean?" She knows full well what he means, but says it anyway. Perhaps just to hear him.

"I'm probably using all the wrong words. I'm probably scaring you, which is not my intent. But to me, last night felt like a year from now, five years from now, a hundred years from now."

She looks away from him so that she won't tear up, and he misreads the gesture.

"I'm sorry," he says, "to frighten you. But to me, last night felt like this empty house, this land, grew bright again. In my dream, we could fly."

"You're not scaring me," she says after a moment of watching his face, blinking to clear her eyes. "You're really not. It's the world out there, Clint. It's the world beyond Doe Branch that scares the hell out of me."

"Well, then, we'll do what we have to do. If we have to hide, we'll hide. If we need to step out into the broad light of day, then we'll step out. If anyone chooses to gainsay us, then the hell with them."

They sit and stare at each other as the morning light floods in through the open kitchen windows. Just at that moment, Nick, the shepherd who cares for no human but him, comes to her side and lays his head in her lap so that she will pet him. Which she does, hiding her astonishment.

MARIAN'S APARTMENT IN TOWN ON SUNDAY AFternoon.

Luke is making spaghetti for a simple supper when Catherine arrives. The two women are free to sit in the small living room, so that Marian can tell Catherine about the conference, about essay writing, about the five-hour drive back. They are surprisingly easy together, Catherine thinks. Slowly becoming more friends than colleagues, even when talking about school.

When Clinton gets there, Marian hugs him and Luke comes out to shake his hand. He and Catherine nod to each other with barely a flicker of a smile.

The only awkward moment comes during supper. Marian asks him if he's heard from Matthew for his birthday. He shakes his head, conscious that Cat has picked up on the tone in Marian's voice and is staring at him.

"He didn't call?" Marian asks. "He told me he would call."

"Nope. I was at the farm most all day yesterday. Phone didn't ring."

"No card?" She, Marian, is determined.

"Nope. I checked the mailbox Friday and yesterday." He can sense Cat nodding; she walked with him down to the mailbox after their ride.

"Well, hell," Luke says reassuringly. "He *is* a man. Probably just forgot."

"Oh, he didn't forget," Marian replies. "I reminded him."

CLINT AND CAT TAKE THEIR LEAVE AN HOUR later, after an apple pie with candles. Still being careful not to show too much affection, too much knowledge. She has parked at the jail so that they can walk the two blocks to her car together, at least that.

"Matthew is your son, right?" she says. And when he nods: "I'm sorry, Clint. I think I almost know how you feel because..."

"Because of your husband?"

"Yes. He doesn't call or write either."

It takes him a breath or two to realize she's joking. And when he does, he stops in the middle of the sidewalk to look up at the sky and laugh. They both laugh, breaking open a tension neither realized was there.

"Well," he says, "at least we didn't give ourselves away."

"Oh, she knows."

"Seriously?"

"When the two of us were alone in the kitchen, cutting the pie, she looked me straight in the eye and said, "How long have you and Dad been...?"

"Been what?"

"She didn't finish the sentence."

"What did you say?"

"About twenty-four hours."

"What did she say?"

"She laughed. But then she said to be careful. *You two are so obvious, it's pathetic.*"

CHAPTER 24

THE DOG DAYS OF AUGUST. HOT AND DRY. THE river is as low as anyone can recall, and the Forest Service is on high alert for fires. Twice now, his deputies have been called out to help put out brush fires around the county.

On the island, the football team has begun practice on the field behind the high school. Catherine is there every day from early to late, and in a few days, Marian and the other teachers will join her for the "work days" prior to school opening.

On a Thursday night, a bootlegger disappears trying to escape from Fender and Norton out on the River Road. When they pull him over, acting on a tip, he tries to take advantage of the low water to swim the river and escape. The two deputies confiscate the car and the liquor, but lose the driver. They find out his identity two days later when his wife comes in to see if he's been arrested. When they tell her about the incident out on the road, her only comment is that the "damn fool can't swim."

In the middle of the following Sunday morning, when almost everyone in the county who isn't hungover is in church, a huge barn on Ammons' Branch burns to the ground. When the call comes in that afternoon, Clinton drives out to the site of the fire. The landowner is a man named Clarence Nix, who also happens to be a county commissioner. Clinton and Nix walk down from the house to the site where the barn stood. Nix is almost beside himself with anger and frustration. Two horses were destroyed in their stalls when the barn collapsed, and the flames spread through dry pasture grass until the fire department had managed to get there and put it out. The barn timbers are still smoking in the hot afternoon sun while Clinton and Nix stand talking.

"Any chance this was an accident?" he asks Nix at one point.

"What do you think, Sheriff? That barn has stood there since my grandfather's day, sixty summers at least, and it picks today while we're all in church to go up in smoke?"

"Not likely," he admits.

"There've been others, right?"

Clinton nods. "Five over the past year. But every other one has been in the middle of the night. Nothing in broad daylight like this."

"Maybe this one is different," Nix admits. "Or maybe the son of a bitch is just getting more careless."

"Careless or brazen. Figures we can't catch him."

"Meaning *you* can't catch him."

Clinton shrugs. "Meaning *I* can't catch him."

"Anything else ties the barns together?"

Clinton considers. "I'll tell you this, Clarence, since we've known each other for as long as we have. Every victim has been a Republican. Not necessarily a prominent Republican, like you, but at least registered as such. I don't know if—"

"What the hell, Clinton? That mean you know who it is?"

"God, no. If I knew..."

"That mean you can't touch him?"

"Slow down. That's not what I mean and you know it. If I find him, he'll end up in the federal pen in Atlanta. All I'm saying is that's the only thing we've found that links all the fires."

They stand and regard each other for a long moment. "You shouldn't have told me that, Clinton. Should have kept it to yourself."

"Why?"

"Because I'll have a hard time forgetting it, that's why. I didn't vote for you, but I was halfway glad you got elected. So, how about you catch this bastard, no matter what he is."

Clinton nods. "I'll do my best," he says. And after a bit. "Can any of the neighbors see your barn from their houses? Any chance anybody saw anything?"

HE SPENDS THE REST OF THE AFTERNOON CIRcling the site, looking for any sign, any clue, as to how the fire started, or more to the point, who started it. Then he begins to work his way further out, onto the hillside behind the ruins. It's almost four o'clock before he finds two footprints in the creek bank fifty yards or so from the site. The left print matches the one from the earlier fire: square-toed cowboy boot. The right print matches the left, but is worn almost flat on the outside. He walks all the way back to the Jeep for his camera, brings it back, and takes careful pictures of both footprints.

WHEN HE ARRIVES BACK AT THE JAIL THAT AFternoon, he finds an older man—sixties perhaps—waiting for him on the steps. Out of sheer disgust with the world and soaked in sweat, he sits down beside the man and leans back against the door.

"Hotter than the furnace of hell, ain't it?" the man offers.

"Yes, it is. And given that, who in their right mind would set fire to something on a day like this?"

"Why, nobody in their right mind, Sheriff. You know that. You been out to see about that barn what burned down, ain't you?"

Clinton nods, which only makes his sunburned neck hurt.

"Well, I can tell you who done it."

Clinton looks over at the old man sitting beside him. He's cut himself shaving a time or two and has an abundance of gray hair growing out of his nose and ears. "What's your name?" he asks.

"My name is Poteat. I just live down the road a ways. Anyways, I was sayin'. I think them Democrats burned that man's barn down. Or Methodists. I ain't sure which."

Clinton snorts. "Maybe it was both—Democrat Methodists."

The man nods. "Makes sense to me."

From where he sits, Clinton can see the bridge to the island, and as if in a dream, Catherine Metcalf's station wagon coming over it, headed to town. He lets himself wish for her, wish to see her, and in another minute, the wish is fulfilled. She pulls up to the curb squarely in front of the jail, cuts off the car motor, and leans out the window to look at the two of them. "You two don't look so good," is the first thing she says.

"That's right, miss," Poteat says. "I was helping out the sheriff here, but we ain't making much progress."

"Why are you really here, mister? Other than this is a handy step to sit on?" Clinton.

"I come to rest myself," he says simply.

"You mean rest by sitting?" Catherine asks.

"No, ma'am. I come to turn myself in to the sheriff."

"You mean *arrest* yourself?" Clinton.

"That's what I said. Rest myself."

"On what charge?"

"Well, what's that called where a man is a no-good, lazy-ass bum? Won't do no work nor nothing?"

"Vagrancy?"

"That's right. That fits me to a T. Vagrancy."

"You look like a vagrant," Catherine says helpfully.

"Smell like one too," Clinton.

"I'm a pretty damn good vagrant, ain't I?"

Clinton nods.

"Can I get rested then?"

"Maybe. Why else are you here?"

"Well, sir, I get the dry mouth. Ever' month about this time."

"The dry mouth?" Catherine asks.

"You mean, you need a drink?" Clinton.

"Bad. I need a drink of that old liquor. But you see—and I hate to tell this in front of the lady—I'm a mean drunk. That whiskey steals my moral facilities. And my wife, she's had enough. She sent me away when she seen I had the dry mouth."

Clinton thinks of Rus, his father. God knows he's familiar with the dry mouth. "So, you want me to arrest you to keep you sober for a few days?"

"If it's not too much trouble. I can do it myself if you show me how."

"Can you come back in the morning?"

Poteat shakes his head sadly. "Too late, Sheriff. I might be a raving lunar-tic by morning."

"Well, hell. Come on in. We'll rest you."

Catherine gets out and slams her car door. "I can help," she says. "Right now, neither one of you looks like you could write your name."

CHAPTER 25

THE BLISTERING HEAT IS FOLLOWED BY A DAY and a night of rain. At one point, the electricity shuts off for several hours, and the only sound in the jail is Poteat in a corner cell upstairs, singing slowly and plaintively one love song after another—"Edwin in the Lowlands," "I Whipped My Horse," "Come All Ye Fair and Tender Ladies"—the last so high and lonely that Gloria Goforth stands at the bottom of the stairs, transfixed.

Twenty-four hours of hard rain and the river gives up what it has hidden from them: the body of Bill Saunders, the bootlegger who disappeared on the River Road, washes up against one of the bridge abutments right in the middle of Marshall. Several deputies and firemen block traffic while Clinton, along with Dwayne Austin, use a grappling hook on the end of a rope to pull the body loose from the pile of brush it's tangled in and slowly, carefully tow it to shore on the island. There, they load it onto a stretcher and into the back of an ambulance for the ride to the morgue.

As they are on school property, Catherine Metcalf comes outside at the end to watch the process from a distance, but they don't acknowledge each other except with a nod and a wave.

Once the ambulance pulls out with the body, Clinton walks back across the bridge to the jail and asks Gloria Goforth to track down Mrs. Saunders's address and send Austin to notify her. After she jots down a note or two, she nods to a young man who has followed Clinton in. "This is Mr. Michael Smith," she says, "from the university. In Chapel Hill."

Clinton automatically reaches out to shake hands and then stops himself. "I've been fishing a corpse out of the river," he explains. "Let me go wash up. Come on in and sit down. Gloria, coffee?"

Normally, she'd yell through the door, *You know where the pot is, Clinton*, but given that they have company—from the university, no less—she calls "Yes, Sheriff," and goes back to the kitchen to get it for them.

Five minutes later, they do shake hands and sit down in his office with the door closed. Smith is a thin young man with a mustache and a ready sense of humor. Wire-rimmed spectacles. Dressed in a wrinkled suit and tie, at Clinton's suggestion, he strips off the suit coat and hangs it on the back of his chair. He explains that he's from the Institute of Government, a branch of the university designed to support local government all over the state.

"What can I do to help you?" Clinton asks.

"It's the other way around, Sheriff. I'm supposed to help you."

"That's good. I'm new at this. Probably use all the help I can get."

"Well, my area of expertise is law enforcement and I'm new at it too. Only been at the Institute for a year."

"Have I screwed up? Is that why you're here?"

"Lord, no. Or if you have, I don't know about it. I'm from Michigan, you see, and I figured the easiest way for me to get to know the state, and get to know all the sheriffs, was to travel around doing what we're doing right now."

"Makes sense. What sort of services do you offer? Training?"

"Yep. That's mostly it. Training and consulting. We offer introductory courses on law enforcement procedures, investigation, arrest and detainment, that sort of thing."

"In Chapel Hill?"

Smith nods.

"Anything up this way? Asheville, maybe? It would be a lot easier to get my boys to attend if it was an hour away rather than five."

"We can talk about that, for sure. A lot of your colleagues in the west are saying the same thing. Also, you see that telephone on your desk?"

Clinton grins. "I'm familiar with it."

"Well, I'm on the other end. When you don't know which way the law twists and turns around something, what you can and can't do, you pick up the phone and call me."

"Hell, I should just hire you."

"I'm not sure my wife is quite ready for Madison County."

"Mine wasn't," Clinton admits and they both laugh. "Let me ask you something. I'm guessing you're a lawyer, right?"

"Yeah, but don't hold it against me."

"I got no problem with lawyers when they're on my side. Do you know a young attorney named Matt Salter? There at the Institute?"

"Matthew Salter? Of course I know him. His office is only two doors down from mine. Good Lord, you're related?"

And suddenly, there he is. Swimming in fast, deep water, like the bootlegger they pulled from the river. "I'm his father," he manages to say.

"That's amazing. I had no idea. I should have guessed, given the same last name, but he knew I was coming up here to visit four or five of the local sheriffs, and he never said a thing."

"He's doing well, is he?"

"Of course he is. Smart as a whip and—I don't know—charming, if you know what I mean. Never met a stranger, and women find him irresistible."

"What did he say when you told him you were coming up

here?" Clinton is struggling to keep his voice perfectly neutral, even as it strikes him that the man sitting across from him knows his son better than he does.

"It was funny. He winked at me and, in a serious voice, said, *Now, Michael, whatever you do, don't let the sun set on you in Madison County.*"

"He grew up here," Clinton says simply.

"I did not know that. He doesn't talk much about—" And suddenly Smith grinds to a halt, sensitive to the fact that he is laughing and Clinton isn't. "Sorry. I hope I didn't say the wrong thing."

"No, no. It's just been a while since I've seen him. I'm glad to hear he's doing so well. It's almost lunchtime, Michael. We usually eat together here, same fare as goes upstairs to the prisoners. Why don't you stay and eat with us?"

Which he does. While Gloria, two deputies, the magistrate, and a stray local lawyer regale him with stories of bootlegging and cattle theft, dead mules and lost wives. When Michael Smith and Clinton part ways after lunch, it's as friends. As he's leaving, Michael asks him if there's anything he can do to help the cause in Madison.

"Can you find me an arson investigator?" Clinton asks.

THAT EVENING, AS DUSK IS BEGINNING TO gather over the river and swallows are circling the chimney of the old mill, he walks across the bridge to Blannahassett Island, where the high school sits waiting. The football team is straggling in from practice, slowly drifting into the lighted gymnasium where their locker room waits. As he walks toward the school, he notices the light in Catherine's office blink off, and just that loss of illumination gives weight and heft to the darkness. Rather than climb the steps into the building, as he'd vaguely planned, he waits beside her station wagon.

When she comes out a few minutes later, he's standing in the shadows beneath an ancient maple that has stood in the middle of the parking lot since the school was built. He speaks her name softly, her full name, and she turns toward him instinctively, recognizing his voice in the dark.

"Sheriff?" she says, just to be sure.

"Me," he says, the single syllable, to reassure her. "Would you like to go for a walk? I need to talk to someone."

"Walk around here?" She glances back at the gym, where a cluster of cars waits for the football players, across at the town, where lights are strung along the few streets, where flood lamps glare at the courthouse. "Be more private if we went for a drive."

"True," he agrees and walks around to the far side of her car. She unlocks her door, slides inside, and reaches across to unlock his. For a moment, he is back in high school, getting into a car with a local girl after football practice, wondering what might happen between the two of them, where her father's car might take them along the way home.

Then he is back here, on the car seat across from Cat. She starts the car and, without speaking, pulls the knob to turn on her headlights. As they cross the bridge toward town, she reaches toward him with her right hand and grasps his left. As if that is the thin lifeline between them, all that connects them, all that sustains them. Just the caress of palm and fingers.

She is tired, he can tell, as is he, and yet...and yet, something flows back and forth, a kind of current that rouses him and stimulates her as well. The sudden, unexpected electrical charge that comes from their unplanned contact.

She turns right and drives down Main Street, past the train depot and on out the River Road, her headlights drilling into the night. Once they are past the lights of town, the nocturnal world is palpable. He rolls down his window to let the cool air off the river flow into the car and over their faces. For a moment, she releases his hand so she can steer with her right and roll down her own window with her left.

A mile further and she pulls off the road and down a slight incline toward the river, down into a gravel lot where once a house had stood, a house that was flooded so many times that it was finally abandoned and now only the brick chimney remains pointing into the night sky. She parks facing the river, cuts off the engine, and then, the headlights.

She scoots toward him on the seat and he puts his arm around her instinctively, protectively.

"Do you feel like you're back in high school?" she asks.

"Yes. What if we get caught?"

She giggles. "You're the sheriff. What are they going to do? Arrest us?" He doesn't reply to her teasing and she remembers what he said back in the parking lot, that he needed to talk to someone. She reaches up and places her left hand on his chest, over his heart. Surprisingly, he is all but gasping for breath. "What is it, Clint?" she whispers. "What do you need to say?" Instantly, she is afraid that it is about her, that he means to break off whatever is between them.

After pausing to clear his throat, he says, "Why does my son hate me?" His voice is suddenly hoarse and she realizes just how serious this is.

"What do you mean? Matthew? Are you talking about Matthew?"

"I tried to be a decent father. No, more than that, I tried to be the best father that I could imagine. My own father was a shit and I swore—I mean, *swore*—that I would be different, that I would be better, that I would be the best father that any son, any daughter could ever have."

"Easy, easy. Breathe and you can tell me. Say whatever you need to say." She massages his chest as she repeats this. He is suddenly so taut that she's afraid for him. "I don't think he hates you," she whispers. "I truly don't."

"He does. His friend was here today. From the Institute of Government in Chapel Hill. Some nice, young man named Smith who knows Matt well, and even though Matt knew he was coming up here, knew he would see me, he never even bothered to mention that we were related. Like I didn't exist in his world, like I'm sort of—I don't know what. A ghost. Why would he do that if he doesn't hate me?" He is still hoarse, but breathing more easily.

"You're not a ghost, Clint. I'm touching you. Can you feel me touching you?" She slides her hand down and rubs at his stomach, meaning him to feel her, meaning him to relax before he tears a muscle. And slowly, slowly, she can feel him ease under her hands.

"I know," he finally manages to say. "But God, it feels like he's trying to erase me."

"What if that's not it? Listen, Clint, I've never met the boy, but Marian and I've talked about this. What if he's not full of judgment and blame? What if he's just so caught up in his own world that he doesn't bother to think about other people at all? You or anybody else."

There is a pause here. She can hear him breathing, almost hear him thinking. "That would be worse," he says finally. "What kind of father must I have been if he doesn't even bother to pretend?"

She is whispering now. "You were a fine father," she murmurs over and over. "*Are* a fine father. Look at Marian. I know you, Clinton Salter. I *know* you. And because of Marian, I know what kind of father you were." Then, more loudly, "Listen to me, Clint. Did it ever occur to you that this is not about you? This is about him." And finally, because she can't stop herself: "We have his mother to blame for this."

CHAPTER 26

CATHERINE ALWAYS GOES TO VISIT HER HUSBAND at the Ivy Rehabilitation Center on Sunday afternoons. The next Sunday, after the visit from Michael Smith from the Institute of Government, Clinton asks if he can go with her.

At first, she is surprised, shocked even. Why would anyone want to share the burden of watching over a living, breathing corpse? But he persists over the phone on Friday night and Saturday until she finally agrees. They meet at a gas station parking lot just over the line in Yancey County, and because she is nervous, she asks him to drive her car.

All of this is new…to both of them. She can tell that he has bathed and shaved carefully for the occasion. This is only the second time he's ever driven her car with her in the passenger seat. Even the place they're going is new to him, a residential care facility outside Spruce Pine. "What do we say if someone sees us together?" she asks as they pass Burnsville. "One or two of the nurses are from Madison."

"We say that after all this time, you're seeking some sort of legal advice about the care of your husband."

"You a lawyer now?"

He smiles, almost laughs. "No, but I have some experience with…end of life decisions. Extended care. Something like that. And we can say that we're friends."

"Are we?" She is nervous. "Friends, I mean?"

"We better be."

Now, *she* almost laughs despite her nerves. "Why are you going with me, Clint? Seriously."

"To share it. After what happened at the farm on my birthday, I...struggle not to think about you. I try not to constantly scheme how to be with you. And it doesn't seem the least bit fair to carry you around inside my head all day without wanting to—I don't know—help you, care for you, share your life."

"Including the worst parts of my life?"

"You listened to me carry on about Matthew the other night. That's the worst part of my life, I think. Even worse than the war. Losing my son when he's still out there, walking, talking, breathing. And it's maddening not to be able to do anything about it because he's in complete control. So, is this the worst part of your life?"

"God, yes. Mostly because it's this weird kind of suspended animation. Like I'm frozen in a photograph from years ago and can't escape. As the years go by, it gets worse instead of better. You'd think it would get easier, but it doesn't because I'm the one who's frozen, not him."

"Do you dream about him? When he was still active?"

"Not anymore. But I have nightmares where I'm the one lying in bed in the rehab center. I'm the one trapped inside my own dead body and can't get out. And *that* is horrifying."

WHAT CLINT SEES INSIDE ROOM 32-B AT THE Ivy Rehabilitation Center is a thin, gray figure lying under a sheet that has been pulled up under his arms and carefully folded. The air inside the room smells of antiseptic and decay. The bed is immaculately made, the pillowcase crisp and clean, as if he has been carefully prepared for viewing. And since Cat always comes on Sunday, that is quite probably the case.

The figure of James Metcalf itself is thin to the point of emaciation, the arms little more than bones with a fragile sheath of flesh. The head is like a skull because the skin has sagged, not into the chin and throat as it normally does in an old man, but rather down through his ears to the back of his head, where it rests permanently on the pillow. The eyes are closed, peacefully closed, but the mouth sags open, revealing gray teeth. The breathing is shallow but regular.

Catherine sits for a few minutes on the side of the bed and holds one of his hands. Because she does this and because he doesn't know what else to do, Clinton walks around the far side of the bed and mimics her. Sits carefully down on the side of the bed and takes the man's other hand carefully into his own. The skin is dry and cool, the bones of the fingers prominent but brittle. *Where is the life?* he wonders. *There's almost nothing that is physical, nothing that changes as day sinks into night and night rises into day. And yet, he's still breathing. How the hell does he breathe?*

"If you're thinking about putting him out of his misery," she whispers, "it's nothing I haven't thought a hundred times."

"It's not that," he says. "I just wonder what's keeping him alive."

"There's an IV portal in this arm. Once a day, they give him a bag of glucose fluid that supports the bodily functions, and somehow that's enough."

"And he never changes? He's..."

"He's been like this for five years. He showed some signs of responsiveness in year two, and the doctors held out some hope that he might recover some awareness, maybe some movement in his extremities. But that never happened. Last year, he developed pneumonia, and the nurses whispered that I should prepare myself, that it was probably the end, but that didn't happen either."

He stands up. "I'm going to step outside for a few minutes so you can have some time alone with him. Say anything you need to say."

"I said it all a long time ago," she replies, "but thank you."

HE WALKS ALL THE WAY OUT TO THE PARKING lot while waiting for her. Suddenly, the inside of the rehab center had begun to feel tight, as though the air was thick with age and death, or *not death* in the case of Cat's husband. Outside, there is the sun again, hot and strong, air rife with birdsong.

When she comes out ten minutes later, he isn't sure what to say to her. Somehow it is worse having been there because it's more real. Yes, he's shared it with her now, but the sharing is of something unimaginable, something dry and suffocating.

She walks up and leans against the car with him, letting the sunlight pour over her. "I'm sorry," he says. "I don't know how you've stood this."

She nods, and when she speaks, it's slowly, as if she's measuring the words. "The hardest part...or I guess there are two hardest parts. One, you wish he'd just let go. I wish he'd just let go." Her arms are crossed tightly across her chest. "I know that people joke behind my back about just placing a pillow over his face and holding it down for a minute or two. But for me, it's not a joke. I've thought about it, even picked up the pillow."

He reaches over and wraps his hand around her upper arm, which is tight with the tension of what she's holding in or maybe beginning to let out. "What's the other hardest part?" he murmurs.

"The other hardest part is that I feel like he's taking me down with him. I didn't resent it when he brought me here, dragged me up to the remote mountains to live off the land, milk the cow, pluck the chicken. His nutty fantasy. Some days, I even thought it was an adventure. But this..." She nods toward the Ivy Rehab building. "This feels like he's trying to drag me down into the grave with him. Like he refuses to die and leave me here."

"Well, we're not going to—"

"Let me finish. Most days, when I leave here, I'm cursing him with every other breath. I used to hate myself for it, but not anymore."

"No need to hate yourself. And now that we've been here, I can do the cursing for you. I imagine I'm better at it." And even though they're standing in the middle of a public parking lot in broad daylight, he pulls her to him and puts his arms around her. She is still stiff with anger and despair, but at least she is shielded against the world.

As they're driving back from Spruce Pine to where they'd left his Jeep, he asks her the question that's been nagging at him. With his eyes on the road, both hands on the steering wheel, he says, "The other night, you said that we had Matthew's mother to blame for the way he is. What did you mean?"

"I shouldn't have said that," she offers. "Not my place."

"I don't care that you said it. I just wonder what you meant."

He can sense her adjust her seat belt so that she can turn toward him on the car seat. "Marian and I have talked about this, Clint. Even before you and I—even before your birthday. I was curious about you and I asked some questions, and she opened up. At least about her brother. She told me that when they were younger, their mother would tell them to leave here, leave the mountains. First chance they got. Get the hell away from here, essentially. She thought it was stupid and said so. Matthew listened."

"So, it's not me that he hates. It's the mountains."

She hesitates before answering. "I didn't say that. I don't think Marian would mind me saying this. According to her, when Gretchen—do you mind if I say her name? Okay, when Gretchen died, he blamed you. He blamed you for, I don't know, bringing her up here, making her live here when she obviously hated it so much. Almost like you'd kept her prisoner or something."

"In this godforsaken, redneck corner of the world?"

"Something like that."

"No, I've heard her use those exact words when she was angry about something. Angry at me about something."

"But she wasn't like that all the time?"

"No, we were happy a lot of the time. She especially liked joking around with Will and making fun of the way I talked. But still, she had her moments when the pipes froze in the winter or there was a brush fire in the summer."

"Well, he must have taken the whole thing to heart and, according to Marian, he blames you."

He sighs. Long and deep. "I think that too. Blames me for being the redneck, clodhopper, hillbilly..."

He can sense her nodding. "And he wants to get as far away from it as he can."

"You mean, as far away from me as he can."

"It's not just you, Clint. It's the mountains. But for him, you're one and the same."

CHAPTER 27

AT THE GAS STATION ON THE COUNTY LINE, THEY buy two Cokes out of a bath of ice and pop the tops off the bottles using the opener on the side of the cooler. She points out a picnic table sitting under a stand of trees at the back of the lot. They sit there, out of the sun and mostly out of sight.

Neither of them gives words to the question both are asking. The picnic table is asking, the trees are asking, her station wagon sitting in the sun is asking: *What are we going to do?*

"We're going to have to see each other," one of them says when their Coke bottles are half-empty. Him. "I can't imagine not seeing you."

"We're going to have to be careful," the other says. Her. "If it gets out that I'm...dating, I'm pretty sure I'd lose my job. In fact, I'd probably be invited to resign the next week."

"Surely, surely there are one or two rational human beings on the school board. Tell me there is."

"There are two Baptist preachers, a banker, a housewife, and your illustrious brother. At the last meeting, they rebuked a teacher from Mars Hill for running a chain saw on Sunday."

"My brother..." he says as if those words alone are enough. "My brother never had a spiritual thought in his life, but he's in the front pew at First Baptist in Marshall every Sunday."

"So, I could resign," she says simply. "Find something else to do."

"Hell no," he says flatly, with almost no inflection despite the profanity. "No, you earned this. You need this. Education is who you are. I'll resign. I came by the job dishonestly anyway."

"*Hell no*, right back at you." Her eyes are a blue blaze. "You may not need the job, but the job needs you. In part, it needs you because you're made of this place, blood and bone. I've watched you grow into the sheriff's office over the past few months, and I can see you becoming more and more determined to do it right. I'm not going to let you quit now."

"But you've been doing education one way or another for twenty years. I've been sheriff for less than one. It's not fair for you to—"

"Just stop, Clint, and listen for a minute. What exactly does a good sheriff do? You've seen it from the inside out now. In a perfect world, what does he do?"

Clinton pauses to think. It's not something he's put words to before. "He runs a clean shop. No bribes, no liquor out the back door. He gets rid of the sorry-ass deputies and replaces them with the best he can find. He gets them some decent training and then sets the best example he can."

"What about those he serves?"

"The people?"

She nods. "Them."

"A good sheriff makes the county as clean and safe as it can possibly be, and when somebody tries to interfere in the lives of others, destroy the lives of others, he puts a stop to it."

"Clean and safe?"

Now it's his turn to nod.

"That's funny. Not laughable, but ironic. That is almost exactly what I thought I wanted to do when I became principal. Get rid of the sorry-ass teachers and replace them with the best I could lure to the island. Get them decent training and create a school that is clean and safe. Somewhere in a journal, I probably wrote exactly those words. And here's the thing: You're already better at your job than anything we've had in a long time. You can't quit."

"I'm not going to let *you* quit either," he says quietly. "So, what do—"

"We do? I don't know."

"We carry on a...relationship until..."

"Until James dies." She finishes the thought when he can't.

He nods. "I don't much believe in sin, but if I did, I imagine it's a sin to wish him dead."

"Oh, I've wished for it. Even before you, I wished for it. I could feel the breath being sucked out of me every Sunday afternoon, but then whenever I stopped going for a few weeks, I felt even worse. Like I'd broken my wedding vows for no good reason." She holds up her left hand and points to her wedding band. "In sickness and health, 'til death do us part."

"I've thought about that. Told myself that I should give you up because I was corrupting you."

She laughs at the thought. Drains the last drops of Coke out of her bottle. "More like you're saving me. Saving me from myself, saving me from him." She reaches over to take his bottle and sucks the last drops from it as well. Then, while he gazes at her, she says one word. "Clandestine."

"What?"

"*Clandestine.* I looked it up last night when I couldn't sleep. Something that is *kept secret or done secretively, especially because illicit.*"

"I know what *illicit* means," he says ruefully.

"I hope so. You're the sheriff. Which means, by the way, that maybe I'm the one who's corrupting you, taking you down with me. I worry about *that.*"

He shakes his head slightly. "I don't think you have it in you to corrupt me. I fell off from righteousness years ago." She is almost smiling and so he reaches over to caress her cheek, hoping to turn the faint curl of her lips into a grin with his fingertips, which, after a moment, he does. There is the gap in her teeth, the round tip of her nose, the cobalt in her eyes. "It's Sunday," he says. "Our day off. Why don't you drive up to the farm? I'll stop by the jail to make sure nothing has fallen down or burned up, and then I'll follow you. Thirty minutes later."

"I'll stop by the store," she offers. "Something for supper. Are we going riding?"

"Something like that," he replies, the heat evident in his eyes.

"Clandestine," she says.

THE DIFFERENCE IS THAT THIS TIME THEY SPEND the rest of the afternoon—right up against suppertime—in bed. She'll need to go home to the rented bungalow that night to be ready for school the next day and to avoid exciting her neighbor's suspicion.

Even without the night to look forward to, this is a wonderful interlude after they've made love and are lying tangled loosely in the sheet on his bed.

While she dozes, perfectly relaxed in late afternoon bliss, he is floating halfway between sleep and wakefulness, his own gut-deep need for her released into a warm and wanton place that exists where he stops and she begins. And now that boundary is more fluid than ever, less certain, more mysterious.

When his eyes do drift closed, he sees within his mind the edge of his upper pasture where it disappears into the depths of the woods, full summer woods woven from strands of green mystery, humming with life and suggesting a depth that is impossible to understand unless your body is on full, sensuous alert. How to penetrate the depths within those shadowed woods or within this woman lying beside you.

Mystery in close relations: The more intimately you are entwined with someone, the more mysterious they become. And the more complete your fall.

She stirs briefly and rolls toward him, pulling the sheet up over his body as well as hers, protecting him, caring for him, finding him easily without opening her eyes. She pushes her face into the hollow of his neck and kisses him there.

As the afternoon sun falls away toward the Divide Mountain, light comes flooding in through the open bedroom windows: warm, yellow, buzzing light, almost fluid in its intensity. And the two of them are one animal, complete against the passage of time. Or so it seems to him. They have a past and a future full within this moment.

When, eventually, she rises to go to the bathroom, a sort of reality returns to the room—less real than the one before, the one they and only they share between them—but real in the world of others. His eyes open of their own accord so that he can watch her naked body move with its dancer's grace and clarity around the foot of the bed.

Here, now, as he regards her, he knows something new. She is sweetly soft, finely made and feminine. But, at the same time... strong. *Her softness is her strength*, he thinks.

CHAPTER 28

A MONTH LATER, ON A THURSDAY MORNING, THE phone rings at the sheriff's office.

Clinton has been there perhaps ten minutes and is drinking coffee with Gloria Goforth in the front office. She answers the phone and when she does, he can tell by the look on her face and the tone of her voice that it's bad. He starts back to his office, assuming she'll patch the call through, but she holds up her hand signaling him to stay. She keeps repeating the phrases, *Calm down* and *Yes, I know*. Again, *Yes, I know, sir*—"exactly where it is. The sheriff is on his way." And then: "Stay there. He'll meet you there."

He gulps the hot coffee, burning his tongue, and walks into his office only long enough to pick up his badge and a notepad off the desk. Then back into Gloria's office to sit and listen. Take notes.

"Do you know where the old Richland Norton place is?" she asks. He searches through his memory for a moment before he lands on a spot in his mental map of the county. "The old, square brick house a couple of miles below Hot Springs on the river?"

"That's the one. Built by Richland Norton back in the day when he cut the timber off all that land from there to Tennessee. His daughter has been living there her whole life, in her seventies or eighties now. Recently her brother's wife died, and he moved in with her. Brother and sister, both in their dotage."

He nods. Writing rough notes on his pad.

"Somebody apparently broke into the place last night and shot them both."

"Dead?"

"Dead. That was his son on the phone. He drove up this morning to check on them and found them. He's down at Jesuit Residence in Hot Springs, and he's hysterical. I told him you'd meet him there before going up to the house."

He nods and stands up. "See if you can catch Way Tipton at home. He's close. Tell him to meet me at the Norton place."

"What about Balis?"

He pauses. "You think he's kin?"

"Likely. He's a Norton and up there, everybody's kin."

"Track him down too. Send him to the house. But tell him that if he gets there before I do, to park at the road and not to go in without me." He starts for the door.

"Clinton?"

"Yes, ma'am?"

"Ambulance?"

"Yes. The big county rig. Assuming they are dead, eventually, we'll need it for the bodies."

He makes it to Hot Springs in twenty minutes.

CLINTON PICKS UP JOHN NORTON AT THE JESUIT Residence and Retreat Center above Hot Springs. Norton, calmer now than he must have been over the phone, explains that he drives over from Tennessee every few weeks on his day off to check on his father and his aunt, Grady and Bonnie. Usually, they were up and about early in the morning and his aunt would fix him breakfast.

"What did you find this time?" Clinton asks him as he drives.

"I went to the back door like I always do, and it was standing wide open. The screen door was tore most off its hinges, and the main door was shoved open. Daddy was lying just inside the door, and Aunt Bonnie was back beside the stove, both of them cold as a fish out of the creek. Blood all over the floor."

Clinton turns to the right off the road to Newport and down a gravel road toward the river below. After five minutes, they come out of the trees into acres of open pasture along the river.

As they drive up and over the railroad tracks, he asks Norton, "Is that the house?"

"Yessir. That's it. You want me to show you?"

"No, let me look around first and take some pictures. Then we'll get you to show us." He pulls the Jeep over to the side of the road before the driveway, across from the house. Way Tipton's Chevrolet is already there, and Way is standing beside the Nortons' mailbox. He asks Way to sit with Norton in the Jeep and take down his statement, starting with when he called his father the afternoon before to say he'd be stopping by.

He carries the camera from the Jeep up to the front porch, careful to walk on the stepping stones that trace the path from the driveway to the porch. Everything there, on the stones, the steps, and the porch, seems completely normal and undisturbed. The front screen door swings open easily, but the front door itself is firmly locked from the inside. There's a pane of glass in the door, and through it, he can see a set of stairs leading up to the second floor and, beside the steps, a hallway that leads to the back of the house.

HE HEADS BACK DOWN THE FRONT STEPS AND around the side of the house farthest from the driveway. The yard is undisturbed on this side, dew still on the grass. Someone, Bonnie Norton, he assumes, has planted flowers along the side of the house. Around back, he comes to a small back porch. Three sagging wooden steps lead up to the covered porch. The gravel on the path leading from the driveway on the other side of the house is scuffled as though someone has carried something heavy or perhaps run along it. He takes a photo of the path and then the steps.

Standing on the porch, he takes a photo of the screen door, which, as Norton has said, is torn from its top hinge and hanging precariously by the bottom one. The screen in the door is torn as well. The inside door, solid wood, appears to have been shoved roughly open, and there's a hole in the door, approximately chest high. The torn wood looks fresh, as if the hole is recent. *Bullet hole*, he thinks.

The door itself is jammed half open by the body of Grady Norton just inside, lying on his back in a pool of what must be his own blood, wearing new overalls and what was probably a white shirt before the blood soaked it. There's a footprint in the blood beside the body, but it's new since the blood coagulated. John Norton's, he assumes. More photos.

To this point, he has touched only the back porch railing, and he suddenly realizes he's not wearing gloves. He edges around the kitchen table to where Bonnie Norton's body is sprawled against the stove. She too has apparently been shot. Twice, judging from the wounds. *To keep her from screaming*, he wonders, *although the sound of the shots...*

He takes more photos of her body and then, from the hallway, of as much of the kitchen as he can manage. He hears knocking from the front door behind him and when he looks back, he sees Balis Norton, his deputy, standing there. He walks down the hallway and, using his handkerchief, unlocks and opens the door.

"They dead?" Balis asks.

He nods. "Have been for quite a while, judging from the blood. You related?"

Balis nods. "My grandpa was a cousin to the two of them—something like that. We used to have reunions down here by the river. When I was a little chap, we used to play in that old barn."

"Well, if you want to see them, walk as far as the kitchen door and take a look, and then I want you to stand by out at the road and keep any curious folks from coming out to the house. Don't let anybody stop and start tramping around sightseeing. I'm going to go change the film in this camera."

"Sheriff?"

"Yeah?"

"One more thing. The old man, Grady Norton. He was known for carrying around thousands of dollars in cash."

"On his person?"

Balis nods. "Yep. When his wife died, he took all his money out of the bank, said he'd never trust lawyers or bankers again. He carried it in envelopes in his overall pockets. Must have kept it here at the house when he was at home."

THERE IS A PHONE IN THE HOUSE, WHICH HE USES to call Gloria at the jail. Send every deputy she can track down to the Norton house, along with medical gloves, a measuring tape, and more film for the camera. Oh, and call the Buncombe County medical examiner and tell him that they're sending him two murder victims, and he needs to know as much information as possible about them as he can provide. And fast, sooner rather than later.

He refuses to let even the ambulance pull into the driveway close by the house but makes the attendants park beside the huge, old barn and wait while he goes carefully over the bodies. Grady Norton was shot once, squarely in the middle of his chest, the bullet apparently fired through the door. And again, through his head, apparently to make sure he was dead. There is nothing in his overall pockets except a string pouch of loose tobacco and a packet of rolling papers, a Boker Tree brand pocketknife with two worn blades. From where he kneels on the floor, Clinton notices a Zippo lighter on the floor under the edge of one of the cabinets, perhaps Grady's, but maybe the killer's. In Grady's shirt pocket, beneath the torn bibs of his overalls, Clinton finds a black-and-white photo of Grady with a woman roughly his age, perhaps his wife. They are dressed up and posing, she smiling, Grady staring straight ahead. No money, no envelopes, no keys, no wallet. Last thing he sees is a small gold chain looped through the buttonhole on the overall bibs. The chain is broken off at three inches, give or take. *Must have fastened the old man's pocket watch,* he realizes, *which means the son of a bitch jerked it off the body.*

He finds a plastic bag in a kitchen drawer and drops the tobacco, the rolling papers, the lighter, the chain, and the knife in the bag. The photo he places in a separate bag.

Bonnie Norton has been shot twice, once in the hip and once in the chest. *First in the hip,* he thinks, *as she comes into the kitchen to check on Grady, and then in the chest, after she's down?* She is wearing a robe over a gown, bedroom slippers on her feet. She has a wad of Kleenex in the pocket of her robe and a packet of Tums. That's it. Except that her glasses have blood on them. She must have reached up to adjust her glasses after she was shot the first time, perhaps to better see who was attacking her and her brother. When he checks her right hand, he sees that her fingers are bloody. The glasses go into another plastic bag.

He stands up and almost turns away before checking her left hand. Her ring finger has a pale indentation from years of wearing the same ring. The ring is gone and her ring finger is dislocated.

He finally lets the ambulance boys into the house, but through the front door and down the hallway, still saving the backyard for later examination. He joins Way Tipton and Balis Norton out on the road while the attendants bring the two bodies down the front sidewalk and load them in the ambulance. "Buncombe County Morgue in Asheville," he stresses to the driver. "The regional medical examiner knows they're coming."

CHAPTER 29

CLINTON GOES THROUGH THE ENTIRE HOUSE WITH John Norton, the son. They move slowly, but Clinton keeps him talking to prevent the shock from silencing him completely.

He starts in the yard with John, going over where he parked his car and which tracks leading up to the back porch are his. Then the kitchen, with how he found things that morning. And yes, the one footprint in Grady's congealed blood is John's.

Then, the rest of the large, rambling, dark, and haunted house: five rooms downstairs and six upstairs. The two bedrooms on the second floor were used by the brother and sister. One of which, Grady's, has been hastily torn apart. *Searched*, he assumes. An old footlocker has been jimmied open and its contents strewn across the floor. A rolltop desk sits against the wall. The rolltop itself, made of beautiful cherrywood, has been smashed at the lock and shoved back.

"That's where they kept the coins," John Norton explains.

"What coins?"

"My grandfather, Grady's daddy, was a lifelong collector of rare coins, mostly silver and gold. When I was a little boy, he would take them out and spread them on the bed for us to play with. He told us some was gold pieces and some was Morgan silver dollars. He gave us an ordinary silver dollar every year on our birthday. They wasn't worth so much as the coins he had in the collection—he just got ours at the bank—but they was to remind us of how special we were and how special all us Nortons are."

"So, whoever broke in here last night knew about the coins. Was searching for them."

Norton nods slowly. "They must have. They come straight here to look for them. Knew to bust open the rolltop."

Family, Clinton thinks but doesn't say. *Check out the various cousins.*

They find the old man's day-to-day billfold—two tens and a five, a driver's license. They find photographs, spare change, and dozens of antiques left over from the Richland Norton generation, when the house was built out of fancy lumber milled on the site. When the family had real money.

So far as John Norton is able to say, there's nothing else missing, at least nothing as obvious as artwork or antique furniture. His grandmother's jewelry box sits quietly on the dresser in her room, unopened.

At midday, they're still at it, combing the yard for any clue as to who was there the night before. He is surprised to see Gloria Goforth pull up in her car. Not only has she brought one more deputy, Sam Ray, with her, she has ten sandwiches from Robbins Drug Store and two large Stanley thermoses of coffee, black and strong. They all gather out by the barn to eat, including John Norton.

After lunch, he intends to interview Norton one last time, who is managing to sip coffee but can't bring himself to eat. When Gloria gets up to go, he walks out to her car with her. "Thanks for the food," he says to her. "God knows we needed it. I wish I knew what I was doing."

"You're doing fine. Is there anybody you want me to call?"

"What do you mean?"

"You want me to call Marian, let her know what's happened? Or that principal of yours?"

Time for him pauses. The breeze in the sycamores down by the French Broad River dies away. In a way, she's asking if he trusts her. Can he let himself trust her? The words *clandestine* and *illicit* float to the top of his mind.

"Everybody on this earth needs friends, Clinton. Surely you know that. You can trust me to call her, if you want her to know what's going on."

"Do," he says. "In fact, if you call her at school, she can tell Marian at three when the bell rings."

Gloria smiles at him. "Good for you. One of life's biggest trials is learning who your friends are."

HE SPENDS ANOTHER THIRTY MINUTES OR SO with John Norton after letting him use the phone at the house to call his wife in Tennessee. Break the bad news to her. The man is exhausted, but still coherent enough to share the history of the house, a showplace when it was built around 1905.

By my Grandpa Norton. Richland Norton.

His daddy, my great-granddaddy, George Washington Norton, once owned two thousand acres from here to Tennessee. Can you believe that? Bought it way back before the Civil War for pennies when this land was naught but wilderness. He left it to Grandpa Norton in his will, which is somewhere in the house.

Around 1900, Grandpa rented out all this land from here on up the river as far as the Tennessee line. Nearly a thousand acres to that logging outfit in Runnion. So much timber that they was a secondary sawmill right here. They built that big barn just to handle the livestock. I think the sawmill sat just over there where that shed is now. And beyond into the fields in back. The narrow-gauge railroad they used ran along this side of the river but up against the foot of the ridge. Right in front of where we're sittin'.

Grandpa Norton worked for the Betts family, who owned the Runnion operation, as a surveyor, foreman, lumber grader, and so on. That's where he learned the business. He was making money hand over fist from selling the timber rights and running the mill here. So, he wanted to build his wife, Nancy—her picture's in there on the wall—the fanciest house this side of Hot Springs.

No, I'm all right. I'd favor a little more of that coffee, though, if there's any left.

Well, sir, he hired a crew out of the loggers working up and down the river, and they pitched in on Saturday and Sunday or anytime when there was a lull in the timberwork. You probably didn't take time to notice, but they used all different kinds of wood. Inside the house and out. The floor, the cabinets, the paneling and such.

His wife thought he was crazy. Walnut this and cherry that. Virgin chestnut from back before the blight. Maple stair rail and so on. Grandma Nancy complained it slowed 'em down, and she wanted to move in. But Grandpa Richland was determined that every kind of wood that come out of these hills would be featured in his house. Like it was a museum of wood.

How am I related? Well, Richland Norton had five, I think that's right, five children but only one son. His son was Grady, in course. And one of the girls was Bonnie. Bonnie was a sweet woman, but so shy she would barely come to the door unless she knew you. Never married. Always heard that she had a fellow that died in the swine flu, and that was as close as she come to marriage.

Anyway, she lived here her entire life. Was born here and never left here. And as time passed, the other three girls moved away. Eventually died, such that Grady and Bonnie was the only two left.

My daddy, Grady, he married my mama, in course. And had me and my sister. All his life, they was two things he hated: bankers, number one, and lawyers, number two. Didn't much like preachers either. When Mama died two years ago, he swore he'd never darken the door of the bank in Marshall again. He remembered the Depression years and feared another bank collapse.

His money? I guess Balis told you that. He carried up to ten thousand dollars in hundreds on his person. Not in envelopes, though, like the stories you hear. In special leather pocketbooks that fit in his overalls.... Pocketbooks is what the old-timers call 'em. Wallets. Leather wallets. The rest of his money he kept in the foot-locker. Thought it was safe 'cause it had a lock on it.

I guess that's what the son of a bitch was after that shot 'em. The money. The coins.

You say there was more than one SOB. How do you know?

"There's at least two, probably three, sets of footprints out in the soft ground at the end of the driveway. Around the tire tracks from a big car or a truck."

John Norton nods. "You're gonna ask me who would've known, ain't you? About the cash money and the coins?"

"Yes, sir, I am."

"Ever'body knew about the cash. Daddy talked about it ever'where he went."

CHAPTER 30

IT IS CLOSE ON SIX O'CLOCK BEFORE HE DRIVES away from the Norton place, having left Sam Ray to guard the house overnight.

He expects to find the jail mostly dark, mostly quiet, but Rosie Maney is still there with Brutus asleep under her feet. Her husband has fed the two prisoners—drunk and disorderly—upstairs and is sitting companionably with his wife in the kitchen.

And, to his happy surprise, Marian and Catherine Metcalf are sitting in the kitchen as well, talking with Rosie and sipping coffee. When he first hears their voices, he thinks for a moment that he's dreaming, wishing, but his wishes are real, and his family is there.

"Meat loaf in about ten minutes," Rosie says when she sees him standing in the kitchen doorway. "Meat loaf and mashed potatoes if you can stand it."

"Those are the best words I've heard all day," he says. And then: "What are you two doing here?" This to Catherine and Marian.

"We came for the food," Catherine says.

"And to make sure you're all right." Marian.

"I have no idea," he mutters, "if I'm all right. It's been a long day. And I'm more confused than I have any right to be."

Catherine gets up and walks to the large, stainless steel coffeepot on the stove and pours him a mug. Adds just the right amount of milk and stirs before bringing it to him. No one in the room would think to notice how precise and comfortable she is doing this, except for Marian, who already knows.

He thanks Cat and says to the room, "I'm going to wash up and make a few notes while the day is more or less fresh in my mind. Somebody yell when the meat loaf comes out of the oven."

Back in his own office, he lays his badge on the desk and sits with the steno pad he's been sketching and writing in all day. He intends to make a chronological description of what he thinks happened at the Norton house, but he discovers that his eyes are too blurry, his hands too cramped from fatigue. Catherine comes in and sits down quietly in the chair across from him with her typical grace, something he isn't too tired to notice.

There is a moment when their eyes meet—hers questioning, concerned—but only a moment before the quiet is shattered by someone blundering through the outer office, calling out and cursing. Someone who can only be his brother. And then Will is in the room, dragging the other office chair over to the desk. "Goddamn, brother," Will says loud enough to be heard upstairs in the cells. "You caught whoever killed those Nortons yet?"

"Not quite yet," Clinton replies, almost in a whisper.

Will seems to notice Catherine for the first time, but doesn't speak to her, rather nods his head at her and asks Clinton, "Who's this pretty young lady? A witness?"

Clinton can't help himself. He almost laughs at how like a rooster Will is. A loud rooster crowing outside your window on some hungover morning. "No, Will, this is Catherine Metcalf. She's the principal of Marshall High School."

Will turns to give her his salesman's once-over. "Well, Mrs. Metcalf, I reckon you work for me then. I'm the chairman of the school board."

Catherine pretends to smile. "No, sir. I work for the superintendent. He works for you."

"Hell, same difference." Will laughs as he says this, perhaps even to suggest he's joking.

"What do you want, Will?" This from Clinton. "I'm in the middle of a murder investigation."

Will glances at Catherine. "Don't look like it to me. Looks like you been sent to the principal's office to me." Again, he laughs. Again, too loud. "I just came by to check on you. Make sure you're still upright. Not every day we get a double murder around here."

"I'm upright," Clinton offers. He stands up. "Lot to do, though."

"I get your drift," Will says and grins. He turns to go, but as he does, he stops to regard the map on the wall. The map that now has six red pins stuck in it. "Maybe the Norton killings are a good thing. Maybe they'll give you something worthwhile to spend your time on," he says. "And you can forget about these damn barns you keep fretting over."

And then he's gone, making just as much noise leaving as he did arriving.

"Why did you say that, brother?" Clinton mutters such that only Catherine can hear.

"Why *did* he say it?" she whispers.

MEAT LOAF AND MASHED POTATOES. PEACH cobbler from the day before set back in the oven to warm. Rosie Maney's plain, delicious hot food. Iced tea or coffee, take your pick. As they eat, he tells them the bare outlines of what happened at the Norton house. And when they ask, he admits he has no notion of who the killers might be, but because of the coins, he has to at least look at family members.

After the cobbler, they stand up and carry their dishes to the sink. Marian offers to wash, but Rosie only nods at her husband. "He'll be here all night," she says. "Needs something to do."

The three of them—Clinton, Marian, Catherine—part ways on the sidewalk. Marian kisses her father on the cheek and tells him to get some rest before walking toward her car. Catherine does not touch him at all but asks quietly if he wants to talk. He nods. "Mrs. Penland's porch?" she asks.

"Perfect," he says.

"I need to go home and change. In an hour?"

"Just right," he says. "That'll give me a chance to wash this day off my skin."

ROCKING CHAIRS, AS BEFORE. BOURBON AND two mugs from the kitchen. Mrs. Penland herself comes out to turn off the porch light. When he introduces Catherine as his friend, Mrs. Penland simply says, "That's good. Everybody needs friends," before saying good night and going to the back of the house.

"What do you think she means?" Cat asks.

"I'm not really sure. Maybe she's giving us permission to..."

"Permission to what?"

"Sit on the porch, I guess. Sip from her mugs. Hold hands?"

Which they do, all three. Quiet for a bit, as she gives him time to come round to whatever he wants to tell, whatever he wants to share. But when he does speak, it's not what she expects. "I don't think I'm up to this," is what he says.

"Us...or the murders?"

"The murders. I'm more than up for us. But all day long, I kept thinking I didn't know what the hell I was doing. Fingerprints, tire tracks, muddy boot prints, bloodstains. I don't know how to handle all that."

"You do if anyone does."

She can feel him shaking his head in the dark. "Cat, when Will first talked me into running for sheriff, I thought all I'd ever have to deal with was weekend drunk and disorderly, plus somebody stealing a tractor or a motorcycle from his son of a bitch brother-in-law. Occasionally a shot fired in anger, but not straight, not that hit somebody. It's been less than a year and we've had a high school kid shot in a parking lot, a grave robbing, and now..."

"Do you believe in providence?" she whispers.

"Is providence another word for God?"

"Maybe. Sometimes."

"Then, no. I don't believe in it."

"I do," she says. "Most days, I do. Although, it's a hell of a mystery when you think about James lying there frozen in time."

"If that's providence, then it sure has a mean streak."

"Yes, it does. But then, on the other hand, we're sitting here. Together. What if this is providence?"

She can hear him snort. A brief, comfortable laugh. "I like this version of providence," he admits.

"What I'm saying is that I think it's providential that you're sheriff. Maybe even that you're sheriff right now. Today. When those poor, old people got killed. I know enough about that Runnion man you ran against to get down on my knees and thank God that it's you and not him. And I know enough about the general riot of humanity, which I see every working day, to think you're it. You're here for a reason."

"Here with you or here as sheriff?" He may be teasing her, hard to tell in the dark.

"Well, both. Here with me. I think I already said that. But what I really mean is that you have no reason whatsoever to doubt yourself as sheriff. What are you really good at, Clint? If it's not fingerprints and bloodstains, what's your talent? I think I know, but I want to hear you say it."

"I guess I'm good with people."

"Thank you. Despite pretending to be just a good old boy from Doe Branch, you're very good with people. Nobody better. For some reason, people like you. They trust you. Look at me."

"Maybe, but what does that have to do with—"

"Talk to the people, Clint. Talk to the people and eventually, they'll *tell* you who killed the Nortons."

CHAPTER 31

THE NEXT DAY, A FRIDAY IN SEPTEMBER, THE AIR is cooler in the morning along the river than it has been since May.

He starts the day at the jail with Gloria. Coffee and a series of clear decisions, directions, and orders. He and Way Tipton will meet the investigators from the State Bureau of Investigation at the Norton house at ten. He will call in at noon to check in with her. She will have all the deputies meet him at the jail at four. *All* the other deputies, whether they were scheduled to be on duty or not. Rosie will feed them, and he has something to say to them.

And then, just as he's about to leave, he pauses in her office. "Gloria," he says. "Of everybody who works here—in the sheriff's office, I mean—who's a Republican?"

"Why do you want to know? Now's not the time to fire somebody for political reasons."

"I don't want to fire anybody. I want to find out something."

She hesitates, but then answers. "Dwayne Austin is a good Republican. And so am I."

He grins. "I thought you said you voted for me."

"I did, but I also never thought you'd win." She's grinning at him now. "And I bet now you're sorry you did."

"Right now, I'm just exhausted. But I've got a job for you and Dwayne."

He picks up Way Tipton on the corner of Bridge and Main Streets as he passes through Hot Springs. Not for the first time, he notices just how quiet and unobtrusive Way is. Almost as if he moves through the scenery without attracting your eye. Seeing without being seen.

Which is a fine characteristic for a deputy, he thinks. Someone you wouldn't even notice...at least not until he needed to be noticed.

When they arrive at the Norton house, he sends Sam Ray home for some sleep, after telling him about the meeting at the jail that afternoon. When the crime scene boys from the SBI arrive in their van, only two of the three boys are *boys*. One is a young woman from Wilmington, who, it turns out, is the fingerprint expert. After a conference around the van out by the railroad tracks, they take over the scene, as they keep calling it.

He leaves Way to stand by and answer questions as they work and walks back across the tracks and along the dirt road that will take him to the Nortons' neighbors. He smiles as he does, recalling Catherine's advice from the night before. And with his badge prominently displayed, he walks up to two houses and three trailers.

He doesn't get dog-bit and he doesn't get shot at, but he also doesn't find out much. One young woman, distressingly pregnant, comes out on her porch with a rifle, but as soon as she grasps who he is and that he isn't interested in her husband, talks his ear off. *Yes*, the Nortons were nice old folks, especially her, but *No*, she didn't hear anything the night they died. *No*, she did not intend on having her baby at home, and *Yes*, she'd been seeing a doctor.

One old geezer named Oettinger, who gets up to piss at least four times a night, *every damn night*, told him that he'd seen car headlights leaving the Nortons' early in the morning of the night they were killed. *Them lights flash up in the woods here where I live cause when an auto-mobile goes over them railroad tracks, the lights rise up and then dive back down again. You get what I mean? Rise up and dive back down.*

Car lights early in the morning. *When it was still black dark outside. Not a glimmer of light in the east.*

The Nortons themselves owned a twenty-year-old farm truck that was still parked beside the barn at their house. An old farm truck, which, according to John Norton, still ran well enough to take the two old folks into Hot Springs once a week. So, the car lights Oettinger claims to have seen—*rise up and dive back down*—are probably connected to the killers, but that's it. All he gets from a hot morning of visiting with the neighbors.

Did the Nortons have any enemies? *Why no, sir.* Any idea who might have done it? *Hippies. Them hippies might have done it. Looking for drugs.*

By midafternoon, the SBI team is finished. They take the back door with the bullet hole, the doorframe itself, and the rolltop desk with them in the van. They also show Clinton two bullets they found embedded in the kitchen woodwork, one of which apparently went through Grady Norton's head and one through Bonnie's Norton's hip. Handgun, they tell him, .32 caliber most likely. They'll know for sure once they're back at the lab in Raleigh. He promises to secure the other bullets from the medical examiner and forward them to Raleigh as well.

And that's it. He and Way are left alone at the Norton farm. Insects buzzing in the hazy afternoon heat. The river valley wide here, with far-flung fields on either side of the river—slow, summer-green water flowing slowly away to Tennessee.

They lock up the house as best they can with the back door and its frame gone entirely. He drops Way off in Hot Springs to pick up his own car, and they drive back to Marshall to meet with the entire department and to consider.

SUPPER IS CHICKEN-FRIED STEAK WITH GRAVY, along with a mess of green beans and biscuits for those who want bread. It's crowded in their jailhouse kitchen and dining room: Lloyd and Rosie Maney, Gloria Goforth, Way Tipton, Sam Ray, Balis Norton, Danny Fender, and Dwayne Austin. Clinton makes nine, not counting Brutus the dog and a stray cat that has also taken up residence.

After most everyone has eaten their fill, Clinton stands up and clears his throat. Everyone quiets down to listen except for the cat, who is loudly licking gravy out of the bowl someone set on the floor for her.

"I appreciate what all of you have done in the last thirty-six hours," he begins. "Every single one of you pitched in and helped, here and out at the Norton farm. Nobody complained and nobody shirked their duty. Quick update in case you haven't heard: The bodies are with the Buncombe County Medical Examiner in Asheville. He says he'll give us something by tomorrow morning. The SBI was out at the house almost all day. Way and I managed to stay out of their way. They should be able to tell us something about fingerprints, ballistics, blood, and so on. They promised less than a week.

"For now, what we know is that the Nortons were each shot twice, probably with a thirty-two caliber revolver, one of the most common damn guns in the world. Motive is probably robbery, since Grady Norton was famous for carrying around large amounts of cash, and there was a valuable coin collection in the house, which is missing. Whoever did this may have been after the money and the coins, but they sure as hell didn't hesitate to shoot both the old man and the old woman, twice each, to make sure they were dead.

"Balis is related to the victims and I hope that you'll extend our condolences to the family. Let me know when the funerals are set and I'll plan to be there. I wouldn't mind if some of the rest of you show up too. Given that whoever did it knew about the coins and where they were kept, we may need to look at who that might be."

"May be family," Balis offers. "I won't deny it."

He nods. "May be family. Or longtime friends. But no matter how you figure, we have a crisis on our hands. We're a small-time sheriff's department in a thinly populated county and this kind of thing doesn't happen, or at least not once in fifty years. So, Gloria and I will stay in touch with the medical examiner and the SBI. That part will take care of itself over the next week or so.

"What I want you all to do is get out and about. Spend most of your days and most of your evenings talking to people. Leave your uniform shirts at home for this week unless you're at the jail. Get out in the community and visit. Friends, relatives, cousins you haven't seen in a while. Don't bring up the Nortons straight away, but let it come up naturally. Wonder out loud who might have done such a horrible thing. And so on.

"You know Madison County. Somewhere out there are a half dozen people who know full well who probably did this. And unless they're scared to death, they tend to talk. And over the next few weeks, word will slowly seep out. What we have to do is listen. Pay attention. Hear what's being whispered, even when it's not being whispered to us. Any thoughts?"

Danny Fender raises his hand. "I been thinking. The Norton place is awful close to the Tennessee line. Maybe the killers are from Newport or somewhere over that way. That's a mean-ass part of the world, makes us look like Sunday School. Sorry, Mrs. Goforth."

General agreement as to Tennessee. Clinton nods. "I'll call the Cocke County sheriff Monday morning. Any other thoughts for now? I'm going up to the farm tomorrow—Gloria has that number—but otherwise, I'm going to be out and about too.

Seeing what people have to say about this mess. If you need me, night or day, call here. I'll make sure Gloria knows where I am."

When their meeting begins to break up, he asks Dwayne Austin and Gloria to come into his office with him. Gloria shuts the door behind them and he points to the map on the wall. There is a black pin now, marking the spot where the Nortons died.

"Listen, Dwayne, Gloria tells me you're a good Republican."

"I am that, but you shouldn't ought to hold it against me."

"I don't. In fact, right this minute, I'm glad of it. I don't want the Norton murders to distract us completely from the fires that have been going on for the past year. Way Tipton tells me that every single one of those pins represents a barn or a house that belonged to someone who just happens to be Republican. It may be an accident, of course, but just in case, while you're out and about talking to everybody who might know about the Nortons, don't hesitate to inquire about the fires as well. What are folks out there saying?"

"Detective work?" Austin asks, intrigued.

"It is. And I think you'll be damn good at it. You and Gloria both. People will talk to you who would never talk to me."

An hour later, he walks across the bridge to the island. Friday night football, Marshall High School versus Mars Hill, and there's still some tension between the two communities from last winter's shooting at the basketball tournament. Sam Ray was scheduled to be at this game, but Clinton sends him on home since Sam spent the previous night with the Nortons' ghosts.

Besides, Clinton still enjoys the electric floodlights bathing the field in an unearthly glow, the drums pounding madly as the band marches out of the gym and through the gates. He played in his day and as strange as it seems—given the war and everything else that has happened to him—he still dreams a few times each fall that he's in the locker room, pulling on the pads, jamming the helmet down over his head. He dreams of what the violent world looks like through a face mask. The sounds, the lights, the full-blooded clash of adolescent boys slamming into each other. So much easier to digest than everything else he's lived through over the past few days.

So, he roams the field, from one set of sideline stands to the other, and after halftime, settles in near the gate on the home side, not far from the concession stand. Munches on some salty popcorn bought at the concession stand. From personal experience, he knows full well that more fights break out here than anywhere else. Here or the parking lot.

As he stands there, letting his thoughts drift away from the game and back again, Catherine Metcalf walks up to stand beside him for a few minutes. She too is on the move, keeping watch over her students. They stand silently, only a few feet apart, watching the game as people walk past. Eventually, she says, "Got any plans for the weekend, Sheriff?"

He smiles. "I thought I'd go up to my farm on Doe Branch tomorrow afternoon. Spend the night. Enjoy twenty-four hours away from the jailhouse."

"You keep horses, don't you?"

"Yes, ma'am, I do. Might go riding."

Almost a whisper: "Want some company?"

"God, yes." Barely a murmur.

She smiles before she continues her rounds. "That's what I hoped you would say...Sheriff."

CHAPTER 32

THAT SATURDAY AFTERNOON IS ONLY THE SECond time they've worked together to saddle Little Joe and Nell, but even so, they are relaxed in the stone barn, as if long acquainted—with each other and with the horses.

As before, the little mare eases when Cat brushes her. Little Joe is as powerful and stolid as ever. They ride further up the mountain this time, through a gate at the top of the upper pasture and along an old logging road through the woods.

The ground is dappled by autumn sunlight strained through red and yellow leaves. It feels as if they're riding through time further into the depths of the season. Suspended between late summer and fall, bathing in the sun-washed colors of the trees.

They barely speak during this part of the ride, for there is nothing that needs saying. Just by being there, they are sharing something bigger than either of them, bigger even than the two of them together.

The old road traces up and over the shoulder of the ridge and empties out into a meadow above the cemetery. The thick grass in the meadow has begun to brown from the chill September nights, and it's as if the horses are wading through fall. They ride by the cemetery and he points out a hawk circling above them in the thin, sun-bright air. Circling and calling to its mate, who answers from afar.

They follow the fence that separates the upper pasture from the lower, and just beside one of the gates, they pause at a shallow, rock-lined spring to let the horses drink the fresh water. They dismount and stand for a moment as he points out deer tracks in the soft ground. Then he notices the boot print in the mud, and the extraordinary brilliance of the afternoon is shattered.

"Damn it to hell." He is whispering, but she is so close that she can hear every word. And when he stands suddenly, she steps back, unsure.

"What is it, Clint?"

"Goddamn him," he says, much louder now. Bearing down on the *damn*.

"Clint?"

He points to the boot track. "Someone has been here!" is all he says.

"Randall?"

"Hell no. It's way too big for Randall. Or you. Or me, even. Look!" He places his left foot carefully beside the print without pressing it down into the muck. "And look at the heel, where it's worn."

"Why does it—"

"It matters. Oh, yes, it matters. It's..." He hesitates.

"Tell me, Clint. Who is it?"

"I'm not sure that..."

"Don't do that. I know it's your land and your house, but it's our lives."

He nods roughly. "It is."

"Then tell me. We hide from everyone else. We can't afford to hide from each other."

"I've found that exact same print twice after a barn has been burned."

The slant, afternoon sun is still there, but the breeze feels cooler now, the air less fragrant.

"Damn," she mutters, almost involuntarily. "Does this mean he knows you're after him?"

"Maybe. At the very least, he knows who I am and where I live."

WHILE SHE FIXES SUPPER—GRILLED CHICKEN, creamed corn, rolls—he brings the shotgun downstairs from the bedroom and gets his army M-1 carbine from the closet in the living room. He lays both carefully on an old army blanket on the dining room table before fixing them each a drink, the old fashioned she favors. While she cooks, he cleans both guns, fieldstripping the M-1.

At one point, she stands in the kitchen door, glass in hand, watching. "Should you do that while you're drinking?" she asks.

He smiles. "I can do this in the dark with both eyes closed… unfortunately."

She nods. "The war?"

"Yep. The war. I'm going to put the shotgun back in the bedroom. Shells in the drawer of the bedside table. The carbine goes in the closet by the front door. The magazine with its shells will be on the shelf above."

"What magazine?"

"I'll show you in the morning."

THEY SIT LATE AT THE DINING ROOM TABLE, FINishing a bottle of wine between them. He tells her about the colonel who became a general, promoted on the spot by Patton when his superior was killed. He tells her how cold the winter was when they drove deeper into Germany and how the Germans became so desperate just to survive. He tells her that he killed men whom he didn't know and didn't hate. How he got the wound on his shoulder. He tells her that by the end, he was sick of it all. But he also learned just how much he loves life, how much he wanted to come back. To the children and to the mountains.

"To Gretchen?" she asks, her voice kind, understanding.

He nods. "Sure. Although curiously enough, it was the mountains I dreamed of. This little valley. Doe Branch. I discovered just how I didn't want to die over there. I wanted to die here...of old age."

"Let's make that advanced old age," she says.

AFTER SUPPER, HE TAKES THE DOGS OUT WHILE she does the dishes. When he returns, he discovers she has freshened the drinks they started before supper. They carry their glasses upstairs and, after only a few words, strip down to their skins and take a shower together. The soap and hot water play tricks on them, releasing them into a kind of reverie. Standing in the shower, their wet bodies pressed together, they kiss as if starving, as if staving off death.

Her lips taste of grilled food and bourbon, an autumn fall of leaves, and a hot fire.

Once in bed, his bed...their bed, she slips down beneath the sheets and takes him in her mouth. And for a few acute moments, her tongue and lips are all the known world to him.

Just when he thinks he might die—and not of old age—she crawls up to straddle him. Takes his sex and slips it effortlessly inside her. And then lies down lovingly over him, only her hips alive now, taking him in slow, muscular waves.

Within the same urgent tick of time, they realize that her body is the perfect skintight sheath for his, and he is complete within her.

IN THE MORNING, WHEN HE GETS UP TO LET THE dogs run and brings a cup of coffee for himself and Cat, he slips back into bed with her.

"Where did you learn all of that?" he asks. "What you did last night?"

She giggles. "Just because I'm a teacher, Clint, don't assume I'm a prude."

"Apparently not. Anything but."

AFTER COFFEE IN BED AND BREAKFAST AT THE kitchen table, he teaches Cat how to insert the magazine containing the .30 caliber shells into the stock of the carbine and click off the safety. They go outside behind the house and—because they're miles from the nearest active church—he shows her how to aim and fire it at a handy fence post. She succeeds in scaring the sheep, but doesn't come anywhere near the post.

"Maybe if you let me shoot at the barn," she says, mostly just amused by the whole process.

"You might hit that," he admits.

CHAPTER 33

CLINTON INTENDS TO SPEND MONDAY MORNING at the Norton place so that he can see it all over again with no one to bother him, no one to interrupt his thoughts. On the way there, he parks on Bridge Street in Hot Springs and goes into the hardware store that sits just beside the Spring Creek bridge. He wants to visit a bit on the way up, and he wants to ask about the Zippo he found in the Nortons' kitchen.

Mr. Gentry, the owner, sells him a new ax handle to replace the one that split up at the farm, plus two pounds of 16-penny nails for some repairs to the lower barn. As he's paying, he asks Gentry if he knew the Nortons.

"I didn't see her but maybe once a year or so," Gentry replies. "She was kind of a recluse, if you know what I mean. I seen him often enough. Once a week when he come into town for some groceries or supplies of some kind. He'd work his way up and down the street a bit, talking to first this one and that one. Liked to sit on that rock wall up there in front of Sunnybank and smoke while he jawed with the old boys who hang out there."

"Didn't he roll his own?"

"He did, he did. He bought loose tobacco and rolling papers over there at the grocery. Bought himself a box of kitchen matches from us every few weeks."

"I thought he used a lighter. A Zippo."

"No, no. He liked to carry a dozen or so kitchen matches in his overalls. He could light one with his thumbnail and fire up a cigarette like it was a magic trick. Can you strike a kitchen match with your thumbnail, Sheriff? I can't."

"I also heard he liked to carry around a sizable amount of cash."

"He didn't just carry it around. He liked to find a way to show it off. Mrs. Gentry or me would ring him up for a box of matches or a roll of bob wire, and he'd out with a leather wallet of hundred-dollar bills, so he could make a big show of pulling one of those Ben Franklins out to pay up. Half the time, we couldn't make change 'til the next time he come in. He'd hold that bill up to the window light like he was making sure it wasn't counterfeit or something—and so everybody else who was standing around could see it too—and then hand it over."

"For a box of matches?"

"Oh, yeah. For next to nothing. You reckon that's what got him killed?"

UP AT THE NORTONS', CLINTON PARKS BY THE mailbox and wanders into the huge old barn before going over to the house itself. In the two days after the killings, nobody had really bothered with the barn, assuming that the answers to all their questions were imprinted in the driveway, the back porch, the house itself.

The Nortons were past farming livestock or anything like a cash crop of tobacco or corn. But Bonnie Norton kept a good-sized garden to piddle around in: corn, beans, squash, tomatoes, her garden patch between the house and the river. Inside the barn, he finds her tools in one corner. A hoe, a garden rake, a shovel—all with handles worn from years of use. A couple of rusty buckets. Three sacks of cow manure. An open sack of Sevin Dust she must have used to dust her tomatoes for bugs. And here is the old toe-end of a stocking she used to dust them with.

It is dark in the barn, the only light coming from the morning sun as it slips in between loose boards on the eastern side.

Dark enough so that he almost trips over the answer to one of his nagging questions. John Norton had said that his father and aunt kept a dog, an old collie named Popper. Clinton has almost forgotten about Popper in the hurly-burly of investigations, questions, and dealing with the bodies. Almost, but not quite... because the dog should have sounded the alarm the night of the robbery, and none of the neighbors mentioned a dog barking.

Here is the answer. Popper's body—brown eyes wide open in shock and surprise. Apparently shot—once...no, twice—and then slung back inside the barn to die. Whoever killed the Nortons also didn't mind shooting a happy-go-lucky collie dog named Popper, for God's sake, just to make their job easier.

He borrows the shovel from the barn, finds a spot of relatively soft ground under a couple of hemlocks at the back corner of the barn, and buries Popper there under several feet of good earth. Then stands by himself in the slant, morning sunlight and says a version of the prayer he's recited over a dozen dogs since his childhood.

...may you run now without faltering. May you eat good, rare steak for your supper. May you bark as loud and long as you like at anything, at a falling leaf. And may you sleep on an old rag rug beside God's own woodstove.

He puts his hat back on and starts back to the barn with the shovel, but then pauses. Takes his hat off again and offers a coda to his prayer for Popper.

...and the son of a bitch who shot you, when you were just doing your job. I'll put him in the ground as well. You have my covenant as to that.

THE HOUSE ITSELF GIVES UP NOTHING, ALthough he spends two hours there, sitting and listening in each separate room. Peering into closets and pantries and cupboards with a flashlight. Sifting through drawers and looking under mattresses. Lifting the edges of rugs to find nothing but dirt and dead bugs.

He does notice one thing they'd missed in the first, hectic hours in the house. In the bedroom with the rolltop desk, one of the pillows has been stripped of its pillowcase and tossed in the corner. So, they used a pillowcase to carry something, he thinks, probably the money or the coins. Otherwise ... nothing.

But perhaps that's not right. Perhaps the house is giving him something after all. The sense that time is suspended inside its walls. That dust motes hang silently in the old, yellow light without drifting to the floor. The clock on the table in the hallway has been wound and is ticking away, but its hands read six-thirty, not the time it is currently or the time the Nortons would have been killed. Keeping its own time by ratcheting forward or back in some haunted movement all its own.

When he goes back outside and reenters the day, he takes a few minutes to walk down along the riverbank. Lets his internal clock slow so that he can think. He pauses to unwrap, trim, and light a cigar. Sometimes, the smoke helps him put the day on pause, while his mind circles back over the small things. The often significant things.

What the house says clearly is that whoever busted in and killed the old people knew exactly what they were looking for—coins and cash—and even knew where to find it. They didn't search because they already knew. And they didn't bother with Bonnie Norton's jewelry because they knew it was probably worthless.

At least one of the two or three killers had been in the house before. Knew the Nortons, knew their dog even. And since old man Norton—Grady—had moved in with his sister only two years before, that meant the killer who knew had probably been there in the past few years.

It is time to talk to the family. And tomorrow, he realizes, is the funeral. He sits on a log by the river long enough to smoke down his cigar, thinking about families, how so much about them is right and yet, how often things go wrong.

Back at the jail, he has Gloria get Lewis Sutton, the sheriff over in Cocke County, Tennessee, on the phone, which takes all of thirty minutes.

"Sheriff, this is Clinton Salter, across the line in Madison County."

"How they hanging today, Sheriff? Call me Lew."

"How is keeping the peace over there, Lew? I heard you had some snake-handling in one of those little brush arbor churches that spring up."

"We did that. One lousy snake, 'bout as big around as your finger. But the damn newspapers made it sound like cobras and bowie constrictors. I threw the thing down and crushed it with my bootheel. Let that preacher do his business in a cell for a week or two. But that ain't nothing to what you got goin' on. One of my deputies said you had a double killing a few nights ago. Boys Home Road, wherever the hell that is."

"We did. An old couple, brother and sister, shot down in the kitchen and robbed. It being so close to the line and all, I wondered if you could give any guidance."

"What do you mean, guidance?"

"Any rough characters over your way up for that kind of thing. Any loose talk about the crime?"

There is a pause before Lew Sutton responds, and when he does, his voice has lost all its humor. "Oh, hell no. Don't you go looking over this way, Salter. I keep my goddamned part of the world scrubbed clean as your mama's turkey platter. Any miscreate that might be worthy of that I sent away a long time ago."

THAT AFTERNOON, HE STEPS OUTSIDE THE JAIL with Dwayne Austin, so that Dwayne can smoke a cigarette while they talk. They sit at a battered picnic table next to the railroad tracks, a battered picnic table covered in cigar and cigarette burns and littered underneath with butts.

"You hear anything about the fires?" Clinton to Dwayne.

"Nothing like a name," Dwayne replies. "But something come up a couple of times that give me pause for thought. Twice, when I was just smacking my gums with some good old boys, talking wild about this or that, somebody said something funny. Once at that little gas station up on Shelton Laurel, one of the old geezers, a rock-solid Republican just like you mentioned. *Well,* he said, *you ought to just ask that sheriff of yours. You got to figure he knows who done it if anybody does.* And the other old geezers laughed like that was the funniest damn thing they'd heard all day."

"Just ask me?" Clinton, incredulous.

Dwayne nods emphatically and then pauses to light a second Camel from the first. "Then I was doing the same sort of detective trick down at Roy Roberts's little store at Hurricane. You know the one I mean—with the tourist cabins—and old Roy hisself said something similar. Said, *Hell, Dwayne, ask Clinton. I have a feeling it's in the family, so to speak.* I wasn't sure what to make of that. *In the family.* What does that mean?"

"I don't know. What did you say?"

"I said, it can't be in the family. He ain't hardly got none. His son is long gone and his daughter is a schoolteacher. Roy just laughed at that."

At four o'clock, when Gloria is ready to leave for the day, he invites her down the street to Robbins Drug Store for a cup of coffee. He sips at his cup while she savors a Coke. After he tells her what Dwayne had said, she shrugs. "He's a better detective than I am. I didn't get that far at lunch with the girls from the courthouse. But I did learn something interesting."

"Tell me."

"You recall our friend Tom Runnion, who you sent packing the very first day you were sworn in?"

"How could I forget him?"

"Well, Mr. Runnion has found a home over in Tennessee, working for the Cocke County sheriff."

"What? You're kidding me. I was talking to that sorry—just this afternoon."

"Oh, it gets better. He told the county clerk before he left that he—now, get this—that he planned *to kick your ass next election cycle and then go on to fame and fortune as the High Sheriff of Madison County.*" She is smiling.

Clinton laughs out loud. "Fame and fortune as sheriff? I had to dig deep in both pockets just to buy you a Coke."

"It would help if you remembered to cash your paycheck. But seriously, Clinton, what do you think he's up to?"

"Who knows. What worries me is that Roy Roberts said, *It's in the family.*"

"The fires, you mean?"

He nods.

"Your brother again?"

"Maybe. It would explain why he keeps ridiculing me for trying to catch the arsonist."

"Strikes me that you two couldn't be more different. And he does like to be in charge."

He shrugs. "Oh, I doubt if it's him with a kerosene can skulking around by the light of the moon. But what if he knows who it is?"

"What if? What are you going to do about Runnion?"

"Nothing. Runnion's a fool."

She stares at him, considering. "Sure, he is," she says finally. "But your brother isn't."

CHAPTER 34

SHE DISCOVERS THAT SHE HAS SOMETHING TO say. To James, her husband.

Here on this Tuesday afternoon, September 14. Room 32-B of the Ivy Rehabilitation Center. Spruce Pine.

It's the day of the Nortons' funeral, but she doesn't really belong there. Not at the funeral home on Main Street or up at the old cemetery on the ridge above Marshall.

So why is she here, on a Tuesday, when school is in session, and she has to leave the whole building in the charge of the algebra teacher who doubles as an assistant principal? Why is she here, when she missed her usual visitation day without a qualm? She didn't get up that morning, planning to go to Burnsville. She didn't dress for it or prepare for it. She didn't intend to leave her wedding ring on top of the dresser in her bedroom, but she did.

In the depths of her mind, she knew, has been whispering the words, louder and louder until she had to speak...or scream.

It's time, James.

Finally, after all these years and after all you put me through, it's time. You, with your pureness of heart and your fine sensibility, your devotion to this and that.

All that got you, and all that got me, was this room. Empty, white, sterile, flushed with the stench of chemicals and rotting breath. There is no god in this room, James. No theology. No night or day. No right or wrong. Nothing.

No birdsong, no running water, no natural clock. The only sound is your breath, and that no longer has any meaning. No longer measures anything other than a few faint ounces of purified air. Nothing...nothing...nothing!

What's that, you say?

Nothing. Exactly. You say nothing.

You said so much when you were alive, burned through words like there was an endless supply of twisting, turning, subtle syllables that you could use to seduce me, hypnotize me, hold the world at bay and keep me close.

Which you did. For years. Because I did love you...or thought I did. I will give you that, here at this low place, this place on the bottom of the ocean like the bottom of a dream. A drowning nightmare. This final place that you brought me to in order to keep me.

I did love you. Was convinced I loved you. But what did I know? That was then. I'm a different woman now, James. And now I know something fierce that I didn't know then.

I know what it feels like to be with a man. I know what it feels like to breathe his breath, to think his thoughts, feel the sharp edges of the world through his hands. You've met him. He was here. He touched you. But he didn't touch you the way he touches me. He touches me everywhere.

What you and I had was some sort of choice. What he and I are is something else, something different that you and all your words could never explain.

It's as undisturbed and inevitable as the weather. You don't control the weather.

Do you know what it's like to feel the cool rain on your naked skin? No, if you ever knew, you've forgotten. Do you know what it's like to feel the wind down through the pasture grass caressing your face, whispering in your ears? Do you?

When he touches me, I am myself. And when I touch him, he becomes something hard and hot and palpable, more real than any word on a page, more real than anything you ever imagined or anything you ever caused me to feel. I didn't summon it—nor did he, for that matter. It came on us unexpectedly, and now it makes us, mends us, binds us. Such that...

I'm alive now, where before I was dead. I am alive, James, being born every day.

And you, husband, are not. Perhaps you never really were. So, it's time for you to let me go. Let this room go, let this great, blistered emptiness deflate for the final time. Go seek that God you were always praying to in the dark.

And leave me to the fire and the light.

CHAPTER 35

AT THE SAME TIME, TWENTY-FIVE MILES AWAY. The Bowman Rector Funeral Home, Main Street in Marshall.

The small chapel is filled to overflowing, not because the Nortons were so well-loved in life, but because they are so widely known in death. Notoriety makes for a packed house.

Clinton sits with Gloria Goforth in the first row behind the family. The other deputies—Austin, Fender, Ray—are standing against the back wall by the door, acting almost as ushers when the crowd threatens to overwhelm the funeral home staff. Way Tipton is outside on the sidewalk, lounging against the wall, casually smoking a cigarette. Watching, watching.

Balis Norton? Balis is a pallbearer. One of twelve, since there are two caskets at the front of the chapel. The family was allowed to see Grady and Bonnie Norton's bodies at a private viewing that morning, but now Grady's casket is closed since the undertaker couldn't disguise the effects of a pistol shot at close range.

The Nortons were not famous churchgoers—she because she was so shy of people, and he because he didn't have time for it except at Easter and Christmas. So, the family has brought in a Baptist preacher from a little fundamentalist church near the Tennessee line. Once the crowd has settled in, this preacher says a quiet prayer and then, as far as Clinton can tell, goes crazy.

LET NOT YOUR HEART BE TROUBLED: YE BELIEVE IN God, believe also in me... In my Father's house are many mansions: if it were not so, I would have told you. I go to prepare a place for you... This in a high, singsong voice, as if this little peacock of a preacher has a woman's vocal cords stretched tight in his ill-shaven throat.

And if I go and prepare a place for you, I will come again and receive you unto myself; that where I am, there ye may be also... And whither I go ye know, and the way ye know... Old Thomas saith unto him, Lord, we know not whither thou goest; and how can we know the way? Preacher man is into it now, jabbing with a stiff forefinger, first at the worn-out Bible clutched in his left hand and then at the crowd of people before him.

Jesus saith unto him, I am the way, the truth, and the life: no man cometh unto the Father but by me! The *me* is a full-throated shout. Clinton is sure they can hear it out on the street.

I never met Brother Grady and Sister Bonnie in this life. No, I was never so fortunate, but I tell you now, I'll see 'em in heaven and I'll know 'em when I see 'em, because we are brothers and sisters in Christ. A-men!

One blood, one family before the throne of God, akneelin' and asingin' in the radiance cast upon us by his face. A-men!

No, no! I'm not worried about Brother Grady and Sister Bonnie. Today we lay them down for their well-earned rest, and on the last day, the last morning, I tell you, they will rise up out of the cold ground to be with Jesus. A-men.

And I will be there. I will be there, hand in hand, with Brother Grady and Sister Bonnie and all them saints, awalkin' up that steep and narrow road to the heavenly gates. A-men!

But where, oh where, will YOU be? Because I tell you today, they is hell awaitin' on the coarse and nasty sinner. They is eternal fire just as they is eternal glory. And the eternal fire is hot, I tell you.

Hotter than anything you ever seen or felt on this earth. And it's awaitin' on you if you don't get up with Jesus. A-men!

Hell is a barn on fire and you tied to the stall. Hell is a lake of flames and you adrownin' in it. Hell is red-hot pokers apiercin' your flesh. Make no mistake. A-men!

No man cometh unto the Father except by me. And that me *is Je-sus. You and you...and you...got to repent where you been and what you done. You got to forswear them unclean thoughts if you ever want to embrace Grandpa Grady and Grandma Bonnie again. The only way you will ever see them again is to give your life to Jesus here today. A-men! And I say again, A-men!*

Let us pray...

Then preacher man is done and collapses back onto his folding chair. As if somebody yanked his plug out of the wall, Clinton thinks.

As ridiculous as this rooster crowing might be to some, he notices that several of the family members are mightily affected. Two of the older women are weeping outright. And one of the men, seated two down from Balis, is bent over with his head in his hands. Clinton can see that his back is shaking with raw emotion.

Another of the Norton family members turns surreptitiously and glances over his shoulder directly at Clinton, almost as if he can feel the sheriff's eyes on the back of his head. He has orange-red hair and a pale face covered in freckles. When Clinton nods to him, the man turns immediately back to the front of the chapel, where Mr. Rector from the funeral home is explaining how to get to the cemetery while the pallbearers stand and file out from the rows of chairs to gather around the caskets. Turns out that carrot-head is one of the pallbearers, standing on the opposite side of Bonnie Norton's casket from Balis. A moment later, when he catches Balis's eye, he nods at carrot-head to mark him. Meaning to inquire about the man later.

At the cemetery, Clinton stands back with Gloria and the deputies while the family members sit under an awning erected by the two open graves. Once the pallbearers lower the caskets onto the ground beside the holes, they step back to either join the family or stand in a line to one side. Except for carrot-head, who glances around and then walks up the slight hill to stand beside the hearse.

Clinton leans over to Way Tipton, so he can whisper. "See the man who just walked behind that line of cars?" Way nods. "Keep an eye on him. He's awfully nervous." Way nods and, after a few minutes, slips away to climb the hill as well.

When they all get back to the jail midafternoon, he calls both Way Tipton and Balis Norton into his office and closes the door. When he asks them about the redheaded man, Balis offers that his name is Jason Fortner, one of Balis's dozen first cousins. Doesn't know much about him except that he's been in trouble a time or two. Not penitentiary trouble, but enough to get the highway patrol involved. Spent the night in jail once or twice.

Way tells an interesting story from the cemetery. He slipped up on Jason Fortner without really trying to, and when he spoke to him, Fortner almost jumped out of his shoes. Way said he was looking for his grandmother's grave, and Fortner allowed that all he wanted was to "smoke a goddamned cigarette in peace."

"Funny thing is," Way continues, "I had to light it for him. He had most of a pack of Camels, but said he'd lost his lighter a few days back and used up all his matches. So, I came out with a matchbook and lit him up. And after that, we were buddies. I offered my condolences and he claimed he didn't know the old people very well, but thanks anyway."

Clinton tells them about the Zippo lighter he found at the Norton house and that Grady Norton lit his roll-your-owns with kitchen matches. A kitchen match with his thumbnail was his trademark.

"Should we talk to him?" Balis asks.

Clinton nods. "Sure. And while he's having a chat with me, you two can search his residence. See if anything turns up, coins or cash."

CHAPTER 36

"HELLO?"

"Hey. It's me."

"I wanted it to be you. That's why I answered the phone at midnight."

"I started not to call, but the later it got, the more I wanted to hear your voice."

"Are you still at the jail?"

"Yeah. I'm going up to Mrs. Penland's in a bit, but I wanted to whisper good night. Did I wake you?"

"Almost. I'm in bed, under the covers, just turned the lights off. I was reading until a few minutes ago. How was the funeral?"

"Strange. Strange in almost every way."

"How do you mean, strange?"

"I've never seen so many people crammed into that chapel. Every chair filled, plus people along the walls, and men and women both out on the sidewalk. Smoking, talking. Reporters from three or four newspapers."

"Good lord, Clint."

"I know. It was stifling hot inside, a cold wind off the river outside. Her casket was open and before the service, people kept walking up front to look at her."

"His was closed?"

"Hmm."

"Because of where he was shot?"

"Yes."

"Why are people so fascinated with the dead, do you think? Why do we want to see their bodies?"

"I don't know. During the war, when there were corpses everywhere along the side of the road or piled on a street corner, we got to where we didn't even notice. Somebody else's problem to solve. We were alive, so we just kept moving."

"But not here. I was at a funeral for a student two years ago, and people stood around the open casket and talked about how natural he looked, as if he were asleep and might sit up at any moment. It was...ghoulish. They couldn't stop talking about how he looked. His mother kept reaching in and patting his hands."

"Maybe we need to see the body in order to accept the plain, simple fact that the flesh is empty. When Gretchen died, I sat in the hospital room and watched everything about her change. I stayed until she was cold to the touch."

Here is a pause, static on the line, before she speaks again. "Did you...see anything that helped with the investigation?"

"Maybe. One of the grandsons is named Jason Fortner, curly red hair. Rough-looking, mid-twenties. He kept glancing over his shoulder at me as if he expected me to jump him during the funeral sermon. Nervous as a cat on a stove. And it seems he's lost his lighter, and there was a Zippo lighter at the Norton house."

"Fingerprints?"

"The SBI has the lighter, and after tomorrow, we'll have Mr. Jason's prints to see if they match. So maybe. What I don't understand, if it's true, is how on God's green earth someone like that would hurt his own family. Hell, shoot the old people outright. And the dog."

"They killed the Nortons' dog?"

"Yes, I buried it yesterday. Promised revenge."

"I can imagine you doing that. Talking to the dog...the ghost of the dog."

They are both smiling. Miles apart, connected only by the whispered impulses of their voices, the sound of their breathing.

"I like thinking of you in bed," he whispers, even though the doors to his office are shut, and the jailer is upstairs with his prisoners. "I've never even seen the inside of your house, but I like... your bed."

"I wish you were here," she whispers as well. "Magically transported."

Again, a pause. And their breath slightly deeper.

"What did you do today?" he asks after a moment. "While I was visiting with the dead. Seeing them into the ground."

"Much the same. Visiting with the dead, that is. I took the afternoon off and drove over to Burnsville. Had a long talk with James."

"Did he talk back?"

"No. But I think he heard me."

CHAPTER 37

JASON FORTNER LIVES WITH HIS MOTHER IN A double-wide trailer set back from the road to Upper Shut In. Off the Newport Highway, ten miles as the crow flies, from Tennessee.

When Clinton—along with Balis Norton and Way Tipton—arrive at the trailer midmorning, they discover that Mrs. Fortner has gone to work in Newport and Jason is still asleep. Balis pounds on the door until Jason appears, drowsy and half-dressed.

At first, Clinton is polite, even friendly. Explains that they're visiting with various members of the Norton family to find out all they can about the old couple and what might have happened to them. They give Jason a moment to grab a shirt off the back of a chair and a pack of Camels from the arm of the couch.

Once he's outside, Clinton shows him the search warrant signed by the magistrate and leads him more or less gently to a rickety picnic table under a shade tree in the yard. Scrawny chickens are roaming about, scratching for whatever they can turn up in the scant grass. Way and Balis are already inside the trailer, intending to work their way slowly from one end to the other.

"Why you need to search my place?" Jason asks as he and Clinton sit down at the table. "Mostly my mama's. I only got one room." His hands are shaking as he pops the pack of cigarettes against the back of a hand to shake one loose.

Clinton nods pleasantly. "Oh, we're searching here and there for anything we can find out about the family. We've not had a murder like this in...well, forever. Two old people shot down in their own kitchen, for God's sake."

"Well, I didn't have nothing to do with it, I'll tell you that. Shit!"

"What is it?"

"I come out without my matches."

Clinton hands him a book of matches from his shirt pocket, watching to see how comfortable he is with them. "What you need is a lighter, Jason. Carry in your pocket."

The man, pale until now behind his freckles, blushes with something like pleasure. "I've got me a good one. A Zippo that I found at work. But I misplaced it a while back. Probably dropped it here in the yard when I come out to smoke."

Clinton nods. "I hear you. I hate losing things." And then, a pause while Jason lights up, clenching his hands together to keep them from trembling. Clinton says, "Let me ask you something. Did you ever see the coin collection that was there at the house? It's gone missing, and we're trying to find someone who can describe it for us."

Jason stares at him in dismay. "What...coin collection?" he finally manages to ask.

"The one that came down through the Norton family. Gold and silver, very old, most of them, according to Balis. It would sure help us if we could find somebody in the family who could tell us what was in the collection."

Jason can't quite meet his eyes, keeps looking down at the cigarette in his hands or over to the trailer. "Wonder what all they're doing in there?" he asks Clinton. "They sure been in there a hell of a long time, and my mama don't like people messing with her stuff."

"Oh, they're very careful, those two. The place will probably be neater after they've looked around than it was when your mother left for work this morning."

"What are they looking for, Sheriff? I don't have much of—"

"Look at me, Jason. No, stub that cigarette out before you burn yourself. Look at me. What do you think they're looking for? They're looking for anything that ties you to the Norton murders."

"Why would they do that? I ain't got nothin' to do with it."

"You know something about it, Jason, or your hands wouldn't be shaking like that. No, don't get up. Sit here with me."

He reaches over and grasps Jason's forearm hard to hold him at the table.

"They ain't gonna find nothing, I tell you. They ain't..."

"Why not? Why won't they find anything, Jason?"

"Cause them Crowders, they took everything. Them mean sons-a-bitches held a gun to my head and took it all. They—" Jason Fortner stops, horrified, and puts his free hand over his mouth.

At that moment, Balis Norton comes through the trailer door, down the sagging steps and walks over to the table. He reaches his fist out toward Jason and slowly opens his fingers to reveal a very old gold coin. "Ever seen this before, cousin?" he whispers.

Jason, with his tobacco-stained hand still clasped over his mouth, shakes his head roughly. Finally, after a long moment, he lets his hand fall to the tabletop and emits a long, low moan. "It was the only thing they give me," he says. "For all my trouble a driving 'em, that Gold Eagle was the only thing they give me. Said it would buy me a tank of gas."

CHAPTER 38

STATEMENT OF JASON RANDOLPH FORTNER

MADE THIS DAY, SEPTEMBER 15, 1965, BEFORE THE following:

- Clinton Salter, Sheriff, Madison County, North Carolina
- James Ramsey, Chief Magistrate, Madison County, North Carolina
- Balis Norton, Deputy Sheriff, Madison County
- Gloria Goforth, Sheriff's Office, Madison County

The following statement was made by Mr. Fortner at the Madison County jail, between two and four o'clock in the afternoon on the above date. Mr. Fortner declined to have an attorney present.

On the night you're talking about, I took them two Crowders, Bob Crowder and his son, Jimmy, out to the Norton house on Boys Home Road, down there by the river. I stayed in the car the whole time they was in the house. I never meant to go in or to be part of whatever evil they was up to, and when I heard gunshots in the house, I knew I wasn't going in.

How many gunshots in the house? I don't know, four or five. I never knew for sure, and I wasn't about to ask Bob or Jimmy, either one.

I first met them boys at the Thunderbird out on the Newport Highway. The Thunderbird is a roadhouse just across the Tennessee line. It ain't got such a good reputation, but a man can get a drink there, if you know what I mean. Not like in this county. You can get a drink over there to wash the road dust out of your throat after a long day working on the highway.

It was back in August, I'm not sure just what day. A Friday night I think, and they was both in there drinking long-necked Buds and playing pool. I like me some pool as well, so me and another boy got up to play them. I teamed up with Bob and the other guy with Jimmy. We played a few games, switching out partners and such, and drank a few beers. I run out of money, and Bob said he'd loan me a ten if I was good for it.

I reckon the trouble all started right then and there cause I said that I sure as hell was good for it. I come from a rich family over on the North Carolina side. Rich, hell, Jimmy said, and started laughing at me. But I said, Oh hell no, my uncle carried around thousands of dollars cash money in his pants pocket and didn't mind nobody knowing it.

Well, that stopped up their smart mouth, and we all sat down to have another beer. Bob asked me, kind of sly-like, you know, about my Uncle Grady, and I told them about Grady and his money, how he didn't trust the bank nor the lawyer. And then, when I tried to explain to them where Uncle Grady and Aunt Bonnie lived, down by the river, they acted all stupid, like they didn't know where I was talking about.

The coins? Yessir, after another beer or two, along with Jimmy running his mouth about how I didn't know what the hell I was talking about, being a damn, dumbass redneck, I told him that not only was there tens of thousands of dollars laying around, there was a mess of old gold and silver coins that was worth even more.

Bob asked could I draw them a map to the treasure house, that's what he kept calling it, the treasure house. I said that I could do better than that, I could show them.

Well, they said that they'd like to go by and visit with Uncle Grady and Aunt Bonnie. Bob said that his father-in-law was an antiques dealer over in Newport, and he loved old stuff like furniture and coins. He'd dearly love to see the coin collection if Uncle Grady was willing to show it to him.

I was pretty drunk by this time. I ended up sleeping it off in my car out in the parking lot. But before we called it a night, I promised them boys that some Friday night, I'd ride them out there to see Uncle Grady and Aunt Bonnie. Just so long as they promised me they'd be nice to them and wouldn't hurt them.

Well, you see, I knew good and damn well what they was up to, but I never dreamed they'd hurt the old folks, and I figured they'd split three ways with me if I was the driver. So, we agreed on a night a couple of weeks later, and I was to meet them at that picnic area down just this side of the line, where they'd leave their car. They told me that nobody'd notice if it was my car because I was kinfolk. But their car might be suspicious.

Well, that's what we done. On the night in question, as you keep calling it, we met up around midnight at the picnic area.

Yes, I can take you straight to it. Show you where we

met up and then parted ways after it was done.

So, I drove them two back down the Newport Road until we come to that little church where you turn off to the Boys Home Road. I asked them again was they going to hurt the old folks, and Bob swore up and down that they had no intent of doing harm to anyone, man nor beast.

Well, that was a lie, cause Jimmy shot the poor old dog before they ever even went into the house.

I sat out there in the car and waited for what seemed like forever. Once I heard the shots, I thought about driving off and leaving them sons of bitches, but I figured that if I left them, they'd track me down to kill me too. So, I sat and waited until they come out.

Oh, I don't know. Best part of an hour, I guess. They come out with a pillowcase full of cash and an old brass-bound box that had them coins in it. Jimmy was almost running, but Bob was walking along like he was coming home from church. Jimmy jumped in the back with the pillowcase, and Bob handed him the box in the back door of the car and then climbed in front with me.

Bob said to get the hell and gone out of there. So, I backed up next to the barn to turn around and drove back the way we come. Jimmy was laughing in the back seat. I guess he had his hands down in that money because later, I found a hundred-dollar bill lying in the floorboard. Bob told him to shut up, but then started laughing too, like somebody just told a joke or something.

By this time, I was good and scared, I tell you. I asked Bob if the old folks was okay, and he said—I'll never forget it—he said they was no trouble at all and was resting easy. Jimmy started laughing again, so I figured it was a lie, but by then they was nothing I could do.

We come to the picnic area I mentioned earlier, and I said are we gonna divide up shares? Bob said, You'll get what you deserve, Jason, don't you worry. So, we got out and sat down at a picnic table there in the dark. Jimmy and Bob went to the car with the sack and the box, and a minute later, Bob come back to the table with one gold coin and laid it on the plank in front of me. He said, There you go, Jason, that's all you get cause that's all you done.

"Tough titty for you," Jimmy says and starts giggling like a girl.

But that ain't fair, I say. We was to go equal shares, and you got the treasure you was after. Then he said, You might of thought we said shares, but all I ever said was we'd pay you to drive us. Buy yourself a tank of gas with that.

Then he turned away like he was going back to the car, but Jimmy said something to him. Something I couldn't hear. He turned back around, and he had that pistol in his hand.

No, I don't know what kind...or caliber. It was pitch-black dark. He held that pistol up to the side of my head with the barrel almost in my ear and said that if I ever talked to anybody, even my mother, about what they done, he'd find me and blow my damn brains out. His exact words, blow my brains out. Did I understand?

I said I understood. Totally and completely. Cause I thought he was gonna shoot me dead right there in the picnic area. But all he said was, good, to keep my mouth shut. And then he went and got in their car, and Jimmy drove them on off.

What else did I do? Why, I came straight home and went to bed. Confused and scared as I ever been in my life.

My lighter? You mean my Zippo? I lied to you about that, Sheriff. I didn't lose it. I loaned it to Jimmy that night, when we first met up at the picnic area, so's he could have a smoke. When I asked for it back, he just laughed and said I could buy me a hundred lighters after that night.

No, I don't know where they live other than it's over in Cocke County. Somewhere around Newport.

Is that all? I guess so. It's the gospel truth, I know that.

CHAPTER 39

TWO DAYS LATER, THEY MEET AS AN INFORMAL council at the jail. Clinton and Way Tipton, plus Jimmy Ramsey, the magistrate, and Judge Gudger.

The question before them is what to do with Fortner's statement. The Crowders, father and son, live across the line in Tennessee, and Clinton has no experience in how to get at them.

"Where's this Jason Fortner now?" the judge asks, after reading over his statement.

Clinton nods upward with this head to indicate the second floor. "Upstairs in a corner cell, away from the two drunks down at the other end."

"He all but begged us to keep him here where it's safe," Way adds. "And the sheriff said not to worry, he was going to be here for a while."

"Even if he never went in the house," the judge offers, "and it played out just the way he tells it here, he's still an accessory to murder. Does he have a lawyer?"

"Can't pay," Clinton says. "Wants a court-appointed attorney."

"Well, you better bring in the district attorney, get him involved, and then set a preliminary hearing for the next session of court. The judge will find him a lawyer, probably some young fool who doesn't know any better. But that's not the problem, is it?"

Clinton shakes his head, no. "The problem is how to get at the two Crowders."

"Well, normally, once you get Fortner sorted out, get the

DA's blessing, and get through the preliminary hearing, then you call the sheriff over in Cocke County and get him to find the Crowders and arrest them. Then he would hand them over to you, and you could start the whole process over with them."

"That could take weeks, Judge. I don't work like that."

"In this case, you do. There's going to be a trial somewhere down the road, Clinton. A major trial. And you can't afford to screw up the procedurals along the way and watch those two walk because we didn't cross all our t's and dot all our i's. But the DA, the court-appointed lawyer, and the Superior Court judge here aren't your problem. Not really."

"What is?"

"The sheriff of Cocke County, that's your problem. He's not known for his cooperation with other law enforcement agencies. In fact, he's not known for his cooperation with other members of the human race."

"So, what do we do if Sheriff Sutton doesn't want to play ball?"

Gudger pauses to consider. "Well, we work our way through the system. Have our DA contact their DA, deliver an arrest warrant that Sutton or one of his deputies is responsible for serving on the Crowders. They take them into custody, and then we have the courts request their extradition so that they can stand trial."

"How many weeks?"

"Not weeks, Clinton. Months."

"There's another little matter that might clog up the pipes too." This from Way Tipton in his characteristically soft voice. "Something that Clinton hasn't offered up just yet."

"I'm all ears," says Gudger.

"Tom Runnion is a deputy in the Cocke County sheriff's office," Clinton admits. "Working for this Sutton character."

"And?" Gudger says.

"And our friend Tom swears that he's just biding his time until the next election, when he's going to come riding over the mountain on a white horse to save us all from ourselves and take back the sheriff's office here."

"Kick Clinton's ass," the magistrate offers.

They all turn to look at him.

He shrugs. "Runnion runs his mouth. Word gets around," he explains.

Gudger whistles. "That changes things, men," he mutters.

"How?" Clinton.

"How do you think? If Runnion wants to run against you in two years, the best thing that can happen to him is for this murder to go unsolved. Your chief witness sits upstairs in jail as the months go by, Sutton denies all our efforts to extradite the Crowders, and Runnion talks it up all over the mountains about what a sorry sheriff you are. Everybody wins but you."

"Damn politics," Clinton says. "Damn Runnion. Damn Cocke County. Anybody else?"

"Sheriff Sutton."

"Damn Sutton. And the horse he rode in on."

Gudger laughs. "Don't blame the horse, Clinton. Here's what we do. We start the process, working with the DA and setting the groundwork for a preliminary trial. Keep your boy, Fortner, safe and quiet here in the jail. Let me talk to some of my legal friends across the line in Tennessee, just to see what's actually going on over there. In the meantime, Clinton, see if you can find us a jurisdiction or extradition expert. You told me about that guy from the Institute of Government. Call him and put him to work on this. All we have to do is somehow get those two across the state line."

"This is going to take a while, isn't it?" Clinton asks of no one in particular.

Gudger nods. "Yes, it is. And my best advice is that we can't let word leak out. Not about holding Fortner in jail. Not even about having a witness, with arrests to follow momentarily. If we spook the Crowders, they'll flee this state and that state too. Just play dumb and act like you don't know anything."

"Should be easy," Clinton says.

THAT AFTERNOON, LATE, HE DIGS MICHAEL Smith's business card out of his desk drawer and calls the main line at the Institute of Government, University of North Carolina. The very nice woman who answers patches him through to Mr. Smith's office, where an answering machine picks up after four rings. He leaves a message telling Smith they need to talk, telling him that Madison County needs an extradition expert.

By that time, it's near five o'clock. He says goodbye to Gloria for the weekend, leaves Way in charge of the office overnight, and admits that he is tired, tired and frustrated. "Patience," Way counsels. "We'll get the sons of bitches."

Clinton nods. "One way or another," he says. When he walks outside, the late September weather has all the early makings of fall. A chill breeze, the sun aslant the horizon. Dry leaves rattling in the trees. On the spur of the moment, he drives the Jeep across the bridge and parks beside Catherine's station wagon.

It's a Friday night open date on the high school football schedule, and the team is running through a minimal practice out on the field. Before walking over to watch them for a few minutes, he finds a piece of paper in the glove box of the Jeep. He chuckles to himself when he realizes that his paper is a blank search warrant. He writes a cryptic note:

Doe Branch.

Tonight?

Tomorrow?

Sunday?

He tucks the note under the windshield wiper of Catherine's car.

He walks over to the empty bleachers on the visitors' side of the football field and watches the boys running through plays. The coaches yelling, directing, blowing whistles. Because there is no real game and no one besides him watching, the boys are laughing and shouting at each other, playing rather than working.

The breeze is blustering into real wind now, blowing in gusts down the valley, off the river. He is chilled and exhilarated at the same time. Autumn and the turning of the year. On the cusp of October...

When he walks back to the Jeep, Catherine's car is gone, but the search warrant is tucked now under his windshield wiper. She has folded it over and written on the back in her much cleaner, more precise hand. *All of the above*, it reads.

CHAPTER 40

HE STOPS IN THE GRAVEL ROAD ACROSS FROM HIS father's house and taps the horn on the Jeep. After a moment, the porch light blinks on and Randall Shelton emerges, as always, with his ancient .410 held down by his leg. "It's me," Clinton calls out. "Come home for the weekend."

Randall steps down off his porch and walks to the far end of the footbridge. "Is it Friday then?"

"It is. And when the sun comes up next, it may well be Saturday."

Randall nods. "I sure hope so."

"Any problems this week?"

"None to speak of, except that the dogs been barking at night. Once, a night or two ago, even old Nick got going, so I walked over and let 'em out to run. They took off to the top pasture, with little Jake barking his head off."

"Bear?"

"Maybe...maybe. But I didn't see nor smell no bear when I went along behind. It was an hour before they come back down, and I let them back in the house. Local boys out hellin' around in the middle of the night, maybe."

Clinton's turn to nod. "I'll keep an eye out the next two nights. You get your rest. And by the way, Catherine Metcalf is coming up in a little while. You'll hear her car."

"That funny thing with wood on the sides?"

"Yeah, that."

"Good."

"What?"

"I said *good*. I'm glad she's coming up."

"Are you now?"

"I am. You been by yourself too long. My opinion."

"That's funny, coming from you, a man who sees his daughter maybe three or four times a year. Doesn't ever go into town."

"I go to the store at Barnard. That's far enough. Besides, I'm an old man at home with my memories. Talk to Jesus and my wife most every evening. He's in heaven and she is too. You, on the other hand, are a young man yet."

Clinton sits and thinks for a moment. Old...young? "Maybe. I feel ten years younger when I'm up here. And another ten years younger when she's around."

Randall nods. "Like I said..."

WHEN HE PARKS BESIDE THE HOUSE AND LETS himself in the kitchen door, the dogs are ecstatic, Jake barking and spinning in circles, even Nick up his hind legs to lick Clinton's face. This is home, he thinks, as he walks back out to the Jeep to bring in two sacks of groceries. The dogs, the food, the whiskey waiting on the sideboard.

And a woman. No, that's not right. Not just *a* woman. *This* woman. The warmth in her sapphire eyes, the gap in her teeth when she smiles, her hair flowing like water when she throws her head back to laugh. This particular woman who molds herself to him and toward whom he moves as if to the moon or sun.

She is on her way, thank God, but the house is cold. The elemental things, he thinks, heat and light. The dark without and the fire within.

Before he does anything else, he turns up the thermostat and then lays a fire on the hearth in the living room. The dogs are still outside when he lights the kindling—making their rounds, ranging as far as the orchard. They'll come in when she does, he thinks, and tell us what's outside.

Two potatoes to bake in the oven, two steaks marinating on the counter, as they rise to room temperature. An apple pie from the grocery ready to go into the warm oven when the potatoes come out.

The front porch light is on.

He hears Jake barking from down by the creek, which may mean her car is close. And in another moment, he hears the station wagon turn carefully off the Doe Branch Road and onto the gravel of his driveway. In this last moment, sure now that she is imminent, he sets the bourbon and the glasses out on the sideboard.

He unlocks the front door and pulls it open. She has a paper sack of groceries under one arm and is fending Jake off with the other hand, laughing as she does so. Her hair is pulled back into a ponytail, something he's never seen before except when they're riding. She is wearing loose-fitting, pale slacks and a thick sweater the color of old apples. Russet, he thinks, her sweater is.

He kisses her, just there, in the open doorway, while her arms are half full of groceries and a dog is jumping up, trying to be part of the greeting. "What else is in the car?" he asks her. "What needs to come in?"

"There's a suitcase in the back seat," she says. "It's heavy."

And it is. He marvels as he lugs it up the front porch steps and through the door. "What in the world is in here?" he asks.

"I brought a lot of clothes and some books," she confesses. "Fall, winter. I had this fantasy that you'd let me use one of your closets."

In response, he goes straight through to the stairway and groans dramatically as he carries the bag up to the bedroom. His bedroom? Theirs? Plenty of room, he thinks, in his own closet, which has been his alone for such a long time.

When he comes back down, she hands him a glass tumbler, two-thirds full of bourbon, some water, ice. She has one just like it and when he sips, the whiskey burns in his throat. Heat and light. And when she kisses him, he can taste it again on her lips and tongue.

He thinks, they both think, about the bed upstairs, but then the fire is coming alive on the hearth. Food waits in the kitchen. So, they sit down on either end of the old leather couch and turn to face each other, drinks in hand. The terrier, Jake, lies down on the rug before the fire.

The potatoes have only been in the oven for a quarter hour, he tells her. They have time enough to breathe, to stop the day and the night where it is, where they are. The fire is warm enough now, the whiskey hot on the tongue, and they can just be. She slips her shoes off and pulls her legs up onto the couch so that her feet rest against his thighs.

He can't stop smiling. At the fire, the drink, at her. But even so, she thinks that his face is testament to who he is, what he has suffered. She can read in his cheeks and chin the knife blade of the war, the puckered scar beside his eye from his father's fist, the sharp chisel of struggle and loss; in his eyes, the despair over his son. All of that in the lines and wrinkles and yet...and yet...he is young tonight. And when he turns toward her, his face opens up like a flame that finds oxygen.

"I sometimes think that I'm what's left of a woman," she says. "Thin, dried-up, like a husk."

He shakes his head and sips his whiskey before speaking. "Nothing could be further from the truth."

"Maybe it's that I was dried-up. Unused. Like a field that has lain—what is it?"

"Fallow?" he suggests.

"That's it. Like a field that's been torn open and lies barren under the sun, but nothing is planted, and it never rains."

"No rain for what, five years?" he suggests.

"Oh, God. Much longer than that. Mine was not a...passionate marriage, Clint. Pleasant, I suppose you would say, but not passionate. Too much mind, never enough body, at least for me."

The whiskey must be having an effect, because he laughs out loud. "Well, you've come to a place of not so much mind," he says.

"And the body is pretty damn fine."

He raises his glass. "The body you're referring to—yours and mine stirred up together?"

She nods emphatically and pushes against his thigh with her sock feet. "Our body. And I like it *stirred up*, by the way."

"What you're saying, about the dry husk of a life. A long season of drought and then the rain falls, suddenly...unexpectedly. That could just as well be me. I've been nothing but a dry stalk standing alone in a field until you."

She has a sudden, almost overwhelming feeling of tenderness toward this man. As if she could take all of him inside her somehow...and heal him. Ease the iron tension in his muscles and erase his scars.

"Are you hungry?" he asks finally, after a pause given over to the shifting firelight and the sweet, autumnal sense of time suspended.

"Starving," she admits after pausing to think about it. "Are you cooking?"

He nods as he stands up, his glass empty. "It's simple, though. Meat, potato, bread. Pie, maybe."

"Wine or whiskey to go with it?"

He can't help but smile at her. "First wine and then bourbon," he says, going into the kitchen. All in the fullness of time.

Food, fire, wine, and then bed? Here... In all the wide world, she thinks, *what else is there?*

SHE OPENS A BOTTLE OF RED WINE SHE HAS brought, pours them each a glass, and sits with him in the kitchen while he sears the steaks. Just as he's about to fork the steaks out of the skillet and onto the plates, there's a scratching at the door.

She gets up to let Nick, the shepherd-husky, in from the night. His nose and his tongue are cold against her palm as she pets him. His fur is full of small sticks and burrs. "He's been far afield," Clinton says. "All the way to woods at the top of the upper pasture. There's something out there he doesn't quite like would be my guess."

"A bear?"

"Maybe. But whatever it is, we should heed what he's saying. Pay attention. After dark, the farm belongs to him."

The food, like the fire, is made of the most basic ingredients. Of the earth and the season. So simple and so pleasing that she eats far more than she ever would in town.

After supper, she fixes them both another drink. Not quite so much bourbon in the glass as before, but enough to last them as the fire burns down. Before her glass is empty, though, she sets it on the end table and crawls the length of the couch to curl against him. He puts his own glass down so that he can hold her in his arms. His hands burrow under her sweater.

In a while—hard to say just how long—one or the other suggests that they lock the doors and go upstairs. They're both yawning.

Even their peace has a grain of passion in it.

CHAPTER 41

WHAT, THEN, ARE THE INGREDIENTS OF TIME? The flight of the sun across the sky? The phases of the moon carving up the night sky in intricate precision? Also the stars, which keep their own kind of tremendous clockwork?

And the seasons, are they part of the recipe? That which hurries us and beguiles us. Restrains and binds us.

Each moment of the present, the most current click of the clock on the sideboard or the watch on your wrist, each moment contains a thousand moments that we call *past*, a thousand moments that we call *not yet*. And from this the current moment derives its mysterious depth. From this, it takes its true meaning. Not the hectic dance that we smear over it.

No sense in confusing the present for all there is. Everything is all there is, and everything is here now.

Lazarus Salter chases his oldest son with a hammer. Nick, the dog, runs through the upper pasture. Clint forgets the horrors of the war, though they return with fire and sword. Catherine forgets the barrenness of the bed she shared with James, even as he gasps for breath. But there is no ultimate forgetting. Heaven and hell are blended into this moment and that. Bliss and agony, God and the devil.

All moments stirred in the recipe of this moment. All are flaming here, on Doe Branch. All chant their long lines and sing in the chorus. The truly astonishing thing about the union of Clint Salter and Cat Metcalf is that in their conjoined body and mind are all the cries of things past and future. Some heard, some unheard, but here, nonetheless.

This night, in bed, it seems to her that pleasure ripples through her body like a strong wind. His skin quivers at her touch while a fox screams on the ridge behind the house.

AFTER A LEISURELY BREAKFAST, THEY BUNDLE up—his barn coat, her sweater—against the cool mountain air of late September. They walk up to the stone barn with the two dogs running and chasing around them. There, they brush Little Joe and Nell. An apple each to crunch on and they are content to be saddled.

Clint ties a pair of saddlebags onto Little Joe to hold the sandwiches Cat made for their lunch, along with a couple of apples and some cookies. A canteen of water. He ties a blanket behind Nell's saddle for their picnic, which causes the mare to prance and pull away until Cat calms her.

They ride down Doe Branch toward Bearwallow Gap and the river until they come to the rocky road up the Divide Mountain and beyond to Anderson Cove. He wants to show her the highlands property that his grandparents left him over the mountain in the very heart of his country.

It's two miles up to the Divide and down through Coley Gap to the valley. They let the horses pick their way up to the top, both because it's a steep climb and because the road itself is washed out in places and more boulder than dirt in others. The dogs range far ahead as they climb, impatient to see and smell the world ahead.

At the top, they dismount and lead the horses along the top of the Divide. He points out an opening on the right where bear hunters gather on Saturday nights in the fall, drinking and telling tall tales while listening to the dogs run deep into the mountains.

They mount again as the trace—it's not much of a road—starts to wind down toward the cove. They pause, sitting at ease in their saddles while he points out the lay of the land below. Where once upon a time before the war, a half dozen families lived and farmed, now, there is a cemetery, a few grand, old barns, and some falling-down houses. He describes it all to her as he traces the folds of the land with his pointing finger. As if he is describing the ocean, she thinks. That deep, shifting and complex.

From Coley Gap, the horses pick their way down to the valley floor. He shows her the huge, two-story log barn that his grandfather built to hold hay and shelter livestock. They pass the orchard on their right hand. Mostly Pippins plus a few Limbertwigs. Even as he's pointing out the varieties, the dogs suddenly chase hard in among the trees, and a yearling bear stands to peer nearsightedly at them before disappearing quietly into the woods.

"We grow the apples for them now," Clint says with a smile. "The bear and the deer."

"Are you ever tempted to come pick them? Even just a bushel or two?"

"I think of it every August," he says, "but..."

"But what?"

"But I don't like to come up by myself. It's not the same." This with a shrug.

"What if I came with you?"

"Then we could have all the apples we'd ever want," he says.

THEY SPREAD THEIR PICNIC ON THE GROUND near his grandparents' house that burned. They hobble Little Joe and Nell rather than tie them, so that they can wander a bit to find the sweetest grass. The dogs seem content to stay close by, Jake eating the leftover scraps of sandwich Cat throws to them.

From where they sit, he points out various landmarks from what was once a thriving community of perhaps fifty souls. And when they stand up to repack the saddlebags and let the horses drink from the creek, he points out the boundaries of his holdings, the two hundred acres, more or less, that he inherited, which includes most of the valley floor.

After lunch, they lead the horses up and around the overgrown road to the Anderson cemetery, where he introduces her to his grandparents and their kin. Two graves in particular he gestures to, one Robbins and one Salter, both survivors of the Civil War, both tough men in their own right. "I'd deputize them if I could," he tells her.

"Why them?"

"They both had a reputation. Whiskey makers, fighters. I need somebody to go over into Tennessee and bring me back the two men that killed the Nortons, and the judge says I can't send a living deputy. Says that I can't go myself either."

"Because?"

"Because of the laws governing jurisdiction."

"Well, good lord, isn't there some kind of law enforcement in Tennessee?"

"Not to be trusted."

"You don't like that, do you?"

"Hell no," he says softly. "It whets my temper like a knife just to think about it. When those two were alive"—he nods at the graves—"they didn't trouble so much with the boundary line between North Carolina and Tennessee. It was all just country. And those bastards across the mountain would have been fair game."

"Don't you do it, Clint."

"Do what?"

"I can tell how much this bothers you by how quietly you're talking about it. You're warning me you may go after them despite the law, aren't you?"

He laughs. "Maybe. I'm thinking about how to get at them."

She stands staring at him, considering. Again, wondering if she should ever be afraid of him. But no, that's not it. Should she be afraid *for* him?

CHAPTER 42

THE SERIOUS MOOD AT THE CEMETERY EASES when they get back on the horses. The ride back is just as slow and quiet as any autumn passage could be, unspooling through a sun-splashed afternoon. Even the breeze along the top of the Divide Mountain, with its hint of cold nights to come, doesn't penetrate. They talk and laugh when the trace becomes more like a road and the horses have room to walk side by side.

That evening, she cooks chicken breasts over brown rice in the oven. After supper, Cat asks Clint about his family: How far back do they go and how deep into the hills? In response, he uses scissors to cut off a two-by-three-foot piece from a roll of brown butcher paper that he finds under the stairs. He spreads it out on the dining room table. She pours them a drink while he makes his preparations. Then they sit together while he draws his family tree, telling stories with each successive generation until the paper is full of interconnected branches and the room is full of ghosts.

At one point, he gets up to scissor off a second sheet of butcher paper so that he can sketch a rough map for her, to give her some sense of what parts of the turbulent, mountain-tossed land west of the river are home to these ghosts. When he does, she pours them each one more splash into their glasses, sweetening their drinks, she tells him. Secretly, her head is already swimming, whether with the whiskey or the stories, she can't tell.

The names that are woven into the telling? Salter and Robbins, Anderson and Goforth, Fortner and Freeman. The

Robbinses, in particular, reach back through the decades all the way to the time just after the war—the Revolutionary War—and they built, bought, farmed, and fought over the land until Clint's elaborate sketch of a map is as intricate and layered as the inside of a rose.

The place names are knitted into the family names. Doe Branch, of course. Big Pine, where there is a mysterious rock house, and Little Pine. Snakeden Ridge, Puncheon Camp Branch, Troublesome. Worley, where there's a store—or was a store. The Divide Mountain. Anderson Cove, where they were that very day. Wooleyshot Branch...

"No," she interrupts him. "You're pulling my leg, Clint. I refuse to believe there is a place in this world named *Wooleyshot.* Whatever the hell does that even mean, anyway?"

He points with his pencil to the left-hand margin of his map sketch. "Right there," he says and carefully labels it. "Runs into Spring Creek."

He then begins to add the cemeteries to his map by drawing small crosses where they lay, scattered onto the various ridges and gaps in the mountains. And the cemeteries, she realizes, or at least most of them, bear the same names as the family tree. She reaches out and grabs his arm.

"Wait," she says. "I just realized something. If you could somehow lay the map over the tree and see both at the same time." She reaches out to do so, trying to show him what she means despite the bourbon. "Then they would... I don't know. Melt together somehow."

"Like those clear plastic pages in the encyclopedia," he replies, staring down at the drawings and lists he's made. "Where you turn the page to lay the organs over the bones of the body."

"And then the muscles and the skin over the skeleton and the organs," she finishes his thought. "We have those encyclopedias in the high school library. That's what this is, Clint. Your people and the mountain land, ridges and coves, branches and creeks and rivers, are just one thing. One body. The only thing that separates the skeleton and muscles from the skin is time." She knows that she's a little drunk now and suspects he is too.

"Time is a myth," he says fiercely. "No piece of this is separate from the rest of it."

She reaches out with one hand to touch the two broad, brown sheets of paper, the rough fruits of their last hour together, of all his inner knowing sketched out for her. And with the other hand, she takes the pencil from him and raises his palm to her lips. Only when she's kissed the fingers that have been so faithfully listing and drawing does she speak. "I think I'm finally beginning to understand," she says. "The people and the land—all the way back to the beginning—truly are one thing."

PART THREE

IS

Madison County
1965

CHAPTER 43

JUST BEFORE THEY GO UP TO BED, CLINT LETS THE dogs out to run. When he does, Nick breaks hell-for-leather straight up through the lower pasture, with Jake barking in his wake. For some reason he can't name, this seems different to Clint, threatening somehow. He dashes past Cat, where she lies dozing on the couch, and slams up the stairs to grab the 12 gauge from the bedroom and buckshot out of the bedside drawer. Down the stairs again. "What is it?" she yells to him as he goes past her, through the kitchen and out into the night.

"I don't know," he calls back to her and is gone.

After a long moment to gather her wits, she sits up, slips her shoes on, and scurries into the kitchen. The door to the outside is standing wide open where he left it. She closes the door and splashes cold water on her face. Then, resolute, she walks back into the living room to the coat closet. She pulls on Clint's barn coat before lifting the shoebox containing clips for the carbine down off the shelf. She digs the gun itself out from behind the coats and jackets hanging there. Somehow, her hands remember what is vague in her mind: how to slide the clip into the bottom of the stock until it locks.

She turns on the front porch light and locks the front door. Then, after turning on the back porch light, she too slips out the back, pulling the kitchen door shut behind her. She goes only as far as the picnic table in the backyard, near the clothesline, where she can see most of the back of the house without being seen.

Lays the carbine carefully on the table and sits down on the cold bench to wait for Clint.

She wonders at herself. At what she's doing. But then, as the cold night air brings her more fully awake, she remembers the boot print in the mud beside the spring that had made Clint so anxious. Angry, even. So, there is a threat, she imagines, something dangerous in the dark. Then, she recalls that as far as the human community is concerned, she can't be seen here. At his house in the middle of the night. In his bed, by implication. *Clandestine*, she thinks to herself. *That's me*. And then, strangely for a woman who isn't used to guns, she reaches out to touch the stock of the carbine before whispering the word out loud. "Clandestine."

CLINT IS AS COMFORTABLE IN THE FIELDS AND woods at night as it's possible for a man to be. Plus, he knows his own farm as well as he knows the inside of his house. He can sense it rising all around him in the dark.

He pauses at the gate to the lower pasture to let his eyes adjust to the dark. The moon is three-quarters full and just up over the ridge to his right. The unshorn grass in the pasture in front of him is glistening with dew, and he can hear the flock of sheep lowing gently near the lower barn.

Jake is still barking from time to time, but not consistently, probably because he's running his legs off trying to keep up with Nick. They're in the upper pasture now, according to the little dog's yelps. He can see the path through the dew where the dogs shot straight up the farm road to the orchard, so he slips through the gate and follows their trail, loading the shotgun by feel as he climbs.

He eases in among the apple trees. At the upper end of the orchard, he pauses, as the trees provide some cover. The war comes back to him now, the hunting of other human beings suddenly fresh and grim in his mind.

And then, the oddest thing. He sees the faintest glimmer of light in the upper pasture. Small, oblique, bobbing along. *Flashlight*, he thinks, *someone walking*. The light is headed toward the stone barn.

He raises the shotgun. As tempting as it is to shoot at the light, he knows he's too far away and it's too dangerous. He holds the stock to his shoulder to absorb the shock and fires one barrel into the night sky, just to send a warning and to rally the dogs. The light blinks out.

He reloads as he leaves the shelter of the apple trees and moves quickly ahead to the fence, slips between two strands of barbed wire, and climbs toward the barn.

Chaos. Nick is barking now as well as Jake. The two horses, Little Joe followed by Nell, gallop downhill past him as he climbs, their hooves a muffled thunder in the thick autumn grass.

IT'S ONLY LATER, WHEN CAT AND CLINT ARE BOTH back in the house, the dogs sprawled before the fireplace and the doors locked, that they can catch their breath and begin to put the pieces together.

Before they go to bed, he tells her about seeing what he thought was a light, maybe a flashlight or a lantern. And that he fired the shotgun into the air to scare off the intruder, whatever it was. She tells him about walking to the end of the driveway after hearing the shot—confused, scared. Should she lock herself in; should she go toward the sound of the shot?

And how, before she could decide, she heard a car or truck engine start out on the Doe Branch Road, fifty yards or so beyond the house. How she then saw an old farm truck drive slowly by the front of the house. And as it passed, it suddenly accelerated with a loud rumble, speeding toward Bearwallow Gap and the river.

"What could you tell about the truck?" he asks her. "Make, model?"

She laughs ruefully. "I probably couldn't have told you that if I saw it in broad daylight."

"Color?"

"Black, maybe. Or dark blue," she replies doubtfully.

Somehow, the anxiety from all of this creeps into the house with them. Was the light real? Was the truck somehow related? What scared the horses, other than the shotgun blast? The dogs? What did they see or smell?

He is restless and unresponsive in a way that she's never seen him before. And his mood conveys to her, such that for the first time, they go to bed out of tune with each other. Not distant, but discordant.

When they fall asleep, their dreams are troubled by mysterious lights, ghosts or spirits awake in the night. The sound of sudden gunshots and car engines revving up to speed away. All this is nothing that either will remember except for the riddle of darkness, the enigma.

WHEN SHE WAKES IN THE MIDDLE OF THE night, the smell of her dream is still in her nostrils. The bitter stench of a weapon that's been fired, the faint tang of expended gunpowder, the thick stink of exhaust from an old truck engine. She rolls toward him for comfort only to discover that his side of the bed is empty; cool, but not cold. He's gone but hasn't been up for long.

She finds him downstairs, sitting alone in the living room. There's only the faintest red-orange light from the simmering coals in the fireplace.

"You didn't tell me everything, did you?" she says.

"Why do you say that?"

"Because I can feel you holding back. And it divides us, hurts us."

He shakes his head. "No, I didn't tell you everything."

"Because you want to protect me." It's not a question.

He nods. "That's right. It seems my job to protect you."

"I'm not part of your job, Clint. I'm part of your life."

He doesn't respond, so she pulls his robe more tightly around her against the chill and goes to the sideboard. There, she pours them each a finger of whiskey—neat, no water, no ice. Hard, like the talk.

While she does this, he rises and goes to the fireplace to throw some corncobs on the coals, along with some slender splits of pine and a few pine cones. When he sits back down, she hands him his drink and sits as well.

"Let's get something straight," she says. "We're adults. Not children. I don't need to be protected, or if I do, you can protect me best by always—always, damn it—being honest with me. I don't care if you scare the shit out of me. It's better than this." He doesn't reply, so she continues. "I was treated like a child before, by that other man. By James."

"The all-but-dead man," he says and smiles ruefully.

"Him. And you see where that got us. Him and me. So, if you want *us* to survive. Us—whatever we are, a couple—then you damn well better treat me like an adult. We're consenting adults."

He sips the bourbon and grimaces before speaking. "More than just consenting," he says. "Willing...determined."

She nods. "I like *determined*... So, what did you not tell me earlier?"

"After I fired off the twelve gauge, straight up, into the sky, the light I saw went out, so I started up through the tall grass, toward the last place I saw it. Reloading as I went. When I got up close to the stone barn, to where it felt like the light was, I tripped over something, something hard. Fell flat on my face... with the loaded gun." He shakes his head at the memory. "Stupid. It's a wonder I didn't blow my own head off."

"Jesus."

"Oh, it gets better. What I tripped over was a five-gallon can half full of coal oil. I left it at the lower barn when I came back down."

"Coal oil? That somebody would use to...?"

"Start a fire."

A pause while she sips from her glass, lets the whiskey pool in her mouth and burn before swallowing. "Is it your arsonist?" she finally asks.

"Just about has to be. Unless we've got two firebugs running around the county. And this is a long way from anywhere for it to be a couple of bored country boys out for a lark."

"So, it was intentional. They knew it was your farm. And whoever was driving the truck that I can't describe dropped them off and picked them up."

"That would be my guess. If they just happened to be driving by, then it would be somebody who lives on up the branch. And you wouldn't have heard them crank up the engine right after they heard the gunshot."

She nods. Gets up and brings the bottle from the sideboard so that she can pour another finger into each of their glasses. "So, Sheriff, what do you think it means?" She sits back down and, this time, leans back onto her end of the couch and brings her feet up.

"It means that whoever has been setting fires for the last year or longer either decided I was a Republican, which makes no sense, or that I was after them, which is true."

"Who knows you're after them? I mean, seriously after them."

"You, me, Way Tipton. Gloria Goforth, plus one or two of the other deputies. And..."

"And?"

"And my brother, who keeps telling me it's ridiculous for me to be chasing after a bunch of random barn burnings. Just an old mountain custom."

"He knows who it is. I meant to ask that as a question."

Clint smiles. The smile becomes a grin, and then, the whiskey warm in his throat, the grin becomes a laugh. "Hell yes, he probably knows who it is, or at least suspects, and he wants to protect them for some reason. Politics, most likely."

"Damn him."

Another laugh. "I've been saying something like that for...oh, twenty years or so."

"So, Clint, my darling, sweet man. All you have to worry about is murder, fire, flood, and all the plagues of Egypt. Plus, you almost had a fight with your...whatever I am."

"Silent partner."

"I'm not always very silent." She laughs now, at the idea of being quiet. "But I do like *partner*."

"I like your talk," he offers, "when it's just you and me. You, me, the dogs, the fire. I think a fine forever could be us talking."

"You like it enough so that you can rest now?"

He sighs. "Maybe. I couldn't sleep before."

She stands up before him, tugs on the belt of the robe she's wearing and lets it fall open. "I know how to put you to sleep," she says.

CHAPTER 44

LATE SUNDAY AFTERNOON, AFTER CATHERINE leaves, Clinton walks the farm with Randall and explains what happened Saturday night. The light, the strange truck, the can of coal oil. Randall grasps the threat immediately and agrees that for the time being, he will sleep by day and stand guard with the dogs by night.

By midmorning Monday at the jail, the weekend Clinton spent with Cat on Doe Branch seems like a dream, something that happened long ago. The peace of their Sunday together—slow and rinsed in autumn sunlight—transformed into something entirely different. Doors banging and phones ringing. Upstairs, their occasional guest Poteat is singing a plaintive ballad from his jail cell, voluntarily arrested to avoid the temptation of liquor yet again. Something about the wagoner's lad. When Clinton pauses at the foot of the stairs leading up to the cells, he can hear faint strains of Poteat's voice, again struck by how high and tremulous the sound.

Your horses is hungry, go feed them some hay,
"Come sit down beside me," is all I can say.
"My horses ain't hungry, they won't eat your hay,
So farewell, pretty Nancy, I've no time to stay."

No time to stay. Gloria is on the phone, trying to make an appointment for Clinton with the assistant district attorney for

Madison County. The magistrate sends over a note from the courthouse that he needs to see Clinton, today if possible. Partway through the morning, Clinton realizes that he should have heard from the SBI crime lab on Friday, and when he calls his contact there, he's told that a detailed report is in the mail. Read it first and call back.

At lunchtime, he sits outside at the battered old picnic table by the river with a hot cup of coffee and a sausage biscuit left over from the meal Rosie had put together that morning for the prisoners and deputies.

The jailhouse cat, Brutus's friend, has come out with him and is sitting on the far end of the table, regarding him solemnly. "Why don't I know your name?" he says to the beast, who yawns and continues to stare. "Do you even have a name, or are you just Cat, like my lady friend?" Another impossibly wide, toothy yawn. "Want to trade places?" he asks the cat. "You do my job, I'll do yours?"

In his mind, he's trying to focus on the rest of the day. The assistant DA, the magistrate (what the hell did he want?), the SBI... when Gloria opens the side door to call out at him. "Phone," she yells. "University, Institute of Government." And it's only at that moment he remembers that he'd called Mike Smith on Friday to ask for advice about jurisdiction. He tosses the last bite of sausage to the cat, crumbles what's left of the biscuit for the sparrows, and carries his coffee inside.

He nods to Gloria as he passes through the outer office and closes the door behind him. When he picks up the phone, a bored female voice asks if he is Sheriff Salter; he says he is, and she replies, "One moment, please," in a plastic tone.

Thirty seconds, a minute, before there's a click, followed by a strangely familiar voice that he can't quite place.

"Sheriff Salter?"

"Yep. You got him."

"This is Matthew Salter at the Institute of Government."

"Who?"

"Matthew...your son."

Clinton can feel his throat constricting so that he almost chokes. "Matt! Son, is everything all right?"

"Of course. I'm calling in response to your request for counsel on legal jurisdiction. You may not be aware, but that's my area of expertise here at the Institute, and your request was referred to me."

"I—I knew that. Mike Smith told me that you knew more about jurisdiction than anyone in the state."

"I see. I had forgotten that Michael spent some time with you up there. And yes, he's correct. I probably do know more about the subject than anyone except one of my law school professors. What, exactly, is your question, Father?" There is a chill formality to Matt's voice that causes Clinton's stomach to clench painfully.

So, it takes him a moment to collect his thoughts. "As you may know, we had a double murder here a few weeks ago. An older couple shot and killed in their home up above Hot Springs."

"I believe I've read something about it."

"Last week, we identified an accomplice, a local boy, who drove two men from Cocke County to the house the night of the killings and then away again afterward. Based on his sworn statement, we think we know who did the killings, and I need advice on how to get at them."

"Cocke County is in Tennessee, I believe. Is that correct?"

"Yes. Newport is the county seat. Just across the line."

"Well, Father, you can't get at them. The two men can only be arrested by the Newport police or the Cocke County sheriff's office."

"What if they don't want to cooperate?"

"Then your hands are tied. Is the SBI involved in the investigation?"

"Yes, I'm expecting a report from them in a day or so."

"You might enlist their aid in your cause. Ask them to request that their counterparts in Tennessee arrest these men so that they can be extradited, but if you push it that far, you had better be certain that they did, indeed, commit the crime."

"Oh, they did it, all right."

"Hmm. Did your witness actually see them shoot the old couple?"

"No, but he—"

"Then, you don't have an eyewitness, do you?"

"Well, hell, Matt, I—"

"Matthew. I go by Matthew professionally. My advice to you, Sheriff, is to tread very lightly in this matter. Let the district attorney up there take the lead and follow his instructions to the letter. Do you know what I mean by *to the letter*?"

"Of course, I know. But you're saying that if we don't find someone on that side of the line to cooperate in the arrest, these two cold-blooded sons of bitches can just sit over there and laugh at us?"

"Leaving out the rather crass profanity, that is almost exactly what I'm saying. Do you have any other questions?"

A pause, and then he decides to try. "When are you going to come up for a visit, son? We'd love to see you."

"I'm afraid that my duties here at the Institute keep me very busy. And I consider Chapel Hill to be my home now. Good luck with the dilemma you are facing. Certainly, we at the Institute prefer to see justice done whenever possible. If you have any other questions in your official capacity, Father, you can leave a message with the switchboard operator here. Goodbye, Sheriff."

Clinton has his own farewell, his expression of love, his desire to see his son, all these words in his throat, but the line is already dead.

THE MAGISTRATE WANTS TO DROP OFF A BUSHEL of potatoes for Rosie to use in the jailhouse kitchen. The assistant DA can see him at four o'clock that afternoon in her office on the second floor of the courthouse. The thick, manila envelope from the SBI arrives at two, special delivery, but sits unopened on Clinton's desk while he sits and stares at the carefully typed address label.

The thing that finally pulls him out of his painful reverie over the conversation with his son is his daughter. Marian. At a quarter past three, she knocks on the door of his office. The high school has just dismissed and for some reason he can't quite grasp—does this have something to do with Matthew?—she wants him to walk down the street for coffee.

"Have you got time?" she is saying. "I need to tell you something."

"I've got almost forty-five minutes," he says, suddenly back in the present, focused on the worry in her voice. He picks up the envelope from the SBI along with the other materials on the Norton case.

At Robbins Drug Store, they get coffee at the counter and carry the mugs to a small table in the corner, away from the hustle of customers getting prescriptions filled and children ogling the rack of comic books.

When they sit, he speaks even before she has a chance to. "I talked to Matt today on the phone."

"Oh, really. How was he?"

"I think the word is *officious*. He was calling from the Institute of Government about a legal matter, and he talked as if he barely knew me." His voice is perfectly even, but she knows how much it hurts him to say this.

"Matt is my brother and all, but you know, Dad, sometimes he can be an ass. A perfect little ass."

Clinton almost smiles.

"Don't let Matt get under your skin, Dad. There's something else I need to tell you." She is whispering now.

He leans toward her expectantly.

"Catherine's husband stopped breathing on Saturday night, and they didn't resuscitate him."

"He's dead?"

She nods fiercely. "Yes, finally. They tried to reach her over the weekend, but she wasn't at home. She got the call at school this morning."

CHAPTER 45

"SHE CAME BY THE ROOM BEFORE SHE LEFT school for the day. She said to tell you that she'd call you tomorrow."

"Was she okay? What about the funeral?"

"She seemed—I don't know, a lot of things. Relieved, confused, harried. Maybe more relieved than anything. Which, given the circumstances, kind of makes sense, doesn't it?"

He nods. "A lot of sense. I visited him once with her and there was nothing left of him except breath. And barely that. What can I do?"

Marian shakes her head. "Nothing. She asked me to help her with the obituary. They may take him back to Durham. He had some sort of family there. She told me twice to tell you not to worry. She'd said she'd call you tomorrow. Did I already say that?"

THE ASSISTANT DISTRICT ATTORNEY FOR MADISON County is named Charles "Charlie" Burns, and he has an office on the second floor of the courthouse. Mid-forties, a workaholic, he is from Ashe County and has earned a reputation among the petty criminals he mostly prosecutes as hard, harsh, unforgiving. Or, as one prisoner in the jail described him to Clinton, "that redheaded bastard in them shiny shoes."

Clinton has dealt with him directly a half dozen times in the nine months since he was sworn in, including bringing Wallace

Sawyer to trial for grave robbing, and their meetings have been cool but cordial. According to Gloria Goforth, the coolness is because Burns is a rock-solid Republican, which accounts for him being appointed to three consecutive terms.

That afternoon, in his office, Clinton goes straight to the point. It's about the Norton murders: He thinks he knows who the killers are, but he can't get at them. The minute he hears the word "Nortons," Burns gets up, tells his secretary not to "let any yahoos interrupt us," and closes the door to his office.

Clinton lays out the whole story for Burns. How they kept noticing Jason Fortner at the funeral. What they found in his mother's trailer, plus what he said by way of a confession. He hands him Fortner's sworn statement and while he reads it, gets up to look out his one window—down Main Street toward the train station.

When he's finished a second pass through the pages of Fortner's statement, Burns clears his throat and Clinton sits back down. "Jesus, Clinton. That was fast. The killings only happened, what, two weeks ago?"

"Something like that. Twelve days ago."

"Do you believe this Fortner character? Seems to me like I've seen him before."

"You probably have. He hasn't got much of what you'd call a life. But yes, I believe him."

"Have you talked to the sheriff in Cocke County? What does he go by...Sutton, isn't it?"

"Lewis Sutton. I talked to him right after the Nortons were killed, mainly because where it all happened is close to the Tennessee line, and several of my deputies thought the killers might have come over from Cocke County."

"Hell of a place, from what I hear."

He nods. "Reputation is worse than ours."

"What did he say?"

"He was nice enough, at least at the beginning. But then he turned off gruff and said he ran a tight ship and that there weren't any such trash as would do something like the Nortons in his county. *Goddamn county*, actually. His words."

"So how do you think he would respond if you called him back with this?" Burns holds up Fortner's sworn testimony.

"I honestly don't know. To me, what Fortner has to say seems clear as a bell, and if you were in the room while he was telling it, you'd have believed him."

"You don't think he's protecting himself? I mean, what if he was in on the whole thing and he's just claiming that he stayed in the car? If he puts it off on the"—he pauses to check the names—"on these Crowders, then he gets off with a much lighter sentence. *Accessory to* rather than *murder one*."

"I thought about that. But to be brutally honest, he doesn't seem that bright. And he would have had to make the whole thing up on the spur of the moment, sitting at a rickety picnic table in his mother's side yard. And..."

"And?"

"And how will we ever know if we don't at least interrogate the Crowders?"

"Granted. Let's look at it from a different direction. Will your boy, Fortner, stand up under cross-examination from a really tough defense attorney? Bailey, say, or Pritchard? Somebody like that."

Clinton shrugs. "I don't know. But if we get their fingerprints, the SBI can put the Crowders in the house, and that should go a long way toward driving a nail in it."

Burns pauses to consider. "Maybe...maybe. Your boy, Fortner, if he was truly never in the house, then he didn't see who pulled the trigger. He can't testify as to which of the two shot the old people, can he?"

"No."

"If we ever get them to trial, that will be a problem."

"I know. Somebody else—a lawyer from the Institute of Government—said the same thing to me earlier today. And what do you mean, *If* we ever get them to trial?"

"I mean we got a long road ahead of us on this thing, Clinton. I don't think your counterpart over there is going to be any help. And if we call up Sheriff Sutton and tell him about this, it's entirely possible he even warns the Crowders if he knows them. So, the first challenge is getting them into custody. And after that, we'll play hell getting a conviction even if they're guilty."

"What are you really saying, Charlie?"

"I'm saying I've got to talk to the boss, the elected district attorney for the six counties. See what he says. One thing I know for sure is that if we do take this to court, he'll be sitting in the lead chair at our table." He pauses to wink at Clinton. "The man loves a murder trial more than milk and honey if he thinks he can win. Get his picture in the papers."

"Fair enough. Everybody keeps telling me to follow your lead. But what the hell am I supposed to do in the meantime?"

"Keep Fortner quiet and out of the way. Tell everybody else who knows about this, the magistrate, the deputies, to keep their damn mouths shut. One thing I do know for certain is that if the Crowders are guilty and they hear about this, we may be looking for them in Texas rather than trying to extradite them from Tennessee."

THAT NIGHT, AFTER DARK, HE GETS IN THE JEEP and drives out of town along the bypass and turns up the road Catherine lives on. He has no idea if she'll be home or not, and he doesn't plan to stop, but for reasons he's not entirely sure of, he wants to check on her. Drive by to see if her lights are on, be close to her for the half minute it takes to pass her little rented house.

The house is dark and the station wagon is not in the driveway where she normally parks. He half-expected this, but then again, over the previous weeks, they'd eased into the habit of letting each other know where they were most of the time, and it's oddly unsettling to him not to have talked to her since the news about her husband.

By the time he parks back at the jail, it's past eight o'clock, and he thinks a hot bath and a stiff drink might help him sleep, so he walks back to Main Street in order to climb the hill to Mrs. Penland's. When he passes the bank beside the courthouse, he glances up at the large clock in front of the bank and then stops to stare. The clockface, smudged and stained from lack of attention, claims it's past midnight, and he has to check his wristwatch just to make sure he hasn't lost four or five hours—or worse, lost his mind entirely. No, his old, beat-up Elgin is ticking, and it's only eight-fifteen.

When he is finally able to sleep that night, he dreams of Matthew, not as an adult—full of condescension and lawyer talk—but as a boy. In his dream, he carries the towheaded youngster on his shoulders across the road from the newly built farmhouse at Doe Branch down to the creek itself, where little Matt loves to play in the water. They are laughing and talking silly talk to each other, and when they reach the creek below the spring house, Clinton takes off his boots and rolls up his pants legs so that he can wade in the water with Matt.

Everything is liquid summer sunshine and birdsong. A cow in the pasture behind his father's old house is mooing for its calf, who is tottering toward mama on as yet spindly legs. The branch is startlingly cold, but Matt doesn't mind. He sits down on the sandy bottom of the creek and tosses handfuls of rushing water up into the air. Water spiders and minnows thread through the gleaming. The smell of creasy greens along the bank. Just here, a laurel bush toppled over where the creek has eaten away its roots.

This is the peace after his return from the war. The peace that comes of the simplest things. The abiding affection he feels for the earth and for his son, the boy who bears his name, who carries his fondest love.

The dream ends quietly, with father and son still playing in the creek, as the light fades into the darker corners of sleep. When he wakes in the middle of the night to visit the bathroom, he is happy to remember the dream in butter-soft clarity. Happy to believe that it actually happened just as he saw it, more memory than dream, over and over again.

And when he returns to bed, he savors the lineaments of the dream, recalls the smell of his son's hair when he was a baby and Clint held him while he fell asleep. How he had fed him his first more or less solid food and lay down beside him night after night as he fell asleep. Read to him countless books, just as he did later for Marian.

Where, when had it all been lost? What had turned their deep and secret bond into something so desperately strange as the heinous phone call that afternoon? So distant and full of sharp and jagged judgment?

What has he done, he keeps asking himself, as he lies lonely in his bed, what godawful thing has he done to turn his son so against him? Or, even worse, what if he's done nothing at all, which would mean he can never repair the damage.

CHAPTER 46

MIDMORNING THE NEXT DAY, TUESDAY, GLORIA Goforth comes into his office and says quietly, "Phone call for you, long distance."

He raises his eyebrows to signal a question: *Who*? She nods and mouths the name, *Catherine*, before going out and closing the door.

"Hey, Clint." Her voice is tired, but full. Full of emotion, he imagines, but strained through a couple of hundred miles of telephone cable.

"Cat, where are you? How are you?"

"I'm at a friend of my mother's in Durham. You didn't know I had a mother, did you?"

"You're coming back, aren't you?"

She laughs, quietly, and he imagines her in some old lady's house. Full of dust motes and eternally hushed except for the occasional sound of a teakettle whistling on the stove. "Of course, I'm coming back. That's home, where you are."

"Are you okay?"

"I'm fine. In fact, I'm better than that. It was a shock, Monday morning, to hear that he was gone, but then... Hang on for a minute, I'm going to close the door." Only static on the line. Then she was back. "Mrs. Daily can't hear except when she wants to. But when she wants to, she can say whole conversations back to you."

"How old is—"

"I don't know. Over seventy. I lost count. Anyway, it was a shock yesterday morning when the call came, and I almost felt guilty when I realized I was up at Doe Branch with you when he died."

"Almost?"

"Almost, but not really. It felt like he died years ago and I'd said goodbye a thousand times. So no, I'm fine. I called his sister in Raleigh and we talked it through. Here's the strange thing. He wanted to be cremated."

"You mean—I've never known anyone who was cremated."

"He thought it was the environmentally sound thing to do, plus he always told me he wanted to stay on the farm, so I was supposed to scatter his ashes over the pasture on some far-distant day when he died."

"Okay. So why are you in…?"

"We're having a memorial service here, with his family and my mother. Looks like Thursday afternoon and then I'm bringing his ashes back with me. His obituary should appear in the Asheville paper tomorrow and the *Madison County Chronicle* whenever it comes out."

"Friday. Comes out Friday morning."

"I sent it in to both. Marian helped me. I figured that it would be a good thing if people knew."

"It might be a good thing for us. I'm sorry, I didn't mean to be selfish."

"No, that's exactly what I've been thinking. We might be free someday."

There is a pause now as some seconds unspool. Two people breathing, dreaming.

"Are you really okay? I mean, I would understand if you're grieving."

"I cried last night when I thought about who we were, who James and I were, twenty years ago. When we first thought that we belonged together. I was young and naive, and he was brilliant. Or so I thought. I cried for all of about five minutes over who we tried to be. Not who we became. Not who I am now."

"When will—?"

"I want to come home."

"When?"

"I just want to come home to Doe Branch and curl up on the sofa and watch the fire burn in the fireplace and listen to you talk to me. That's all I want." She is whispering now.

"Come on, then."

"Friday afternoon. Friday night at the latest. Will you be there?"

"I'll be wherever you want me to be."

CHAPTER 47

THURSDAY MORNING, THE MORNING OF JAMES Metcalf's memorial service in Durham.

In the middle of that morning, Clinton's reveries are interrupted by a phone call from Charlie Burns, assistant DA for the county. Could he come to Burns's office at one o'clock that afternoon? His boss, James Eastman, is driving down from Boone to hold a strategy session.

"Oh, and Clinton—"

"Yes?"

"He goes by James, not Jim or Jimmy. And you better start out with Mr. Eastman, which is what you'll hear me call him."

"Formal, is he?"

"At times, very."

Clinton is alive to the irony—Catherine being the only other person who would catch it—that at the same time they're saying goodbye to one *James, not Jimmy* they're welcoming another into their lives.

JAMES EASTMAN IS TALL, FORMALLY DRESSED IN fine slacks and an expensive-looking wool blazer. His tie is conservative and perfectly knotted. He and Clinton get off to a rocky start, as Eastman introduces himself with, "University of Virginia plus UVA Law, district attorney for the Northwestern District of the State of North Carolina for twelve years, and veteran of a half dozen capital cases." Clinton replies with, "Marshall

High School, Mars Hill College, sheriff for eleven months, and veteran of the First Infantry Division, European operations."

They stare at each other for a long, increasingly tense moment without smiling before Charlie Burns offers, "Play nice, gentlemen. We're on the same side." Both men smile a little, the ice somewhat broken, and they begin.

From the moment they sit down, Eastman runs the meeting and for long moments, Clinton wonders if he's on trial. When he says as much, Eastman shakes his head and says, "No, but your evidence is."

They go over Fortner's sworn statement, along with how Clinton and his deputies identified Fortner and brought him in so quickly. They go over the collection of evidence from the SBI, including how soon they were on the scene and whether it was relatively undisturbed when they went to work. They go over the presumed series of events again, with Clinton defending his instincts and intuitions as well as the evidence thus far accumulated.

At one point, Eastman points out that if, indeed, Fortner never entered the house, then he can't testify as to who might have pulled the trigger on the old couple. He's not an eyewitness in the strictest sense of the word.

"Yeah, well," Clinton replies, "that's the third time this week I've heard that, once from Charlie here. Does it matter?"

"It matters because the two Crowders may be tried separately, if at all, probably with two separate attorneys, and each will blame the other. Best case, we nail them both; worst case, they both get off easy while blaming the other. *I was in the bathroom when Dad pulled the trigger*, and *I was upstairs when Junior lost his mind and fired*. That kind of thing. It would be better for us if Fortner was standing in the kitchen when it all went down."

"How do we get our hands on them?" This from Burns, although it was the question Clinton was dying to ask.

"Who's the sheriff in Cocke County?" Eastman asks. "I can't believe that's actually the name of the place."

"Good old boy named Lewis Sutton," Burns replies. "I've done a little research since Clinton and I talked on Monday. Prominent Republican family, if there is such a thing in Cocke County. Old-school mountain sheriff. Hates outsiders, especially longhairs. Manages to overlook most of the bootlegging and cock fighting that goes on while throwing kids in jail over a half dozen pot plants."

"Have you ever talked to him?" Eastman to Clinton.

"I called him right after the murders happened, just because the Nortons only lived a few miles from the state line. He was friendly at first, but when I let slip the killers might be from over his way, he sulled up fast."

"Sulled up?"

"Turned sullen. Offered that he ran a tight ship, and if there was anybody in his county who was even capable of such a thing, he would know about it."

At this point, the conversation pauses. Burns and Clinton wait on Eastman to comment. Which he finally does. "Give me a day or two to think this through, and I'll call my counterpart over there. Get a feel for Sheriff Sutton from him. With any luck, if the DA for Eastern Tennessee tells Sutton to arrest the Crowders, then he'll have to do it. And then we can probably extradite them without much trouble."

At this, Eastman stands up, and the proceedings take on a less serious tone while he packs up his briefcase. "I've got to say, Sheriff, that you and your boys worked fast to ID Fortner and get a statement out of him. Sure you weren't in the military police in the army?"

Clinton grins at this. "No, but I had some dealings with them once or twice. Or rather, they with me."

Eastman smiles with more warmth than before. "I only know one other Salter. An attorney in Chapel Hill, probably not in your circle."

"Is his name Matthew Salter?"

"Sure is. At the Institute of Government. You know him?"

"I raised him. He's my son, although he doesn't get home very often."

"Well, tell him I said hello next time you talk to him. Everybody down that way thinks he's got a future, in politics if nothing else." Eastman pauses to shake hands with Charlie Burns and then, more warmly now, with Clinton. "Young Mr. Salter just might be of some help to us in this case too, if we run into problems on the jurisdiction side of things."

"WARMED RIGHT UP WHEN HE FOUND OUT I was Matthew Salter's father, not just some army roughneck with a forty-five strapped to my hip and chaw of tobacco in my mouth." Clinton is telling Gloria Goforth about the meeting. "*Young Mr. Salter just might be of some help to us...if we run into jurisdiction problems.*" He says this last part in a prissy tone of voice, what Clinton imagines might be associated with the University of Virginia School of Law.

"He said politics?" Gloria asks. "Matthew has a future in politics?"

Clinton nods morosely. "What he said."

"Republican or Democrat?"

"How the hell would I know?"

"Ask Marian, why don't you. I'm curious."

HE DOESN'T ASK MARIAN, EVEN THOUGH SHE shows up at the jail around five to ask him if he'll buy her supper. "I just can't cook another meal. I'm tired, and I'm worried, and I need my daddy."

"Is the Rock Cafe good enough, or do you want me to drive you over to Mars Hill?"

"The cafe is fine. If he'll give us a quiet table. I do want to talk to you about Catherine, though."

"Let's talk as we walk. Say anything clandestine along the way."

"Clandestine?"

"That's our code word. Tongue in cheek. It means—"

"I know what it means. Jesus, Dad."

"You *are* tired."

She nods. They're on the sidewalk now and, without needing to plan it, turn right on Main Street rather than left, giving themselves a few minutes alone to exchange the news before entering the maelstrom of the Rock Cafe.

"Have you talked to her?" Marian asks.

"Yesterday—no, Tuesday. Said she'd be home tomorrow afternoon. She's bringing his ashes to spread up where they used to live."

Marian nods. "What she told me too. You know, I helped her with his obituary. He wasn't a fool, like you might expect. He was educated, learned even. Divinity school."

"She would never have married him if he was a fool." Clinton sighs. "He was probably brilliant in his own way. Even if he couldn't grow corn and beans."

"You're brilliant in your own way, Dad."

And for the first time that week, he laughs. Not just laughs, but stops, puts his hands on his knees, leans over and laughs straight out of his belly.

"I'm serious," she says, but even as she does, she starts to giggle as well. "Luke thinks you're brilliant. The dogs think you're brilliant."

Which only sets him off again. "I grant you—" He's having a hard time talking. "I grant you the dogs are a hell of a lot smarter than most people, but still..."

"She wants to come home," Marian manages to say after a moment. "And I get the feeling she thinks home has something to do with you."

"I want her to come home," he says finally. "In the worst way. Is it all right, Marian? I mean, is it all right with you that we're... *You*, Marian. Catherine and I both keep expecting you to wake up one morning and kick up an immortal fuss over... You know what I mean."

"It's fine with me, Dad. Truly." They are standing stock-still in the middle of the sidewalk. "She's my best friend, I think, even though she is my boss. And you're my dad. My only father. If I could ever have imagined it, I would have suggested it."

He nods, puts his arm around her shoulders. "So, here's what I think. I think that you, Luke, and I should plan a welcome home dinner for her."

"Friday night? She told me that she would probably be home tomorrow afternoon. I could cook."

"No, honey, I think Saturday. Up at the farm. You, me, Luke. The dogs." He hands her a folded slip of paper that he's carried around in his shirt pocket since Gloria handed it to him. On it, in Gloria's handwriting, is the message that Catherine left for him late that afternoon:

Tomorrow afternoon. Maybe late.

Doe Branch. Very tired and need to rest.

Please and thank you...C.

They eat easily together at the Rock Cafe: chewing, swallowing, smiling. As they eat, they agree on a special supper Saturday night at the farm. Reluctantly, she agrees to let him cook. She'll bring a dessert, and she'll bring Luke.

Over coffee, she tells him that they have something they want to talk to him about on Saturday.

"You mean you and Luke?"

"Yep, the two of us. And actually, Luke and I need to talk to both of you."

"Catherine and me?"

She nods. "You better prepare yourself," she says.

CHAPTER 48

HE COMES TO A DEEP REALIZATION FRIDAY AFternoon as he cleans the house, feeds the stock, and brings in enough wood for the fireplace to last the weekend. As he washes two potatoes to bake, as he marinates two chicken breasts in Worcestershire, salt, and pepper. Waiting until he knows her timing before committing all of this to the oven.

He assumed up until that afternoon that he was giving the farm to her as their lives unfolded. Or at least sharing it with her. As they spend more time there—day by day, night by night—he is giving himself to her by giving her the place. But that afternoon, having felt so far away from her for a week, the weather different in her absence, the temperature unexpectedly cold, the wind sharp and biting, he realizes that all this time, she's been giving the farm to him.

It is as if the farm, the real farm, had flown off into the night sky after Gretchen died and he was the only one living there. It had slowly disappeared into some other time, some other dimension, and he has been living alone in the shadows of the farm. It seemed to exist, it seemed real, but only as something has reality in a dream—deadened, muffled. He loved the steep pastures and fields and he took his strength there, but it wasn't the same as when he shared it with someone. So, there is a sense in which she is giving the land to him at the same time he is giving it to her. His deep, sensual relationship to Doe Branch—which is his relationship to himself—is returning to him.

CATHERINE CALLS HIM AT THE FARM JUST AFTER four o'clock from her mother's house in Asheville. She's leaving there in a few minutes to drive home.

"Home?"

"Where you just answered the phone, Clint. Home."

"Are you okay?"

"No, but I will be when I get there. It should be..."

"Figure ninety minutes. Five-thirty if you leave now."

"I'm leaving now. I need a drink."

AT FOUR-THIRTY, HE PUTS THE POTATOES IN THE oven to bake. At five, he puts the chicken in as well. She'll want cornbread, he knows, for a homecoming, so he spoons Crisco into the skillet and puts it in the oven to heat while he mixes the batter. Five-fifteen, he pours the hot oil into the batter, mixes the bread, and puts the skillet back in the oven.

Why is he so anxious, he wonders. She's an adult, she's a careful driver, she knows the way.

The hell with this, he thinks. *With this waiting.* Pulls on his old barn coat, jams the battered, wool fedora on his head, and with the dogs, strikes out up the road in the direction she will come. The dogs are beyond excited, as they normally don't get to explore in this direction. They are under the fences and into the woods on either side of the road, barking at rabbits, chasing in the leaves stirred up by the strong wind. The clouds threaten rain, he thinks.

When he reaches Bearwallow Gap, he stops at a curve in the gravel road where he can see down the other side of the hill toward Big Pine Creek and the pavement there. It is from here, leaning against a roadside boulder, that he hears the whine of the station wagon engine as it strains against the climb. The dogs recognize the sound too and come running to stand beside him, as ready as he is for her.

"WHAT WAS IT LIKE?" HE ASKS LATER, AFTER they have unloaded her car and rushed into the house ahead of the first heavy drops of rain and eaten hot food with the wine she brought. After she had changed into old, very comfortable clothes from the upstairs closet while he fed the fire on the hearth. After he made them each an old fashioned—doubles so that neither would have to get up off the couch anytime soon.

"What was it like?" he asks again, but quietly, unsure if she's ready to talk.

"Which part? Traveling with my mother? Dealing with his family, whom I hadn't seen in years? The actual memorial service? Missing the dogs?"

Nick regards them regally from the braided rug just in front of the fire, but Jake has managed to insert himself between them on the couch.

"Any of it," he replies. "All of it."

She pauses to think and he can tell she is only now beginning to relax. She sips her drink and tongues the whiskey before replying. "The weirdest part of the whole experience was that it kept hitting me that I was a stranger. No one knew me, not the me I am now."

"Even your mother?"

"Oh, she figured out that I had changed, even in the past year. We talked on the way back; I'll have to tell you about that later. But no one else. Everyone assumed that I was the grieving widow. That I would be distraught. That I would need their support and counsel. At the memorial service, people kept handing me Kleenex even though I wasn't crying. Afterward, I hugged his sister, shook hands with his cousins, said all the appropriate things about being in touch, always remembering, and so on. And on. Knowing full well that I'd probably never see any of them again. It was strange, Clint. Like some episode of *The Twilight Zone*, where I was playing myself, but the self I was playing wasn't me.

"Oh, and one more thing. I found out that they all blamed me for him running off to live in the middle of nowhere. They assumed that their lovely boy, James, had lost his mind when he met me and that I had somehow convinced him to give up a promising future to become a dirt farmer. That's what his sister called it, *dirt farming*. I tried to explain to his aunt that it was exactly the other way around, but she only nodded knowingly and said, *Then why are you still there, honey, if it wasn't you in the first place*?"

She is smiling ruefully at the memory and he laughs at the look on her face.

"So, it was all your fault?"

"It was all my fault that their darling boy ran off to wear overalls. Even though the boy was way over thirty at the time. And then here I was at his funeral, apparently not the least upset that he had died. You could tell they wanted tears, remorse, grief, something, and I had none to give. I almost tried to fake a tear or two, but couldn't quite bring myself. My mother cried for both of us."

"Do I want to meet your mother?"

"Oh, lord!" She laughs now and he can tell the heat from the fire and the bourbon are having their effect. "Someday, you'll have to meet her, I suppose. But not tonight. God forbid. Not tonight. Tonight, I just want to sleep."

She sets her glass on the coffee table, which causes him to take the last sip from his own and place his glass there as well. He shoves Jake off the couch gently so that she can ease over into his arms. They stretch out side by side so that he can hold her, adding his own warmth, his own breath, to that which comforts her.

IT'S ONLY IN THE MORNING, WHEN SHE HAS SLEPT soundly through the night, that he asks her about the day. He has been up once during the night, after the storm blew through, to let the dogs out. And is up early again to let them run outside at dawn. And while they're out in the new-made weather, he brings her coffee in bed, as has become, almost, their custom.

She sits up when he comes back into the bedroom and he remembers that the night before, she managed to slip on a pair of his underwear and one of his T-shirts to sleep in, an outfit that she gives a different sort of meaning to. "Good morning," he whispers. "Welcome home."

She smiles sleepily and caresses his fingers when he hands her the coffee mug.

He goes back downstairs for his own mug and brings his coffee back up so that he can sit with her. In this early, easy time, he tells her their plan: that Marian, Luke, and he want to give her a welcome home supper. Not, perhaps, a memorial service, but a party after the service, where she can relax and just be.

"Tonight?" she asks over the rim of her mug.

He nods. "Tonight, if that's okay."

"Mmm. More than okay. Who's cooking?"

"I am."

"Why don't we do it together?" she asks, and when he starts to protest, "After this week, I want to do a hundred things with you, Clint Salter, and cooking is one of them. I've missed you."

"Together then. Marian is bringing dessert. And Luke. Oh, and they have something serious they want to tell us."

"Tell us—or tell you?"

"Us, apparently. Marian said *us*, as in you and me."

She sits up suddenly and sloshes some coffee out onto their blankets. "What do you think it is?"

He shakes his head. "That they're leaving, maybe. Graduate school? That he's taken a job somewhere, and she's going with him?"

"You don't think they're getting married?"

"Maybe, but they have yet to seem like the marrying kind."

"Hmm. Okay. Do you have any champagne, just in case?"

"God, no. I hate champagne."

"An expensive bottle of wine then?"

"Yes. That I have. I bought it for when you came home."

"That's sweet. So, we'll save the good stuff for the announcement, just in case it's something to celebrate." She pauses to drain her mug. "Clint, can we do something else? I mean, today?" She's awake now...and excited.

"Sure. What is it?"

"Will you call Marian and ask them to come on up early afternoon? I thought we might all go together up to the head of Anderson Branch. I can show you where I tried to live for seven years. And we can let dear old James Metcalf's ashes fly across the countryside."

"Are you sure?"

"Very sure. I don't want to do it alone. I want to do it with *my* family. Not *his* family and definitely not my mother. I want to do it with you and Marian, Luke too. Is that okay? Do you think I'm crazy?"

He laughs, partially at her excitement and partially at the idea of their made-up, folded-together family. "That's not crazy at all," he says finally. "I've been wondering where you lived."

THEY LINGER FOR A BIT LONGER, SHE NESTLED beneath the covers, he fully dressed on top. Each aware of the other, each thinking of ways to induce the other to stay, go deeper. But she's too excited about the day to linger long in bed.

When she stands and stretches, walks around the foot of the bed in her makeshift pajamas, he watches her as if it is the first time he's ever really seen her—in this form, in this light. Long-legged, supple, flowing, every bit of her a dance.

CHAPTER 49

MIDAFTERNOON, THE FOUR OF THEM DRIVE TOgether in the Jeep from the farm on Doe Branch down to the river at Barnard. Then, rather than crossing the bridge back toward Marshall and points beyond, Clint turns right up Anderson Branch. They pass a small, hard-shell Baptist church partway up the branch, and just at the top where the old Ben Freeman farm once lay nestled into the top of the cove, Catherine directs Clinton to turn to the right up an even sorrier excuse for a road.

Clinton points out the path to the Freeman Cemetery on the left, and they keep going, bucking and bouncing over the ruts and rocks, down into a wide, overgrown field, which fills up the next cove and then rises again through tall grass and weeds to the top of a second ridge, where Catherine directs him to park beside a rusted-out hay rake. Clinton can tell where fences ran the edges of the property from the joe-pye and ironweed stalks, along with a few remaining locust posts.

From the Jeep, the four of them walk through the high, tousled weeds to a small house, built long ago and falling now into disrepair. There's a porch of sorts, collapsed on one end, a gaping open doorway, and two busted-out windows on the front. A rock chimney on the closest end that stands straight and true, such that you know it will still point to the sky long after the rest of the house falls in beside it.

"This is it?" Marian whispers.

Catherine nods and grins. "I know. It's not what you expected, is it?"

"It's...tiny."

Catherine laughs. "Marian, honey, trust me, it's even smaller on the inside."

Clinton is standing beside Catherine, watching the side of her face as she regards the house she lived in for seven summers and seven winters.

"How many rooms?" Luke asks.

"Depends on how you define *rooms*. Three, really. What you might call a living room/bedroom, a kitchen with a woodstove in it, and a bathroom about the size of a large closet. Did have running water, though."

"Electricity?" Clinton asks.

"Do you see any power lines?" She is still grinning, enjoying just how stunned they are.

"He brought you to this?" Marian.

"He did. The plan was always to camp out here until we could build a house further along the ridge. He still had some trust fund money at that point, and we were going to use it to build a beautiful house with views in every direction."

Luke and Marian turn to look around them at the mountains. Clinton and Catherine turn to look at each other. "Lord, Cat," he whispers. "I had no idea."

"It was a dream," she says back to him, ever so quietly. "The man could dream."

"And in the winter?"

"In the winter, it was a nightmare."

When Marian and Luke turn back to the two of them, Marian can see the sadness in Catherine's eyes, but also the smile flickering at the corners of her mouth. Catherine holds out an inexpensive wooden container, roughly the size of a cigar box, and says to all of them: "I say we walk a little way along the ridge and give dear old James Metcalf back to his version of paradise."

"However you like," says Clinton.

A moment later, when she lifts the lid and holds up the box, the wind off the higher ridges whips the ashes away over the field below and scours the empty box.

"Now, he can stay here in peace," Luke offers, all any of them can think of to say.

Catherine tosses the box back in the direction of the tumble-down house and tucks her hand under Clinton's arm. As Marian and Luke start back down the slope toward the Jeep, wading through the tall grass, she reaches into her jeans pocket and holds up her left hand where only Clint can see it. She's holding something loosely between her fingers—her wedding ring—which she tosses after the box.

"Sure you don't want to keep it?" he asks.

She laughs, lets him see her whole mouth, her whole face, while she turns it up to the sun and shakes her hair free in the breeze. "Quite sure," she says. "It belongs right here, among the ruins."

AFTER CLINTON AND CATHERINE PUT POTATOES in the oven to bake and start a pot of green beans boiling on the stove, he goes outside to build a charcoal fire in a stone grill that is as old as the house. While he and Luke are outside collaborating on cleaning out the grill and starting a blaze under the charcoal, Catherine and Marian have a few minutes alone in the kitchen.

"I saw Matthew last week," Marian says, "and I'm trying to decide whether to tell Dad or not."

"Where did you see him?"

"Luke and I went into Asheville for dinner Wednesday. And lo and behold, we ran straight into my brother at the restaurant."

She pauses, but Catherine doesn't interrupt her train of thought.

"He was here for some big Democratic planning meeting. Preparing for something called the Vance-Aycock Dinner next month. At first, he didn't have much to say to us, didn't want to introduce us to the men he was with, but once he got going, we could tell he wanted us to know just how big a deal it all is. How big a deal he is."

"Why not tell your dad?"

"I don't know. I always feel like it hurts his feelings to be reminded that Matt was right here, less than an hour away, and he never even bothered to let us know. In particular, he never bothered to let Dad know."

Catherine shrugs. "Tell him. If you don't, then you end up keeping secrets from him as well. It's not going to hurt his feelings any worse than Matthew has already. Besides, I don't keep things from him. Now that you've told me, it's as good as telling him."

"I know, I know. Sometimes I'd like to slap my brother. He's just so damn different from the rest of us. When I was a kid, I thought he might be adopted."

THE MEAL IS AS PERFECT AS A MEAL CAN BE. THE steaks come in smoking from the grill, tender and succulent. The potatoes are steaming on the inside and crusty on the outside. Salt and pepper, swimming in butter. The green beans are savory with bacon grease. Clinton gives what, for him, amounts to a little speech over the bottle of cabernet. Bought for Catherine, shared with those who love her.

The conversation flows truly and well, through school and work, the progress of the Norton murder case, Catherine's memories of the coldest winters she spent in the house they saw that afternoon. How she hung her school clothes in the barn so they wouldn't stink of woodsmoke, and how she had to park all the way down on Anderson Branch so her car wouldn't get snowed in.

When Clinton and Catherine serve ice cream for dessert, Marian tells her dad about seeing Matthew three nights before in Asheville. Big Democratic meeting. The Vance-Aycock Dinner. That Matt might go to work for the governor's office. Clinton masks his surprise as one revelation follows another, shows no emotion other than curiosity. "He has the right kind of personality for politics," is all he says.

They stack the dishes in the sink for later and Clinton lets the dogs out to run for a bit. The four of them settle in the living room. Clinton builds an old fashioned for Catherine and one for himself. He offers wine or whiskey to Marian and Luke. She accepts another splash of wine, but Luke refuses since he still has to drive them back over the river to civilization.

Once they're all comfortable, Clinton smiles warmly at his daughter, whom he loves. "Is that what you wanted to talk to us about?" he asks. "About Matthew, I mean?"

Marian shakes her head. "No, Dad, it isn't."

CHAPTER 50

DESPITE THE WARMTH, DESPITE THE FLICKER OF firelight, despite the food and drink, a wave of tension washes through the room. Nobody speaks. The only sound is the crackle of the wood on the hearth being consumed in flame.

Everyone's eyes are on Marian now. She, in turn, is focused on her father's face.

"How would you feel about being a grandfather?" she whispers.

He clears his throat. "What?"

"I said, How would you feel about being a grandfather?"

He closes his eyes, as suddenly there is more light in the room than he can withstand. He feels the rush of adrenaline rising through his body, and he can sense his hands begin to shake.

"Oh, Marian." This from Catherine. "This is the most—"

"He's crying," Marian says. "Dad, are you crying?"

He opens his eyes and nods. "Maybe," he mutters.

"Are you upset?" Catherine asks him.

He shakes his head. "Happy," he manages to say. "Just happy."

"Aren't you mad?" Marian asks. "Or scared or—at least frustrated at Luke and me for being so stupid?"

His head is still shaking back and forth and his eyes are closed again. "No," he whispers. "Why would I be?"

"What he's trying to say," Catherine offers, "is that he loves you two. That he wants what you want. And even if this is...

unplanned, it can still be one of the best things that could possibly happen."

"Sir." Luke clears his throat. "In front of these witnesses, I would like to ask your permission to marry your daughter."

Clinton can't help himself; he laughs outright. "It's a little late for that, son, don't you think?"

"Too late for getting married?" Luke looks stunned.

"No. Too late for asking. Getting married, you should probably consider. And, of course, you have my blessing. Today and all days."

And soon, Catherine thinks but doesn't say. *Knowing public opinion and the damn school board.*

AFTER A TOAST TO THE FUTURE, THEY SEE MARian and Luke out to their car. It's so late in September as to flirt with October, and the dusky dark is cold, the leaves in the maple beside the house rattling in the wind. There is much hugging on the porch, including a hard, chest-to-chest embrace between Clinton and Luke. An even longer squeeze between the women, who whisper fiercely to each other.

When they are back inside and the dogs with them, Cat tells Clinton just to leave the dishes. "I'll wash them in the morning, I swear," she says. "Is there any bourbon left in the bottle?"

He holds up said bottle before the light of the fire and then nods. "A splash for you and one for me. Enough for a toast."

Glasses in hand, standing in front of the hearth. "This feels like more of the future," he says and she grins.

"Yes, it does. I don't quite know how we get there from here, but God knows. How do you feel about being a grandfather?"

"I'm already there," he says. "We're going to teach this child to ride and shoot. To walk in the woods, to gather apples up in Anderson Cove. He or she, I don't care which, is going to spend the summers right here on the farm, with us. And read more books than anyone ever could imagine."

"*Us* who?"

"You and me, his grandparents."

"What are you saying, Clint?"

"I don't know what I'm saying exactly. But the only way I can imagine it is with you. Here."

She is terrified, just for a moment. And elated. Just now, the elation outlasts the terror, burning it away in a flicker of golden heat. She holds out her glass toward this dear man she's only recently come to know. "To the future then," she says.

They click glasses. "Was. Is. Will be," is what he says in return.

The whiskey touches them equally, burning cold and smooth on their tongues.

"God, Clint," she says. "Lead me upstairs and take me to bed. Make love to me like you mean it."

"I will always mean it," he says. "Until the day they roll me in a hole and throw dirt on me, I will mean it."

CHAPTER 51

For once, he sleeps soundly and she is restless. Twice during the night, she gets up, wraps herself in his robe and stares out the bedroom windows, listening to the wind toss in the trees outside and shove against the side of the house. The wind, when it truly gathers itself to push down from the ridges above, moans under the eaves and around the corners. Listening, she can sense winter lurking on the mountain.

She can hear the hooting of an owl from up near the cemetery. If Clint were awake, he could tell her what kind.

After all this time alone, alone both before James Metcalf's accident and even more so after, she is surprised to find how easily she has slipped into a life with this man. The man sleeping there under the covers. It is surprising to her that she isn't more afraid than she is, more anxious about their future. More reluctant to give herself to him, so soon and so completely.

But here she is, listening to the wind, and there he is. Close, very close. How to go through, she wonders, from here to there? How to make this sacred place into future days and future nights?

And so it is, on this morning, that it's her who is downstairs early, her who lets the dogs out the kitchen door, her who brings him coffee in bed, just as he's stretching into some sort of wakefulness.

They sit up in bed together, sipping. She in his old wool robe, he naked, the cool air prickling his skin. The coffee hot on the tongue.

"I think there are a lot of things we need to talk about," she says, after giving him a few minutes to come alive. "Before I go back to town this afternoon, I think there are a lot of things..."

"Do we need an agenda?" He is half serious, half teasing.

She nods, still serious, though there is humor in her voice. "Probably. I have items and I bet you do too. Once you stop to think about it."

"What are some of yours?"

"First thing, practical thing, is to get them married. You're from here and know better than I do, but it seems like people will accept a baby being born eight months after a wedding. With, you know..."

"A wink and a grin."

"With a wink and grin. But I don't trust the preachers on the school board for one second. And if she's going to keep on teaching, and she told me last night she has every intention, then it should happen soon."

He nods. "You're right. So, item one is a wedding. What's two?"

"Depends. Depends on how you feel about Matthew, what Marian told us last night about seeing him in Asheville. About... politics. Do we need to talk about it, do anything about it? Will Marian invite him to the wedding?"

He shifts uncomfortably in bed and pulls the quilt up to his chest. "I talked to him last week, and it was..."

"It was...?"

"Awful. For me, at least. I'll tell you about it over breakfast. It had to do with the Norton murders. And for now, I'm just angry."

"Angry at Matthew?"

He nods and drinks from his mug. "Oh, yes. At Matthew. And I don't imagine getting over being angry anytime soon."

"That's probably healthy." And then, after a pause: "Are the murders on the agenda?" she asks.

"Have to be. For me, anyway. Things are starting to get very complicated, and I have no intention of letting the Crowder boys slip through the cracks just because everyone else thinks they can't be touched."

"Complicated?"

"More so every day."

"Well, whatever you do, Clint, you have to be careful. You know that, right?" She sets her mug on the rickety bedside table and turns around to sit cross-legged, facing him. "Do you even know what *careful* is?"

"I hear you," he finally says. "I understand. What else is on the agenda?"

"Us."

"What?"

"You and me. We're the last item on the agenda."

He grins. "What's there to talk about?"

She closes her eyes and lets her face open to him, even lets her grin broaden so that he can see the gap in her teeth as she starts to giggle. "In case you haven't noticed, Clint, I'm a woman. I'm in love and I need to talk."

"You're in what?"

"You heard me."

AFTER BREAKFAST, THEY BUNDLE UP AND GO FOR a walk with the dogs, down to the road in front of the house, where they pause to wave at Randall Shelton, who is standing on his porch regarding the morning.

"You going to church?" Clint calls to him.

"Maybe," Randall replies. "Maybe I'll let it come to me."

Once they turn to walk up the hill toward Bearwallow Gap, the dogs race on ahead, chasing myriad smells in the chill autumn air. When they reach the gap where Clint waited for her on Friday night, they pause to catch their breath. "What are you thinking about Marian's wedding?" he asks her.

"Maybe it's because I'm a woman," she replies, "or maybe it's because I've been in the public eye for years, but I think that the sooner they get married, the better. I laid awake at one point last night counting on my fingers, and the baby should come almost at the end of school in June."

"We can't wait until Christmas?"

"I'm not sure we should wait until Thanksgiving."

"Will you talk to her about it?" He puts his arm around her shoulders, partly out of plain, physical affection; partly because of what he's asking her to do. "You're better at it than I would be."

She nods. "I thought I'd call her as soon as I get home this afternoon."

"Home?"

"Well, it's not really home. The little house on Roberts Hill Road. I haven't been there since Monday afternoon, and I have to somehow get organized for school tomorrow. Get myself ready for life out there." She points in the general direction of the river and beyond.

"Will you call and tell me what she says? What the two of you decide?"

She nods. "Of course, I will. Are you staying here tonight?" And when he nods yes, they start walking up the old road toward the Divide Mountain. "Tell me about the murders now, will you?"

He does. The Fortner boy's confession. His implicating the Crowders, father and son. The reaction from Sutton, the Cocke County sheriff. Two meetings with the district attorneys.

"Where does Matthew figure into it?" she asks. "You said you spoke to him about all of this."

"He called me from the Institute of Government after I asked them for advice on jurisdiction. What I could and couldn't do. Turns out, Matthew is an expert on jurisdiction."

"But that's good, right? You actually got to talk to him."

"I don't know if I talked to him. It was mostly *him* talking at *me* in my official role as sheriff. No, that's not right. He lectured me. Told me my hands were tied and that I'd better stay out of the way and do what the DA told me. 'Follow his instructions to the letter,' he said and then asked me if I knew what *to the letter* meant."

"Oh lord, Clint. I'm sorry. I want to meet this young man."

"You may get a chance if we're going to have a wedding. I might even get to see him myself."

"You *are* angry, aren't you?"

"Yes, but me being mad doesn't touch him, apparently."

"Maybe. I'm not so sure." She reaches out to take his hand as they walk. "Oh, one more agenda item we forgot this morning. What about the barn burnings, whoever it was in the upper pasture that night? What was it, a week ago?"

"Seems like a year rather than a week, doesn't it? I haven't had time to think much about it since. Randall's been standing guard at night. But it's always there in the back of my mind. It's personal now and I mean to put an end to it."

They pause while he points out the Big Pine valley on the far side of the ridge, where the road follows the creek up toward Worley. It's quieter there in the trees, although they can hear the wind like a freight train further up the ridge. He lets go of her hand to put his arm around her shoulders again, and she leans into him. "What about us?" he asks her. "Now that you're free in the eyes of the world and you've had a week to think about it, what about us?"

"What I think is that in six months, give or take, we can go anywhere we want in public."

"Months? I was thinking more like six days."

"You do live in your own world, don't you, Clint? If you weren't the sheriff and I wasn't the principal, we might get away with it. But I don't think anybody, even the Madison County school board, would argue with six months. People will still talk, still speculate on how long we were seeing each other before James died, but what the hell. Let them talk. At that point, I don't think it matters. I do wonder what being involved with me will do to your chances of getting reelected."

"I don't want to get reelected if it means giving up my life."

"Yes, you do. We've had that conversation before. But truthfully, what I worry about is how we'll do when we're out there in the world where people stare at us and gossip behind our backs. Like we're in some sort of shooting gallery. Known, recognized, talked about. We're pretty damn good at *clandestine*—sometimes I think we even relish it. But will we be as good at normal?"

"I know the answer to that," he says.

"There's more. If you really want me—and I mean it, Clint, really want me all in your life—and we're together all the time, or at least as much as our two jobs will allow, will you get tired of me?"

"I think—"

"All week I've been scared that...now that you know me, do you even want me? You didn't get a chance to say because I cut you off, twice."

He's laughing by this point. Laughing at just about everything about her: her voice, her fears, the look on her face.

"Stop laughing at me." She is trying not to smile.

"Can't help it." Playfully, he puts his free hand over her mouth. "Since you're in love and we're talking, let me say something."

"Hmm."

"I think I told you yesterday, last night—hell, sometime in

the last twenty-four hours, I can't imagine my next life without you. I meant it when I said it. No, let me finish. Can't imagine much of any life now without you. We both know what it is to be unhappy, right?"

He lets her nod yes.

"And we know what loneliness is. And now, to have somebody. To have each other. There's nothing in these last weeks that makes me think we can't handle people staring at us and talking about us. Like you said, the hell with them. And there's nothing we've done or felt together that makes me think we won't be even happier when we don't have to say goodbye on Sunday afternoon. I think we've earned the right to be happy seven days a week, not just one or two."

"Do you think you'll ever get married again?"

"Does it matter?"

"It might. In time."

"You're not pregnant, are you?"

It takes her a moment to realize he's teasing. "Nope. Don't think it's possible. But there are other reasons why people get married."

"There are?"

"You know good and damn well there are, Clinton Salter."

He squeezes her hand. "I might find a rich widow to marry," he offers.

"I think you better give up on the rich part," is all she says.

CHAPTER 52

TOGETHER, MARIAN AND CATHERINE PERFORM a small miracle of planning and preparation.

The wedding is set for Saturday, October 9, two weeks after Marian breaks the news about her delicate condition to her father and Catherine. Two o'clock in the chapel at Mars Hill College, where the groom, Luke Spencer, teaches mathematics. After meeting with the young couple, the college chaplain—a staunch Baptist preacher old enough to be their grandfather—agrees to perform the ceremony.

Clinton's brother, Will, and his family are invited. Luke's parents and his two sisters from over in Tennessee are invited. All twelve teachers at Marshall High School are invited. Marian's brother, Matthew, and his high-society girlfriend are invited...twice.

Catherine writes to Matthew in her role as maid of honor and receives no reply at all. Marian calls him at home the weekend before and gets a maddening response. *Maybe...probably not...very busy...will be in Asheville on the twenty-third for a political event... might stop by then if schedule permits...will let her know.* Marian is so mad when she tells Catherine about the conversation that she calls him a "precious little prick," and Catherine doesn't disagree. They decide to tell Clinton that Matthew can't attend on such short notice because of his schedule but sends his love.

October 9, 1965, dawns bright and cold, but by that afternoon, the sun has warmed the autumn air into a suffused radiance. The college campus is especially beautiful, and everything goes off without a hitch. The chaplain performs the ceremony without preaching a sermon, the organist from the music department provides a sweet, slow rendition of "Amazing Grace," and Marian herself is simply radiant.

After the ceremony, everyone gathers in the college cafeteria for a reception provided by Marian's fellow teachers, where Luke's family blends effortlessly with the Salters, Catherine, and Marian's teacher friends. It is as if, for a few hours, everything is just as Catherine and Marian hoped it would be. And perhaps only Clinton remembers to miss Matthew, who, by all rights, should be there—for his sister, if no one else.

During the reception, Will works the room as if he's a politician running for office, such that any innocent bystander would assume he is the father of the bride rather than Clinton. In particular, he goes out of his way to remind all the teachers present that they work for him, even while Catherine keeps quietly reassuring them that it's not true. Clinton and Catherine are friendly, but no more than that, behaving toward each other more or less as they act in relation to the others who are there. Even so, Luke's mother makes the mistake of assuming they are a couple and apologizes when Marian explains that one is her father and the other her boss.

After Marian and Luke leave for a night at the Grove Park Inn—Clinton's present—he and Catherine are the last to depart, having cleaned up the cafeteria and paid the chaplain. She drives away first while he stops to talk to a group of students in the parking lot.

LATER THAT NIGHT, HE CALLS HER FROM THE farm. She's at her bungalow, where she's been sleeping for the past two weeks while she helped Marian prepare for the wedding.

"Are you still awake?" he asks her.

"Reading," she replies. "Waiting on the father of the bride to call."

"As the father of the bride, I'm thanking you."

"You already thanked me, twice at least."

"Three times, then. You made today happen."

He can hear her chuckle, soft and breathy. "It was what we hoped it would be," she says.

"Are you in bed?"

"Yes, and just this side of asleep. But I'm sitting up now because I want you to tell me something."

"What's that?"

"What do you plan to do about the Crowders? I've asked you a couple of times over the past ten days, and you very neatly, very cleverly avoid the question."

"Well, the DA is trying. His counterpart in Tennessee is stalling and we figure it's because the sheriff won't pick them up."

"So, you're stuck?"

"We're stuck. Eastman, the DA, says it could take weeks, if not months, and we're all afraid that the sheriff will warn the Crowders. Probably related to them somehow. Cousins or something. Are you sure you want to know what—"

"Yes, Clint. I'm sure I want to know what you plan to do. I worry more about what I don't know than what I do."

"I plan to lure them across the state line and arrest them myself."

"How in the world?"

"There's a little picnic area just this side of the line, where our boy, Fortner, picked them up and dropped them off that night. Where they threatened him within an inch of his life. I plan to have him call them and tell them he's in trouble and ask them to meet him there."

"Surely they're not that stupid."

"Surely they are. Or at least surely they might be. Plus, when I go back and reread Fortner's statement, the son comes across as a thoroughgoing sadist. The father not much better. Nothing they would like better than the chance to shut Fortner up for good."

There's a pause while she's thinking. Then: "I have two questions. One, are you sure it's legal? Isn't luring them over the line entrapment or something like that?"

"What's your other question?"

"Isn't it dangerous? I mean, you just said they are sadistic killers and you're going to be right in the middle of it, aren't you?"

Now, it's his turn to pause. "One, I think it is legal. Judge Gudger says it's legal enough for this part of the world. And once we have them in custody, we can separate them and see if they won't incriminate each other."

"Dangerous, Clint? The picnic area?"

"Yes, I'll be there. I can't ask a handful of deputies to do something I wouldn't do myself."

"Oh, Clint. When?"

"Soon."

CHAPTER 53

"PUT YOUR DADDY ON THE LINE, JIMMY. I AIN'T talking to you. None of your damn business. I need to talk to your daddy."

Jason Fortner is sweating even though it's cool inside Clinton's office. He's sitting at Clinton's desk using Clinton's phone, and he has Jimmy Crowder on the line. Judge Gudger, Way Tipton, and Gloria Goforth are all seated around the outside of the room. Gloria is taking notes. Clinton sits beside Fortner to steady him. And write him directions on the pad in front of him if necessary.

"Bob, is that you? Bob? I ain't call you if it wasn't a goddamn emergency. The sheriff's been out here all morning searching and asking questions. They think I killed Uncle Grady and Aunt Bonnie. I know they do."

A pause.

"I didn't tell them nothing 'bout you and Jimmy. I did just what you said. But I got to get out of here... What?

"You heard me. I said I got to get the hell out of here. I'm going to Florida or some damn place like that where they'll never find me. But Bob—listen to me, Bob. I got to have some money. I'm stone cold broke...

"Gas, food, enough to get across two or three states. I'm telling you—"

A long pause. Fortner's hands are shaking. Not just with fear, Clinton thinks, but with anger now too.

"You got to help me, Bob. If they take me in, I'm telling them everything you done. You hear me—

"Naw, I ain't coming over there. You'll let Jimmy kill me. What? Naw, I ain't coming to no Thunderbird neither. Meet me at that little campground where we left your car that night."

Clinton scrawls the words *PICNIC AREA* on the pad in large, block letters.

"You know where I mean, that picnic area where we split up after— When? Tonight, goddamn it. Tonight! Salter and his bunch will be all over me by tomorrow...

"All right. Nine o'clock... Yeah, I know how to tell time. Nine...o'clock. And you'll never see me after. I'll be to hell and gone."

Fortner starts to say "goodbye," but everyone in the room can tell the line is already dead.

Judge Gudger hauls himself up out of his chair, walks over, and places his hand on Fortner's shoulder. "You should get an Academy Award, son," is all he says.

"What's that?" Jason Fortner asks.

CLINTON'S DILEMMA IS WHETHER TO TELL CATHerine before or after. After Fortner is safely back upstairs in his cell and the group has dispersed, he calls Gloria in to ask her advice.

"I think you know her better than I do," Gloria says. "What has she said about it already?"

"She says she worries more about what she doesn't know than what she does."

"There's your answer, Clint. You better tell her and in person. And don't, for God's sake, write her a note or leave her a message."

Round about three-thirty, when he suspects Catherine to be winding up her day, Clinton walks over the bridge to the island

and climbs up the stairs to the first floor of the high school. For once, luck is with him, and he finds her alone in her office, her secretary already gone for the day.

He steps in, closes the door behind him, and sits down on the other side of her desk.

"Sheriff Salter?" she says, nonplussed for a moment. "What can I do for you?"

"I just wanted to let you know that we're picking up the Crowder boys tonight."

"Damn you, Clint," she whispers.

"Cat, I need to."

"I know. You promised the dog."

"I did."

"What time?"

"Nine. Out near the state line."

She looks down at her hands where they rest on her desk. Then looks back up to meet his eyes. Nods. "All right. Please, for my sake, be careful. And call me afterward, no matter how late."

CLINTON DRIVES THE DEPUTIES HARD THAT AFternoon. He sends Way Tipton to Asheville with Jason Fortner, transferring Fortner for the time being to the Buncombe County jail. He sends Dwayne Austin and Danny Fender up to Fortner's mother's place to borrow Fortner's car for the night. And then he rides up to the picnic area with Balis Norton to inspect the lay of the land.

By eight o'clock that night, they are all in place. They park Fortner's old Chevy roughly where he met the Crowders the night of the murders. Thankfully, it is tucked away from the two Forest Service streetlights, so it won't be obvious there is no one in the car. Sam Ray is waiting in the Jeep a couple of hundred feet down the road, parked in the trees, ready to pull in behind the Crowders and block the exit. The rest of the deputies are scattered in the trees around the spot itself, and all are armed. Clinton has given them a stiff lecture about not shooting first, but protecting themselves if things get hot.

Tensions rise and fall as various cars from the Tennessee side drive in around the curves and pass the entrance to the area. At eight-thirty, a carful of teenagers from the North Carolina side turns in at the entrance, the kids obviously looking for a place to party. Clinton sends them on their way in language so strong that the two boys and two girls in the car quite likely go straight home and never have a "picnic" there again.

Eight forty-five, and a car matching the description Fortner gave them approaches from Tennessee, slows, and turns into the area. From where he stands behind the trunk of an ancient oak, Clinton hears the engine of the Jeep cough into life farther down the road, and he knows the entrance will be blocked shortly. "Come on," he keeps whispering to himself over and over, "come on," as if watching an animal approaching a trap, sniffing the bait.

The Crowder vehicle pulls up two spots down from Jason Fortner's car. The headlights blink off, even though the engine is still running. Someone, presumably Jimmy Crowder, gets out of the passenger side, eases around the back of the vehicle and approaches Fortner's car. He is calling out in a weird, high, sing-song voice, "Jason, oh, Jason, come on out, Jason. We brought you some sweet cabbage for your trip."

Clinton's eyes are well enough adjusted to the dark, so he can see that the man approaching the car holds something that looks like a pistol out in front of his body, but even so, he isn't prepared when the figure steps up to the side of the car and opens fire straight through the glass of the passenger-side window. Shattering the glass on both sides and filling the car with bullets, laughing like a lunatic the whole time.

The smell of cordite fills the cold night air and for a flash-lit moment, Clinton is back in Germany, with death on the ground.

"Go," he shouts so loud he can feel his vocal cords straining. "Go now!" And he is running, straight around the back of Fortner's car, with the .45 in hand. Jimmy Crowder hears him as he is pausing to reload, having just emptied his gun. When Clinton rushes at him from the back of the car, Jimmy points the empty pistol at him and pulls the trigger repeatedly, still laughing like he is deranged.

Clinton tells him twice to drop the damn gun, and when he doesn't, steps forward, still gasping for breath, and clips Crowder over the ear with the cold, hard barrel of the .45. Once and then a second time backhand, which finally knocks the boy to the ground.

The old man backs up hard, spitting gravel over a wide swath and slams his car straight into a tree. When he jumps out, cussing, and begins to run for the entrance, Danny Fender tackles him to the gravel road just like he tackled a ballcarrier ten years before, playing football for North Buncombe High School. Tackles him so hard that he cracks the old man's wrist and sprains his own ankle.

It is midnight before everything is sorted out, with Robert Crowder (father) and James Crowder (son) of 47 Lawson Road, Newport, Tennessee, locked in separate cells on the second floor of the Madison County jail.

It's one in the morning when Clinton calls Catherine, his voice hoarse from yelling, his back and neck aching with fatigue.

"Yes, hello! Clinton, please say it's you."

"It *is* me. It is."

"Are you...?"

"I'm fine, I swear."

"Why are you so hoarse?"

"There was a lot of yelling. Me mostly."

"Who were you yelling at?"

"The deputies, directing traffic. And then the son, Jimmy Crowder, was either strung out on something or just...crazed." He pauses to clear his throat.

"Was anyone else...?"

"No. No one was killed. The old man may have broken his wrist when Fender threw him on the ground, and Fortner's car was shot to pieces, which is nothing but evidence now. But no, everyone walked away, with our Tennessee friends in handcuffs."

There is a pause. Both exhausted, both reaching out tenderly with their minds toward the other.

"When can I see you?" It's her voice, husky now as well. "I want to make sure you're as okay as you say you are."

"Tomorrow night." His voice is speaking almost without his mind, which is exhausted. "Let's meet outside of town, go somewhere for supper."

"Sit and talk?"

He's nodding and then remembers she can't see him through the telephone and so speaks, hoarser now than before. "Sit and talk. Like two old friends, who..."

"Enjoy each other's company." She finishes his thought.

"That. Just that."

Again, silence. Comfortable and breathy.

"I'll call you tomorrow at the jail," she whispers. "When we're not exhausted. We'll figure something out." She imagines that he's nodding yes, and perhaps nodding toward sleep. "Good night, Clint," she whispers. "I'm glad you're alive."

CHAPTER 54

"WHAT THE HELL DO YOU MEAN, CLINTON, *They're in custody*?"

"I mean that the Crowders came over into North Carolina of their own free will, and when they did, we picked them up." Thursday morning early, and Clinton is on the phone with the assistant DA, Charlie Burns.

"Why is it that I don't quite trust that nice, simple Mayberry version of events? How did you trick them into coming over? No, don't tell me. Are you at the jail?" He pauses long enough for Clinton to answer in the affirmative. "Then come on over to the courthouse. I'll get some coffee going."

"Give me thirty minutes, Charlie. I'm expecting a call back from the SBI. Thirty minutes, and I'll know more than I do now."

THE SBI AGREES TO SEND THE SAME CRIME LAB team as before to the picnic area. The Park Service has locked the gate there; Dwayne Austin and Sam Ray are standing guard. The Fortner car and the Crowder car are right where they were after the events of the night before. Untouched. Neither Austin nor Ray have had any sleep, and Clinton has promised Danny Fender and Balis Norton will relieve them by noon.

When the lead agent on the SBI crime scene team calls Clinton back, he explains the situation in detail and tells him what's there: fingerprints, bullets, shell casings—everything but Jimmy Crowder's .32 revolver, which was carefully bagged by gloved hands and is locked away now at the jail. "Not bad, Sheriff, not bad. We're in New Bern now. We should wrap up here late this afternoon. We'll leave Raleigh first thing in the morning and be there before noon tomorrow. Don't let anybody touch those cars."

CHARLIE BURNS IS NONPLUSSED AT FIRST, BUT after he assures Clinton that yes, indeed, he does want to know the whole story, Clinton tells him. In plain, unadorned language. How Jason Fortner sat at Clinton's desk and called the Crowder house and asked for money to leave the state. The Crowders agreed to meet and when they showed up—in North Carolina—they didn't stop to talk but shot Fortner's car full of holes.

"Have you interviewed them?" Burns asks.

Clinton shakes his head, no. "Thought you'd want to sit in."

Burns nods. "Boy, have you ever got that right. Let's talk to them separately. Anybody hurt in this little fracas?"

"Junior has some knots on his head where I knocked him down with the barrel of my .45, and the old man hurt his wrist when a deputy tackled him as he was running away. We had a doctor in this morning already, and he splinted the wrist."

Burns nods. "Good. Nothing to gain a jury's sympathy. Let me call the boss. Assuming he gives the go-ahead, then we can start on them. Get a preliminary statement from each, and I can instruct them to call an attorney, etcetera."

Clinton stands up to leave.

"One more thing," Burns says. "My boss, Eastman, may raise a little hell about how you lured them across the line. Just let him talk. No mountain jury is going to fuss about that, especially if all the evidence comes in on our side. But from here on out, we've got to do everything by the book. Because this is a capital case, it could end up in an appeals court down the line, and we want to have everything, and I mean *everything*, just right. Savvy?"

"I savvy. Now that we've got them in hand, we'll treat them however you say."

Burns nods. "Good. Perfect. I'll be over there as soon as I can track down Eastman on the phone."

THEY BRING THE OLD MAN, BOB CROWDER, DOWN to Clinton's office first. Charlie Burns introduces himself as the assistant district attorney for Madison County. Almost immediately, he and Clinton fall into a natural pattern of good cop, bad cop: Burns playing the tough, driving, never-satisfied bastard while Clinton offers to bring Crowder a cup of coffee, some water, aspirin for his aching hand.

Crowder claims only to have met Jason Fortner twice, once at the Thunderbird roadhouse, playing pool, and once when they came over the line the night before to offer to help the poor boy out of a jam, where they were ambushed by the North Carolina sheriffs. He'd never heard of the Nortons, he was sorry they got themselves killed, he respected the elderly and would never harm a hair on the head of a granny lady or an old grandpa. Oh, and he thinks his wrist is broken, hurts like hell.

"Sorry about your wrist, Mr. Crowder," Burns says. "I got a couple of things for you. One, when we match the bullets your son fired last night to the bullets we pulled out of the Nortons, and when we match up all the fingerprints you two left at the scene, it's going to be pretty obvious you were there. Two, when we bring your son down here in a few minutes and talk to him, he may have a better memory than you. He may start singing like a mockingbird. Ever thought of that? So, if there's anything you want to tell us now, before the walls start closing in on you, it will help your sorry case later."

"I ain't going to hang this on my son. What kind of father would do that?"

"Was it your son that pulled the trigger on the old couple?" Clinton asks quietly. "He was sure blazing away last night."

"He ain't quite right in the head sometimes," Crowder says and then stops himself from saying more by slurping coffee from the cup Clinton has brought him. "I want a lawyer. We both do."

"You got one in mind?" Burns asks.

"I'm from Tennessee. Don't know no lawyers over here."

"Doesn't matter. We'll get you in front of—" He glances at Clinton.

"Gudger is standing by," he says.

"We'll get you in front of Judge Gudger this afternoon. If you can't afford an attorney for your defense, he'll appoint one for you. And boy, are you ever going to need one."

"What are the charges?" The old man has perked up again and is showing some spunk.

"Breaking and entering, robbery. Murder. I'm sure there's more, but murder is the one that matters. See you around, Mr. Crowder."

THE SON, JIMMY CROWDER, IS NERVOUS, EVAsive. His hands are shaking so hard the cuffs are rattling when Way Tipton leads him in and sits him down. Clinton does the math in his head and guesses that the boy, for he is little more than that mentally, is in his mid-twenties.

"My head hurts," the boy whines, "where you done busted it open last night."

"I don't see any blood," Clinton offers offhand.

"Would you like me to get you some aspirin?" Burns asks in a surprisingly soft voice. When Clinton glances over at Burns, he winks and nods at young Crowder. *Your turn,* he seems to say. And their roles are reversed.

"You shoot those old people, Jimmy?" Clinton begins. "Cause if you did, now's the time to say so."

"I don't know nothing about those Nortons," he says, gruffly. "Ain't never heard of 'em."

"How'd you know their names?"

"Read it in the paper. Seen it on the TV. Somebody shot 'em, but it wasn't me."

"Your old man?"

"Naw. He's a tough old son of a bitch, but he goes to church now and again, and he wouldn't pull no trigger on the elderly."

"What about the dog?"

"What dog?"

"The Nortons' dog. You shoot him?"

"Damn dog wouldn't shut up," Jimmy says, eyes wide. "Deserved what he got. Besides, it ain't no crime to shoot a dog."

"In my book, it is," Clinton says evenly. "Why did you go crazy last night and shoot Jason Fortner's car full of holes?"

"That wasn't me."

"Four of us saw you, Jimmy. We were there."

"I don't remember."

"Why did you try to shoot me?"

"I'd never seen you before. I didn't know you was a sheriff. You come at me unexpected with...with a gun in your hand."

Burns cuts in smoothly. "Does your head hurt, Jimmy?"

"Yeah, he whipped me with his gun barrel." The boy gestures roughly at Clinton with his cuffed hands.

"Were you afraid?"

"I was afraid of him." He nods at Clinton.

"Did you kill the Nortons, Jimmy?"

"I don't remember. I mean, I don't know nothing about that."

"It's okay if you're confused, Jimmy. I understand and I can help you."

"How?"

"We're going to arrange for you to have a lawyer this afternoon. I'll help you with that. And I can talk to the judge for you." Burns nods reassuringly.

"Will you keep me away from him?" Nodding at Clinton.

"I can keep him from hurting you anymore."

The boy nods. "Okay. Can I go now? I got to pee."

Burns nods. "I'll be with you in court this afternoon when you go before the judge."

WHEN WAY TIPTON HAS TAKEN JIMMY BACK UPstairs, Clinton turns to Charlie Burns. "What was that about?" he asks. "You suddenly turning from vinegar into sweet tea?"

He smiles benignly at Clinton. "Don't you know?" he says. "Every boy needs a friend." And then, after he stands up to go: "I'll check with Gudger and set a time. When we're ready, get those two into orange jumpsuits and walk them right down the middle of the street to the courthouse. Let them sweat a bit." At the door, Burns turns again before leaving. "You heard him confess to the dog, didn't you?"

Clinton nods.

"Be ironic if that's what sends him to the chair."

"Be justice," Clinton says.

CHAPTER 55

THE APPEARANCE BEFORE JUDGE GUDGER IS SET for three o'clock in the main courtroom at the Madison County courthouse, a block away from the jail.

Catherine calls him that afternoon just after two. Gloria patches the call through and then winks at him before pulling the door closed behind her.

"Are you exhausted?" Catherine asks him.

"Maybe. Hard to tell since the whole day has been on the run."

"Are you sure you still want to have supper?"

"More than ever."

"Remember the Weaverville Milling Company?"

"Where we went after the trial in Asheville?"

"That's the place. How far away do you think it is?"

"Thirty, forty-five minutes."

"What if I were to pick you up at Mrs. Penland's at seven? It'll be dark by then and we can ride together. I'll drive in case you fall sound asleep on the way home."

He closes his eyes and sighs. For a brief moment, he can imagine riding through the dark in her car, their only connection to the outside world the headlights stretching out ahead of them. "Thank you," he mutters into the phone.

"Is that a yes?" she asks.

"That's a yes."

THE ARRAIGNMENT HEARING GOES OFF THAT AFternoon without a hitch. Clinton, along with Way Tipton and the jailer, walks the Crowders the two hundred feet to the courthouse, up the stairs, and into the largely empty courtroom. There, Judge Gudger explains that the district attorney's office, as represented by Mr. Burns, has filed felony charges against them, including breaking and entering, robbery, and murder. Do they understand? They are each required to respond verbally. He explains that they have been charged separately and will be tried separately.

He then explains their constitutional rights, including the right to legal representation. Can they afford an attorney? No. Then he will appoint one for them by early the following week. He reassures them that he will arrange the best court-appointed legal representation available because this is potentially a capital case. Do they know what this means? No. He explains that the state has charged them with first-degree murder, which may be punishable by death.

"We ain't even from this state," Jimmy Crowder cries out. "Hell no."

Gudger ignores him and continues. They will have a chance to meet with their lawyers during the next week or two. Once they have done so, Gudger will schedule a second hearing or hearings, in which they will appear separately and enter pleas—guilty or not guilty—to each of the charges filed against them. Their attorney can and should appear with them during these hearings. Bail for each will be set during the second set of hearings.

Do they have any questions?

"Can we at least be locked up together, or beside each other?" Bob Crowder asks. "We're family."

Gudger glances at Clinton and Burns, both of whom are shaking their heads, no—Burns much more emphatically.

"No, sir, I'm afraid not," says Gudger. "Since you are being tried separately, from here on out, you and your cases will be treated separately. In addition, this time alone will give you an opportunity to meditate on what your lives have come to. Anything else?"

Charlie Burns replies with, "No, Your Honor," and "thank you, Your Honor." The whole proceeding lasts maybe thirty minutes.

For Clinton, that night feels like an island. Downstream from Marshall in the French Broad River is a lonely place called Mountain Island. It's as large as Blannahassett Island, where Marshall High School sits on hard, flat land, but Mountain Island rises majestically over three hundred feet out of the middle of the river. For years, a hermit—no one now alive knows his name—lived on the island in a half-cave, half–lean-to shelter that he built out of driftwood and fallen logs. Every time Clinton has visited the place, he is struck by just how quiet it is there. Except for the rushing away of the river and the occasional passing train, Mountain Island sits alone in the middle of the world. Any season and in all weather, it is quiet there. Peace drops slowly there.

As he is describing it to Catherine while she drives the two of them along the dark, lonely roads, south toward Weaverville and the Milling Company, she interrupts him to say, "This night feels like that. Quiet...peaceful."

"I think that's what I'm trying to say," he offers. "The world is rushing by, dazed and confused in the dark, frantic to be and do something, and yet, we're here, apart."

"On an island?"

"On an island, at least for a few hours."

He tells her about the day, the interviews with the Crowders, their arraignment before Judge Gudger. He tells her that the SBI will be on the scene tomorrow and that the bigwig district attorney, Eastman, will be there on Monday. Now that the Crowders are caught, the world beyond their island is speeding up rather than slowing down.

The Weaverville Milling Company is everything they hoped. They request and are seated at the same table where they sat once before, when they were first flirting with the idea of meaning something to each other. "Our table," they call it, close by the fireplace. There's a small salad before the main course with hot bread and soft butter. Then they both order trout. She wants hash browns, he a baked potato. Two glasses of a dark, red cabernet just because it's cold outside.

"Do you think there are seasons in people's lives?" she asks, once they've eaten most of their fish and potatoes.

"Um. Yes. There are dark, cold times, and there are warm, sun-drenched times. I had thought the rest of my life would be barren, honestly. A dry field. Until Christmas Day last year."

"Christmas Day?"

"Remember? At the farm. You came with Marian and Luke. We walked up to the rock barn and talked to the horses. You said you wanted to go riding. I don't know why exactly, but it felt to me like there was a spark. Not much, nothing dramatic, but it was as if someone somewhere was trying to light a lamp with a box of matches."

"I know what you mean," she says, warmed by the wine and the fire. "I went home to the bungalow that night and wondered about you. I wanted to ask Marian a hundred questions, but I knew I couldn't, not then. I didn't know if she'd let me anywhere near you, but there was something. Light, like you said."

"A season of light? Imagine if we'd met five years sooner or five years later."

"I don't want to think about that. I want to believe that we met at exactly the right time. I'm scared to death to say it. I almost bit my tongue off when I said I was in love the other day. Why you don't run for the hills, I have no idea."

"It never occurred to me to run." He says it simply, easily, without much thought. And then smiles at the thought.

The waitress visits their table and they agree that he should have a second glass of wine but she would not. Driving.

"Are you exhausted?" she asks. "You were up most of the night."

He yawns.

"See what I mean?"

"I am tired. I meant to take a nap before you came to get me. Took a bath and laid down across the bed at Mrs. Penland's, but it didn't work. Too many thoughts chasing too many worries."

"Finish your wine," she says. "Let me take you back."

He nods. Takes two long, meditative sips from the wineglass. "Can you come to the farm this weekend?" he asks. "I mean to go up there tomorrow evening, no matter how late. I need to get away from it all."

"What if I come up Saturday morning? Spend the night."

He smiles, sips again. "I'm afraid to tell you this, but I..."

"What is it? Clint?"

"When I ran in on Jimmy Crowder, the son, he drew down on me with the thirty-two he'd been firing into Fortner's car. Pointed it straight at me and pulled the trigger over and over. It was empty, or we wouldn't be sitting here. Even so, it took me straight back to the war. My whole body shook then, and—" He holds up his right hand where she can see it tremor. "And talking about it even now brings back the shock. The echo of gunfire. Somebody yelling in German."

She grabs his hand in both of her own and begins to knead his fingers. "Oh, Clint. I'm sorry."

"That's not the worst of it. The worst of it is that on some level, I knew he was trying to reload. Some part of my mind knew he was fumbling in his pocket for shells, but when he turned, I almost shot him anyway. I thought he was German. The safety was off on the forty-five, and my finger was in the trigger guard."

She holds his hand to her lips and kisses it. "But you didn't kill him, did you? You stopped yourself, didn't you? My precious man."

"Are you mad at me?"

"Of course not. Being there is who you are. I'm learning to accept it, that you do what you have to do. But I'll never stop nagging you about being careful." She kisses his hand again and holds it against her cheek.

He grins in the flickering, yellow light—candles reflecting the fireplace—and then laughs. "Take me home, Cat," he says. "And on Saturday, we'll go for a ride and pretend the rest of the world isn't real."

CHAPTER 56

THE SBI CRIME SCENE VAN ARRIVES JUST AFTER noon. Clinton gives them Jimmy Crowder's .32 caliber pistol, still bagged, and the investigators follow Clinton in the Jeep out to the picnic area where the Crowders were arrested.

Even though it's been over thirty-six hours since Jimmy Crowder shot Fortner's car full of holes, the SBI team is all but slavering over the amount of evidence at the scene. After watching them work for an hour or so, Clinton leaves Balis Norton to keep stray picnickers and curious neighbors out of the area and drives back to the jail.

The night before at Mrs. Penland's, he dreamed that the farmhouse at Doe Branch was on fire and he, Catherine, and Marian were trapped inside. The nightmare seems so real that he actually calls the caretaker, Randall Shelton, from the jail that morning to check in. Randall just laughs and says that the house was fine when he went over to let the dogs out that morning.

Even so, the dream haunts Clinton, and when he gets back to the jail that Friday afternoon, he decides to drop by his brother's house on Little Pine before heading up to the farm that night. Visit with Will and see what he can pry out of him about the ghost arsonist.

IT'S CLOSE ON FIVE O'CLOCK WHEN HE PULLS UP the long gravel driveway to Will's house in Little Pine. Will's wife comes out even before he gets out of the Jeep to tell him that

Will is down at the barn with their son, Willie, throwing out hay to the half dozen head of beef cattle they keep there. She invites Clinton to stay for supper, but he politely declines, telling her he wants to get up to Doe Branch before dark.

He drives the Jeep around the house and on down the mostly dirt road to Will's barn, where he stores hay and feed. He can see ahead of him the ten-year-old farm truck Will and Willie use on the place and that Willie drives to school when he bothers to go. It's a cloudy, dirty black, and he's reminded of the truck Catherine saw on Doe Branch the night they scared off the intruder with the coal oil. Did Willie's truck look like that truck? If so, the coal oil truck would blend perfectly into the dark.

He pulls up to one side of the barn, not wanting to block Willie in if the boy needed to get his truck out. Will sees him from the open barn door and waves. "Be right with you," he calls out. "Soon as we throw out another bale or two."

Clinton is walking from the Jeep to the barn door, thinking vaguely of helping his brother and nephew, when he sees it: the thing that will change most everything in their world.

It is simple enough. The ground between the barn door and the parked truck is worn down to dirt by constant traffic and muddy from recent rain. Among the pointed tracks left from Will's old cowboy boots are those of his son, and one of his son's heels is worn entirely away on the outside. Clinton's mind is slow to process—indeed, is numb with a sort of certainty. He casually walks over and places his own shoe beside Willie's boot track. It is a perfect match for the one he's been chasing for months.

Clinton turns to stare at the truck behind him. *Black or dark blue*, Catherine said on the night of the intruder.

Will and Willie walk around the corner of the barn from where they've been breaking bales and tossing hay to the cattle. Willie pulls off a pair of leather work gloves and tosses them casually back through the open door onto the barn floor. He has a chaw of tobacco in his cheek and turns his head to spit before moving on toward the truck.

"What can I do you for, brother?" Will asks Clinton.

"Need to talk to you about something."

"Need my advice, do you?" Will says and laughs. "Go on up to the house, Willie. Tell your mom I'll be along in a few minutes."

Willie climbs into his truck, cranks the engine, and wheels around to drive back up the road toward the house.

Will leans on one hand against the side of the barn. "I heard you may have solved the Norton killings," he says conversationally.

"Maybe. The SBI has some work to do, and the DA's office has to see their way through, but maybe."

"Who was it done the killing?"

"I tell you who it wasn't." Clinton is barely able to keep the anger out of his voice. "It wasn't the son of a bitch who's been burning up people's property."

"What are you saying, Clint? You best be careful."

"I'm saying you acted all along like you might know who it was and that I'd better mind my own business and let it go. But I never dreamed it was your own son."

"Like I said, you'd better back up a step or two. You got no proof and Willie is family. Besides, even if it was him—or some of his friends—it's our enemies he's been burning out."

"What do mean, *our enemies*?"

"Republicans, you idiot. The same goddamn Republicans who are determined to keep the county in the dark ages for the next fifty years. The same goddamn Republicans, by the way, who voted for Tom Runnion in the last election. Whoever's burning those barns is trying to help you, for God's sake."

"*Whoever's burning those barns* is breaking the law, Will, and he just climbed in that truck and drove up the hill."

The two brothers stare at each other, both panting with emotion, anger and fear radiating off their bodies. Will takes a step toward Clinton and shakes his fist at him. "You stay the hell away from my son, Clinton. You hear me?"

"Is that why you wanted me to run for sheriff?" Clinton asks suddenly. "Because you figured out what he was doing and you wanted to protect him?"

"Of course it was," Will says. "What the hell do you think? You're my brother and all, but sometimes, you're the most naive son of a bitch on the face of the earth."

"Damn it, Will. Did it ever occur to you I might arrest him?"

Will takes a step closer and reaches out to poke Clinton hard on the chest with a stiff forefinger. "If you do, you'll regret it, by God. You lay a hand on Willie, and that skinny little piece-of-ass school principal you been running around with will be out on the street looking for a job."

Clinton reaches out and takes a fistful of Will's T-shirt. He can feel his right arm beginning to tense up, gathering for the punch. "What the hell did you just say?"

"That skinny little piece of ass, Cathy Metcalf, or whatever her name is, that you been screwing on the sly. We don't take to that kind of immoral behavior in Madison County, and in case you're suffering from insomnia due to your war injuries, I'm still the chair of the goddamn school board. We'll run her out of town."

"How the hell do you—" Clinton begins but then remembers that the same night Catherine saw the black truck, whoever was driving the truck saw her in its headlights and maybe her station wagon in the driveway. He lets Will's shirt go and steps back. Breathes. "Here's the lay of the land, Will." He's hoarse to the point of choking. "If you hurt her in any way—*any* way at all—I will nail your hide to that damn barn behind you with your own hammer. I don't care if I go to jail for it. Make sure you understand that. Willie will go to prison and you, you conniving son of a bitch, will wish you were in there with him."

Will snorts. "You can't lay a hand on me and you know it." He reaches out and starts to pat Clinton on the cheek, but then thinks better of it. "We need each other, brother, just like we did when we were boys. There's a lot about our family relations over the years you might be just too blind to see. How about you leave Willie be, and I'll let Mrs. Metcalf keep right on educating the young people?"

"Maybe," Clinton says. "Maybe. I'll have to think about it. But I'll tell you one thing: You better rein him in. If anything so much as a chicken coop goes up in flames in the coming months, he'll find himself chained to a bench on the second floor of the jail before he has time to turn around."

"I'll talk to the boy," Will says and shrugs. "Tell him his uncle is on to him. How about you take care of your little household, and I'll take care of mine."

Disgusted, Clinton turns away. When he climbs into the Jeep and sticks the key into the ignition, Will asks, "You gonna give me a ride back up to the house?"

"You can walk," Clinton says grimly. "It's not that far."

As the Jeep passes the front of Will's house, he happens to glance at the front door. Just as he does, his nephew, Willie, steps out onto the porch, laughing at something. He takes his right hand out of his jeans pocket and raises it. Clinton assumes he's going to wave, but instead, Willie extends his arm and lifts his middle finger.

CHAPTER 57

CATHERINE GETS TO THE FARM ON DOE BRANCH in the early afternoon on Saturday. When she arrives, Clinton's blood pressure drops, the tension begins to drain out of his shoulders, and the dogs—Nick and Jake—go boiling out of the house to greet her.

Somehow, in a way that neither can really articulate, this day and night together are different. They each need this time. To escape, to breathe, to believe.

She has eaten lunch. He has not, so she laughingly sits him down at the kitchen table while she makes him a peanut butter and jelly sandwich and watches him eat it. She pours him a glass of wine to wash down the sandwich, and they end up sharing it, passing the glass back and forth between them.

It's October 16, and despite the season, the afternoon air is washed by the sun and warmer than you might expect in the high mountains. She unpacks far more clothes than she can wear in two days, adding more layers to what she's already deposited in the closet upstairs. They smile at each other while she unpacks. Their smiles turn into grins when she asks him if they're going riding.

"Of course," he says. "I think you came to see the dogs and the horses more than you came to see me."

So, they dress accordingly—she in jeans and a blue, wool sweater that reminds him of her eyes and he in a pair of jeans that are holed at one knee and worn out at the cuffs. A flannel shirt from another decade.

He has every intention of telling her about the confrontation with his brother as soon as she arrives, but he can't bring himself to break the mood. Each time he opens his mouth to broach the subject, the words stick in his throat. She's so happy, visibly relaxing before his eyes, that he can't bear to invoke the outside world.

They walk up through the orchard, hand in hand, picking a few late apples for the horses, saying nothing out loud, while their bodies whisper to each other. Each breath, each beat of their hearts, seeks a shared rhythm. They're simply together, with no one to distract them except the dogs, who are running far afield.

The horses, Little Joe and Nell, do nothing to interrupt the mood. Rather, after much petting and brushing, they relax into the flow of this October day, these two familiar people. And before they know it, Clint and Cat are on horseback, riding out of the upper pasture onto an old logging road that takes them further up into the hills behind the farm. They follow a route they've ridden before, over the ridge and around, back down by the cemetery. At one point she asks him if he's wearing a watch. He shakes his head. "No," he says. "You?"

"No. I don't want the time to pass."

"Let the sun tell time," he suggests. "It moves more slowly this time of year."

"Sun time, then," she says.

Time doesn't pass; although the sun is closer to the ridgetop when they reach Doe Branch and turn to ride a bit further up along the road. Without thinking, he asks her if this is where she saw the dark truck on the night of the intruder.

She nods. "There was a lot going on that night, but it sounded to me like it was parked right along here somewhere, almost as if waiting for something...or someone."

"Makes sense. Probably waiting for whoever was in the upper pasture." They ride on for a few paces. "There's something I need to tell you about after supper," he says.

"Want to tell me or need to tell me?"

"Need."

Just before the old Doe Branch Church and the abandoned school building, they turn the horses around and ride just as slowly back down the way they came.

"Meat loaf," she says after a bit.

"What?"

"Rosie at the jail showed me how she makes her meat loaf, and that's what we're having for supper. Unless you're tired of it."

"It makes my stomach moan just to think about it." He laughs and the chill that came over them earlier dissipates.

"HE SAID *WHAT*?" SHE IS INCREDULOUS.

It's eight o'clock or thereabouts. Full dark outside. They're sitting in front of the fireplace, drinks in hand.

"He admitted that it was Willie, had been Willie all along. And that one of the reasons he wanted me to run for sheriff in the first place was to protect him. Probably the main reason he wanted me to run."

"Are you going to arrest him—Willie, I mean?"

"I don't know. It's complicated."

"Complicated because he's your nephew?" She sips from her glass.

"No. More complicated than that. Worse than that."

"What do you mean?" They're seated at each end of the couch, the couch where they first made love. She turns now, as she likes to do and extends her legs toward him, her sock feet against his leg.

"He threatened to get you fired if I go after Willie."

"Son of a bitch." It's more groan than speech. "Chair of the school board."

Clinton nods. "He pointed that out."

"What did he say, exactly?" Her legs are rigid; he can feel the pressure against his thigh.

"Exactly?"

"Yes, remember, we're going to honest with each other."

"He said that if I lay a hand on Willie, that skinny, little piece-of-ass school principal I been running around with will be out on the street looking for a job. And then some bullshit about how we don't take to that kind of immoral behavior in Madison County. It's a wonder the hypocritical bastard didn't choke to death over his own words."

"Oh, lord, Clint. It's like our worst nightmare. What did you say?"

"I said that if he harmed a hair on your head, I'd nail his ass to his own barn with his own hammer. And I meant every word."

"No, you didn't."

"Don't be too sure. He basically called me a naive idiot and you..."

"At least he called me *skinny*."

He glances up and she's actually smiling.

"Did he call me a whore?" she asks.

"Nope. *Skinny piece-of-ass school principal*."

She's still smiling, ruefully. "Well, that's something. And it's sweet that you offered to...what? Nail him to his own barn."

He has to smile back at her. "I did that."

They each pause to take a swallow of the bourbon, although their eyes never leave each other.

"Don't worry, Clint. It's simple enough. I'll just resign. Leave at Christmas."

He shakes his head. "No. I don't want that. Truthfully, you don't either."

"I want that before I'll see you compromised by your... brother."

"*Asshole* brother?"

"That might be the word I was thinking."

"Let's wait. See how it plays out. I can still threaten him with arrest for fixing the election."

"No, you can't. You were the one who got elected. Listen to me. I can get a job in Buncombe County or Yancey County and commute. I walk away and he loses his control over you."

She sips her whiskey and watches while he thinks, shaking his head the whole time. "I still say *no*," he says finally. "And I'll tell you why. I didn't particularly want to be sheriff in the first place, but now that I'm in, I figure to do some good, and I sure as hell don't want to be forced out by him. You, on the other hand, are brilliant at what you do. You run the best school in Madison County—hell, probably western North Carolina. It would devastate Marian if you left."

The thought of Marian gives her pause. "Then what do we do, Clint?"

"We wait him out. See just how much control he has over Willie. If he really can rein him in, then I'm satisfied for now. In the meantime, I am going to find out who else is on the school board and get to know them. See if he does have that kind of leverage or if he's just bluffing."

She sighs. "Maybe. I hadn't thought about that."

"And another thing..."

"What other thing?"

"You said we had to wait six months before we are seen together."

She nods.

"I asked Gloria Goforth, who was born here and has lived here her entire life. You want to know what she said?"

A smile is slowly emerging on Cat's face. "What did she say?"

"She said that, given the circumstances, Christmas should do it. I watched her do the math. Over five years since the accident and over three months after James finally died. She reminded me that this is, after all, the twentieth century. People aren't so puritanical as they used to be."

"Christmas?" The smile on her face has blossomed now and Clint glimpses the gap in her front teeth that he loves. "What else did she say?"

He blushes. Even in the faint light from the fireplace, she can see that he is blushing. "Well, she actually thought I was asking how soon we could get married, when she said Christmas. But I...straightened her out."

Cat laughs. "She thought we could get *married* at Christmas! Why did she think we even wanted to?"

"I don't know. She said I was besotted, so she just assumed."

"*Besotted*? Good. I like besotted."

Another pause while they each think about what's just been said, the words that hang before them in the flickering light from the fire.

"But wait, Clint, what does that have to do with your brother and his arsonist offspring?"

"What it has to do is this: By Christmas, we're a couple. We're...standing right there in front of everybody. And all of a sudden, Will's threat to get you fired loses its power. He's got nothing."

"And you can go after Willie..."

"If I need to. If a doghouse or an outhouse burns down anywhere in the county, I'll arrest him."

Cat sighs. "So, I don't get to make a grand dramatic gesture and quit?"

"Nope. You and me together in public will be dramatic enough."

CHAPTER 58

THE NEXT MORNING, SUNDAY, IS AS QUIET AS Clint's ever known it, both in the house and outside as well. When he gets up at dawn to make coffee and let the dogs out, the farm itself seems still to be asleep. He stands in the kitchen doorway, listening for a few minutes, and hears only the faintest breath of wind in the orchard trees and a quiet *bah* from one of the ewes.

As he's pouring the coffee, he hears the commode flush in the upstairs bathroom and water running in the sink. He pauses at the foot of the stairs to see if Cat is coming down. She doesn't materialize, and so he climbs carefully with the two mugs of coffee in his hands. While climbing the stairs, he notices that even the house itself is quiet. Resting, he thinks, settled and still.

The morning for Clint and Cat passes so slowly and luxuriously that it seems eternal. It is only when dark clouds blow in from the river at midday and it begins to rain that they consciously admit, first to themselves and then to each other, that eventually their day must end, and they must return to the rest of the world.

She leaves in late afternoon and he early the next morning, going straight to the jail and arriving in time for breakfast.

LATER, HE WOULD THINK BACK TO THE DAY AND the week that followed as if he had jumped off the deepwater railroad trestle above Hot Springs into the spinning, swirling rapids below. From peace, sun-dappled and secure, into swimming hard in fast water. Time doesn't just accelerate. It explodes.

On Monday morning, he prepares for his meeting with the regional DA, Eastman, who is scheduled to be at the courthouse at ten. That meeting lasts into midafternoon, with only a thirty-minute break for lunch. Both Burns and Eastman end up praising Clinton and his deputies for corralling the Crowders, but only after twice going over the events leading up to their arrest. At the end of the meeting, Burns suggests that the Crowders be moved to a larger jail, where they can be kept isolated from each other, and Eastman agrees. The Crowders will be moved later in the week, and Jason Fortner will be brought back to Madison County, where his mother can visit him in jail and Clinton can keep track of him.

As soon as Clinton gets back to the jail, closer to four o'clock than three, he receives a phone call from Sheriff Lewis Sutton from Cocke County, Tennessee. It's not a friendly call.

"I hear you've got two of my local citizens locked up in that rinky-dink jail of yours. What did they do, spit on the sidewalk?"

"If you're talking about the Crowders, they're charged with murder, among other things."

"Murder? You talking about that old couple that got robbed? Makes no sense. Now, I'll admit the son—what's his name, Jimmy? He's got a mean streak. Gotten into a few altercations. Likes to hang out at cockfights and such, but if there'd been any killing, I'd have heard of it. Plus, them boys are good Republicans, voted for me every time."

"Funny you should say that, Sheriff. When I called you about the Norton killings, you didn't think there could be any connection to your part of the world."

"I'm not convinced there is. Anyway, if you thought it was the Crowders done it, why the hell didn't you ask me to pick them up for you?"

"To be honest, I wasn't sure you'd do it. And I didn't want to tip them off."

"What the hell are you implying, Salter? And just in case you haven't quite got the lay of the land yet, being new and all, you got no jurisdiction this side of the line. You even heard of *jurisdiction*?"

Clinton snorts. "I've been lectured about it more than once during the last month. Just to be clear, we arrested Robert and James Crowder in North Carolina."

"Where?"

"Doesn't matter where. But I will tell you that it was on state-owned land, so there's no confusion about which side of the line."

"The hell you say. Well, you may have 'em, but I doubt you'll keep 'em. I got me a deputy over here, Tom Runnion, tells me that you're a goddamned pantywaist, and the only reason you're even sheriff is that your brother voted half the dead people in the county to get you elected. What do you think of that?"

"I think you should be careful who you listen to, Sutton. Don't count on seeing Bob and Jimmy Crowder anytime soon. Pleasure talking to you." And he hangs up before Sutton has time to reply.

Gloria Goforth has been standing in the doorway to his office for most of this conversation, listening to his half with a grin on her face.

"Exchanging pleasantries with your counterpart over in Tennessee?"

"If exchanging pleasantries means getting cussed out by Lew Sutton, then yes, that's exactly what I've been doing."

"This about the Crowders?"

Clinton nods. "I think our instincts were right. If we'd asked Sutton to pick them up, he'd have warned them and they'd be long gone."

"You're smarter than you look, Clinton. Did you know that?"

"I'm not sure that's a compliment. Didn't you tell me something about Tom Runnion?"

"You know perfectly well what I told you. He's working over there while preparing to kick your ass in the next election. His words, not mine. And now I'll tell you something else."

"What?"

"He's a moron, but keep in mind, he's the kind of moron people around here like to vote for."

CHAPTER 59

THE JAIL. WEDNESDAY MORNING.

Clint has just made arrangements with the sheriff in Buncombe County to manage the prisoner transfer. Buncombe deputies will bring his star witness, Jason Fortner, back home to Madison that afternoon and pick up the Crowders. In a sense, they will no longer be his problem; they can become the district attorney's headache for the weeks leading up to their trial.

Clint is back in the kitchen, drinking a cup of coffee and petting the jailhouse cat when Gloria Goforth comes to fetch him. "Phone," she says.

"Not available," he replies and nods at the cat. "Interviewing a suspect."

"You're available for this," she says. "It's from the Institute of Government."

He carries his coffee back into his office and Gloria shuts the door behind him for privacy.

As before, there is the bored voice of a university secretary, followed by a half minute of static.

Then, a voice he knows well is on the line, and as before, it is filtered through a sort of antiseptic, professional veil, impersonal to the point of insult.

"Is this Sheriff Salter?"

"Yes. Matt?"

"This is Matthew Salter. Calling from Chapel Hill. Good morning, Father."

"Morning, Matt. It's good to hear from you." Not really, he thinks, not like this. "Are you calling about the suspects we arrested? We picked them up on this side of the line. In Madison County, as a matter of fact."

"That's what I heard. Mr. Eastman, the DA called to tell me. Quite a coup on your part. Congratulations."

"Thank you."

"No, I'm calling about a political matter. Something I've discussed with both James Eastman and with the governor." Matthew pauses, perhaps to let the weight of the word *governor* have its effect.

Which it does, but probably not the effect Matthew has in mind. Clinton can feel his blood pressure rise at the mention of politics. "What's that, son?" Clinton asks slowly.

"I don't know if you're aware, but the Vance-Aycock Dinner is Friday night at the Grove Park Inn in Asheville, and we all thought it would be a good idea for you to put in an appearance. It's the biggest Democratic event in the state, and a show of solidarity from Madison County would be much appreciated."

"Appreciated by whom?" Clinton can sense his own voice taking on Matthew's tone, formal and correct.

"Well, by Eastman, certainly, and by Governor Moore. You know he's from up that way, and he's particularly interested in the western region. I've talked at length about this with Uncle William, and he feels strongly about it as well."

"You mean my brother, Will?"

"Yes, I thought that you could even ride over with him if you like."

We'd kill each other, Clinton thinks, but doesn't say. Rather: "Are you going to be there, son?"

"Yes, the governor has asked me to attend. This could be of great advantage to you politically, Father."

"Well, here's the thing, Matt. I'm a farmer and, these days, a lawman, but not a politician. Never have been. And it would be hard to dress me up as anything that I'm not."

"It would give us a chance to converse as well," Matthew says. "Talk about my future in politics as well as your own."

Clinton pauses. This is different, almost personal. "I don't think I belong at the Vance-Aycock Dinner, son, but I'll tell you what. I'll be glad to sit and talk with you about your future, even my future, but only here, at home. And since you're going to be in Asheville for the weekend..."

"What do you mean by *home*, Father? The jail in Marshall?"

Clinton can't help but laugh. "No, even though I spend so much time here, you might think I live in a cell upstairs. No, I mean the farm at Doe Branch, where you grew up. Come on over to the farm on Saturday, spend the afternoon with me. I'll invite Marian and Luke out for supper, so you can congratulate them in person. Besides, there's someone I'd like you—"

"Father, you should know that I don't really think of...the farm...as my home anymore. Chapel Hill and Raleigh are my home."

"I know that," Clinton says simply. "You've made that abundantly clear. But even if this is not your home, it is your family. Your sister just got married and would love to see you. Hell, I would love to see you." There's a considerable pause. Clinton can almost feel Matthew weighing his options. He adds: "You and I can discuss politics that afternoon, son. Give you a chance to explain to me how I should be thinking, what I should be doing."

"All right," Matthew says finally. "I suppose that could work. I'll check with the governor to make sure he doesn't need me on Saturday, and if my schedule is clear, I'll plan to visit with you at the farm on Saturday afternoon and evening. I think it's important that we discuss your future."

"Fair enough," Clinton says, thinking that Principal Catherine Metcalf has more to do with his future than Governor Dan

K. Moore. "You can spend the night if you like, if it gets late."

"I'll probably drive back to Asheville after dinner, and I need to confer with Uncle William while I'm there," Matthew says. "But thank you for the invitation. I will confirm our plans via telephone on Saturday morning."

"No need for all that," Clinton says. "Just show up. We'll talk."

"Good day, Father. And let me know if you change your mind about the Vance-Aycock Dinner." Matthew's voice is gone, replaced by the sputter of static before the line goes dead.

When Clinton opens the door to the outer office, Gloria Goforth looks up. "Well?" she asks.

"It's a sad damn day," he offers, "when the only reason your son will come to see you is to discuss your political future."

"I'm sure it's more complicated than that," she replies.

"Apparently, it is. He's developed a sudden fascination with Will as well."

Gloria stares at him speculatively for a bit before answering. "It makes sense. He's the political side of the family, Clint. And you most decidedly are not."

CHAPTER 60

WITHIN THEIR SMALL GROUP—CLINTON, Catherine, Marian, even Luke—speculation swirls around Matthew's homecoming. Why now? Why politics? Catherine and Marian begin calling it the return of the prodigal and joking about killing the fatted calf for supper Saturday night.

Clinton catches himself wondering just what his son will look like. Will he have changed? His hair, his clothes? Certainly, the voice he's heard over the long-distance line has been strangely like and strangely different from the version of his son's voice that he carries inside his head.

He drives up to the farm on Friday night, and Catherine joins him there Saturday morning. It has rained hard during the night, drenching the land, but morning brings the sun in a clear, clean sky.

They plan a meal together—chicken breasts over wild rice and mushrooms—baked in the deep iron skillet Catherine likes to use. Wine? Yes, except for Marian, who's sworn off alcohol for the baby. And Catherine insists on making an apple pie because it's Clint's favorite. With ice cream. Vanilla.

Catherine worries about Clint, how he'll react to having Matthew at home again, but also, and more importantly, how Matthew will treat his father, the man she loves. And in the midst of her worry, while they're cleaning the house for company, she realizes just how nervous she is. She's meeting her lover's son for the first time, and as complicated as it all is already, she wants

Matthew to like her, accept her. Even though Christmas is two months away and she isn't anything officially to Clint...yet.

"Who am I in all this?" she asks Clint suddenly, speaking almost frantically. "And if Matthew does spend the night, should I stay here or go home? And if I stay, where do I—?"

"Stop," he says, almost laughing. "Just stop. I think we have to be who we are. You're my..."

"Girlfriend?"

"Is that it? With all the resources of the English language, that's all there is?"

"You can't say *lover*. Not to your son. And besides, I'm not officially anything."

"You're my friend."

"Do you sleep with all your friends?"

"No, just my best friend. And you belong here, with me. And if he spends the night, which I hope he does, then he can sleep in his old room, and we go to bed just like we always do when we're here."

"Are you sure?"

"Yes, I'm sure. If we're not consenting adults, who is?"

"He's going to hate me," she says, half under her breath.

"Why in the world?"

"Don't be silly, Clint. I'm replacing his mother. He's going to hate me."

"I hadn't thought of that. Well, he already hates me, so we'll just ride it out together. Besides, once he gets to know you, he'll love you."

"Are you sure you want me to stay? Think before you speak for once. For supper? For the night?"

"I'm much more certain about us, Cat, than I am about him and his political business. To be perfectly honest, you belong here now more than he does. He's told me clear as a bell that this is not his home."

MATTHEW ARRIVES A LITTLE AFTER TWO o'clock, driving a state car. He brings in a briefcase, but not a suitcase. The young man is mostly what Clinton had led Catherine to expect—tall, thin, stylishly dressed. Thick black hair combed neatly back behind his ears, hanging almost to his shoulders. She can see immediately the resemblance to Clinton. But then there's the lopsided, flirtatious grin that is either from his mother or entirely his own.

Clinton introduces her as Marian's friend—well, boss and friend—as well as his own close friend. Matthew flashes the grin and says, "Marian warned me that I might get to meet you. Father's sweetheart. It's a pleasure, and I hope you don't mind me monopolizing the old man this afternoon. I have some thoughts I want to share with him."

"Go right ahead," she says. "Talk his ear off. I'm going to walk up to the upper barn and visit the horses. Give you two some time alone."

There's an awkward moment after Catherine slips out the kitchen door, bundled up in Clinton's barn coat against the late October wind. Awkward in that the two men don't quite know what to do with each other. Clinton, feeling that an embrace would probably not be welcome, shakes his son's hand, almost as if meeting him for the first time.

Matthew refuses the offer of a beer or a glass of wine. "Maybe later," he suggests.

"Want to sit, then?" Clinton asks. "I built a fire earlier in the afternoon."

"Sure, sure," Matthew says and Clinton has the uneasy feeling that he's about to receive some sort of sales pitch.

"How was the dinner last night?" he asks, steering for normalcy.

"Excellent. Governor Moore delivered a truly inspirational speech. Leading us into the future. North Carolina joining the ranks of the progressive Southern states.... One of the things I wanted to share with you, Father, is that I've been invited to join the governor's staff at the first of the year, and after due consideration, I've decided to do so."

"Congratulations, son. That's wonderful." Clinton is truly moved, his words warm and genuine.

"I'm glad you think so. I think Mom would be pleased as well, don't you?"

"I'm sure she would. She always wanted success for you in the outside world. Not trapped in the mountains."

Matthew pauses with his mouth half open—the unexpected insight in his father's comment catching him off guard. Then: "In my new job, I'm responsible for building support for the Democratic agenda in the western counties. Old Fort to Murphy. And I need your help."

"How can I help you? I'm nobody important."

"Oh, you'd be surprised. You're the popular sheriff in one of few counties in the west that is leaning Democratic. Uncle William raves about the progress that the two of you have made in the last few years. Finally bringing the mountains in line with the rest of the state. He sees a bright future...new roads, new schools, infrastructure of all kinds."

Clinton has to grin. "I've heard him on the subject, more than once."

"But here's the thing, Father. It's important that we all pull together in the west. It's important that we're clear about leaving the past behind—barns and banjos—and blazing a path into the future." Matthew has grown so enthusiastic that he's almost blushing, and Clinton isn't sure just how to respond.

"What sort of future?" he asks.

"The development of towns and cities in the west. A newer, better airport. Roads you can actually drive on, not like that donkey path outside. In twenty years, the mountain region could look a whole lot like the Triangle if we play our cards right."

"The Triangle?"

"Raleigh-Durham-Chapel Hill. The center of everything that matters in the state."

"Oh, I see. Who are *we*?"

"We?"

"The *we* who need to play our cards right. That *we*—"

"The North Carolina Democratic Party. That's the key. Up here, the Republicans are living in the past. They think Abraham Lincoln is still alive. The Democratic Party is the future of the state. And you're a registered, voting, successful Democrat."

"I am registered and I do occasionally vote. Don't know about successful."

"That's where you're wrong. Uncle William and I have talked about this. You're the face of the Democratic Party in Madison County, and you could be the face of the party in western North Carolina. The old-timers respect you, even when you offer something new."

"That's where *you're* wrong." Clinton can't help himself. "I'm not the face of anything. I'm the sheriff. That's all. My job is to protect people from each other, keep some semblance of peace. And, as much as it sometimes surprises people, I'm the sheriff for everybody, Republican or Democrat, doesn't matter. I've gotten to the point where I don't much care anymore which is which."

"You better care, or you won't be reelected."

Clinton shrugs. "I have my army pension and I can make a living farming."

"Backward, backward, backward. Stop looking back, Father. This is exactly what Mom warned me about." They have come to something deep and personal between them, something neither has ever dared say to the other.

There is a pause, one that stretches out between them, while Clinton watches his son's face closely. He sees some obscure hurt there, almost as if Matthew is pouting. Clinton senses the presence of the boy he had helped raise, the boy who loved to play in the creek. "What did she warn you about, son?" he whispers.

"That you would always be stuck here, refusing to come out into the world. And that if I gave in to the temptation to stay as well, I'd never amount to anything." The boy was gone, replaced by the man, and with the man came the formality, the haughtiness.

"Am I the backward redneck she warned you about?"

"You are when you talk about not caring if you're reelected. Not caring about the future of the state."

"I just don't think I am the future of the state," Clinton offers. "Maybe you are."

Matthew pauses at this, intrigued. "Think of it this way, then," he says. "This would be a huge help to me, Father. Did you ever think about that? You taking on a leadership role in the party would give me leverage in the governor's office. It would help me make a career here."

"Here?"

"Here in North Carolina. I'm asking *you* to help *me*."

Clinton nods at his son, whom he loves, whom he has always loved. "That's different," he says. "I'll do anything I can to help you. Unlike Will, I'm no politician. You should know that. I'm an old soldier and farmer. But if you need me, I'll be there regardless."

And for a brief moment, there is a bridge between them, these two who are so close and yet so different. Matthew reaches out and when Clinton grasps his hand, the son is shocked by the work-worn calluses in his father's palm.

They can hear the outside door in the kitchen open and close, the sound of the dogs lapping water, and Catherine laughing at them.

CHAPTER 61

DESPITE SOME ANXIETY ON THE PART OF ALMOST everyone present, supper that night is the communion that both Catherine and Marian hope for. Luke opens up under the influence of the wine, Marian is glowing in the presence of her father and her brother at the same table. Catherine is sly, funny, gracious. Clinton is quiet for most of the meal, but his face never loses a slight, grateful, satisfied aspect. Matthew goes out of his way to be charming—to his sister, to his new brother-in-law, to the mysterious Catherine. And to his father, which wins him points with both Marian and Catherine.

They don't reveal to Matthew that his sister is pregnant. He hasn't returned that far into the good graces of the family, and Marian has whispered to Catherine that she doesn't want him to know. Not yet. But even so, there is a secret light inside Marian and her father, Luke, and even Catherine. The glow that comes with the advent of the next generation. Life to come.

Night falls early this late in the year. At eight o'clock, it's full dark outside, and cold. When Catherine slips away into the kitchen to dish up pie and ice cream, she finds Nick, the husky-shepherd, and Jake, the terrier, standing at rigid attention by the back door. Nick's head is up and his nostrils are quivering. Sensing her presence behind him, he turns to her and barks once. She knows immediately that he doesn't like something in the air and that he wants the door open. Doing what she's seen Clint do a dozen times, she automatically opens the door for the dogs, and they're off, sprinting straight through the orchard toward the high pasture.

It's only when she looks up to follow their path that she sees it. The thing that has finally come to destroy them.

The rock barn in the upper pasture is a torch. *How?* she thinks for a brief moment. *How when it's stone?* But then, *It's the roof,* she realizes. "Oh my God, the horses—" This last, she whispers out loud. Then screams. "Clint—fire!"

He's beside her almost immediately. "Oh, no, no," he mutters under his breath. "Tonight of all nights." And then he's gone, sprinting through the dining and living rooms, onto the stairs, and she knows that he's gone for the shotgun.

As he tears past the dining room table, only Marian has the presence of mind to speak. "What?" she says. "What is it?"

"Somebody torched the rock barn," he shouts from the stairs. "Maybe headed toward the house."

Matthew looks up suddenly, more than surprised. Shocked. "But he promised me they wouldn't..." he mutters. Both Marian and Luke hear him but, in the hectic dance of the moment, don't grasp what he means.

Then Clinton is back through the room, stuffing shells into his barn coat pocket, the double-barrel 12 gauge long in his hands.

"Dad! Be careful!" Marian calls, knowing full well that he won't hear her. He's already at the back door, lacing up his farm boots, headed out into the dark.

And then the strangest thing that Marian has ever seen occurs just in front of her. Catherine Metcalf, her best friend, her father's lover, strides through the living room cursing under her breath and tears open the coat closet door. She reaches first up onto the shelf where hats and gloves live and pulls down a mysterious metal object, mysterious only until she unearths a rifle from behind the coats and clicks the magazine into its stock. *My God*, Marian thinks, *she knows what she's doing.*

Catherine wheels around, the rifle, some sort of military weapon, pointed at the ceiling. "You," she says, pointing at Marian, "and you," pointing at Luke, "down into the basement. Stay there! Keep her safe, Luke! You," pointing at Matthew, "across the road for the caretaker. We may have to fight a fire!"

Catherine doesn't pause to see if they follow her orders. She is gone after Clinton, into the kitchen and out the door. The pie sits on the stovetop, the ice cream melting on the counter.

Marian and Luke make eye contact. "You and the baby come first," he whispers. She leads him toward the door to the basement steps, which is under the second-floor stairs. As they go, they are vaguely aware of Matthew grabbing up his coat and, strangely, his briefcase. Aware of him pulling open the front door and rushing out. Only later will they realize that instead of alerting Randall Shelton, he starts up his state car and drives away.

CLINTON IN THE LATE OCTOBER DARK, STANDS at the edge of the orchard, one hand on the gate to the lower pasture.

He has the strangest feeling that he's been here before and then, for a split second, like a lightning flash, he remembers the previous invasion of their life and land, when someone—his nephew—attempted to fire the horse barn in the upper pasture. But now—*now*—the roof of that same barn is fully aflame, a torch against the black flank of the mountain.

He breaks open the breach of the shotgun and checks with his fingers to be sure it's loaded. Buckshot, which will tear apart anything it hits at reasonable range. He clicks the breach closed and even as he does, sees a horrible sight. Forty feet away, the back corner of the log barn, the barn closest to the house, suddenly flares up, flames licking and climbing up the ancient, notched logs at the corner.

He unlatches the gate, steps through, and automatically pulls it closed behind him. As he does, the silhouette of a man, larger than he expects, steps around the corner of the barn. The shepherd-husky, Nick, leaps at the figure out of the darkness, tearing at his arm. The man kicks the dog viciously away, points a pistol at him and fires.

Nick rolls over and over in the pasture grass, crying in pain.

Clinton steps forward and shouts—aiming to be heard over the crackling of the flames and the screams of his dog. "Drop the damn gun, you son of a bitch."

"Fuck you, old man," the figure yells and casually points the pistol at Clinton.

Clinton feels the impact of the bullet more than he hears the shot. It drills through his left side, scorching across his ribs, burning...burning. And in that moment, he's again in Germany, staring straight into the blistered maw of his own death. He does what he was trained to do. Drops to one knee, raises the shotgun to his shoulder and takes careful aim at the midsection of the man's body. Holds his ragged breath steady and pulls the trigger on first one load and then the other, spaced so close together that it might be one blast.

Tom Runnion dies as he lurches backward against the barn.

A second figure steps up beside Runnion's body in the lurid light of the fire. Vaguely, Clinton realizes this is the one he expected. Bowlegged, slouching. He cracks open the breach of the shotgun, his left arm shaking now, and reloads. He's confused. Will he kill his own nephew?

Jake, the terrier, rips into Willie's leg, furious at the fire and enraged by Nick's cries.

Clinton slips slowly over onto his side, unable to hold himself upright any longer. From where he lies on the cold, wet ground, he can just make out Catherine standing over him, firing the carbine shot after shot after shot at the fleeing figure of Willie Salter and hitting nothing but the burning barn.

PART FOUR

IS

Asheville and
Madison County
1965

CHAPTER 62

Memorial Mission Hospital, Asheville. For the first two days after he is shot, Clinton is treated in the trauma wing, room 313. Catherine only leaves his side when Marian drives over from Marshall to spell her for a few hours.

He's not in danger, the doctors keep reassuring her, but they have to deal with the infection drilled into his body by the .38 caliber slug and lying afterward in a cold, wet mixture of mud, manure, and fertilizer.

Between the infection, which rages hot through his body for the first day and a half, and the painkillers, he is only marginally conscious even when awake.

Of what does he dream? As he is lying there, high on antibiotics and morphine, what visions come to him?

The answer is simple enough—he dreams of rivers.

The Laurel, where it flows down past Hurricane and into its tight, granite-walled gorge. Splashes, tosses, runs wild until it meets the French Broad, his home river, the matriarch of rivers.

By the second night, the doctors assure Catherine that the infection from Tom Runnion's bullet will subside and—eventually—the pain in his ribs. One last sweet, severe dose of morphine feeds his river dreams and the next morning, still groggy, he tells Cat that there are two French Broad Rivers, not one. The first they can see because it flows over the surface of the earth. Ripple and rapid, fish and kingfisher.

She takes his hand as he talks and caresses his palm, not at all sure that he is in his right mind.

But there is another one beneath the first...subterranean. "Don't you see," he says, smiling wistfully at her. "Somewhere around Asheville, part of the river seeps down through fissures of the earth into hidden passages, veins and arteries, but still flows north. Flows north under the surface, close to the heart of things, where it is hellfire hot. Oh, Cat, I've been so hot."

"I know, Clint, I know." She fetches a cold, wet cloth with which to wipe his forehead and sits to take his hand again.

"The other river, the buried river, is heated by the fire of it, you see, before it rises to the surface again at Hot Springs..." He's speaking slowly, dreamily. "...where it returns to the surface to join its brother. Rising again into the light. But purified now by the darkness and the minerals and the heat."

He rolls on his side in the hospital bed before she can restrain him. Reaches out to her and she leans over him to embrace him awkwardly. Lays her cheek against his, sandpaper rough with three-days' beard.

"That's us," he whispers to her. "Sweet Cat, that's us. We have been hidden underground these last months, navigating those dark places, that deep passage, and we're superheated. We have been near the very heart of the earth, and we are seared from it."

She helps him roll onto his back again and then sits herself, resisting the urge to lie down on the bed beside him. "How do you know all these things?" she asks. "About the two rivers?"

"Last day or so, I've been talking to the river," he says. More clearly now. Maybe more awake than before.

"Does the river talk back?" she asks, smiling at him.

"Oh, yes," he says. "It's always talking, mostly to itself." He watches her face, treasuring the sight of her in the thin morning light. He reaches out again, and when their fingers meet, he pulls her hand to his sore, cracked lips. "Sometimes, Cat," he says into her palm, "I can hear the river singing."

Only later, after she helps him sip chipped ice in cold water, after they both doze for a bit, he curled on his good side and she in her chair, "And are we rising now?" she murmurs while her eyes are still closed. "To the surface? Bringing our heat into the light?"

"Yes," he says. "We must...to survive."

ON THE MORNING OF THE THIRD DAY, THE DOCtors are pleased with his progress, and they move him into a standard room—still a private room, however, because he is a celebrity. The sheriff who was shot down defending his home and family.

On that morning as well, he is allowed other visitors. Among the first are Judge Gudger and Way Tipton. With Catherine's help, he describes for them, in detail, what happened. The judge allows that he will convene a grand jury to investigate the death of Runnion, but he doubts seriously if there will be formal charges. People expect mountain sheriffs to shoot their political opponents.

In front of the judge, Clinton tells Way Tipton to go to Will's farm on Little Pine and arrest Willie Salter as a serial arsonist.

"You sure about that, Clinton—I mean, Sheriff?"

Clinton glances at Catherine, who leans against the window frame. She nods. They have discussed this.

"I'm sure," Clinton says. "He was there. And it's his boot print we kept seeing at other sites."

"Yes, but he's—"

"I don't care. It's time. Take Danny Fender with you in case Will or Willie gives you any trouble. Fender was a man when he was twelve years old."

"Go armed?"

"Yes. The judge here will give you a warrant."

WHEN THEY ARE GONE AND CATHERINE MOVES back to the bedside chair, he looks long at her and sighs. "Is Nick dead?" he asks finally. She realizes that between the pain and the morphine, he's forgotten about his dog. Forgotten, that is, until they retold the events of the night.

She grins. "No, he's not dead. The vet in Marshall had to amputate his leg, but he's already back home, hopping around the house on three legs. Half-crazed because we won't let him outside except on a leash."

He laughs. For the first time since the night of the fire, he laughs, and she with him.

"Help me," he says after a moment. "Get me up and let's go for a walk around the ward. Maybe they'll let me go home too if I walk on a leash."

"Two days," she says as she slowly helps him sit up on the side of the bed. "Doctor says maybe two more days. If you cooperate."

BY THE AFTERNOON OF THE FOURTH DAY, THE doctors are satisfied. He can go home the following morning, so long as there will be someone with him twenty-four hours a day until they are sure he can care for himself.

The debate that ensues takes place over his bed; over his body, really. The two women he loves most in the world, one on each side.

"Luke and I can just stay at the farm for a week or so," Marian says.

"You both have to teach," Catherine counters.

"Then who?" Marian.

Catherine raises her eyebrows—all she has to do to signal her intent.

"Oh," Marian says. "But you have to go to work too. If you don't show up for a week, what do you think people are going to say?"

"They're already saying it, I would imagine." This comes from Clinton, but they pay him no mind.

"I could take a few days off," Luke offers from where he sits in the corner. "Take care of—" He almost says *the old man* but catches himself in time.

Catherine and Marian both turn to look at Luke and then, simultaneously, shake their heads.

"Love you, honey, but..." Marian begins.

"Not a nurse," Catherine finishes.

It appears to be a stalemate.

"How about I take care of myself? The dogs will be there." Clinton speaks, flat on his back. "All I want to do is go home."

The women don't bother to reply to the dogs, don't even look down, but Catherine does lay a hand on his shoulder.

"Let's split it," Marian says.

Catherine nods, at first slowly and then with some conviction. "I'll do nights. You do days. I'll go to school during the day."

"Will you teach my two senior classes?"

Catherine nods. "And you go home to your husband at night. You're newlyweds, remember?"

And you go home to yours, Marian almost replies but catches herself, first frowns and then smiles at the thought. And says instead, "There's some strange sort of symmetry in all this, isn't there?"

Catherine nods. "I know. I feel it too."

There's a significant pause, as each one in the room thinks about what's to come.

"What day is it?" Clinton asks after a bit.

"Wednesday, maybe Thursday," says Catherine.

"Wednesday," Luke confirms.

"October twenty-seventh," adds Marian. "On Saturday, Luke and I will have been married three weeks."

"Good Lord," Catherine says. "All the more reason for you to spend these nights at home."

THEY MANAGE TO GET LUKE AND MARIAN OUT the door, Marian to return the next morning to take her father home to the farm. Catherine is left alone with Clint.

"You too," he says. "Go home for the night. Please."

"But will you—"

"No, no. You've slept in a chair for three nights straight, if you can even call it sleeping. They're going to come in shortly with a tray of hospital chow, and in another few hours, I'll be sound asleep."

"Dreaming of rivers?"

He nods. "Dreaming of rivers. Dreaming of us." She takes his hand, and he squeezes her fingers. "You're so tired you can barely stand up, Cat. Go home to your place, take a hot bath, and sleep. I'll see you..."

"You'll see me late tomorrow afternoon, as soon as school's out. At the farm."

"It will seem like heaven after all this."

She bends over to kiss him, the first time she's placed her lips directly on his since he was shot. Just that much touch, and her eyes are damp. "God, I'm glad you're alive," she whispers.

CHAPTER 63

EARLY THE NEXT MORNING, WHILE CLINTON'S still picking at his breakfast, he has a visitor: William Deaver Salter, his younger brother.

Clinton has been up since dawn and sitting in one of the chairs in his room. Will pulls the other around to face Clinton.

"I came by to check on you," Will says in what, for him, is a quiet tone. "See how you're making out."

Clinton nods and pushes the tray with his breakfast, mostly untouched, to one side. "There's a biscuit and some gravy there if you want it," he says to Will, caught up still in the long habit of taking care of him.

"Naw, I'm all right. I ate something at the coffee shop downstairs. I was a little nervous about coming up to see you, after what happened the other night."

For a long, tired moment, Clinton isn't sure what to say. Then: "It's a miracle that nobody in the family was killed. Willie, for one."

"Or you," Will says simply. "Brother."

"Or me. I guess it's a good thing Runnion couldn't shoot straight."

"Runnion was drunk," Will offers. "So was Willie, truth be told."

"We've had a lot of trouble with the truth these past years, Will, seems to me." Clinton shifts slightly in the hard hospital chair, trying to ease the pain in his ribs.

"You all right?" Will asks. "Want to get back in the bed?"

"Nah. I can sit a while longer. Good for me." And then, after another pause: "What are you doing here, Will? There's no votes to be had in the hospital."

"Believe it or not, I come to make peace." Will sighs. "I had to do a lot of thinking the last few days. Then Tipton and Fender showed up at the farm late yesterday. Took Willie. Gave me some more to think about overnight."

"It's a rough damn time. I'll give you that. But I warned you. If Willie touched another match, he was going down."

"I know you did. And I warned him, threatened him within an inch of his life, but it didn't do no good. Something's bad wrong with that boy, to tell the truth."

"Truth again, huh?"

Will nods. "Maybe we need to just be honest with each other. Part of what I've had on my mind is how we started out. You and me. Fighting just to survive. I know that. I know I owe you, and I don't want us to turn on each other now. I'm here to say I'm sorry for my part of it."

Clinton stares at his brother in wonder. He's never heard him apologize for anything, not since he was a small boy. "Where do you think we went off the tracks?" he asks. "The war, when I was gone?"

"I think it was before that." Will is oddly decisive when he says this.

Clinton searches through the hazy files of memory. "Before? When we were both just starting out? What do you mean?"

"I've carried around the burden of something for a long time," Will says, slowly, carefully. He is rubbing his hands together now, so hard that the muscles in his arms and shoulders bulge from the tension. "Something that nobody living except me knows about. And here lately, I've decided it's poisoning us. You and me. Come between us."

"What the hell, Will? Tell me."

"Back before the war. A year or so after you and Gretchen got married. Before I met Martha." Here he comes to a dead stop, his mouth open to speak, but the words choking in his throat.

"Go on."

"Me and Gretchen, I mean Gretchen and me...we had a fling."

"You mean like an affair? You slept together?" Clinton can feel his stomach draw up tight, the pain searing through his ribs.

Will nods, staring straight into Clinton's eyes. "Yeah, that's what I mean. Not so much and not so long. Six months, maybe. She was miserable because she hated the mountains, and you were working night and day."

"It makes a kind of sense that she would do it," Clinton admits after a moment, his mind spinning back through those years, remembering what a fuss she'd made over Will, always inviting him to meals, always answering the phone when he called. "But why in the hell did *you* do it?"

"Cause you've always been better than me. That's why, damn you. Better at school, better at sports. Better at everything. Hell, better with girls. You always finished everything. Even college. And for once, just once, here was something you weren't better at. You didn't even understand your own wife. And I did. I understood her. She turned to me, talked to me. Sought me out when you didn't have time for her."

Clinton has tears in his eyes. Anger? Sorrow? Maybe some guilt. More sorrow, he thinks, than anything. At the sheer, unmitigated waste of it all. Time and emotion...his own stupidity.

"I wish I hadn't done it," Will says and coughs to clear his throat. "And I would understand if you hated me for it."

Clinton feels his head shaking even before the words come. "No, little brother, I don't hate you. Been a few times lately when I wanted to kill you, but I don't hate you."

"Will you accept my apology for what I done?"

"I don't even know for sure what that means, Will."

"Part of what it means is that sleeping with—with what happened back then is that it made me feel superior to you all these years. Made me think I was smarter than you, that I knew things you didn't. That you were the naive one, the Boy Scout, and I was the one who knew the way of the world. Eventually, I decided that I could make you sheriff and then make you do what I wanted. I guess you could say what happened back then stained my mind, corrupted me."

"I guess you could say that. Maybe *she* corrupted you."

"I'd like to start over. See if we could ever get back to where we were."

Again, Clinton marvels at his brother. The single human being on the face of the earth he's known longer than any other. And again, he fears that there are tears in his eyes. "Equals," he says finally.

"What?"

"What if we start over as equals? Or at least try to. And speak the truth to each other."

Will nods, is still nodding when they hear a knock on the hospital room door. Neither speaks, but both are nodding in some silent agreement of the blood.

Following the knock, Marian shoves the door open with her shoulder. She's carrying a duffel bag, ready to get her father dressed and out to the car. Ready to get him started on the arduous journey home.

"Uncle Will," she says, surprised. "What are you doing here?" And for a moment, the reverberations from the firefight at the farm are just here, in the room with them. Muzzle flash and flame.

"We were just visiting," Clinton reassures Marian. "Talking about the past."

"I've come to help your father if I can," Will says to her.

CHAPTER 64

THE FARM AT DOE BRANCH. THURSDAY AFTERnoon.

Randall Shelton comes to sit with him on the porch and reports that the roof on the stone barn took most of the damage. But he's been working on it each day and has removed the charred timbers along with the scorched and twisted tin. A Goforth boy named Josh from Big Pine is coming on Saturday to help him, and they should have the roof back on by the end of the weekend. He also confirms that the horses are fine, although Nell has turned off skittish again since the night of the fire.

The news about the log barn is not so good. Only the back right corner burned, but the back wall collapsed next day from the weight of the roof, and he reckons the whole thing will have to be replaced.

"Daddy Man?" Clint asks, and Randall looks down.

"He was crushed when the back wall collapsed, Clint, and it's my fault."

"What do you mean?"

"He busted out the night of the fire, but I found him next day and put him back in his stall. Should never have done that. Should have seen the structure won't stable."

"Were you able to bury him?"

Shelton shakes his head. "Didn't have to. Barn did it for us."

"Smell?"

Shelton shrugs. "Pretty bad when the wind is right. I reckon I owe you for his loss."

Clinton shakes his head. "Of course not. You had no way of knowing. Insurance will buy us a new ram. And we'll rebuild the barn in the spring. Maybe two stories this time. Can you knock together some sort of lean-to shelter for the ewes in the meantime?"

LATE AFTERNOON, MARIAN PACKS UP FOR THE drive to Marshall, where she and Luke are slowly transforming her small house into a place for the two of them. She realizes her father is tired and tries to talk him into coming inside and resting on the couch, but he is determined to wait for Catherine on the front porch. "I've been inside for days," he tells her, "and the fresh air alone is delicious." In response, she brings out a quilt from the couch and wraps it around his legs.

When Catherine's station wagon pulls into the driveway, Marian goes down the front steps to meet her, and together they bring in another suitcase load of Catherine's clothes along with sacks of groceries. Once everything is inside, the two women gang up on him and convince him that it will be dark before long, and both he and Nick need to be inside where it's warm. Once both dog and man are settled, Marian leaves.

Clinton naps while Catherine puts up all the groceries and begins to brown chunks of stew beef in the cast-iron skillet. She turns on the radio that sits on the kitchen counter, tuned to a county music station out of Tennessee, and lets it play quietly as she cooks. She realizes as she boils the potatoes and cuts up the onions just how much she likes caring for him, cooking for him. Yes, the onions make her cry, but there's no sadness or hurt in those tears. When he wakes, she'll fix them both a drink and carry his into the living room. Something that simple, that elemental, and she is filled with a sort of homecoming even as she anticipates it.

Part of what she's realized these past days, since the fire and the shooting, is that he cares for her the same way. That he wants to do for her in the simplest manner possible, to cook for her, to pour her whiskey and carry it to where she sits. Climb up the stairs to bring her coffee in bed. To serve her. And somehow that knowledge, that he cares for her comfort and her pleasure, opens her to him. Brings her into rhythm with him.

She knows she can't match his cornbread, so she rolls out and cuts biscuits to bake to go with the stew.

After a bit, she hears him stirring, and when she tiptoes into the living room, she finds him up and about, building a fire in the fireplace. He still mostly holds his left arm close to his side, where the doctors have his fractured ribs tightly wrapped, but he's moving more easily, using his right hand to toss corncobs and split pine kindling into the firebox.

"Are you supposed to be up and doing like that?" she asks, but easily, easily.

He nods. "Yes, I am, Doctor. It's so we can sit up later on the couch. I have one good arm, which I mean to wrap around you."

"All right, then. When the fire catches, sit back down, and I'll bring you a drink. You can drink, can't you?"

"Yes, I can. I have officially replaced morphine with bourbon. And the doctor says I am to take my medicine or suffer the consequences."

LATER, AFTER SUPPER, THEY DO SIT TOGETHER on the couch, both with their old-fashioned medicine. Both relishing the sense of being truly home, being in the one place on the face of the earth where they are left alone to be themselves.

"What do you reckon happened to Matthew that night?" he asks her at one point. "I don't remember him at all once the fun began."

She describes for him what she told Matthew and then, after

some hesitation, what Marian reported to her later on. "He said something like *he promised me they wouldn't* or...*they promised me they wouldn't unless*.... Then he grabbed up his coat and his papers and drove away. Scattered gravel getting out of the driveway." Then, after a bit. "What do you think it means?"

Clinton sighs. "I think it means he'd been talking to his Uncle Will or maybe even Willie. And that he knew about the fires, but thought Willie and Runnion wouldn't try to burn us out. Or at least wouldn't try to burn us out until he'd had a chance to make his pitch, sell me on his goddamn politics."

"Have you heard from him since?"

"Marian says he called her on Sunday and asked if everyone was all right. She gave him the casualty list along with a piece of her mind. Says she called him a coward for running away. He said he was worried about his reputation, didn't want to lose his job with the governor. Couldn't afford to get mixed up in any redneck incident that might make the papers." And then after a moment, adds, "Plus I guess it was his worst nightmare: feuding in them there hills."

"I'm sorry, Clint. Truly I am. He was so nice at supper that night. Good to you and sweet to Marian."

"There's something else here, Cat, that might be connected."

"What do you mean? Something you're not telling me?"

"I haven't had a chance until now. I haven't seen you since it happened."

"Does it have anything to do with Will coming to the hospital? Marian told me she walked in on you two this morning."

"She did. More or less in the middle of something."

"She said you weren't fighting."

"Not with each other. Wrestling with the past, maybe."

"What?"

"He told me that not long after Gretchen and I got married, the two of them had an affair."

"He didn't!"

"He did. Said he'd had to do a lot of soul-searching, if you can imagine such a thing, and even though he was the only living person on earth who knew about it, he felt like the secret was killing us."

"Us?"

"The two of us. Our relationship. Felt like it had poisoned everything that has happened between the two of us since."

"Do you think he's telling the truth?"

"It seems incredible, but why in the world would he lie?"

"Just to hurt you."

"No, it wasn't like that. He was serious. Watching Willie get dragged off to jail may have finally torn something loose inside him."

She sips her whiskey, pausing, thinking. "When did the affair happen exactly?" she asks finally, carefully.

"I know what you're thinking," he says. Sighs. "You might as well say it." He takes a bite of his own drink and lets the bourbon sit on his tongue to burn.

"Is it possible that Matthew is...?"

"Is his son and not mine?"

She can only nod. "That."

"I suppose it's possible. It might explain some things."

"Christ, Clint. Are you okay? First, you get shot and then you get...this."

He sighs and almost smiles. "When I was younger, we'd say it's like getting kicked in the balls by a mule."

She laughs because he means for her to. "That's what I meant. Shot and kicked."

"I think I am okay. I've had since this morning to think about it. I don't know if I need to know right now, one way or another. He acts more like Will's son than he does mine, and that's the part that hurts."

It takes her a moment to reply. Then, she says, "He did come back to you eventually, though."

"I know. I felt it. But I also think he wanted something. Some help that he thought—or somebody thought—I could give. If he was worth a damn, he would have been there at the hospital this week."

"He's young yet, Clint. You know that."

"He is. I admit it. I'd walk a hundred miles to get him back, regardless of...of that other thing. But I don't think he cares about us. He lives in Will's world, not mine. He should have been right where you were, boot-deep in the mud, scaring off Willie and Tom Runnion."

"When you do eventually meet my mother," she says, "I want you to describe that to her. Boot-deep and firing away."

WHEN THEIR GLASSES ARE EMPTY, SHE OFFERS to make up a bed for him on the couch.

"I want to sleep with you," he says simply. "I may not be of much use right now, but I'd give a pound of flesh just to be able to reach out in the dark and touch your arm. Know you're there."

"You already gave the pound of flesh," she says, "last Saturday night." And after a languid moment spent staring into his face: "Come on, then, soldier, let's drag you up those stairs."

CHAPTER 65

By Sunday, Clinton is much improved. According to the doctors, he's past needing Catherine to spend the night, but it's Halloween, and the long afternoon is haunted. By suppertime, it's clear that she doesn't wish to leave, nor does he want her to. When darkness falls, it is riven with moon and starlight.

The wind is in the trees tonight and howling along the ridgeline. Everything outside the walls of the house suggests death in life, past in present, and the somber, restless chanting of ghosts.

Following the doctor's prescription, Cat unwinds the tight wrapping from Clint's ribs that afternoon and replaces the thick bandages with a lighter dressing. They are celebrating being alive and warm inside the house while goblins rule the pastures and fields outside.

After supper, when they sit with their drinks before the fire, she tells him about her visit from the superintendent of schools on Friday afternoon. "He's a nice man, though harried," she says. "And he asked me about us."

"You and me?" Clinton asks.

She nods, smiling ruefully.

"None of his damn business," Clinton says. And then after a breath or two, asks, "What did you say?"

"Said I met you through Marian, and that after my husband died, we became close friends. When you were shot, I helped her take care of you."

"What did he say back?"

"Said that he understood. Was entirely sympathetic. But that given our small-town mentality and the makeup of the board, it might be a good idea if we were more discreet."

"Discreet! How in the hell could we be more discreet and still breathe?"

"Yes, discreet. Or that we consider..."

"Consider what?"

Here, a distinct pause. She is not at all sure that she wants to say it out loud. "Consider getting married."

He laughs. To which she smiles, sips her whiskey.

Later, after he hauls himself to his feet to feed the fire and add a splash of Halloween bourbon to their glasses, she asks him if he remembers what he said before when she asked him about marriage.

He goes into the kitchen without answering and lets the dogs out, speaking softly to both, but especially to Nick, who is steady on three legs but not yet strong. When he returns to the living room, he is nodding. "Yes," he says, "I recall something like that. However..."

"However, what?"

"However, I would only marry you."

"What does that mean, Clint? Will you or won't you?"

"Hmm. I don't know. What do you think?"

She sets her glass tumbler carefully down on the coffee table, struggles slightly as she rises to her feet. "What do I think!" she whispers. "What do I think? I think that I wish you'd make up your mind."

He realizes suddenly that she's near to tears. He's been teasing her, certain that she knows he's only playing. But somehow, he's missed the signs, and this is all deadly serious to her.

He struggles against the pain in his side to drag himself upright. "Cat, you know—" This with a groan.

"Sometimes, I don't know, Clint." Still in a voice barely above a whisper. "Sometimes I'm not sure what you're thinking. And I hate myself for having to ask." Then, just as he manages to stand, she turns and walks away from him into the kitchen. He hears the outside door open and close.

HE STANDS ALONE IN THE LIVING ROOM FOR A long, muttering moment. Reaches into his pants pocket to reassure himself that the thing that he secreted there hasn't fallen out into the couch cushions. He pulls on his old barn coat, which feels appropriate to the night, and takes with him her thick wool sweater from the coat-tree.

There's a heavy flashlight by the kitchen door. He takes that as well.

When he steps outside, the voice of the wind increases by half an octave, haunting and restless. The new moon is a week old and sitting just over the ridge to the east, troubled by rafts of clouds blown across its face, its pale light coming and going over the fields.

Which way would she go, alone and in the dark?

He turns the flashlight on to see if she's sitting at the picnic table in the side yard or anywhere close by, but when it reveals nothing, he clicks it off again. Something tells him that the electric torch won't guide him, that she won't respond to that harsh light in her eyes. Besides, his own eyes will adjust more quickly to the dark if he leaves the light behind. He sets it down behind him on the back steps.

He walks out to the edge of the orchard, one of her favorite places on the farm now that the fallen fruit has rotted away and the grass has grown tall again around the apple trees. The yellow jackets of summer are long gone, the twisted old trees mostly free of their leaves. Each tree has a different personality, or so she tells him. And her favorite is the last, gnarled tree at the upper end, which stands alone, facing up the mountain, watching out for the horses. So she says.

He walks slowly up, between the reaching, grasping branches of the trees, listening to the leaves that are left rattling when the wind whispers to them. When he reaches the end of the orchard, a dozen feet or so below her tree, he stops to listen, and the wind seems to pause as well. In that pause, he can hear her, sighing perhaps, or crying.

He speaks her name, loud enough to be heard on this uneasy night, steps softly toward the tree, where he finds her sitting on the ground, leaning back against its rough trunk. He kneels in front of her and reaches out to wrap the bulk of the sweater around her arms and shoulders. "You're shaking," he says to her. "Here." And he pulls off his coat to wrap around her legs.

She frees one hand to swipe at her face. "You don't want me," she says plaintively. "I just have to get used to the idea that at the end of the day, you might not want me."

He shakes his head in the dark. "That's ridiculous. You're the smartest person I know, but sometimes..."

"If you wanted me, you'd say it. You'd quit pouring liquor and cigar smoke down that throat of yours, and you'd open your mouth and just say it."

He can hear the dogs barking up at the cemetery—by the sound of it, a bear. Or a ghost... Nothing alive that threatens them here.

"Can't you tell how much I want you?" And even as the words spill out of his mouth, he realizes that's not what she's asking. He tries again. "I want you, Catherine Carter Metcalf."

"For what? You don't like my cooking, and you don't need a nurse anymore."

The devil inside him raises its head one last time. "I love your cooking, but...it's mostly for sex," he says, smiling at her whether she can see his face or not.

"If I could get my arm free, I'd slap you," she mutters, trying to keep the humor out of her voice.

"Will you marry me?"

She has already started to speak but now has to clear her throat. "What did you say? It's awfully windy out here."

"Here, pull your hand—your left hand—out from under your sweater. Let me have it."

"Why?"

"I need it. What I said was, *Will you marry me*? I'll keep on saying it."

"What are you doing?"

"I'm trying to slip something on your finger."

"What is it? Clint?"

"It's a ring. It's my mother's ring, almost the only thing I have left that's hers."

"Are you giving it to me? Here, let me help."

"Does it fit?"

"I think so. It's a little loose. I just need to be careful."

"Will you—"

"What are you saying?"

"I was going to ask you tonight, in front of the fireplace. I had the ring in my pocket. But then you ran out the door."

"I did not run. I slipped away like an ethereal spirit. This is better, anyway. Here, sit beside me, and we'll cover up with your coat. The sweater. Here, hold my hand so the ring doesn't slip off. This is better."

"Why is this better?"

She sighs. "Because we're sitting on the land, Clint. This is who you are. The house is fine. I love the house. But the side of the mountain will always be you. The dirt, the trees, the smell of the wind."

She can feel him starting to nod. Admitting she's right.

"You never answered. Are you going to marry me?" he whispers into her hair after a bit.

"I suppose I might. Since you asked."

CHAPTER 66

THEY'VE BEEN DEBATING, CATHERINE AND MARIAN. Christmas or Christmas Eve? In a church? Catherine says she'd like a church, and Marian supports her.

Back and forth, arguments for this and arguments for that. Which, to be frank, Clinton doesn't understand. Why be married at Christmas? And why, for God's sake, in a church? But Christmas has taken on a kind of spectral power in Catherine's mind. And Catherine and Marian have moved on to discussing which church, not whether a church.

Until, finally, when he can abide it no longer, Clinton himself makes a suggestion. "Old Christmas," he says. "We live in the mountains. Why not Old Christmas?"

They are sitting around the Thanksgiving table at the farm. Marian has just served her pumpkin pie. The three of them, plus Marian's Luke, who is following the conversation closely but hasn't joined in until now. "What's Old Christmas?" he asks.

Marian glances at Catherine, who points with her fork at Luke. "I'm glad *you* said it," Catherine says. "I know I'm supposed to know but I don't.... Marian?"

"It's in January, I think. New Year's, maybe. Dad?"

Clinton clears his throat with mock seriousness. "Apparently, I exist in a vale of ignorance so deep and so wide that—"

"Just shut up and tell us," Marian interrupts him.

"How can I both shut up and—"

"Tell us. Or you're going to get married on Christmas Day."

"Eve," Catherine corrects her.

"Old Christmas is when the old-timers celebrate. Not just the birth of Jesus—most agree to celebrate that on December twenty-fifth. But it took time for the wise men to ride those camels cross-country, and they didn't arrive until twelve days after he was born."

"The twelve days of Christmas?" Luke asks.

"Exactly. Thank you, Luke. Christmas only *begins* on December twenty-fifth in the mountains. It doesn't end until January sixth. My grandpa and grandma up in Anderson Cove expected us to visit them on the sixth, and they wouldn't give us our presents or candy until then. That was before my mother left and before my father—" He looks away suddenly and Catherine can tell that he's tearing up. She's noticed lately how any mention of his parents moves him, and she touches his mother's ring on her finger. They've had it sized and she wears it now without fear. Wears it proudly.

"It's Epiphany," Catherine says quietly.

"What's...Epiphany?" Marian.

"In the Episcopal church, where I grew up, it was celebrated. I guess on January sixth. The arrival of the Magi and the revelation of the Christ child."

Marian, ever the English teacher, asks, "But isn't it also...the revelation of truth? The sudden realization of something vital."

"The essential nature of things," her father says. "Epiphany is when things are revealed. And if it's on Old Christmas, it's also when the animals talk. Perhaps it's the animals who reveal the truth."

"What?" Hard to tell who says this first, Marian or Catherine.

"Out in the mountains, the old-timers still believe that at midnight on Christmas Eve, the animals speak, especially the farm animals who were there when Jesus was born. But since those same old-timers believe that the true magic happens on Old Christmas, it's midnight on January fifth, the eve of the true holy day. Kings Day or Revelation Day."

"Are you an old-timer, Papa?"

Clinton gazes fondly at his daughter. "Yes," he says eventually. "I may be the only one in the family, but I stand with the old ways."

Catherine grins at him. "He does belong up here rather than in town," she says to Marian. "Plus, he's superstitious as hell." She screws up her face as if considering a dilemma. Then, with tenderness in her voice: "I'm changing my vote. Let's get married on Old Christmas."

Marian and her Luke watch the older couple carefully, almost afraid to break the spell between them. "What about a church?" Marian whispers finally.

"I think I've found one," Clinton replies promptly.

"*You've* found one?" Marian asks skeptically. "You hate churches, Papa."

"More like I don't *trust* churches. Or preachers either, for that matter. But I sort of favor this little church."

"Where is it? Which is it?" Marian.

"I'm going to take Cat to see it this afternoon. I went and sat in it not long ago, and I think it might be all right."

"You're not going to show it to Luke and me?"

"Not yet. Let's see if Cat approves. Her opinion is the one that matters."

An hour later, Marian and Luke pack up for the drive back to town. Clinton helps Luke carry a bag and basket out to their car, and while the men stand talking beside the car, they can see the women on the porch whispering to each other. "I'll call you tomorrow," Catherine promises Marian. "Once I see what he's up to."

WHAT HE WAS UP TO INVOLVES WALKING through the orchard to the upper pasture and through the pasture to the stone barn. It has a new roof since the fire, along with a new selection of tack, including a new saddle for Catherine, hers having been scorched beyond repair.

As they brush and comb Little Joe and Nell, Catherine finally asks the question that's been hanging in the air. "I thought we were going to visit a church this afternoon."

Clinton nods. "We are."

"This is a church we can ride to?"

"We can."

"Does it have four walls and a roof?"

"It does." He can't help himself. He starts laughing, which sets her off as well.

They lead the saddled horses out a side gate to the pasture that opens close to the family cemetery. There, they mount up and ride down the dirt cemetery road to Doe Branch, where they pause to let the horses drink from the creek.

"Which way?" she asks eventually, her curiosity growing.

He nods up the Doe Branch Road in the direction they rarely take when riding or walking. And after a few minutes, the horses satisfied with blowing and playing in the water, they ride at a steady walk on up the road, past the nearest neighbors and past a few lonely mailboxes. A mile or so further up, where the road veers to the right, away from the branch, they begin to climb. As they come to the top of the ridge—not very far and not very steep—they find a small church house on the top of the hill to the right of the road.

It's a small, concrete-block building, perhaps thirty feet wide and fifty feet long, with a wooden steeple. Over the door is a hand-painted sign that simply reads DOE BRANCH CHURCH. Beside the double front door, under the small overhang, someone has stacked firewood. Silently, they dismount and tie the horses to a poplar at the edge of the clearing.

He isn't at all sure how she'll react and is afraid to speak before she does. He hasn't had much, if anything, to do with the church in any of its many forms since Gretchen's death, and he's unsure if this lonely place will answer for Catherine. As they stand considering, a blue jay chatters at them from a tall oak beside the structure, and the somber mood shifts.

"Is the door unlocked?" Catherine asks.

He nods. "I think so."

She steps closer and takes his hand. "Let's look," she says.

He twists the simple knob on the right-hand door, which swings easily open. When they walk in, it seems to her that they've entered a haunted place. Like a house that was suddenly abandoned, half-empty plates of food still on the kitchen table. As if she and Clinton might have interrupted a congregation of ghosts singing silent hymns and passing an invisible collection plate. There is an open Bible on the pulpit and hymnals open face down on several of the benches. And yet, there are cobwebs everywhere and a layer of dust over all.

At first, she isn't sure they should be here, but he walks easily forward down the center aisle to a woodstove that rests in a box full of sand near the pulpit. He opens the stove door and slowly, carefully, lays a fire inside the belly of the stove: wadded pages from a wrecked hymnal, pine splinters and broken branches. She watches, arms crossed against the chill, while he brings matches out of the pocket of his barn coat and kneels to light the fire.

"Is that all the heat there is?" she asks, knowing the answer even as she frames the question.

He nods, looks up at her, and grins. "I suppose that in the winter, they sat up close, in the front pews."

"Who are *they*?"

"Folks who lived up and down the branch, mostly dead and gone now. I asked Randall, and he says the last service he knew of was at Easter last year, but then the old preacher passed away, and nobody comes here anymore. People say it's haunted."

"I don't doubt that." She watches his face carefully. "Do you come here?" she asks wonderingly. It seems so unlike him.

Before answering, he opens the door to the stove and pushes in two larger chunks of firewood, apparently brought in from the stack on the porch. He sits down on the front pew a few feet from the stove and motions with his head, suggesting she might join him. Which she does, seeking warmth, from the stove and from him.

"Since I got shot," he says quietly in response to her question. "And I thought I might die, I come up here every so often when I'm at the farm by myself. Sometimes, I sit for a while and think my thoughts. Grateful not to have died. Grateful for Marian and Luke, for the baby. Grateful for you. I never in my life expected something like you."

"Sounds to me like you're praying, Clint Salter."

"Maybe, although I don't follow any pattern. I just think about how lucky we are. About all the people who've come before and how we're the sum of who they were and what they did. And as crazy as it seems, I've come to really like this little place, this church, I guess it is. As if it's some sort of shelter left here just for us, some sort of haven untouched by time."

"Sanctuary," she whispers.

He nods. "That's the very word. I never dreamed that you might care for it since it's so rustic. But I liked to think about how it would be to bring you here, share it with you."

She sits close beside him now, thigh against thigh, her arm intertwined with his. "I like it here," she says. "It's peaceful." The only sound beside their voices is the fire in the stove and, occasionally, the wind at play in the trees outside. Listening to the wind, she thinks of the long and tumbled road that has brought them here. She touches the ring on her finger. "Did your mother go to church here, Clint?" she asks.

"I believe she did. Dad wouldn't get close to a church."

She sighs. "Well, then."

After a quiet moment—the fire murmuring, and the wind—she notices an old bird nest up under the eaves. "Where is the bathroom?" she asks. "And please don't tell me the woods."

"No, no," he offers. "There are two outhouses just behind the church, one for men and one for women. They're labeled with signs like the one over the church door."

"You're kidding, right? Come on, Clint, it's 1965."

"Nope. They're downright modern—for outhouses."

She starts to laugh, tickled at just how ridiculous this all feels, how ridiculous and how right. He can't help himself, and after a moment, starts to laugh with her, until they are both bent over at the waist, eyes damp with mirth. When finally they catch their breath, she leans closer to kiss his cheek and nuzzle his neck.

"I guess..." she whispers into his collar. "I guess all we need now is a priest of some sort."

CHAPTER 67

IT'S 1965 AND THE YEAR IS WINDING DOWN. November rolls over into December, and the nights grow longer and colder. The wind that pours down from the high peaks is full of teeth now. It bites at any exposed flesh and tears the hat off your head.

December 8, the moon is full.

Willie Salter was arrested and charged with arson while Clinton was still in the hospital. Public opinion runs hot against the boy, in part because he was there the night their sheriff was shot, and he was on the wrong side of the argument. Once bail is set for his son, Will arranges to bail him out awaiting trial. The boy is chastened, at least initially. It's hard to tell what goes on inside his cloudy mind. Clinton's deputies—Danny Fender in particular—have let him know that next time, they won't be so gentle with him.

The Crowders, father Robert and son James, are awaiting trial for murder in the Buncombe County jail. Any remaining ambiguity about how and where they were arrested has faded entirely away under the ongoing publicity about the cruelty of their crime: killing Grady and Bonnie Norton in cold blood for a sack full of rare coins and less than five thousand dollars in cash. The evidence collected by Clinton and analyzed by the SBI crime lab has given District Attorney Eastman everything he needs to send one, if not both, to the electric chair. Clinton has never forgiven them for shooting Popper the dog.

Judge Samuel Gudger conducts a brief but thorough investigation into the shooting death of Thomas Runnion on the night of the fire on Doe Branch. After taking sworn statements from all who were present and consulting with the assistant DA, he concludes that Sheriff Clinton Salter acted in self-defense and had no choice but to fire on Runnion. There will be no prosecution or trial. The outside world is fascinated, even titillated by the scandal. Inside Madison County, however, public opinion is clearly in Clinton's favor—after all, a man must defend his own property—long before Gudger formalizes it.

WHILE ALL OF THESE PROCEEDINGS TOUCH Clinton in the day-to-day of his job, neither he nor Catherine, Marian nor Luke, are overly concerned. Rather, they are making plans for Christmas—both New and Old—and, with some consternation, trying to decide who to invite to the wedding. Marian's penciled list looks something like this:

Catherine's mother (though we have never met her)—Yes.

Catherine's sister, Molly, if she will come.

Matthew (plus girlfriend Chrissy)—Yes. (Bite my tongue.)

Uncle Will and his family—Yes. Dad insists. (Hope they don't come.)

Dad's deputies—Maybe. Dad says count heads, see if they'll fit.

Judge Gudger—Yes. And his ancient wife.

Luke's parents—I say yes. His sister too.

Gloria Goforth—Yes. Dad & Catherine vote yes.

Handful of Salter kin—Yes. Get the addresses from Dad.

Teachers from school—No. Catherine says not enough room. Wait 'til you see the church. (Give her a shower instead?)

December 12, a Sunday, Catherine takes Clinton into Asheville to meet her mother, a visit she has been dreading for some obscure reason, perhaps because she's afraid her mother will find a way to insult Clinton, call him a hillbilly or worse.

They are invited to tea at the North Asheville home of Mrs. Jacqueline Carter. On the drive over, Catherine dips back into her past to answer some of his questions, fill in some of the blanks. Her father was a successful attorney and a genuinely nice man, at least to his daughter. Smoked a pipe all his life and died of brain cancer, leaving her mother relatively well-off. Her mother always asks if she needs money and she always says no—except when she and James were at their lowest points.

Her mother goes by Miss Jackie most of the time these days, plays bridge at the club, drinks rosé, and gossips unmercifully. She's a good Episcopalian and her boyfriend, if you can call him that, is a retired Episcopal priest who squires her around town, still wearing his black suit and clerical collar. He goes by Father David.

"Do I have to call him Father David?" Clinton asks.

"We'll see," she replies.

As it turns out, Miss Jackie has obviously had her hair done for the occasion and is on her best behavior, chatty with Catherine and sweet to Clinton. It only takes Father David about ten minutes to realize that he and Clinton have the Green Bay Packers in common, and he asks Clinton to call him Dave. At one point, the two men go out on a screened-in porch so that Dave can fire up a Marlboro. He asks Clinton about his wound, and Clinton waves it off with "just some cracked ribs and a lot of blood."

They work their way back to the Packers. Dave argues that Bart Starr is the heart of the team. Clinton disagrees firmly. Ray Nitschke, he offers instead. Defense versus offense. They laugh. Maybe it's defense *and* offense.

"Listen," Clinton says after a bit. "Before we go back in, I'd like to ask you something."

"Sure. Do I have time for another cigarette?"

"Go ahead. We can stall if we need to. Do you still marry people?"

"Not so much," Dave replies, blowing his smoke to one side. "Only on special occasions."

"Does the special occasion have to be in an Episcopal church?"

On the drive home, Catherine asks Clinton what he would think about asking Father David to marry them. Her mother suggested it, and it might help Miss Jackie get over the location of the wedding.

"You mean a tiny little chapel in the middle of godforsaken nowhere?"

She smiles and nods. "Yes—that and the outhouses. I didn't tell her about the outhouses. I know that you don't care much for the clergy in general, but you and David seemed to get along. And it would make Mother so happy she'd split her girdle."

"She wears a girdle?"

"Oh, please! Of course, she does. She has a special girdle for church... So, what do you think? Could you live with David and his clerical collar?"

"If by David, you mean my friend Dave, I think I already asked him."

"Seriously? Good—although you might have checked with me first."

"I only sort of asked him. I did have in mind to confer with the bride. What did your mother have to say while Dave and I were outside talking football?"

"She was impressed. She said you were nothing like what she expected and that you were very nice for a man with a violent past and a—"

"Red neck?"

"She might have used that word. But she did whisper it, so it's almost like she never said it."

CHAPTER 68

MIDWINTER IN THE DEEP MOUNTAINS, THE AFternoon of Old Christmas, January 6, 1966. In the mountains, it matters little the day of the week. What matters is that it's the twelfth day, the day of revealing. When night falls, the moon will lack only a sliver of its full, round radiance. Its effect, even in late afternoon, is extraordinarily powerful.

THIS, THEN, IS THE PLACE.

The Doe Branch Church is lit by twelve oil lamps: two in the back, two in the front, and four on each side. Each lamp sits on a high shelf, with a mirror affixed to the wall behind it to reflect the lamplight out into the room. The church is heated solely by splits of red oak and walnut burning hot inside the woodstove in front of the foremost pew on the right. A fresh supply of wood waits neatly stacked on the porch, and the fire has been burning since midmorning.

The entire space is warm against the iron cold that waits outside. The air is lamplit yellow and the orange of old flame. Randall Shelton is the keeper of the flame, trimming the wicks and lighting each lamp in turn. He, along with Clint and Luke, have scrubbed the inside of the church as for a warden's inspection, and since they expect Miss Jackie, a warden's inspection is what they'll receive. For this day, Randall has resurrected a suit from another era and shaved so close that he bleeds from a half dozen cuts.

The room is scented with pine boughs, cut the day before and arranged on the pulpit and along the pews. It smells like Christmas, flaming wood, and scented lamp oil. There are ten pews, five to a side, and each might hold four or five adults. Or so they hope. Fifty are invited that Clinton is aware of, and Marian, assisted by Catherine, has done her math over and again.

The handwritten invitations went out by mail and by hand, assisted by telephone, although, ever since Clinton and Catherine went to the courthouse to apply for the license, half the people in Madison County have known. Most approve.

Said invitations gave three o'clock as the bewitching hour. Shortly after two, Clinton arrives in the Jeep with Luke and the dogs. The dogs go roving outside before coming in to lie by the stove. Luke and Randall do their best to calm Clinton down. He is convinced at this last moment that Catherine will come to her senses and run for her life. They assure him that she is obviously out of her mind, but will arrive in good time. Mostly to distract Clinton, Luke goes over the plan once again.

Father David and Miss Jackie will arrive soon, two-thirty or thereabouts. Catherine will come with them if it appears they are uncomfortable on the lonely gravel road. If they are okay, Catherine will come with Marian, her matron of honor, not long after that. Quarter 'til, perhaps. The other guests will arrive along the way. There is a bonfire to be lit in the parking area in front of the church so that all will find the way. The deputies will attend out by the fire if there is not enough room along the benches.

"So, Marian will stand up with Cat," Clinton says, deep in some other place. "Who's standing up with me?"

"I am," Luke replies patiently. "You asked me."

"You're right," Clinton says. "I did." He reaches over to grip the young man's hand. "Thank you." Then he reaches in his outside jacket pocket and brings out a battered metal flask.

He hands the flask to Luke, who unscrews the top and pretends to take a swig. Hands it on to Randall Shelton, who swallows in earnest. "Jesus, it's homemade," he mutters. Hands the flask back to Clinton, who also partakes, also in earnest. "Yes, it is," he coughs and says. "Freeman boys gave it to me for the occasion."

After a bit, Randall and Luke go out to light the bonfire, intending to give some heat as well as guidance to the guests as they arrive. For a few, spare moments, Clinton is alone in the sanctuary. There is, he thinks, a muted splendor to the place in the warm, lambent light. He thinks of his father, who should be here. And of his mother, gone away. It occurs to him to wonder if Matthew will put in an appearance, prodigal that he is.

Then suddenly, Miss Jackie and Father David are there. Randall stays out by the fire while Luke escorts them in. Father David embraces Clinton and busies himself at the pulpit. Miss Jackie collapses onto the front pew by the stove, and Jake, the terrier, immediately jumps up beside her to lick her face. For the next few minutes everything is a blur. People coming in and claiming seats. The back, left-hand pew is piled high with coats. Clinton stands by the door with Luke, shaking hands. Hugs... laughter. Will arrives with his wife, and the two brothers grip each other's hands, neither letting go for a long moment. Perhaps there is some mutual forgiveness here, some recollection of who they once were and might be again.

A lamp flickers out, and Luke perches on a pew to relight it. The stove is glowing now, radiant with heat.

Matthew, his son Matthew, whom he hasn't seen since the night he was shot, arrives with the Atlanta girlfriend, Chrissy. The two young people are dressed expensively, beautifully even, but not warmly. He and Matthew shake hands. He resists the urge to embrace his son, knowing the boy won't like it. Strangely, the girlfriend asks if there are snakes in the church.

It is nearly three, Clinton thinks. *Will she really come? Catherine, will she actually marry me? Here, now?* He steps outside and walks over to the bonfire. It's blazing now, a beacon light in the darkening afternoon. Way Tipton and the other deputies are there with Randall, apparently more comfortable outside than in. Who can blame them, for the fire throws out a haven of heat. The deputies embrace him, and it occurs to Clinton that in their own simple way, they love him.

As he does them.

THEN, CATHERINE'S STATION WAGON PULLS IN and stops beside the Jeep. Marian climbs out the driver's side, and Catherine emerges from the passenger seat. He saw her late the previous day, but now, she has an unexpected and unearthly radiance.

Just for a moment, he imagines wings.

CHAPTER 69

CLINTON SITS ON THE FIRST PEW ON THE RIGHT with Luke. The young man's presence there is reassuring, comforting even, but for a brief moment, Clinton wonders if he should have asked Matthew to stand up with him as well. But then the boy might have refused. Still wounds there to heal.

Catherine sits on the first pew on the left with her mother and Marian. When Father David stands up to speak, she imagines that his words hang in the air, their significance not in their meaning, but in their music.

Dearly beloved, we are gathered together here in the sight of God, and in the face of this company, to join together this Man and this Woman in holy Matrimony; which is an honorable estate...signifying unto us the mystical union...adorned and beautified with his presence and first miracle...reverently, discreetly, advisedly, soberly...

They are standing now with Luke and Marian, and Catherine is surprised to see that Marian is crying quietly. Even Luke, staunch Luke, is blinking. Then the young couple sit down, leaving only the original two, Clinton Stuart Salter and Catherine Carter Metcalf, standing before Father Dave.

Wilt thou have this Woman...comfort her, honour, and keep her...this Man...to live together...in the holy estate...Wilt thou love him...to have and to hold...I plight thee my troth.

His ring is a simple gold band. Her ring is, of course, the one Clinton slipped on her finger in the orchard on Halloween night. His mother's ring, which, in turn, offers them both a kind of connection.

Bless, O Lord, this Ring, that he who gives it and she who wears it may abide in thy peace, and continue in thy favour, unto their life's end.

They stand now, holding hands, both still in a sort of reverie. Sanctified and joined in some new way that they don't yet understand. The man before them, his voice coarsened from years of cigarette smoke, closes his little blue prayer book and seems to suddenly notice the open Bible on the pulpit. What he sees there surprises him, and so he reads a bit.

Beareth all things, believeth all things, hopeth all things, endureth all things.

Strangely, the old man, the priest himself, is crying. What he is thinking is impossible to say, but he is moved almost beyond words. He reaches up one hand to swipe away the tears and cover his mouth while he recovers himself. Finally, he looks up to stare hard at Catherine and Clinton, as if regarding them for the first time.

You two are so incredibly fortunate.... To have found each other now. To have survived several lives already, to have outlived the sorrow and loss, and then to have found each other. With all your lives to draw on, you are uniquely capable of recognizing what you have. Oh, how I envy you. Everyone in this church loves and envies you. But none would take from you that which you have earned and what you have made. Why? Because you are our possibility.

AFTER THE SERVICE, THE BRIDE AND GROOM INvite everyone back to the farmhouse, where there is food aplenty and much to drink. When they walk out into the late winter afternoon, the dogs chase around the parking lot barking, thrilled with release. *Though it's not midnight,* Catherine realizes, *the animals are speaking.*

Clinton himself steps back inside the sanctuary and reaches above the door for the bell rope. Perhaps he is the only one who has noticed it during these last days as they cleaned and prepared the little church. Perhaps he is the only one who knows it is there.

But he knows, and he reaches up to grasp the rope, pauses for a moment, and then begins rhythmically to pull. Such that the iron tongue of the bell metes out full-throated celebration. *Let the world know*, he thinks, *what we do here.*

In that ringing moment, time expands and expands and expands—until winter darkness heaves into new life, and light returns to the land.

WILL BE

Coley Gap
October 1970

"WHAT DO YOU THINK HE HEARS?" CATHERINE asks him, nodding toward Nick, the shepherd-husky.

They've come out on the front porch of the farmhouse to look at the moon. Nick is standing at attention on his three legs, focused intently on something beyond their range.

"When he whines like that, he's usually listening to the bear dogs running on the other side of the Divide Mountain."

"He wishes he were with them?"

"He does. Sometimes he'll howl. I figure it's when they get frantic because they've treed a bear."

"I wish we could hear what he hears."

Cat and Clint are standing side by side, looking out at the world with the dog. Now he turns to regard her face. "We can, you know."

"How?"

"Have you got any plans for Saturday night?"

"Sleeping with my husband. Are we going bear hunting instead?"

BY THE FOLLOWING SATURDAY NIGHT, THE RISEN moon is near full. The hills are in the grip of Old October. The chill winds of fall have brushed a dozen ancient colors through the trees: yellow gold, russet red, orange flame. The mountains themselves loom ancient and magnificent.

Just at dusk, they load the Jeep with blankets, a couple of folding chairs, and a thermos of coffee. When she reaches into the pocket of his old barn coat, as she often does to warm her hands, she finds his battered old metal flask, full—she is certain—of the bourbon they both enjoy.

The top is up on the Jeep, of course, but that's not enough to keep out the cold, and they run the heater full blast while they maneuver up the dirt and gravel trace that climbs to the Divide. He stops at the bottom to shift into four-wheel drive, for even the Jeep won't climb that mountain without it.

On this haunted night, they aren't going all the way over into Anderson Cove. He's taken her there before to see the property his grandparents left him and to visit with them in the cemetery. On this night, he explains, they're stopping at the gap of the mountain, where they'll meet some friends of his.

It takes thirty minutes of tough climbing, the Jeep clawing its way over hard granite, into and out of ruts that would swallow her new station wagon. When they are almost at Coley Gap, she sees what appears to be a fire on up ahead at a clearing he showed her years before. "That's where we're going," he explains.

At the Gap, they park beside an ancient Chevy truck that has a couple of mules tethered to it. The mules are saddled. Somebody, or rather a couple of bodies, has ridden them there. Each of the mules has a bucket of steaming mash in front of him, and they share a bucket of water. "Aren't they cold?" she asks Clinton.

He smiles. "They're mules, honey. They're too damn stubborn to get cold."

They leave the Jeep beside the truck. He pauses to rub the noses of each of the mules and cautions her not to walk behind them. "They'll kick," he explains, "if they don't know you. And sometimes if they do."

As they walk up with the chairs and blankets, she can see there's a half dozen men sitting around the fire on a collection of rocks and logs pulled up for the purpose. They're talking and laughing together, the fire burning high, gnawing away at splits of oak and maple. Sparks of humor, she thinks, along with the jots of fire floating up into the stars.

"God a'mighty, it's the sheriff." One of the voices by the fire. "Run for it!" Hoots of laugher. "And look, he brought himself a damn easy chair to sit on. Must be getting old."

"Watch your language, boys, it's Mrs. Sheriff too."

She laughs at them, while Clinton unfolds a chair for her, just close enough to the fire to warm without getting scorched. "Don't worry, gentlemen," she says, "I'm used to it. Remember who I live with."

"Uses filthy language, does he?" More laughter.

"Well," she says, "I'd call it salty."

They laugh so hard one falls off his rock onto the cold ground. Clinton grins. They've been here five minutes, and already she's settled in. He wasn't so sure that she'd like this high, lonesome place, but here they are. Now she leans over to him. "I brought you something," she whispers. "Here, I'll trade you for the flask." He passes her the flask, and she hands him a cigar, still in its cellophane wrapper. The cigar and a box of matches. "I know you love them," she says, "but won't let yourself smoke them at home because of me."

"Tonight's the night," he says to her, and then, loud enough for all to hear, "tonight is the night." He trims the cigar with his pocketknife and uses a blazing twig to set it on fire. He can hear her take a swallow from the flask as he does so.

"Who's trailing along with the dogs tonight, Harold?" he asks through the smoke.

"Don's boy's out there," Harold Anderson replies. "And one of the Buckners. Lee's boy is with them. You know Gordon and

Lee Robbins, don't you?" He points out two men on the far side of the fire. "And my brother, Don?" He points to a sprightly man who's feeding the fire. "Boys, this is the high sheriff hisself, Clint Salter. And Mrs. Salter, if I make no mistake."

"Just Catherine," she says. "We came to hear the dogs."

"Why, you picked a good night then." Don Anderson. "My two are out there. Nate and Nan. Brother and sister Plott hounds. Plus, Gordon and Lee brought in three of the finest dogs I know. Famous hounds. Call 'em out for Catherine, Lee."

"Well, there's Caesar and Hector, two boys in their prime, and they're running with their mama, a long-legged bitch named Old Soul."

There's a pause in the talk, which Catherine suddenly realizes is from a kind of reverence.

"Old Soul is famous," Clinton explains to her. "All over the mountains, here to Tennessee, south to Georgia."

"North to Virginia," Harold adds. "You forgot goddamn Virginia."

"When you hear her, you'll understand why," says Clinton.

"She has a famous voice, plus she favors to fight when it comes to it. Bear drops down out of a tree, and it gets to be Old Testament time, she turns into nothing but teeth and claws." This from Gordon, with pride.

She hands Clinton the flask. He takes a swig and hands it back. "Don't they get chewed up?" she asks. "By the bears, I mean?"

"Chewed up, clawed up. Killed outright. We've buried many a dog back up in the woods, haven't we, men?"

"Old Soul's had forty-three stitches over the years." Gordon. "Once, she—"

They would never know what once she did, because at that moment, Lee shushes Gordon and the rest. They listen in utter quiet, only the fire daring to breathe as it gnaws at the wood.

Below them, on the far side of the cove, sounds a long, wavering cry. "That's Nate," Harold whispers. "Or Nan."

A series of rapid yips and then a howl to still the blood in your veins. Harold turns to Gordon and Lee. "Is that—?"

"Hector and Caesar. Joining in."

"What are they saying?" Catherine asks.

"Well, Nate or Nan spoke out first," Don explains. "Said, Come over here and smell. Is this what I think it is? Then along come Caesar and Hector to take stock, noses to the ground. And by God, they say, I believe it is. Big bear come through here, and it's time to chase."

"What about Old Soul?" she asks. "Is she...?" She pauses, realizing that the men have fallen silent again.

There is a chorus in the air now. In the valley below, but moving, coming closer. The thin, quavering of Nate and Nan, the yipping of Hector, the breathless howls from Caesar. And then, as if in answer to her unspoken question, comes a long, high, impossibly sharp cry that is not of this earth. In it is the scream of all life and near death. When it fades, comes the stillness after breath ceases and before it begins. Even the fire falls silent. Again comes the ancient, primal cry of Old Soul, telling the bear that they are on his trail, coming to kill him.

"Jesus," she whispers and reaches over to grasp Clinton's hand.

"That's her," he mutters. "Now you know."

THE DOGS PASS OVER THE DIVIDE A HALF MILE from their fire. Then down into the still vast wilderness on the other side, where Doe Branch itself originates. Eventually, the dogs run beyond mere human hearing, still on the trail.

The talk resumes. Now Clinton gets up to stir the fire and feed it several splits of fresh wood.

"Does your side ever bother you, Clint?" Don Anderson asks him quietly after he sits back down.

"Yeah, it does. When the weather changes, it aches sometimes."

"Pistol, was it?"

He nods. "A thirty-eight. Slug bounced off a rib or two and went all the way through. Ruined a perfectly good shirt."

"It scared me to death," Catherine says suddenly. "He's gonna act like it was nothing, but I was sure I'd lost him. I screamed and screamed that night, standing in his blood."

Silence.

There is a sudden gust of wind from Anderson Cove through the gap, and the fire leaps up in response. For a long moment, it's clear that the blaze itself has sentient life and is speaking to them. But then the wind dies down again, and the fire is just a fire.

"How's that high school of yours carrying on, Mrs. Salter?" This from either Gordon or Lee, hard to tell.

"Most days, we manage to teach them something," she says in a normal tone of voice, relieved to change the subject. "We'd do just fine if the school board would quit politicking and leave us alone."

"Can't your husband arrest the goddamn school board? Lock 'em up?"

She laughs. "You don't know how many times I've suggested that. But he doesn't seem to want to, for some reason."

"Well, the next time you got to go before 'em, you call us, and we'll go with you."

"I wish you would."

"We'll bring the dogs."

"I believe Old Soul would tree a school board member, don't you, Lee?"

"Or chew his leg off," Lee says.

At midnight, Clint and Cat rise to go. The cigar is long gone, the last inch tossed into the fire, and the flask empty.

As they are falling asleep that night, warm now in their own bed at the farm, she murmurs sleepily, "Do you hear that noise, faint in the wind?"

"I hear it often," he replies after a moment's stillness.

"What do you think it is?"

"I know what it is. It's the bell at Doe Branch Church."

"Is a ghost ringing it?"

"Maybe. Or the wind. All I know is that I hear it ever so often, late at night."

"What does it say?"

"Says we're safe now. That all is well."

ACKNOWLEDGMENTS

IN THE DOWNSTAIRS LIBRARY OF OUR HOUSE OUTside of Asheville, North Carolina, hangs a topographical map of the beating heart of my fictional world, which stretches from Asheville north into the wilds of Madison County. Significantly, *In the Fullness of Time* is set primarily in the county seat of Marshall, which lies just beside the French Broad River. Catherine Metcalf's high school sits on an island in the middle of that river. On September 27, 2024 (after the novel was finished but before it was published), Hurricane Helene swept through these mountains, and the French Broad rose to the highest level ever recorded, devastating both Marshall and Hot Springs.

Story is a powerful and lasting antidote to destruction and loss. My hope is that *In the Fullness of Time* will become part of the narrative record of what this place was like before the flood. Perhaps it will serve not only to eulogize what we've lost but also to help to recreate what was and will be again. After all, this is a novel about the mysteries of Time.

Those readers who are familiar with the history of Western North Carolina will recall that politics in Madison County from the 1950s through the 1980s were more or less ruled by the Ponder family, one of whom was repeatedly reelected as sheriff. Although there are echoes in the political landscape and in the various shenanigans that went on (dead people voting?), Clinton Salter is definitely not E. Y. Ponder, nor is Will Salter a fictional portrait of Zeno Ponder. The deeper you read and the more you know, you will see that any similarities exist only on the surface.

A number of good friends offered first-hand insight into Madison County life and politics while I was working on *In the Fullness of Time*. I would be remiss if I didn't thank Jim Baley, Steve Greene, Steve Metcalf, Joe Penland, Jim Rumbough, and Mike Smith for telling their wonderful stories. Many more helped these stories become a novel. Wendy Ikoku read the manuscript closely, as always. Margaret Sutherland Brown offered such cogent insight and then represented the book beautifully. Amanda Chiu Krohn and Ashlyn Inman worked their editorial magic at Turner. Lynn, of course, lived with Clint Salter and Cat Metcalf for months.

Finally, it's important to acknowledge the good mountain people whom we lost to the storm and the many strong mountain people who continue to rebuild. *In the Fullness of Time* is dedicated to them.

ABOUT THE AUTHOR

TERRY ROBERTS IS THE AUTHOR OF SIX CELEbrated novels: *A Short Time to Stay Here* (winner of the Willie Morris Prize for Southern Fiction and the Sir Walter Raleigh Award for Fiction); *That Bright Land* (winner of the Thomas Wolfe Literary Award, the James Still Award for Writing About the Appalachian South and the Sir Walter Raleigh Award for Fiction); *The Holy Ghost Speakeasy and Revival* (Finalist for the 2019 Sir Walter Raleigh Award for Fiction); *My Mistress' Eyes are Raven Black* (Finalist for the 2022 Best Paperback Original Novel by the International Thriller Writers Organization); The Sky Club; and most recently, *The Devil Hath a Pleasing Shape*, released in October 2024.

Roberts is a lifelong teacher and educational reformer as well as an award-winning novelist. He is a native of the mountains of Western North Carolina—born and bred. His ancestors include six generations of mountain farmers, as well as the bootleggers and preachers who appear in his novels. He was raised close by his grandmother, Belva Anderson Roberts, who was born in 1888 and passed to him the magic of the past along with the grit and humor of mountain storytelling.

Roberts is the Director of the National Paideia Center and lives in Asheville, North Carolina, with his wife, Lynn.